W9-BWU-442

Newfoundland Area Public Library

Newfoundland, PA 18445 (570) 676-4518

DISCARDED

L'AMOUR

A COLLECTION

L'AMOUR

A COLLECTION

Louis L'Amour

BANTAM BOOKS
NEW YORK

Reilly's Luck, Over on the Dry Side, and *Son of a Wanted Man* are works of fiction. Names, characters, places, and incidents either are the product of the author's imagination or are used fictitiously. Any resemblance to actual persons, living or dead, events, or locales is entirely coincidental.

2010 Bantam Books Hardcover Omnibus Edition

Reilly's Luck copyright © 1970 by Louis and Katherine L'Amour Trust

Over on the Dry Side copyright © 1975 by Louis and Katherine L'Amour Trust

Son of a Wanted Man copyright © 1984 by Louis and Katherine L'Amour Trust

All rights reserved.

Published in the United States by Bantam Books, an imprint of The Random House Publishing Group, a division of Random House, Inc., New York.

BANTAM BOOKS and the rooster colophon are registered trademarks of Random House, Inc.

The books contained in this volume were originally published separately in paperback by Bantam Books, a division of Random House, Inc., in 1975, 1970, and 1984.

ISBN 978-0-345-52570-3

Printed in the United States of America on acid-free paper

www.bantamdell.com

2 4 6 8 9 7 5 3 1

First Edition

Maps by Alan McKnight

Reilly's Luck

ONE

It was dark and cold, the only light coming from the crack under the ill-fitting door. The boy huddled in the bed, shivered against the cold, listening to the low mutter of voices from the adjoining room.

Outside everything was buried in snow. The window was thick with frost, shutting out what light there might have been. Once he heard boots crunch on the snow as a man walked back from the street.

Suddenly Ma's voice lifted, strident and impatient. "I've got no time for the kid! Now you get rid of him! Let one of those farmers have him. They all seem to want kids. Lord knows they have enough of them."

Then Van's voice, quiet, even-tempered as always. "Myra, you can't do that! He's your son. Your own flesh and blood."

"Don't be a fool! There's no place in my life for a kid." After a moment of silence, she added, "What kind of a life could I give him? Batting around from cow town to mining camp? Get rid of him, Van." Her voice rose sharply. "You get rid of him, or I'll get rid of you."

"Is that all it means, then? I knew you were a hard woman, Myra, but I thought I meant more to you than that."

1

"You're a fool, Van. Without me, you'd be cadging for drinks around the saloons. You take him out of here right now, and get rid of him. I don't care how you do it."

The boy tried to huddle into a tighter ball, tried to shut his ears against the voices, to close out the growing terror.

"All right, Myra. I'll see to it."

There was a mutter of voices again, and then he heard Ma go out, listened to her retreating steps as she walked along the path toward the street. For a few moments there was silence, then the faint clink of glass in the next room; the door opened, letting a rectangle of light fall upon the bare plank floor.

"Val? Are you awake? We've got to get you dressed."

"All right."

Anything was better than the cold bed, but he dreaded going out into the night, and dreaded more whatever was to come. He liked Van, and he trusted him. Sometimes when they talked Van referred to themselves as the two V's.

Van was slim and tall, with a sort of faded elegance; there was a puffiness around the cheeks, and an ever-present smell of whiskey; but his easy good manners never failed him, and Val admired him for that, and for the stories of his boyhood that he often told Val when Ma was not around. She detested hearing Van talk about anything that had happened before they met, and would not tolerate any mention of his family or the schools he had gone to. His family had been wealthy, and the schools had been good schools.

Van struck a match and lighted the lamp. In the light, the bare room looked even more bleak and empty, even emptier than the rooms on the farm where he had stayed until a few weeks ago.

It had been cold there, too, although there was usually a fire in the fireplace, and the farmer and his wife had been kind. Then the farmer's wife had become ill and nobody had any time for Val.

When he was dressed, Van took him into the other room. The boy rubbed his eyes against the stronger light, and then the outer door opened again and Myra came in. She did not look at him or speak to him. All she said was, "Get him out of here."

Van shrugged into his buffalo coat, and then he picked up Val and carried him to the door.

There Van hesitated. "He's only four years old, Myra. Can't you—?"

"Get out!" her voice was shrill. "And close the door after you!"
"Myra, I'll say he's mine. Nobody will know—"
"Get out."

It was icy cold in the barn. Van saddled his horse, lifted the boy to the saddle, and mounted behind him. He hesitated again, holding the boy to him and waiting while Val wondered when he would start. At last he touched his heels to the horse and they moved out of the barn. Van turned the horse to reach over and push the door shut, then they moved away toward open country.

Wondering, Val snuggled down inside Van's buffalo coat. Why were they going that way? There was nothing out there but open plains, but he trusted Van, and in the warmth against him he closed his eyes.

They had been riding for several minutes when suddenly Van swore, and wrenching the horse's head around, he turned back upon their trail. Snow was already covering their tracks, and it was bitterly cold.

"Are we going back, Van?"

"No, Val, we can't go back. At least you can't. We're going visiting."

When the lights of the town could again be seen, Van said, "Do you remember Will Reilly? I think you'll be staying with him tonight."

Val did remember him, a tall, wide-shouldered young man, not much older than Van, but somehow stronger, more forceful. He was a man who rarely smiled, but when he did his whole face seemed to light up. Val not only remembered him, he liked him. Maybe more than anybody, but he could not have said why that was so.

By the time they reached the hotel Val was chilled to the bone. Not even the heavy buffalo coat could keep out the bitter cold. Van tied the horse to the hitch rail, and carried Val inside to the stairs.

The clerk looked up. "Mister, you'd better not leave that horse out there. It's forty below."

"I'll only be a minute."

They went up the stairs and down the carpeted hall. Van stopped and rapped at the door. When the door opened a wonderful warmth came out.

"Will, I've got to ask a favor."

Will Reilly stepped back and let them come in, closing the door behind them. The chimney from the huge fireplace in the lobby came right through this room, accounting for the heat.

Reilly was in shirtsleeves and vest, and a gold watchchain draped from pocket to pocket of the vest. "What is it, Van? You know I'm expected downstairs. Couldn't this wait?"

"It's the kid, Will. Myra told me to get rid of him. He's cost her plenty in the past few days, and she told me to get rid of him or not come back."

"All right, take my advice and don't go back. If you need a stake I'll give you the stage fare to Denver and enough to make a start."

"At what? Thanks, Will, but no . . . no."

"Well? What do you want me to do?"

"Keep the boy until morning, will you? I couldn't think of any other place to take him, and the boy likes you."

"What do you think I am, a nurse? All right, put him down on the bed, but you be almighty sure you come back to get him in the morning, d' you hear?" Then more quietly he added, "She's a fool. That's a mighty fine boy there."

Van put Val down on the bed and helped him undress; then he covered him up. The warmth of the room after the cold Montana night made him very sleepy. It seemed as if he had been cold as long as he could remember.

There was a moment or two of subdued talking, then the door closed and Val heard the sound of footsteps going away.

Val opened his eyes and peeked at Will Reilly as the gambler combed his black hair, and buckled on his gun belt and holster. He caught Will's eyes in the mirror and quickly closed his own.

"All right, Val. Quit faking. I know you're awake."

Val opened his eyes and Will grinned at him in the mirror. Then Will came over to him and gently ruffled his hair. "You go to sleep, boy. You'll be all right here."

Reilly picked up a small holster with a derringer in it and buttoned it at a special place inside his belt. "A bit of insurance, Val, boy. We live in a harsh world.

"Always give yourself an edge, boy. You may never need it, but it saves a lot of worry. Learn to depend on yourself, and if you expect nothing from anybody else you will never be disappointed."

He sat down on the bed beside Val. "Remember this, son. *You* are all you have. Learn . . . learn everything you can, then you will always know a little more than they think you know. Most people in this world are out to take you. It isn't always their fault, but it is the way they live. If you know that, and make allowances for it, you won't go far wrong."

He got up and reached for his coat. "I am a gambler, Val, and I'll be gone most of the night. If you want a drink there's water in the pitcher and a glass beside it. But you can rest easy—nobody will bother you here."

After Will left the room, Val lay awake only a few minutes, studying the flowered wallpaper. A dresser with an oval mirror stood against one wall, and there was a huge old wardrobe filled with clothes . . . Val had never seen so many. Will Reilly had more clothes than Ma. Several pairs of polished boots and shoes were on the floor of the wardrobe.

There was a Winchester standing in the corner, a rifle that had seen much use, by the look of it, but a rifle that had been cleaned and cared for. There was a big black trunk against another wall.

It was broad daylight when Val opened his eyes, and Will Reilly was sleeping in the bed beside him. Will lay on his side with the holster near his hand, the pistol grip only inches away. Carefully, Val eased from the bed so as not to disturb the gambler.

On a stand near the window were six books, all much worn. Val picked up one of them and turned the pages, but he was disappointed to find no pictures. Then he went to the window and looked out.

He had walked that street several times with Van, but never with Myra. She had not wanted anyone to know he was hers . . . if he was. Val had never been sure about that, but it might be that he just did not want to believe she was his real mother.

From up here the street looked very different. He could look right down into the wagons, and if they were not covered by canvas tarps he could see what was in them. He had never been able to do that before.

The men standing in front of the stage station wore buffalo coats or mackinaws, and most of them had ear-flaps. He could see their breath in the still, cold air. One of the men turned his face toward Val—it was Van. Just as Val saw him, Ma came from the stage station and got on the stage, scarcely waiting for Van to help her in. Van gave one quick look toward the hotel, then followed her into the stage.

The door closed, the driver cracked his whip, and the horses lunged into the harness and went down the street with a rush, turning the corner at the bottom of the street and disappearing from sight.

Val stood staring after it, feeling queer. They were gone. Van had left him behind.

Until a few days ago he had seen Ma only a few times. He had lived with the people on the farm, and once in a while Ma came out to visit, and once she brought him some candy. She would sometimes pat him on the head, but she would never listen to anything he wanted to tell her. Then she would leave again, very quickly. He seemed to remember other people in other towns.

Then a few days ago a black shiny carriage had come to get the lady where he lived, and there were other people too, all wearing black, and after they had all gone away the man brought Val into town and left him with his mother.

He was standing at the window now, staring after the stage, when he felt eyes upon him, and turned around.

Will Reilly was lying awake, hands clasped behind his head, watching him. "What do you see, Val?"

"Wagons. Lots of wagons. I can see right down into them."

Will indicated the book Val had taken. "Did you like it?"

"There weren't any pictures."

Will smiled. "I suppose pictures are pretty important in a book."

"Anyway, I liked to hold it."

Will Reilly gave him a thoughtful look. "Now, that's interesting. So do I. I have always liked the feel of a good book. It's like a gun," he added. "When a man opens a book or fires a gun he has no idea what the effect will be, or how far the shot will travel."

He sat up. "I'll get dressed and we'll go downstairs for break-fast. Van will be coming for you."

"They aren't coming."

Will Reilly glanced at him sharply. "What do you mean?"

"They went away. I saw them."

"Oh?" Then, realizing the boy's position at the window, he said, "You saw the stage leave?"

"Yes, sir."

"Well, I'll be damned."

Will Reilly dressed slowly and with care, trying to hide his anger. That would be like Myra. Like Van, too. Van had been dodging responsibility all his life.

He looked at the boy, who was dressing slowly, clumsily. "Did you go anywhere before you came here last night? I mean, did Van take you anywhere else?"

Val pointed toward the wide-open plain. "We rode out there, a long way out."

Out *there?* In this kind of cold? Could the first idea have been to abandon the boy, leave him to die in the cold? At forty below that would not have taken long.

Did Myra know he was alive, then? Will considered that, and doubted it. If Myra had planned for the boy to be abandoned— and she was just the woman who could do it—Van would never dare tell her what he had actually done.

Will Reilly swung his gun-belt around his lean hips. His anger at being left with the boy was gone. It was far better that they had brought the youngster here than to leave him out there to die. But was it, really? What kind of a chance did the boy have?

Will Reilly's own beginning was scarcely better, and he had survived. How he had done it was not pleasant to remember, but he had survived. Did this boy have the guts it would take? Could he be tough enough, resilient enough, and wily enough to make his way? Will turned and looked thoughtfully at him.

There was a lost and wistful look about him, but there had been no tears, at least there were no traces of any now. He looked— well, he looked pretty much as Will Reilly might have looked at that age.

Will Reilly was an immaculate and coldly handsome young man who had the reputation of being an honest gambler—and no man to trifle with. He had had his bad times and his good, but he knew cards and he knew men, and he won much more often than he lost.

His father had been killed in a boiler explosion in Pennsylvania when Will was fourteen, and for the next six years he had worked as a common laborer, moving from job to job until he discovered he could do better playing poker. He had begun it on the jobs where he worked, moved from them to the river ports, and finally to the cities, and on to the Isthmus of Panama, South America, and then California and the mining camps.

"We will have breakfast, Val, and then we will decide what to do." He put on his coat and straightened it. "What's your name, Val? I don't believe it was ever mentioned."

"Valentine. Ma said my pa's name was Darrant."

"Darrant? Yes, that could be. Well, you've got some good blood in your veins. I knew Darrant, and he was a good man, a brave man."

Will straightened his cravat, trying to remember what he knew of Darrant. He had been a French-Canadian of good background, an educated man, to judge by his conversation, and a traveled one. He had been a soldier, but Reilly had no idea when or where, and briefly he had operated a newspaper. Like many another man in the mining camps, Darrant was looking for a rich strike, but somewhere along the line he had vanished from the picture. It was unlikely he knew he had a son.

Val was quiet at breakfast. He liked the tall, easy young man who talked so readily yet took the time to listen to him, too. Reilly talked of his steamboat days on the Mississippi and the Missouri, and Val listened with rapt attention.

There were few people in the dining room. Several of them spoke to Reilly and all looked curiously at Val.

Reilly presently fell silent, thinking of the problem. He was a gambling man, drifting from town to town as the occasion demanded, and he had no idea what to do with a small boy, but he had no idea of shirking the responsibility that was suddenly his.

His anger at Van had departed quickly. Undoubtedly the man had shrunk from abandoning the boy, and he had brought him to the one strong person he knew that he felt he could depend on.

Myra was a tough-minded, hard-souled wench who had chosen her life's work from preference, and neither of them should have anything to do with rearing a child, especially a sensitive boy like this.

Reilly considered the people he knew who might perhaps be equipped for the job, but he came up empty. The local minister was a fire-and-brimstone gospel-shouter who saw evil in all things, and who would never allow the boy to forget who his mother had been.

Ed Kelley, a good man with three children, had a wife who was ailing.

After three days had passed, Will Reilly was no closer to a solution. The boy had the run of the hotel, and was liked by everyone. And a curious fact brought itself to Reilly's attention. The arrival of the boy coincided with a consistent run of luck that left him a substantial winner. The pots he had been winning had not been large, but they had been several percentage points higher than was reasonable.

He was a gambler who knew to perfection the odds on filling any hand he might pick up, and he played according to those odds, so when anything unusual happened he was aware of it at once. Will Reilly was not a superstitious man, but neither was he one to fly in the face of providence.

On the morning of the fourth day, Loomis, who operated the hotel, stopped him on his way to breakfast. "Will, the Reverend was inquiring after the youngster. He declared you were no fit man to have a child, and I think they're fixing to take him from you."

Will Reilly was nothing if not a man of quick decision.

"Thanks, Art. Now about that buckboard of Bronson's? Did you ever find anyone to drive it back?"

Art Loomis was not slow. "I can have it hitched up and out back waiting, Will. I'll even pack for you."

"I'll pack. You get the buckboard hitched, and while you're at it, stop by Ferguson's and buy a couple of bedrolls for me and about a hundred rounds of .44's. I'll also need a camp outfit."

Dunker would know all about the boy. The Reverend had preached the funeral sermon for Mrs. Schmitt. The Reverend Dunker's allies would be Mrs. Purdy, and probably the wife of Elkins, who operated the Ferguson Store. Elkins himself was a good man, but Reilly had no use for the Purdys, for Mrs. Elkins, or for Dunker. There was little of the milk of human kindness in any of them.

He stepped out into the brisk morning air and paused briefly in front of the hotel. Because of the early hour, there were few people about. He turned abruptly toward the store.

Jess Elkins got up when Reilly walked in, and from the expression on his face Reilly knew that he himself had lately been under discussion.

"I'll need some warm clothes for the boy," he told Elkins. "You have a nice town here, but it is cold this time of year."

"Yes, sir. He's about four, isn't he?"

"He's about five. Give me four sets, complete. And he'll need a warm coat and a cap."

Elkins glanced up at him. "You sure you want to spend that much? After all, he isn't your boy."

"In a sense he is." Will Reilly was not one to hesitate over lying in a good cause, and it would give them something to worry about, something that might keep them in doubt until he could get away. "The boy is my nephew."

"Nephew?" Elkins was surprised. "But I thought—?"

"You thought he was Myra Cord's boy? He is, of course, but his father was Andy Darrant, my half-brother. Andy asked me to care for the boy. That was why Van Clevern brought him to me."

He paid out the money, and gathered up the parcel and started for the door.

"You're Darrant's half-brother? Why, I never—"

"Be in tomorrow," Reilly said. "There's some other things I need for him. Tablets, pencils, and such."

He walked quickly back to the hotel, his boots crunching in the snow.

It was very cold, too cold to be starting out in the snow on a long drive. And if it snowed any more the buckboard would be a handicap. But he had his own ideas about that, and when he reached the lobby he glanced around. It was empty, and there was no one at the desk. He walked right through to the back door.

Art Loomis was coming in from the back. "Everything is ready, Will, but if I was you I'd hole up right here. It looks like more snow."

"Can't be helped. The wolves are breathing down the back of my neck, Art."

"Ain't you even waitin' until dark?"

"No. As you say, it may begin to snow. Art, if they come around asking questions tell them I said something about driving out to Schmitt's to pick up some clothes for the boy."

It required only a few minutes to pack, and Loomis took the trunk down the back stairs himself. Then Reilly bundled Val into the seat and tucked a buffalo robe around him.

"Good luck, Will," Loomis said. "You'd better look sharp until you're over the pass."

"Thanks."

"Will?" Art Loomis was staring at him. "*Why*, Will? Will you just tell me why?"

Will Reilly looked at the horses' backs for a moment and then he told the truth. "Art, I never had a kid. I never had anybody, never in my whole life. This is a fine boy, Art, and I figure he came to me for a reason."

He slapped the reins on the horses' backs and the buckboard started off fast.

He did not turn down the main street, but circled the livery barns and left by the back way. It was bitterly cold, and it was thirty miles to the nearest shelter of any kind.

TWO

The horses were grain-fed and strong, and in the intense cold they moved off at a good clip. Reilly glanced back only once. Somebody was standing in the street looking after them as they mounted the rise outside of town. When he had put three miles behind them, he drew up and broke open the package containing the boy's clothing.

"Put these on, Val. No, put them on right over what you're wearing. Then get into this sheepskin coat."

It was wide-open country, without landmarks except for the trail left by the stage and several freight wagons. The ground was covered by only an inch or two of snow, but the temperature was hovering around ten below zero.

He trotted the horses, walked them, trotted them again. From time to time as they went on he glanced back.

Dunker was the kind of man to organize a pursuit, and the sheriff was under his thumb, but the sheriff was also a very lazy man who would have no desire to get out in the cold.

Three hours, and perhaps twelve miles out of town, it began to snow. Only a few fine flakes at first, drifting slowly down. Then it began to fall faster and faster, and soon the horses were white with it.

He was not more than fifteen miles out when the snow became so thick he could scarcely see. The going was heavier, and the horses slowed down. For some time they had been climbing steadily, and now they had left the flat land behind them and were in the low foothills.

Reilly looked down at the boy. Val was awake and sitting up, peering into the snow.

"Cold, Val?"

"No, sir."

"We're in trouble, Val. The snow is getting too deep for the buckboard, and the horses are tired. We'll have to find a place to hole up until the storm is over."

"Is there a place?"

"There's an old cabin, if I can find it. It was off the road to the right, and among the trees. But that's a few miles further on, almost at the top of the pass."

Val huddled in his warm clothes and the buffalo robe. Only his nose was cold, but he succeeded in keeping it back of the sheepskin collar most of the time. The horses were making hard work of it now. Several times they stopped and had to be whipped to make them move.

"Have to do it, Val. If they stop here they'll freeze, but they don't know any better."

They were almost to the crest of the ridge and the wind was rising when the horses stopped again. Will Reilly got down from the buckboard and, taking them by the bridles, he led them on.

Once, screened from the worst of the wind and snow by a wall of pines, he came back to the buckboard.

"How are you making it, boy?" he asked. "Are you all right?"

"Yes, sir. Can I help?"

"Just stay warm. And Val, remember this. If you stop pushing on, you lose. If we keep going, there will be shelter. It is always a little further to the top than you think."

For what seemed like a long while they plodded on. They seemed to be lost in time; in the blowing snow there was no perspective, no way of judging time or space, for they moved inside a whirl of blowing snow in a white world where most of the time Val could not even see Will Reilly.

Finally Reilly took an abrupt turn. For a moment the buckboard canted sharply and Val hung on, wildly afraid that it would tumble over. But the buckboard righted itself and they were out of the wind behind a shoulder of the mountain.

For thirty or forty yards they had clear going on a ridge that fell away on both sides and was blown free of snow. Then they were under the trees, in a thick stand of timber.

Reilly came back to Val. "You'll have to sit tight. If you see me go on ahead, you stay right in the seat. The old Ebbens' cabin is just up ahead, but if we don't make it soon the trail will be blocked.

Reilly moved back and forth across the road, trampling down the snow where it was too deep, then leading the horses on.

Suddenly a black bulk of rock showed before them, and close to it a slanting roof and a doorway. Surprisingly, a thin trail of smoke rose from the chimney.

Will Reilly stared at it, then with numbed fingers he unbuttoned his coat. Tucking his right hand into his armpit, he warmed his fingers while Val watched curiously.

Why didn't they go on, he thought. It would be warm inside the house, and he was cold now, especially his toes. After a few minutes Reilly walked on. He did not go right to the door, but veered off along a beaten path that led to a stable. He opened the door and went inside. When he came out he walked back to the buckboard.

"Val," he spoke quietly, "I don't want you to be afraid now. There are some men in there, and they may be outlaws. No matter what happens to me, you be friendly with them and they will take care of you. There are mighty few men who wouldn't be good to a little boy.

"There are three of them. Probably I will know them when I see them. They may even try to rob me, but you'll be in a warm place, and we haven't any choice. I'll put the horses up first." He started off, but paused and looked back. "Don't worry too much, Val," he said. He slapped his waistband. "I can handle this sort of thing pretty good."

He drove on to the stable through the steadily falling snow, and Val watched as Reilly stripped the harness from the horses, and then rubbed them down with care.

"Always take care of your horses first, Val," he said. "You never know when you may need them in their best shape."

He flexed his fingers a few times. "All right, let's go see what kind of a hand we've drawn."

Their arrival had been muffled by the snow, which covered and banked the cabin. Reilly's knock brought sudden silence within. He pounded on the door. "Open up in there! It's cold! I've got a boy out here."

There was the sound of a bar being removed, then the door swung inward. Will Reilly pushed the door back further and walked in, holding Val's hand in his left one, then releasing it.

He pushed the door shut behind him, still facing the three men who sat around the room. They stared at Reilly, then at Val.

"Looks like I drew a pat hand," Reilly said quietly. "Val, this is the Tensleep Kid. He's one half Irish, one quarter Dutch, one quarter Sioux Indian, and he's four quarters bad. But he's a strong man and he's honest with his friends."

Tensleep chuckled. "I'm not all bad, kid. I got a liking for kids and gamblers." He looked up at Reilly. "How'd you find this place, Will?"

"I grubstaked Ebbens a couple of times."

"Anybody else know of it?"

"I doubt it. Ebbens wasn't a talking man, you'll recall."

"It's mighty cold to be travelin'," one of the others said. "Maybe you'd like to tell us how come?"

"This is Myra's boy. Van left him with me when they skipped town, and the sky pilot down there was going to take him away from me. I like the boy, and I don't like Dunker."

The man was heavy-set, with powerful shoulders. "I don't buy it," he said, looking hard at Reilly, "and I don't like you."

"Your privilege, Sonnenberg. I don't like you, either."

"Then get out."

"No." Val was afraid of that thick, bearded man, but when he looked at Will he saw his friend was smiling. Will Reilly was not afraid. "We're staying, Henry."

Sonnenberg started to rise, but Tensleep's voice cut the movement short. "Let him stay, Hank. We'd put no man out on a night like this, would we, Tom?"

The third man was tall and lank. He looked around lazily, "No, we wouldn't. Forget it, Hank."

Sonnenberg swore. "How do we know he ain't a spy?"

"Reilly?" Tensleep chuckled. "Reilly's a gambler."

There were bunks enough. The outlaws had added bunks when they chose the place, and Ebbens had had several in the beginning. He had always planned to hire help.

"We'll leave when the storm is over," Reilly said. "I'll make some runners for the buckboard."

"I don't like you, Reilly," Sonnenberg said again. "I never did."

"Nobody asked you to, Henry. I'll try to keep out of your way, and you keep out of mine."

"Or . . . ?"

Will Reilly smiled. "I can shoot as quick and as accurately as any man in this room . . . and it's a small room."

"He's right, Hank," Tensleep said. "I've seen him shoot. I've also seen him use a bowie. I saw him carve three men into ribbons before they could get off a shot . . . and they were sent to the table to get him."

Henry Sonnenberg looked thoughtfully at Reilly. "Well, now, maybe I underrated you. Maybe you're better than I thought."

"It's kind of close in here," Reilly said. "I think we'd both get hurt, Henry."

The heavy man stared at him with reluctant admiration. "All right. You got nerve. Only don't cross me."

Val had edged close to the fire. He was beginning to get warm all the way through. Though he had not admitted it to Will Reilly, he had been cold for hours. He was still afraid of these men, although Tensleep smiled at him.

"I didn't know Myra had a kid," Tom said suddenly.

"Nobody did. She kept still about it and the Schmitts cared for him until Emma died. Then Myra told Van to get rid of him."

They were shocked, and showed it.

"That's right," Reilly continued, "only Van wasn't up to it. So he brought him to me to keep overnight, then they skipped out."

"I knew Myra had a streak of mean," Tensleep said, "but a *kid!* She'd do that to a kid?"

"She's a strange one," Tom said, and added, surprisingly, "I knew her family."

Reilly glanced at him. "Where was this?"

"Back east. She came of good people . . . well-off. But she was always a mean one. She skipped out and never did go back."

When Val woke up the cabin was light and he was lying on a bunk with blankets tucked around him. Tensleep was sitting by

the fire with his feet propped up on a stump that did duty for a
chair. He glanced over when Val moved. "Mornin', boy. When
you get right down to it you're an almighty good sleeper, you
know that?"

"Yes, sir."

"Sir. Now that's right nice. Who taught you manners, boy?"

"Mr. Van did, sir."

"Well, I reckon he was good for something, after all. But a
pleasant man, too, a right pleasant man. I never did talk to
anyone who was easier with words . . . unless it was Will Reilly.
You got a friend there, boy. You stick to him. A man never has
many friends in this life and he had better hold onto them."

"You have friends."

Tensleep chuckled dryly, and gave Val a quick, sidelong glance
tinged with ironic humor. "Yeah? You might call 'em that. We
work together, boy, and they're good at what they do, but I was
talkin' of friends you can turn your back on."

"Mr. Reilly likes you."

"Reilly does? Now, why do you say that, boy?"

"I can tell by the way he talks to you and looks at you. He likes
you, all right."

"I'm honored. Will Reilly is a man sparing of his likes. And
what about you, boy?"

"Yes, sir. I like you."

"How about Hank? An' Tom?"

"I don't like Hank . . . Henry. I don't think he likes me,
either. I don't know about Tom."

"Nobody knows about Tom. Not even Tom." He got up and
added wood to the fire. "You keep shet about your likes an'
dislikes, boy. Though I don't s'pose it will make much dif'rence,
one way or t'other."

The snow had stopped, but outside the window, which he
could scarcely see through because of the frost, everything was
white and still. He could hear an axe being used, and from time
to time the sound of voices. He could see big chips lying on the
snow, and a couple of long poles, curved on one end. Will Reilly
had chosen young saplings with a slight curvature for the runners.
Now he was trimming them to smooth the surface that would ride
on the snow.

Sonnenberg, Tom, and Reilly wheeled the buckboard into view

and Reilly went to work to remove the wheels. The buckboard had been built so that runners could be mounted for winter use.

After a while they all came in. Tom went to work preparing a meal, and Reilly tilted his chair back against the wall. "I've got some extra grub," he said, "and we're obliged for your help. If you stay here until you get a chinook, or spring comes, you'll need more than you've got."

"It would help," Tensleep agreed.

"I can leave you a couple of slabs of bacon, some frozen beef, maybe half a dozen cans of beans. We didn't pack flour because we didn't figure to have any place to bake."

"See?" Tensleep said. "I told you he was all right. You never lose anything if you stand by Will Reilly."

Reilly drank coffee, and then nodded to Val. "Get bundled up, Val. We're pulling out."

"You got a long drive." Sonnenberg studied him warily. "How do we know you ain't just goin' out to meet the sheriff some place?"

"If you knew Daily Benson," Reilly answered, "you wouldn't worry. You couldn't get him three miles from town in this weather for twenty thousand dollars. He's a warm-weather sheriff . . . and he isn't looking for you boys, anyhow."

Reilly put down his cup and got to his feet. "Come on out, a couple of you, and I'll give you what I can."

Outside he loaded Sonnenberg down with the bacon and beans, and while the outlaw went inside, Reilly said, "Thanks, Tensleep, I'll remember this." He dug into the buckboard and came up with a ten-pound sack of dried apples. "Take this for an added benefit."

"Thanks." Tensleep started to turn away, then came back. "I just recalled, Will. You be careful down to Helena. The Gorman boys are down there."

Henry Sonnenberg stood by sullenly, but Tom stepped forward and picking up Val, placed him in the buckboard, and tucked the buffalo robe around him. "You ride warm, son. You've got a cold drive ahead of you."

"Thank you, Tom," Val said. "Thank you very much."

Will Reilly stepped up into the buckboard and sat down, then he clucked to the horses and slapped them with the reins. "You boys take care," he said. "And scatter some snow after I'm gone."

He drove down the trail toward the main road, and Val saw his

coat was still unbuttoned and the flap loose on Reilly's holster.
Will Reilly was a gambler, they said, but he did not gamble in
every sense, and it was only when they had put two good miles
behind them that he buttoned his coat.

For a few miles they rode in silence, and then Will glanced
down at the boy. "Are you cold?" he asked.

"A little."

"Did you watch what happened back there, Val? It is always
important to watch . . . and listen."

"Yes, sir."

"Do you know why we're alive now, Val?"

"They were afraid of you."

"No, they weren't. Especially, Tensleep wasn't. But neither
were the others. What was important was that they knew I wasn't
afraid of them, and that they couldn't injure me without being
injured themselves.

"And there was something else, Val. A man who is strong has
to know when to use his strength. I did not challenge Henry
Sonnenberg. If I had challenged him he would have felt he had to
prove me wrong. There would have been a fight, and some of us
would have been hurt. In such a case it is a fine line one must
draw, Val. I accepted Sonnenberg as a dangerous man, while not
yielding in the least."

"Yes, sir."

"Of those men back there, Val, Sonnenberg is the toughest and
meanest. Tensleep is the best with a gun, and by far the most
cunning, but Tom is the most dangerous."

"Why?"

"Because he is not right in his mind. He looks all right, and
most of the time he acts all right, but you can't count on what he
will do under strain when it comes to a tight spot. He could very
easily go wild and kill everybody around him. Afterward he might
be sorry for a little while, but more than likely he would forget all
about it."

After that they rode in silence again, but presently Reilly said,
"Val, you are alone in the world. Don't ever forget that, and don't
forget that he who stands alone is the strongest. It is a wonderful
thing to have friends, but you must know who your friends are.
Learn to judge men, Val. If you do, you will live longer . . . and
better."

The air was crisp and clear, and the horses moved briskly. Val burrowed down in his warm clothes and watched the ears of the horses. From time to time Will Reilly talked of one thing or another.

This was only the first of many rides, in buckboards, on trains, on steamboats, and on horseback, and on every occasion Will Reilly talked. He liked to talk, and Val was a good listener.

It was only a long time later that Val began to realize that Will Reilly was doing his best in his own way to teach him the things that he himself valued. Among these things were to have responsibility and courage, to be a gentleman always, and to realize that a man's word is his bond. There were many other things, too, little things about working at various jobs, getting along with people, noticing the mannerisms that men develop, the tricks of expression or gesture that may indicate when they were lying, or when they are uncertain or afraid. In the hit-or-miss way of the gambling table, the steamboat and the mining camp, Will Reilly's own education had been gained the hard way.

On that first night in the strange hotel in Helena, Will Reilly dressed to go out. As he turned away from the dresser he opened a fresh pack of cards and handed them to Val.

"Take these. Shuffle them a hundred times tonight. Learn the feel of them, learn how to handle them easily. Even if you never play cards it will make your fingers more agile, your eyes quicker." Reilly went out then, and Val was alone.

He went to the window and listened to the crunch of footsteps on the snow, remembering what Tensleep had said about the Gormans. Would they find Will? Would they kill him? Would he never come back?

He watched the lights on the snow, and he thought of all that had happened—of Myra and Van, of Tensleep, Henry Sonnenberg, and Tom . . . did Tom have another name?

Then he began to shuffle the cards. He shuffled, dealt, gathered them up again . . . a hundred times, and a few more.

And so it was to be, night after night. He learned to handle the cards smoothly and with dexterity, to deal, second-deal, to deal off the bottom. He learned to cut cards and shift the cut, to build up a top stock or a bottom stock from which the hands he wanted could be dealt.

"A gentleman never cheats, Val," Will Reilly told him the next night while brushing his hair, "but you will not always play with gentlemen, and it is well to know when you are being cheated; and to know that, you must know what it is possible to do.

"If you suspect a game of being crooked, get out. Use any excuse, but leave it. Don't call a man on cheating, because if you do you'll have to kill him, and a dead man doesn't rest easy on your mind.

"Train your memory . . . and observe. Learn to know and recall every card that has been played, and who played it; but above all, notice people, places, things."

Will Reilly had turned from his hair brushing. "Go to the window, Val, and look out."

When the boy had stood looking out for a minute, Will called him back and said, "All right, how many buildings are there across the street? That you can see from that window?"

"I don't know. I think . . ."

"There are seven that front on this street. Three of them are two-storied, two have balconies."

Will Reilly put on his coat, straightened his tie. "Don't just look out the window, Val. You must learn to see, and to remember.

"Now let's go to dinner."

THREE

By the time he was eight years old, Valentine Darrant knew everything there was to know about a deck of cards. He knew that, in draw poker, when holding a pair and drawing three cards, his chances of making three of a kind were eight to one, his chances of four of a kind, three hundred and fifty-nine to one. He knew all about check-cop and hideouts, and he could detect the whisper of a bottom deal as well as Will Reilly himself.

He had ridden horseback more than a thousand miles over the roughest kind of country, and he had ridden the stage three times that far. He had ridden steamboats from New Orleans on the Mississippi to Fort Benton on the Missouri.

He had followed a dozen rushes to boom towns, had seen those towns born and had seen them die. He knew hundreds of the professionals of the frontier, the gamblers, the bartenders, the shady ladies, and the law officers who drifted from town to town.

Will Reilly liked to sing, and Val had learned dozens of songs which they sang while riding across country, and he knew as many poems, some of them fairly long, that Will was given to reciting to pass away the long hours of travel. Will had read a lot, from anything available, and he had a ready memory for facts gleaned from histories and almanacs. This had begun as a pleasure, but had developed into another source of gambling income, for he had learned very early that men will back their opinions with money, and that the memories of most men were hazy as far as historical facts were concerned. He was also a fine athlete, and an extremely fast foot-racer.

Foot-racing was a favorite frontier sport, and such races could be set up at a moment's notice, and they were features of every frontier celebration. Will Reilly kept a small black book in which he listed the vital facts about the racing and fistic abilities of hundreds of men.

"Percentages, that's the important thing," he told Val. "Always play on the percentages; and never be enticed into a bet when you're angry. Don't ever risk money on sympathy or anger.

"Now you take Ray"—he indicated a stocky man who sat across the room, a dead cigar in his teeth—"Ray is one of the fastest men on his feet west of the Mississippi. He isn't smoking that cigar. He never smoked or drank in his life. It's all for show. He looks fat, but he isn't really. And he can run like a bullet out of a gun—for a hundred to two hundred yards. Beyond that he's no good. For him, the short distances are best."

The black book also listed the speed of known horses, many of which were taken around the country and brought into town hitched to a buckboard or a farm wagon to fool those who might be led into betting.

"Never buck the other man's game, Val," Reilly said, "but watch the percentages. It is not one or two pots that make a poker player, but the consistency with which he plays. Winning big pots, while it can be spectacular, can also attract unfavorable attention. Thieves may decide you're fair game, or some may get the idea that you are cheating."

By this time Val had noticed that Will usually won several small pots during several days of play, and often would seem to let the big ones go by. "The secret of gambling, Val, is to gamble as little as possible. Nobody has to be dishonest to win. It is a matter of card sense, good memory, knowledge of people, and just a shading of luck."

Will Reilly was strict, too, with Val. He demanded cleanliness, neatness, and gentlemanly conduct from him, and he made sure that he got them. What schooling Val got, he received from Will himself, for they rarely stayed anywhere long enough for the boy to enter a school.

Will taught him how to read, although he had already begun to learn, when he came to him, and how to cipher, and to make quick, accurate calculations of probabilities and percentages. And always there were the lessons in observation. Rarely a day passed when Val was not suddenly called on to describe country they had passed through, the clothing of a man, or the location of articles in a store.

"I don't want you to be a gambler," Will commented, "but the handling of cards will give dexterity to your fingers, improve your memory, and give you a quick grasp of a situation."

Will never mentioned Myra, and Val did not ask about her. Actually, it was Van he remembered best, because Van had been kind when no one else had been.

Will Reilly had an Irishman's addiction to eloquence, and a natural love of politics. He had memorized passages from dozens of speeches, and on their long rides they often recited together, or one of them would begin a poem, the other would complete it.

They were eating in a restaurant and talking of poetry when a bearded man at the next table turned around in his chair. "What you tryin' to do, make a mollycoddle out of the boy? Teachin' him all that sissy stuff?"

Will Reilly looked at him coldly for several seconds. Then he took the cigar from his mouth and placed it on the edge of a saucer.

"My friend"—his voice was cold—"I read poetry, I like poetry. Do you wish to call me a mollycoddle?"

The bearded man started to speak, and his companion kicked him under the table. "*Jeff!*" he said warningly, but Jeff was not listening.

"Now maybe I might. Just what would you do about it?"

"I will tell you what I'd do about it," Reilly replied coolly. "If you had a gun, I would kill you. If you did not have a gun, I'd whip you within an inch of your life."

The big man had been drinking, which destroyed any natural caution he might have possessed. Suddenly he dropped his hand to his boot and flashed his knife.

Val never saw Will's own hand move, but suddenly his blade was out and the big man's hand was pinned to the table. The bearded man gave a choking cry of pain, and a trickle of blood ran from his hand.

"Val," Will Reilly spoke calmly, "hand me that copy of Tennyson, will you? I believe this gentleman should have his education improved."

Taking up the bottle on his table, he filled a glass and handed it to the bearded man. "Use your free hand, and drink that," he said, "then listen."

Val never forgot those next few minutes. With the man's hand pinned to the table, Will Reilly leafed through the pages of Tennyson, one volume of a two-volume set he had recently acquired, and then read slowly, in a strong, beautiful voice:

> It little profits that an idle king,
> By this still hearth, among these barren crags,
> Matched with an aged wife I—

Slowly, while men gathered around and watched in awe, Will Reilly read the whole of Tennyson's "Ulysses."

Then he reached over and grasped the hilt of his knife and said, "Let that be a lesson to you, my friend, and if I were you I would cultivate the study of poetry. There is much to be learned, and poetry can be a companion for your lonely hours."

He lifted the knife clean from the man's hand and the table and, reaching over, wiped the blade clean on the big man's beard. "I am a quiet man," he said, "and prefer to eat and talk in peace."

He got up. "Come, Val. And bring the book."

They went outside. Val felt sick at his stomach, and he was trembling.

"I am sorry, Val, that you had to see that, but the man was a trouble-hunter and he might have forced me to kill him, which I would not want to do."

They walked slowly down the street together. "I do not like violence, but ours is a time of violence, and there are some men who understand nothing else."

At daybreak they were on the stage to Silver City.

The driver had walked to the station with them when the last stars were fading. "You won't be crowded none, Will," he commented. "Not many riding the stage these days. Skeered of the 'Paches."

"I put my faith in you, Pete," Will said, smiling. "If you can't outrun them, you can outfight them."

"Me? You're funnin'." He glanced at Reilly. "That true, about you an' Jeff Reinert?"

"I met somebody called Jeff last night," Will admitted. "He didn't tell me his other name, and I didn't ask."

"Heard you pinned him with a blade and then read poetry to him."

"Something like that."

"You're a hard man, Reilly." They walked a few steps further. "You come close. Reinert killed a man over to Tubac a few weeks back, an' they do say he cut up somebody over to Yuma."

"He was a reckless man." They had reached the station. "It is never a good idea to call unless you have some idea of what the other man is holding."

The driver glanced at Val. "You want to ride topside with me, young feller? Glad to have the company."

"Nobody riding shotgun?"

"Later. We'll have two good fightin' men, at least, an' goin' through the Pass we'll need them."

Val was swung up to the box, and he looked back, watching Will Reilly get in. Whenever they were apart, Val waited in a kind of fear, worrying that Will might be separated from him and not come back.

He thought back to Van, who had left him, and he wondered why he had done it. Was there something about him that people did not like? Why didn't his mother like him? But Will Reilly liked him, he knew, and seemed to enjoy having him with him.

The horses were restless, and when the driver swung up to the box, Val clutched the handrail excitedly. He had never ridden on top of a stage before, but he knew it was considered a privileged position. Pete gathered the lines and took up his whip. The whip cracked, the driver shouted at his team, and they were away, at a fast pace. After a short run they might slow down, but most drivers liked to leave town with a rush.

The air was clear, the day cool. It was early autumn, with occasional cloudy days, but today the clouds were far away, and one could see for miles upon miles.

"You're travelin' with quite a man there," the driver said to Val. "He kin o' yours?"

"He's my uncle." They had agreed on this story, and it satisfied people they met. Then Val added, "I like him."

"Reckon you do. I like him myself. He don't bother nobody, but he can sure take care of hisself when trouble comes. He's a well-thought-of man, and you can bet it gives me comfort to have him riding inside there in Indian country."

"Why?"

"Will Reilly? Ain't a better rifle or pistol shot in the country, boy. You look at him now, a-settin' back there like he was goin' to meet the queen, an' you'd never guess that out in rough country he could out-Injun the Injuns. Reminds me of stories my pa used to tell of Colonel Jim Bowie."

It was thirty miles to Cienaga, the first stop on the way east, and when they drew up at the stage station Val marveled at the speed with which they changed horses. It was there two riflemen emerged from the stage station and strolled out to watch the hitching of the fresh team.

Will Reilly and Val had gone inside, and then paused under the overhang to get a cool drink from the olla that hung there. The water was cold, delightfully so, for it was cooled by even the slightest of passing breezes.

Pete talked a moment to the two riflemen, and to another man who looked like a miner.

Inside the low-ceilinged room there were two tables, some benches, and a short bar. A man in a business suit, with a linen duster over his arm, stood at the bar, while a woman and a small boy sat at the table. Evidently they had just finished eating. The boy looked curiously at Val.

"You ridin' the stage?" he asked.

"Yes." Val was hesitant, but curious. He had rarely talked to anyone near his own age; this boy might be a year older.

"Those are kind of sissy clothes. You a sissy?"

Val glanced at Will, who did not appear to be listening, but Val knew very well that he was hearing every word. The realization gave him confidence. "No, I'm not. You don't judge a man by his clothes."

The words were right out of Will's mouth, but Val had the feeling they were good words for him to use.

The boy had gotten up and walked over to Val, who was standing by himself. He was half a head taller than Val, and sun-browned and tough-looking. Val felt vaguely uneasy, but he did not know why.

"I think you're a sissy, and I'm going to wallop you in the dust."

Now, one of the things Val had learned from Will Reilly was not to talk in such a situation. If you were going to fight, you must land the first blow.

He doubled his fist and swung hard. The blow was quick and it was totally unexpected. It landed on the bigger boy's cheekbone, and then Val threw a second punch, which was to the body. The bigger boy backed up and sat down hard.

Will Reilly stepped over and caught Val by the arm. "That's enough now. Let him alone."

The other boy was up, his eyes blazing. "You turn him loose, mister. I'll show him!"

"You just be glad that I don't turn him loose," Will said. Then he tipped his hat to the woman at the table. "I am sorry, ma'am, but boys will be boys."

With a hand on Val's shoulder, he walked him outside and to the end of the overhang, away from the others.

"I suppose you think you won that fight?" he queried, giving Val a quizzical look.

"Yes, sir. I knocked him down, sir."

"You did put him down, but he was surprised and off balance. You did not win the fight. I won it for you."

Val stared at him.

"He would have whipped you, Val. He is a little older, a little bigger, and a whole lot tougher. That boy has worked hard all his life, and he has nerve. I could see that as he started to get up.

"Understand, you did the right thing. He was pushing you. He was hunting trouble. You hit him right, but not hard enough, and the first punch should have been in the belly. The second blow was not hard enough to hurt him. He would have whipped you, Val."

Val was unconvinced.

"The time will come when you have to take a licking, Val, so just see that you take it like a man. No whimpering, no crying—at least, not until you're alone.

"I did not want you to take that licking now, so I stopped it. I've only taught you a little, and in not a very serious way, but I see the time has come. The next town where we stop will be the beginning of some real training."

The stage was loading. Val walked out and got on with Will. There was a moment before they got into the stage when one of the riflemen nodded, "Howdy, Will."

Reilly glanced at him, then nodded, "How are you, Bridger. Been a long time."

"Long time, Will." He gestured to the lean, slope-shouldered man with him. "This here's Bob Sponseller. He's from Australia."

They shook hands, and Sponseller measured him with cool gray eyes. "You ever been in Sydney, Mr. Reilly?"

Will Reilly smiled. "Why, that's a possibility, Mr. Sponseller, it is indeed; but then there are a lot of Reillys in Australia, no doubt."

"Aye, but there was one a few years back had himself a fuss with the Larrikins down in Argyll Cut when the Cut was a new thing."

"What's the Larrikins?" Bridger asked

"It was a name for the street gangs," Sponseller said, "and they had a running feud with the sailors ashore from the ships. There was this young chap named Reilly who set his cap for a girl on Playfair Street, a girl one of the Larrikin chiefs had a preference for. There was a brawl, they say, that started with the two of them, and ended with half of Sydney fighting."

"That is quite a story," Reilly said. "Has that man Reilly been back again?"

"He daren't go back. That's one man they have their eyes ready for, and after their eyes, their fists and clubs."

Will chuckled. "Then if he goes back he had better carry a gun."

Sponseller smiled grimly. "Now, that would be a likely thing to do."

Sponseller mounted the box with the driver, and Bridger Downs got inside. The whip cracked and the stage started to move. The boy Val had fought and his mother rode on the seat facing Will and Val. Bridger rode beside Val, while the miner and the man in the business suit sat on the seat in the middle.

It was twenty miles to Tres Alamos, where they had scarcely

time to stretch their legs before the stage was rolling on toward Steel's Ranch, the last stop before the dreaded Apache Pass.

It was quiet inside the stage. Val dozed, woke up, dozed again. Once he woke up and saw the other boy staring at him. "My name is Val," he said.

"I don't care." Then after a minute, and rather sullenly, the boy said, "I'm Dobie Grant."

His mother was sleeping, and so, apparently, was Will Reilly. The miner looked over at Val. "Boy, would you like to swap seats? I'd surely admire to lean back and catch some shut-eye."

"Sure," Val said, and moved.

The miner sat down where Val had been and leaned back. Almost at once he was asleep.

"That was a nice thing to do," the businessman said. "Are you traveling far, you and your uncle?"

"To Silver City, then El Paso."

The man glanced at Will Reilly again, started to speak, but subsided. After a moment he looked over at Bridger, who was watching out the window, his Winchester between his knees. "Where you going?" the man asked.

"Through the Pass . . . I hope."

"Is it as bad as they say?"

"Worse. Maybe we'll be lucky. It's a narrow trail and built for ambush. If they want us bad enough, they'll take us."

"I can shoot," Val offered.

"No better than me," Dobie declared belligerently.

"You may have to shoot, both of you," Bridger said.

"One thing," the businessman said, "we've plenty of guns and ammunition."

Bridger Downs did not reply. Maybe that fellow thought so, but with Apaches you never knew.

They rolled into Steel's Ranch as dawn was breaking, and got stiffly down from the stage, standing in the chill air of morning to stretch their muscles. Val trudged sleepily after Will Reilly as they went inside.

A coal-oil lamp with a reflector behind it was burning on the wall, and a lantern stood on the table where the hostler had left it when he came from the stable.

"Breakfast'll be on soon," he said, and then added, "It gets right cold of a morning here."

Bridger Downs lounged by the door, watching outside, for this was Apache country, and they might not wait for the Pass. Sponseller was standing under a paloverde tree, watching the changing of the teams.

The driver strolled over to the Australian. "Did you know Reilly before?"

Sponseller shrugged. "There was a Reilly came ashore from a Frisco bark, and he made a play for a girl . . . or she made it for him . . . and her bloke took exception. There was a pretty bit of a brawl, and Reilly won, which nobody thought he could do, and then the Larrikins took after him."

"What happened?"

"Some of them caught him . . . the worse for them."

"He got away?"

"Oh, they'd have fixed his tripe if he hadn't, but the girl smuggled him aboard a China clipper that left whilst they watched the bark he'd come in. The story's often told down along the Cut and in the dives around Circular Quay. I don't know if it was him, but they've the same look."

"He's a good man to have along, going through the Pass," said the driver.

"What's the fat feller got in that bunch of long boxes?"

Pete shrugged. "I wouldn't know. They're heavy."

"Gold?" Sponseller speculated.

"Doubt it. Hasn't the feel of it, somehow. Gold is heavy, all of a chunk. You know when you pick it up. This hasn't the same feel."

The sun came gingerly over the mountains, and the sky and the ranch yard were pale yellow. Pete looked at the mountains for smoke, but saw none.

He looked around again. With Reilly, Sponseller, Bridger Downs, and himself, there were four good rifles. The miner was a likely shot, and as for the fat businessman with the mutton-chop whiskers—there was no telling, although he had a keen eye and did not, somehow, have the look of a tenderfoot.

The horses pawed earth, and Pete went over to take the lines from the hostler. Reilly walked outside and lit a thin cigar and squinted at the mountains. He was wearing a black broadcloth suit, a white planter's-style hat, highly polished boots, now somewhat dusty, and a dove-gray vest.

"If they're riding, Val, you have to lead them a little. And if they're up in the rocks, aim a little high and watch your bullet strike. There's a tendency to shoot low."

"Yes, sir. Do you think there will be a fight?"

Will Reilly shrugged. He glanced at Sponseller, who had taken off his hat to run his fingers through his curly blond hair. "Do you still favor red shirts?" Reilly asked, and he walked to the stage.

Sponseller swore softly, then grinned. "I'll be blowed," he said.

"What did that mean?" Bridger asked.

"He was the one," Sponseller said. "I was wearing a red shirt all the time in those days. I was one of the Larrikins. It was our chief that he whipped . . . whipped him fairly, too."

They mounted up. The driver glanced once at the station, touched the brim of his hat with his whipstock, and they left the station at a brisk trot.

With the horses occasionally walking, then trotting, the stage moved toward Apache Pass. Val now sat by a window, with the words ringing in his ears: "If you see an Indian, or anybody else does, you get out of the way, and fast!"

He liked looking at the desert and the mountains. A roadrunner kept pace with them for some distance, seemingly amused by racing along; sometimes it ran ahead of the stage, sometimes beside it.

The air was cool; the dust stayed behind them. There was a faint smell of horse and leather, and the hot, baking smell one sometimes gets from old painted wood in the sunlight.

Quail flew up . . . a buzzard swung wide circles in the sky. The rocks of the pass began to take on detail. The trail dipped into a hollow, emerged suddenly, and wound among boulders and brush.

"All right," Will said, "we'll change places." He had moved to sit by the window when the stage suddenly gave a lurch and they heard the driver's wild yell, "Hi-yah! Hi-yah!" And almost simultaneously the boom of a rifle sounded right over their heads.

Crouched near the floor, Val could see nothing, but he could feel the grind of the wheels over gravel and stones, and hear the rattle and creak of the stage as the horses fled eastwards.

Suddenly Bridger Downs fired, then fired again and again. Will was holding his fire, as was the miner. The drummer had drawn a pistol.

All at once there came a ripping sound, and there was a bullet hole in the side of the stage right above Will's head. At almost the same moment the stage gave a leap as though it were taking off to fly, and then it came down with a grinding crash, a wheel splintered, the stage plunged forward, and slowly fell on its side.

How he did it, Val never knew, but Will was suddenly outside. He had lost his grip on his rifle, but as the Apaches came charging down upon them he stood erect, and when Val scrambled through the door, now on the top side of the stage, he saw Will fire. An Indian, dashing toward them on horseback, was struck from his horse.

The Indian fell, hit the dust and slid, and then, surprisingly, started to get up. Coolly, Will shot him again.

The others in the stage were scrambling out. Will Reilly stepped over quickly and pushed Val to the ground among the rocks. "Stay there!" he said sternly.

Pete was sprawled in the dirt half a dozen yards from the stage, and he lay still.

Dobie and his mother were crouched close against the bottom of the overturned stage, and the boy's eyes were bright and hard. There was no fear in them, but rather curiosity and a sort of eagerness. Val wondered how he himself looked.

Turning his head, he picked out the men. Bridger Downs had quickly found himself a spot, and kneeling on one knee, he was waiting for a good shot. Sponseller, who had jumped clear when the stage started to go, was about fifty feet away among the rocks, in a somewhat higher position.

The miner, crouched near Val, was favoring an arm, and there was a slow staining of red on his coatsleeve, but he had his rifle in position, partly braced by the fork in a shrub.

The drummer had crawled to the back of the stage and was trying to get one of his long boxes off the roof of the stage.

He turned to Val. "Boy, can you help me? Crawl over here."

Val moved over toward him, and lying down, managed to crawl over and unlash the other end of the box without exposing himself to the Apaches' fire. He pushed the box, the drummer heaved, and it crashed to the ground. The drummer picked up a rock and began to pound on the edge of a slat.

Val crawled back and looked around again. The stage lay just off the trail, forming a partial wall on one side, while on the other side was a bank of rocks and brush. One of the stage horses lay dead almost under the stage, and it must have been his fall that sent the stage into its wild careening.

Val lay crouched close to the ground as the Indians worked closer. He could smell the dust and the powder smoke. Something splintered behind him; the long box broke open and the drummer began taking out rifles. He had twelve brand-new rifles, and from another box he began taking out ammunition.

"Come on, son, help me load these," he said. Val moved over to help, and Dobie joined him. As fast as they could load the rifles they passed them to Will, Bridger, and the miner.

Val kept one rifle himself, and so did Dobie. Filled with excitement, the boys waited for the next rush of the Indians.

"Ma'am," the drummer said, "if you can load these rifles for us, we'll teach those redskins a lesson."

Bridger, with his own rifle and two others beside him, suddenly opened fire. He was making a demonstration as much as anything else, deliberately firing rapidly to show the Apaches what they had run into.

When an Indian showed himself Bridger Downs fired six times as rapidly as he could work the lever, then spaced his shots until the magazine was empty. Then he picked up his second rifle and did the same thing.

Suddenly three Indians moved at once, and the drummer, firing with almost negligent ease, dropped two of them and dusted the third.

Then, very deliberately, he picked up a chunk of slate and tossed it into the air, smashed it with a bullet, and smashed one of the pieces before it could touch the ground.

Will Reilly chuckled, and picking up an empty bottle, tossed it into the air, smashed it, then smashed the neck while the drummer broke one of the fragments.

Sponseller called out: "What the hell you fellers doin', play-actin'?"

Hoping some Apache would understand what he said, Will Reilly yelled back in English, and repeated it in Spanish. "We've got forty rifles an' two thousand rounds of ammunition, so we might as well have some fun!"

One Indian, who lay in plain sight where he had fallen, suddenly leaped up, blood showing on his skull, and made a dive for shelter among the rocks.

Val shot . . . he never knew whether he hit the Indian or not, for four rifles spoke as one and the Indian threw up his hands and plunged forward against the slope, then rolled over twice and lay sprawled, arms flung wide.

Val turned. "I want a drink," he said to Will.

Reilly looked at him and was about to speak when Downs spoke from the corner of his mouth. "Boy, you forget it. That's the one thing we ain't got any of!"

FOUR

The sun was high, the few clouds disappeared, the heat in the bottom of the canyon grew oppressive. No Apache showed along the rock walls. The five remaining horses stood in their harness, heads drooping, unable to leave, for they were still hitched to the overturned stage by one trace chain.

The Apaches evidently needed the horses, for they made no attempt to kill them. Nor did they make any further attempt to dare the fire power of the little group behind the stage.

But the Apaches knew they were out of water. Among the first shots they had fired had been the ones at the waterbags suspended beside the boot. So they had only to wait—and an Apache can be as patient as a buzzard.

Pete was dead—there was now no doubt of that. The miner, whose name turned out to be Egan Cates, had been wounded twice.

Val loaded the miner's gun, and replaced it for him. "That's a good lad," Cates said. Then he looked closely at Reilly. "You any kind of an Injun, Reilly?"

"Why?"

"There's water yonder." He pointed north of their position.

"There's a spring over there, but there's a tank up yonder in the rocks."

"Don't try it." Bridger Downs was emphatic. "You'd never make it. Once it gets dark they'll draw the net tight around us. You wouldn't have a chance."

A slow hour passed, and then another. Only one shot was fired, and that was from the Apache side.

There was no sound from Sponseller, and from their position they could not see him. Whether he was alive or dead they had no way of knowing.

Slowly the day grew cooler. Shadows began to reach out from the rock walls. Val lay against the earth, feeling his heart beat, and listening to the sounds. Would they ever get out alive? He tried to remember the stories he had heard. There were not many who had escaped the Apaches . . . but there had been a few.

His mouth was dry, so dry he could scarcely swallow. Will picked a smooth pebble from the sand. "Put this in your mouth, Val. It will keep you from being so thirsty."

The pebble felt cool, almost cold. Saliva began to flow, and he did feel better.

A star came out, and the night air grew more chilly. Will glanced over at the woman. "Ma'am, did you have anything to eat with you?"

"Yes, there's some bread and coffee, and some jerky."

"There's some'at in my parcel in the boot," the miner offered. "You can get at it easier, but without water it won't help much."

Val thought of the olla back at the stage station, and its deliciously cool water. Then he tried to forget it and think about other things. He tried to remember Myra, but the only thing he could recall was her voice, how harsh it had sounded on that last night.

More stars came out, and they seemed like distant campfires on the field of the night sky, as though a vast army camped out there, far away.

Will Reilly sat up, wrapping his arms about his knees. "Don't worry, Val," he said easily. "I have been in worse spots. Although not many," he added, more grimly. "At least, they won't attack us in the night."

He added, "When this is over I think it will be time to go east again."

Val said suddenly, "I might be able to crawl to the water."

Will looked at him. "You'd try it, too, wouldn't you?"

"Yes, sir."

"Don't. That would be dangerous, even for an Indian."

"I'm small, sir. I take up less room than you, sir, or any of the others. When I lived with the Schmitts, we used to play Indian all the time. I could crawl and hide better than anybody."

"You just wait."

"We need water, sir. I know there'd be Indians there, but they wouldn't be looking for a boy."

"No," Will Reilly said firmly.

Then Val slept, and when he awoke it was very cold. He dug himself deeper into the sand and tried to turn his jacket collar higher. For a long time he lay awake, thinking about the rocks where Egan Cates had said the water was. They formed a steep wall, but they were very broken, with cracks and chimneys everywhere; there were fallen rocks all down the mountainside. A boy could hide where a man would have no chance.

Val would never forget that night. The stars seemed brighter and closer than they ever had, or ever would again. Presently he heard a vague stirring, and then what sounded like a scuffle.

After that there was somebody panting nearby, and he heard Bridger Downs's voice. "In the side . . . I don't think it's bad. He had the same idea I had."

"Did you kill him?"

"I killed him. Oh, he was tough and slippery. He got the knife into me slick as a whistle, but I grabbed his wrist and held on while I clobbered him with my fist. Then I got hold of his throat, dug my fingers in, and smashed his head against the rocks."

"How are the horses?"

"They seemed all right, but they'll be needin' water."

Finally Val slept again, and was awakened by the slam of a gunshot, and he saw Will holding one of the new rifles. The drummer was loading another. "I thought our little demonstration of shooting might scare them off," he said.

Will lit the stub of his cigar with his left hand. "Apaches don't scare worth a damn," he said. And he added, "Although they take notions."

"Notions?"

"Watch for their chief. If you kill their chief they'll back off until they've chosen another. They might leave altogether."

There was no attack, and no Apaches were seen. Val grew restless. He thought the Indians were probably gone. His mouth was parched and his skin was hot, but he did not complain. Nobody else was complaining, and he was determined not to be the first.

They waited, sleeping by turns. It was midafternoon before Will Reilly suddenly reached over and shook Downs awake. "They're coming."

"You sure?"

"I'm sure. They've been filtering down from the rocks, working closer and closer. I think they're going to try a rush."

Egan Cates pulled himself up, his face white and strained. The miner had lost blood, and the lack of water was not helping him.

Will turned to Val. "You and Dobie load. Make every move count now. I believe they're planning to do us in."

When they came it was from scarcely thirty yards off. They seemed to spring directly out of the rocks. They fired a volley and charged.

All the guns were loaded, and the Apaches were met by a crashing volley, the men firing as fast as they could work the levers on their rifles. Val knew the attack would have to be beaten back or they would not survive, and he emptied his rifle as swiftly as possible.

Three Apaches made the circle of rocks. A barrel-chested one vaulted the rocks from behind and rushed at Will's back, a knife in his hand.

Val, unable to think what to do, threw his rifle at the Indian's legs, and the man stumbled and went to his knees. Both boys leaped on him, Dobie striking hard with a rock.

The Apache threw them off and lunged to his feet. They grabbed his legs and he swung down with a knife at Val's back. Will, hearing the scuffle behind him, wheeled and fired his Winchester at point-blank range.

The heavy slug caught the Apache squarely in the chest and he fell back. Will fired again, then turned and clubbed his rifle at one who was fighting desperately with the wounded Cates, who had only one useful hand. The butt caught the Apache behind the neck and he went down, his skull crushed right at the top of the spine.

The two Apaches were tossed over the rocks. The remaining one of the three was backed against the rocks with Bridger Downs's .44 jammed into his belly.

"Hold him, Bridger," Reilly said. "We mustn't let him go to warn the others. Our boys haven't had time to get around to the other end of the pass. If he gets away and tells the others about all the rifles and ammunition we've got, they'll know it's a trap."

The drummer was quick. "We'd better send up the signal for the attack. As for him"—he gestured toward the Indian and drew his knife—"we'd better let him abscond right here."

The Apache lunged suddenly, springing to the top of the rocks, then leaping over. Reilly fired a shot in the air, and let him go.

"Let's hope it works," the drummer said. He glanced at Bridger. "I had to trust you knew what abscond meant, and I was sure the Indian would not."

Bridger Downs spat, and gave the drummer a hard look. "I know what abscond means, my friend, and if I was you I'd forget what it means."

The drummer smiled. "Of course. This is all among friends, isn't it?"

There was a sudden rattle of horses' hoofs, and they saw the dust of the fleeing Apaches. The trick had worked.

"Come on." Will Reilly got to his feet. "We'd better go while the going is good."

"Just for luck," Cates suggested, "throw a fire together. The signal smoke will sort of help them along."

Sponseller came down from the rocks. He had a bullet burn along his ribs, but was otherwise unhurt. He helped get the horses ready, and when they were all mounted up they moved out, three of the horses carrying double.

It was a good fifty miles to Ralston's, and Val never forgot that ride, nor the walking he did on the way.

After that it was Silver City, where Val went riding with Billy, the son of the woman who kept the boarding house. Dobie was with them, too. They raced their horses through the streets and out into the hills beyond the town.

"You people stayin' around?" Billy asked.

"Nope," Dobie said. "Ma's going over to Las Vegas. Her sister—
my aunt—lives there. Ever since pa died we been traipsin'."

"You better hope your ma doesn't marry again," Billy said.
"Mine did, and he's drunk most of the time. He beats me when
he can lay holt of me . . . which ain't often."

"We're going to El Paso," Val said. "Maybe to New Orleans."

They circled around the town and came in from the other side,
talking about Indians. "I never seen any real wild Injuns," Billy
said. "There was some in Kansas folks said had been wild a while
back, but the ones in Colorado were mostly just hanging around."

After supper they stood outside the Antrim House and Ash
Upson talked to the boys. "A pleasure," he said, "a real pleasure
to talk to Will Reilly. It isn't often we find anyone with his
knowledge of literature. He's an admirer of Scott, as I am."

The other boys did not know who Scott was, but Val recalled
Will's mention of him. After a while Will came out. "We're
leaving tomorrow, Val."

Then came a week in El Paso, three days in San Antonio, and a
ride on a steamboat from Indianola, Texas, to New Orleans. It
was a fortunate time for Will Reilly. The cards ran his way, and
he played them carefully, arriving in New Orleans three thousand
dollars richer than when he left Tucson.

After that there was Mobile, Savannah, Charleston, Philadel-
phia, and New York. . . .

And then a year in Europe. Val was growing taller and stronger, and he learned to speak French, picked up some German and
Italian. As they traveled, Will Reilly gambled in every city in
which they stayed. Yet sometimes weeks would pass during which
he would not touch a deck of cards, nor enter a gambling hall,
though even during such times he never really released himself
from the hold of gambling.

His wagers were polite ones, developed during conversations,
and often evolving from some casual discussion of history or
genealogies; on these, too, he was well informed. Often the fact
that he was an American gave his antagonists greater confidence,
as did his manner, which was almost apologetic, though insistent
at such times. Somehow—and Val often wondered how it
happened—it was always Will who was challenged. But Will
Reilly was not a man to allow himself to grow slack in his physical

condition. He boxed, he fenced, he went to shooting galleries, he rode horseback, he wrestled.

But Will Reilly was changing. They were in Innsbruck now, and one night after midnight he returned from the gaming rooms in a black mood. He threw a handful of money on the table in their room. The gesture was one of irritation, even of disgust.

He looked at Val. "You should be asleep. You're too young to keep such hours."

"I wasn't tired."

Will glanced at the book. "*Faust?* Where did you get hold of that?"

"It was a lady. The one you were talking to this afternoon. Louise, I think you called her."

"You talked to her?"

"Yes, sir. She was asking about you. If I was your son."

Will Reilly was silent for a moment, then he muttered to himself, "So she didn't believe me? But why should she? I'm a gambler." His tone was filled with self-contempt, and Val watched him curiously. He had never seen Will like this before.

Will gestured at the book. "Read that—and then read Byron's *Manfred*. That's the only Faust who acted as if he had any guts. The rest of them were a pack of sniveling weaklings who learned nothing that was of any help to them."

Val never knew why he said what he did, but he knew his friend was in trouble. "Have you learned anything of any use to you?" the boy asked.

Will gave him a quick, hard glance. Then he chuckled. "Why, now, there's a likely question if I've ever heard one. Yes, I've learned a lot, but there are some situations where all a man knows is of no use to him. Val, I've been an ungodly fool. I've stepped in where I had no business, and the best I can get out of it is the worst."

"What are you going to do?"

"Play my hand out . . . as far as it will take me. I've taken chips in the game, and I'll not back out now."

"And if you fail, sir?"

Reilly gave Val one of those flashing Irish smiles that lit up his face. "Why, then, Val, I'll need a lot of luck and a fast horse."

Well, Val thought, it would not be the first time they had left town in a hurry. And he wondered if Will had actually given any thought to the fast horses.

Val was not yet ten years old, but he had been reared in a hard, dangerous school. The next morning when he saw Will mount up and ride off toward the forest alone, he went over to the stable where horses were for sale or for hire. He had talked to the hostlers before, and the owners, too. There were two gray horses that he particularly liked, and he stood looking at them now.

"Would you sell those horses," he asked, "if I could get my uncle to buy?"

"The horses are for sale." The hostler was an Italian, and friendly. "Everything is for sale if the price is right."

He waited until another hostler, a German, walked away and then said, "Your uncle should be careful. He is making a dangerous enemy."

"You are our friend?"

The Italian shrugged. "I like him . . . your uncle. He is a man."

"Then sell me the horses and say nothing about it."

The hostler stared at him. "You are serious? You're only a child."

"Sir, I have traveled with my uncle for a long time. I know how it is with him. He lets me do things."

"Yes, I have seen that." The man rubbed his jaw. "You have the money? It is quite a lot."

"Yes, sir. I can get it."

They haggled briefly, but it was largely a matter of form. Val knew he would have to pay a little too much, but he remembered what Will Reilly often said: "The cost of something is measured by your need of it."

"And the horses? Where will you keep them?" the Italian asked.

"Take them tomorrow, when nobody is watching, to the red barn. I shall want them saddled and ready."

That called for some more haggling but to a boy who had spent his life among men, and who had more than once watched Will make preparations for a hurried leave-taking, it offered no problems.

The old stone barn was deserted, a place where, as Val knew, the Italian hostler often met a girl friend. Sometimes Val had walked to the barn with him and they had sat talking and looking across the valley until the girl came, at which time Val would leave them alone.

So, sitting in the pleasant shade of the barn, or in the sunlight, if the hour was early, Val had indicated his impression that the mountains before them could not be crossed into Italy, nor into Switzerland. This the Italian was quick to deny.

"There are smugglers who cross them all the time," he said. "They have secret paths over the mountains. In fact," he added, "I know some of the smugglers, and have used some of the trails."

Now he said after a while, "Why do you think my uncle is in danger?"

Luigi shrugged. "It is plain to see. Your uncle is a handsome man, a strong man. The woman he is in love with, and who, I think, is in love with him, comes of a very important family in Russia, and it is said she is to marry a man here who is of a very old family. This is arranged by her cousin, Prince Pavel, and all is well. Then comes your uncle.

"The lady is out riding. They meet, and your uncle comments on the view. The lady replies . . . and it had begun.

"I was riding with her to be sure all goes well with her, and when we have passed the lady asks me about him. They meet again. By accident? I do not think so. This time they talk of mountains, of the Urals, the Rockies, and these Alps. Your uncle talks well, very well.

"Again they meet, and again. Someone with nothing better to do speaks of it, and her cousin, Prince Pavel, is furious. It is his wish for his cousin to marry the German, who is very rich and of noble family. The lady is warned . . . I know it is so, although I did not see it—only their faces afterward.

"They meet again, and then your uncle is warned."

Will Reilly warned? They did not know him as Val did. He was a proud, fierce man under that cool face he showed to the world.

They warned Will Reilly, who had killed three men in gun duels, and another with a knife in a dark room where they fought to the death? Who had fought the Sioux and the Apaches?

Suddenly Val was afraid. He was afraid for Will, and he was afraid for those others who did not know Will Reilly as well as he did.

FIVE

Val had walked out very early in the morning to see if the gray horses were in the barn, and when he returned he strolled along to the café where he was to meet Will.

He loved the quaint old town which had been a trading post, which had been founded in the twelfth century, or before. He loved standing on the bank of the swift-flowing Inn River, and watching the water. He loved the mountains that loomed so close to the city, and the picturesque buildings of a bygone time. Sometimes he thought he never wanted to leave Innsbruck, but he knew the wishing was useless, for they never remained long in one place.

In Innsbruck Will had done no gambling. Here he thought only of Louise, and Val liked her himself. He had met Louise twice, and they had talked for a long time on both occasions. The first time was at the Munding, and she had bought him a pastry. That was when she had merely met Will Reilly when riding, and had not really known him at all. She had been very curious, but Val was used to that; women were always curious about Will Reilly.

Val never said that Will was a gambler. He was a mining man, a story in which there was some truth, for Will did have a mining claim in Nevada, and he owned shares in several mining ventures.

45

Val walked along the Maria-Theresien-Strasse to where it became the narrow Herzog-Friedrich-Strasse, and went on until he came to a little café where Will told him Goethe used to come to sip wine. He went inside and found a table near a window where he could watch the street.

A man came walking briskly along the street, but when he was opposite the café he stopped and loitered idly.

Val was curious. For more than five years Will Reilly had been training him always to observe anything that seemed unusual or out of place, and this man had been hurrying as if he was afraid of being late, and then had stopped and merely loafed. The hour was early, the café had just opened, and there was no one else about.

Then another man strolled up the street and, without paying any attention to the one who waited outside, he entered the café and seated himself at a table facing that of Val, with the doorway between them.

A couple of minutes later two men came up the street and stopped outside to talk.

Val had eaten breakfast at that café for several consecutive mornings, and had never seen any of these men there before. Suddenly, he was frightened, and he remembered what Luigi, the Italian hostler, had told him.

He started to get up, but the man facing him lifted a hand. "Stay where you are, boy. You will not be hurt."

"I am going because I do not wish you to be hurt," Val said.

The man seemed amused. "Us? Hurt?" he said, and added, "I am sorry you have to see this, boy, but your uncle must be taught a lesson, and it will do you no harm. You may learn from it."

"My uncle has learned a great many lessons."

"But evidently not the essential one. Ah, here he comes."

Will Reilly strolled up the street with that casual elegance that was so much a part of him. As he opened the door Val started to cry out, but a rough hand was placed across his mouth, stifling his shout.

Will stepped through the door and the two men on the street pivoted sharply about and stepped in after him, seizing both his arms from behind.

Will did not struggle, but merely glanced at the man at the

table, who was obviously directing the operation. "Where is the Prince? I am sure he would want to witness this."

They were somewhat taken aback by his calmness, but Val was not. He had seen Will Reilly face such situations before, although not for the same reason.

No one else had appeared in the café, nor was there anyone on the street. They were taken outside to a carriage that appeared from nowhere driven by the man who had arrived first. Inside the carriage were four men, one of whom held a pistol. Will and Val were put in the carriage and the two men who had held Will got up behind the carriage and the leader mounted the box beside the driver.

Val sat very stiff beside Will, trying not to show his fear. Yet in spite of his fear he found himself a little contemptuous of these men. Obviously hired for the job, they were so inept that they had not even searched Will Reilly, and they were utterly unaware of the kind of man they dealt with.

How could they know? He seemed merely a handsome, well-set-up young man, well-dressed and poised. How could they know what lay behind him?

Their destination was only a short distance beyond the limits of the town. Val glanced out of the coach window and across the fields. Just over there, not half a mile away, was the deserted barn with their two horses. The coach came to a sudden halt beside a small grove, where two saddle horses were tied.

Val saw Will give them a quick glance, and knew what he was seeing. One of the horses was the one Louise rode. Was she to be here?

They walked through the trees to a small clearing, perhaps half an acre in extent. Across the clearing, in riding clothes, stood Louise and a tall young man. She wore a gray riding habit, and looked lovely, but her eyes were wide and frightened.

The young man wore a beautiful fur-trimmed coat, which he now removed and dropped over a rock.

Louise spoke, "Pavel . . . *please!*"

"No, my cousin, we are going to teach this American some manners. I hope you will also profit by the lesson."

"Pavel—"

"Remove his coat, if you please," he said to the men holding Will. They stripped off his coat, and he made no resistance. The soft material of his white shirt was ruffled by the breeze. He was smiling.

Val, unnoticed by the others, had edged nearer.

"Now, peasant, you are going to get a whipping. The kind of whipping we reserve for such as you."

"This is rather absurd, don't you think?" Will asked. "If you wish to call the whole thing off, Prince Pavel, I will accept your apology."

"*My* apology!" Pavel's features went taut with anger.

"I must have heard about you, Prince Pavel. I have heard you do not pay your gambling debts, and that you will marry your cousin to this wealthy man so he will pay them for you."

"Stand back," Pavel said to the others, "and give me the whip."

It was a long whip, not unlike the western black-snake or bull whip.

Val was amazed, not so much that they should plan to whip his uncle, but that they were so sure they could.

"Let me do it, sir." The man who stepped forward was a husky brute, and Val saw Will glance at him, marking him for future attention. "I have some skill at such things."

"Of course not," Pavel replied shortly. "I reserve the pleasure for myself." He coiled the whip, drawing the lash almost lovingly through his fingers.

During his early years Will Reilly had made a trip over the Santa Fe Trail, working as a teamster. He had used just such a whip, and he had seen and participated in the brutal whip battles fought by teamsters, who could flick a fly from the shoulder of a bull without touching the skin.

He knew the tactics well, and when Pavel swung the whip and shot the lash at him, Will stepped an easy pace forward, blocked the whip with his forearm, and the lash coiled about it. Instantly his hand dropped, grasped the whip, and gave a tremendous jerk.

Prince Pavel was jerked off balance, the whip flying from his hand as he went to his knees on the turf.

One of the men lunged toward Reilly, but Val promptly tripped him. Will reversed the whip and snapped it viciously at Pavel. The tip of the whip snapped at the young Russian, ripping his shirt and starting blood from his shoulder.

Pavel screamed and, moving lightly as a dancer moves, Will Reilly stepped about quickly. The husky man who had begged for the chance at the whip was next, and the lash whipped his shoulders, snapped at his belly, laid open his cheek.

The action had been so swift that the others had been caught off guard. They were not fighting men, as such, just strong bullies hired for a job. Will moved, now a deadly dancer, his whip a darting snake that drew blood wherever it landed. It struck Pavel's cheek, ripping the flesh, and the Prince screamed again, clapping his hands to his face. The lash popped again, and this time the end dug into his forehead.

Suddenly the man who had been the leader of the group, the one who had sat opposite Val in the restaurant, dug a hand into his coat pocket and came up with a pistol.

Will stepped back closer to Val. "Now!" he said, and from under his coat Val took the pistol he had carried for Will, and tossed it to him. Deftly, he caught it with his left hand even as he moved.

The man had leveled his gun to fire, and Will Reilly fired, almost casually. The man rose on his tiptoes, his gun went off into the turf, and he fell forward on his face in the grass.

At the sound of the shot, its report echoing against the mountainsides, there came a silence. It was no longer a few men giving a whipping to a man for a price. It was death.

Prince Pavel was on his knees, blood streaking his face and neck, his shirt soaked with it. He was staring at Will, stunned horror in his eyes. "Don't . . . don't kill me!"

The other men were backing away, looking for a chance to run. "You'll pay for this!" one of them shouted. "You will never leave the country alive!"

Will Reilly dropped the whip, and walked over to where his coat lay. He put it on, shifting the gun from hand to hand as he did so.

Only then did he look at Louise, who stood shocked and white, unable to believe her eyes.

"I am sorry, Louise, that this happened in your presence," Will Reilly said. "I am not a man to accept a whipping for any reason—least of all, for loving you."

"You have killed him."

"He would have killed me. He was armed, and he was intending to shoot. I had no choice."

He glanced at Pavel. "Had he challenged me, I would have

fought him. Or we might have met together and talked of this. Instead, he chose this method."

"I fight only with *gentlemen!*" Pavel was on his feet, shaken, but with a show of confidence returning.

"Judging by the company you keep," Reilly said coolly, "you need have no fears."

He turned to Louise. "Will you come with me now? I shall return to my own country."

She seemed to hesitate, and stared at him.

"No!" Pavel shouted. "You can not!" He grasped her arm. "He is a murderer! He will be hunted down and thrown into prison, then executed! You would ruin us all!"

Will Reilly stood quietly, while Val shifted from one foot to the other, anxious to be away. Some of the men were already away through the trees, and it was no more than thirty minutes of fast walking to the edge of the city. And these men would be running.

"Louise?"

"No . . . I can not."

One long moment he looked at her. "Good-bye, Louise." He had thrown in his hand, and Val knew it.

"Come, Val." He turned, thrusting the gun into his waistband. He stumbled once, and glancing up, Val saw Will's face was drawn and pale.

Val caught his hand. "We must hurry, Uncle Will. Those men will have almost reached Innsbruck, and people there may have heard the shot."

With Val leading the way, they turned abruptly from the road and went down a path that led across the fields, partly concealed by a line of trees.

"Wait a minute." Will stopped. "We've got to get horses—"

"They're waiting in the barn over there," Val pointed. "I had Luigi put them there. I paid for them," he added, "out of your anchor money."

That anchor money had been a joke between them. It was a little money Will Reilly always kept for a road stake in the event he had to move swiftly. He had once jokingly referred to it as his up-anchor money, but the phrase had somehow been trimmed over the years.

They walked swiftly. Will Reilly was no fool. He was a traveler with no local standing, and no influence, while Prince Pavel came from a powerful family with connections in many European countries. If Will Reilly was arrested now there would be small prospect of escape.

"We're going to be in trouble," he said to Val. "I haven't been gambling lately, and I've spent a good bit. I wish we dared go back and get that anchor money."

"We don't need to," Val replied, "I've got it here."

They dipped down through a stream bed, crossed a stone wall, and went up the grassy slope to the barn. Luigi got up from where he had been sitting. "The horses are saddled," he said, "but you must hurry."

There were three horses, and Luigi said, "You would never get over the mountains without me, and if I take you over the mountains you might take me to America."

"That we will," Reilly said, and swung into the saddle.

They followed footpaths and cart roads to the village of Axams, then across country toward the Sellrainer.

It was clear and cool. The wind from off the Alps was fresh, the horses lively, eager to go. The meadows were matted with wild flowers. The mountain slopes were dark forests of pine. Once a small blue butterfly lit for an instant on the mane of Val's horse and then was gone.

There was no sound but the beat of hoofs. How long before their route would be discovered? How long before pursuit could be organized? A man was dead, and another man of power and influence had been beaten with a whip. They would come, Val was sure of that.

Will led the way Luigi had pointed, and Luigi fell back beside Val. "Tell me. What happened?"

When Val had told him, his only comment was, "It is what I said, he is a man, that one!"

"Where are you taking us?"

He pointed at the vast wall of the Stubaier Alps. "Over that. On the other side is Italy; or if you wish we can go west, and there is Switzerland."

"But they will follow us."

He shrugged. "They will try all the roads first. It will give us time. Not many know the way we are going, although the mountaineers would guess. They will not know at first that we are mounted, and they will try to close the best-known roads. By the time they know what we have done, we shall, with luck, be lost back in the Alps."

When they reached the Sellrainer there was a good cart road that followed the stream as far as the village of Gries, where a footpath continued on up the gorge of the Melach. It was wild and picturesque. Somewhere near was the hunting lodge of the Emperor Maximilian I, but they had no time to think of such things. Soon they would leave the horses at the farm of a man known to Luigi, and from there on it was walk all the way.

"We can get what we need from my friend," Luigi said. "He has warm clothes, boots, packsacks . . . everything."

"I will want a good rifle," Will said.

Luigi shrugged. "That, I think, is impossible. We will have enough to carry without it."

They were climbing steadily. Around them the high fields were green, and there were many butterflies, mostly of the small blue variety, and many birds. Twice he saw what Luigi told him were golden eagles, and once the feared *lammergeier*, or bearded vulture.

The farm of Luigi's friend was a pleasant place when they came to it, a barn for the cows, sheepfold, and a rather larger than usual house with white walls and an overhanging roof. They rode into the yard and a short, stocky man appeared in the doorway, studied them carefully for a moment, and then came down the grassy slope to meet them.

"Friends of mine," Luigi said, "they are going over the mountain."

The man scarcely glanced at them. "Come in, then." He turned his back to them, went back inside, and they followed him.

Seated at a table cleaning a rifle was a young man with a buxom woman, and two equally buxom flaxen-haired girls. A fire was going, for the evening was chill at the altitude. "You will spend the night," the man said. He glanced at Val. "The boy is too young. It is a hard climb."

"He is a strong boy," Will said. "He is accustomed to mountains."

The man took his pipe from his mouth. "I have told you," he said simply. He turned to his wife and spoke to her in Italian.

"He is Tirolean," Luigi explained, "but his wife is Italian . . . from Merano. They have many friends," he added, "in Italy as well as in Switzerland. He knows everybody."

Luigi left the room with the Tirolean, returning after a short time. "He wants too much," he said, "but he will accept the horses."

"I'll bet he will," Will said. "And everything else he can get."

"We can make a deal on the horses because I have threatened to take them back to Gries, where I know a man who will buy them." He accepted a cup of coffee, and added, "There is no fooling him. Men do not come this far into the mountains at such an hour without a special reason."

"Did you tell him what happened?"

"He does not wish to know. You come, he sells, he knows nothing . . . he does not suspect anything, you see? If the police ask he will tell them nothing important. He is a master at it."

They were silent then. Will Reilly sipped his coffee and stared into the fire, remembering. Val dozed, woke once, and dozed again.

After a long time Luigi spoke again. "You know what lies ahead, do you not? The trail is narrow, part of it is all right, part is very steep, very rough. And there can be storms—and if you have not seen a sudden storm in the Alps, you have seen nothing."

Will shrugged. "Is there an alternative?"

"No."

"Then . . ."

SIX

It was dark and cold when Val woke up. Will Reilly was sitting on the edge of his bed, dressing. "Better get dressed, Val. We've got to be moving."

"Where is Luigi?"

"I don't know. His bed is empty."

Val put his feet to the floor and dressed in silence. He might have expected this, for Will was moving true to form. Always the unexpected . . . always the quick start, and then travel faster than anyone could expect.

When he was dressed he went into the kitchen. Will was making coffee. "A warm drink will do us good. Get your gear together, Val. You'll be glad of those heavy boots before the day is over."

"Will we be in the snow?"

"Not until dark, I'm thinking."

"What happened to Luigi?"

"He's around, I believe, but if he isn't, we will move out on our own. I'm ashamed, Val. I was tired, and that and the fresh mountain air made me sleep sounder."

They heard someone stirring in the other room, then the door

54

opened and the Tirolean came out, stuffing his shirt into his pants. "You make free," he said.

"We hoped we would not disturb you," Will said, smiling. "After all, why should you and your family get up just because we must? And we thought an early start would be advisable."

The man looked sour, but whether it was the early hour or something gone awry with their plans, Val could not guess.

He dragged their packs to the door, then went to the table. Will had made chocolate for him. There was bread, jam, and some cold meat on the table.

"You cannot see. It is early to walk on the mountain," the Tirolean said.

"Oh, we'll manage!" Will had not seated himself, Val noticed, and knowing the ways of his friend he held himself ready to move quickly. Anything unusual made Will Reilly wary, and Luigi had no reason to be gone—or none they could think of.

Suddenly Will put down his cup. "All right, Val. Get your pack on."

"You leave without Luigi?" the Tirolean protested.

Will shrugged. "He's probably waiting for us. If not, he'll catch up."

Never turning his back on the man, Will helped Val with his pack, then held the door open for him and stepped into the doorway after him.

"Thank you," he said, smiling pleasantly. "You have no idea how we appreciate this." And he drew the door to behind him.

Will moved out at a good pace and Val was hard put to keep up. It was a cart track, then a herdsman's track, and almost at once it began to climb steeply. Each of them had a staff, which helped.

Below them a few lights showed in the village, and then they rounded a bend. Will slowed his pace. By now they were about half a mile from the village.

"What happened?" Val asked.

Will paused a moment, looking back, giving Val a chance to catch his breath without mentioning it. "Val, most people are sadly, weakly human. Don't ever forget that. All but a few mean to be honest, but sometimes their ambition, their greed, or their need for more money will lead them into error. Probably there is a simple explanation for Luigi being gone. Probably the Tirolean was annoyed because we were up before him, in his own house, and made so free as to prepare our breakfast.

"On the other hand, they may have had second thoughts. Prince Pavel would probably pay a good sum to know what became of me, and after all, the police will be after me. They may have persuaded themselves they should report me."

"I don't think Luigi would do it."

"Maybe not. I don't like to think so, either. Let's give him the benefit of the doubt, and keep moving while we are doing it."

They walked in silence for better than a mile, and then paused for a brief rest.

The stars were out, although far up in the sky over the mountains it was growing light. Presently they could distinguish one tree from another, and they could see where they were putting their feet. The green valley of the Otz lay far below them now, shadowed still, although they walked in sunlight. Val was a good walker, and at one time or another he had done a lot of walking. He had always loved the mountains, and much of his walking had been done at much higher elevations than this. He had gone over passes twelve or thirteen thousand feet up in Colorado; and if what he had heard was correct, few of these passes were anywhere near that.

The men who lived in this region were all mountain men who hunted on these high slopes, and would be making better time if they tried to follow, but as Will told him, "We've a good start, Val, and they know I am armed. Most of them are family men who would have little sympathy with such men as Pavel Pavelovitch."

Will kept their pace easy, and made frequent stops. Shortly after noon they made a longer one, ate a little bread and cheese, and drank from a cold stream that ran off the mountain nearby.

By mid-afternoon, Val was having a hard time of it. His legs were tired, and the climb had become steeper, or so it seemed to him. Once, when they had stopped, they sat watching a golden eagle swing against the vault of the sky.

"It's almost worth it, Val. We'd never have taken this hike otherwise."

"Will, I've been thinking. Won't they send word over the Brenner Pass? A rider or a coach could make the trip to Merano, and officers could be waiting for us when we cross into Italy."

Reilly smiled. "Yes, you are right. That's why we aren't going into Italy. At least, we'll see. There are two ways, and the shortest and probably the best route does take us into Italy, but for just a few miles."

The wind off the mountain was cold. Val plodded on, no longer thinking of anything but the moment when they would stop. Will seemed to be looking for something, and suddenly it was there . . . a narrow ravine that fell away steeply for about a hundred yards, and then ended in a precipice. He turned and descended the ravine.

"Careful now, Val," he said. "One slip, and it will be the end of you."

They came abruptly to another crack in the plateau that ran diagonally into the ravine they followed. Will Reilly took Val by the hand and climbed down into this smaller ravine. Under an overhang was a small stone hut.

Lifting the latch, Will went in, and Val followed. The place was snug and tight. There was a fireplace and a stack of wood sufficient to last for days, for the hut was built against the cliff, and the overhang was deep enough for a storage place for fuel.

"How did you know about this place?" Val asked.

For a moment that Irish smile came over Will Reilly's face. "I listen, Val, as I have taught you to do, and sometimes I cultivate strange company. You might wonder why, but I've learned always to keep one hand on the door latch, mentally, at least.

"There are smugglers' caves and hide-outs all over the mountains. You see, we're near the meeting place of three borders here, Austria, Italy, and Switzerland, and smuggling can be profitable."

He built a fire. He was quick and sure, as always, and his fire flared up with the first match.

"I've brought some tea. We'll have tea and then we'll bathe our feet and wash out our socks. That's the first thing on a long walk, boy. Keep your feet happy, and a change of socks will help."

They started off again before daybreak, and it was piercing cold. They struggled against the wind, but after a while it began to let up and snow began to fall. After an hour of that they could scarcely see. In any event, their tracks were covered. During lulls in the storm they could catch glimpses of a vast sweep of peaks, some looming amazingly near, some far off.

*   *   *

Many times in the years that followed Val tried to reconstruct that escape from Austria. They branched off at the head of the Venter and went west of the mountain, into Italy. They went through small villages—villages they did not know the names of—and passed a fourteenth-century castle; then over a steep pass, and they were in Switzerland. It was footpaths and dim trails most of the way.

After that there was Zurich . . . Paris . . . London—and New York. . . .

Will Reilly was never quite the same again, and he had never quite forgotten Louise.

He was colder, harder, and he laughed less often. He kept Val with him, and they were just as close; they talked of books, they went riding and shooting together. Will Reilly gambled, and he led a gambler's life, and over the next few years he paid attention to a dozen women with the casual ease that was typical of him, but he was serious about none of them.

When Val was fourteen they parted for the first time, when Val hired on at a cattle ranch in Texas. It was hard, grueling work, but he loved it, working from sunup to sundown, with only occasional rides into town. Will was operating a gambling house in New Orleans, but after six months he sold out and rode west to Texas.

Val was now a tall boy, broad in the shoulders and strong in the hands. Fantastically quick with a gun, he had never drawn one in a gun battle; expert with cards, he cared nothing for gambling.

"It's good to see you, Val," Will said when he saw him. He looked at him thoughtfully. "You're growing up, boy."

With Will there, it took little urging for Val to quit his job, and with a pack horse they started riding west to San Antonio. As they rode, Will kept watching their back trail. He was silent for a long time, but after a while he said, "They're hunting me, Val."

"Who is?"

"That's the hell of it. I don't know."

That night in the Variety, Will told him more. "Somebody took a shot at me in New Orleans. They missed. Two days later they tried it again, and they missed again. . . . I didn't."

"You got him?"

"I killed a man I had never seen before, and you know that I never forget a face. I would swear I never ran across him anywhere, let alone gambled with him."

"Mistaken identity."

"No . . . it was me he wanted. He lived long enough to say that they hadn't told him I could shoot."

"They?"

"That's what he said."

"So it's over?"

"No. Two weeks later they tried again, while I was in a card game. They burned me that time, and they got away."

"They?"

"There were two of them." Will Reilly rubbed a hand over his face. "So I quit. I sold out and drifted west. How can a man gamble when somebody he doesn't know is shooting at him? If you have an enemy you know it, and you know him; and if it is a matter of shooting, you shoot. This is different. Anyone who walks in the door may be the one, and they can't all miss."

Val had never seen Will Reilly worried before, but to sit in a gambling game knowing that any one of the players, or any bystander, may be there to kill you . . . well, how do you concentrate on' your cards?

From San Antonio they drifted to the German settlements around Fredericksburg. They camped three nights on the Pedernales to see if there was any pursuit. When none appeared, they rode to Fort Griffin. There, in a poker game, Will Reilly won sixty dollars, and Val won twenty at handwrestling. Although still only a boy, he had an unusually powerful grip, and had the arms, shoulders, and chest of a grown man.

They rode the grub line west, and then they hired two wagons and four skinners and went up the Canadian to hunt buffalo. As both of them were dead shots, they did well. They followed the buffalo with a few other hunters, banding together for protection against the Indians. A tall young man named Garrett was one of them, and he was a good shot with a rifle.

Val, who had a natural aptitude for weapons, and who had done a lot of shooting, killed nine buffalo at his first stand, eleven at his second. When the herd became nervous he stopped shooting for a few minutes to let them get over their uneasiness.

He had made his stand near a buffalo wallow where the buffalo were scattered over the grassy plain below. He waited, enjoying the warm sun after the cool of the night, and watching the huge, shaggy beasts grazing.

Will Reilly was half a mile away at the other corner of a triangle of which the apex was their wagons. Suddenly a rider appeared, a tall man with long flowing hair to his shoulders, riding a magnificent black horse.

"How are you, boy?" He glanced over the terrain. "You have a nice stand here. Why aren't you shooting?"

"I'm letting them get settled down. They were in half a mind to stampede."

The man studied him thoughtfully. "Nice rifle you have there. May I see it?"

"No, sir. I never let anybody look at my guns."

The man smiled. "Are you Will Reilly's boy? I heard he was out here."

Val got to his feet slowly, and the tall man noted how the boy wore his gun, and the stance he took.

"Will Reilly might be around. Who should I say is looking for him?"

"You tell him Bill Hickok wants to talk to him."

Val studied the man. Hickok was a friend of Will's, he knew. In fact, Will had loaned him a horse one time when he had been badly in need of one.

"Mr. Hickok," Val said, "Will said you were a good friend of his, so I take that as truth, but if you've become one of those hunting him, you'd better know you'll have two of us to face."

Hickok looked at Val for a moment, then he nodded. "As a matter of fact, I came to warn him. Will Reilly was a friend to me when a friend was needed, and I hoped to return the favor. There are three men over on the Arkansas, and they are hunting him."

"We'll ride over and talk to Will," Val said.

Will Reilly left his buffalo stand and came to meet them and he listened while Hickok told him the news. "One of them is Henry Sonnenberg," Hickok said. "He said he'd know you when he sees you."

"And the others?"

"Thurston Peck and Chip Hardesty. But don't underrate

Sonnenberg. He's been building a reputation out in the Nevada gold camps. He killed some stranger out at Ruby Creek stage station, and another one in Pioche."

After a short silence Will Reilly said, "Bill, I've got a favor to ask. If you can, without stirring up trouble for yourself, find out who is back of this. They're being paid, and I want to know who is doing the paying."

"You don't know?"

"I haven't the foggiest idea. That's what makes it so bad."

They rode back to camp, put coffee on the fire, and started stirring up some grub. The skinners were still out.

After they had eaten, and Hickok and Will were lighting cigars, Wild Bill looked over the match at Will. "Do you know a man named Avery Simpson?"

"Should I?"

"He was in Wichita for a few days, then traveled to Hays. I understand he has ten thousand dollars to be paid to the person who kills you . . . no matter how."

Will Reilly just stared at him. Val got up to bring more fuel for the fire. When he had put the buffalo chips on the flames, he said, "Maybe we ought to look him up and ask why?"

"Yes," Will said. "The hell of it is knowing that anybody may try to shoot or knife or poison you, and not even knowing why."

"Want me to talk to him, Will?" Hickok asked.

Reilly smiled, without humor. "I'll admit, Bill, that this business is getting under my skin, but not that much. I can still fork my own broncs."

"Of course." Hickok leaned back on his elbow. "Don't forget Sonnenberg while you're looking for this man Simpson. From what I hear, Sonnenberg is a sure-thing operator. If I was you I'd shoot on sight."

Bill Hickok stayed the night with them and rode on in the morning. The next morning they rode out, too. Only this time they rode east, and then north.

Val and Will rode into Hays on a frosty morning, and went to the hotel to make inquiries. Avery Simpson had checked out, leaving as a forwarding address the Peck House, in Empire, Colorado.

"All right," Will said quietly, "we'll go to Empire and find out what Avery Simpson has to say for himself."

Val walked to the window. There was a terrible sense of foreboding in him. Why did Avery Simpson want to have Will Reilly killed?

And did he want to kill Val too?

SEVEN

The Pecks had arrived in Empire with considerable means, and over the years they had enlarged their house, imported furniture from the East, and lived in a degree of comfort known to few in the mining regions. For nine or ten years they entertained travelers, known or unknown to them, until bad times came to the country and the Pecks turned to entertaining for a small charge.

The Peck home, always the center for everything in that part of Colorado, had now become a hotel, and it was there that Will Reilly and Val arrived late one evening.

A fire was blazing on the hearth, for the night was cool. It was a pleasant room, and after the chill of the long ride on the stage it felt comfortable.

Val looked around the room thoughtfully. He saw a young girl, perhaps younger than himself, and there was a man, obviously an easterner, who sat in a big leather chair reading a newspaper and smoking a cigar.

The girl was small, with large eyes, and was very pretty. Val went over to her. "Do you live here?" he asked.

"No." She looked at him with interest. "Do you?"

"We travel," Val said. "In this country—and we spent a year in Europe."

"I've never been there, but I will be going, one of these days."

"I'm Val Darrant," he said. "What's your name?"

"Maude Kiskadden." Her chin lifted proudly. "I am an actress."

"An *actress?*"

"Yes, I am. So is my mother."

Will Reilly had come up to them. "How do you do?" he said, offering his hand. "I am Val's uncle. Did you say your father's name was Kiskadden?"

"Yes."

"I knew a Kiskadden up in Montana. In Virginia City."

"That was my father."

Will Reilly looked at her curiously. "Your mother was named Virginia? Who used to be married to Joe Slade?"

"No, sir. My mother is named Annie. She's an actress."

"Sorry. I guess Kiskadden must have married again." He glanced around the room, then his eyes came back to her. "Are there many people stopping here?"

"Only four. There's my mother and me, and there is a mining man from Denver, and some easterner."

"I had expected more. . . . This easterner now—can you describe him?"

"He is a tall blond man, sort of heavy. He smiles a lot, but I don't like him," Maude Kiskadden said.

Val watched Will Reilly go up the stairs, his face serious. Two hours later, at the supper table, they saw Avery Simpson for the first time.

He came into the dining room after Will and Val were already seated. The Kiskaddens were there too, and Simpson nodded to them, then seated himself at a table at one side of the room and lighted a cigar before opening his paper.

Will Reilly got up. "Excuse me a minute, Val. I will be right back."

He crossed the room to Simpson's table. "Mr. Avery Simpson, I believe?" Will drew back a chair and sat down.

Simpson took the cigar from his mouth and looked at Reilly. "Do I know you?"

"Apparently you do not, or you would be a wiser man."

"What does that mean?" Simpson asked.

"I understand you have been offering ten thousand dollars to have me killed. I am Will Reilly."

The cigar almost dropped from Simpson's lips, and he fumbled for it. His face had gone white. "I don't know what you are talking about," he said.

"You know perfectly well, Mr. Simpson, but if you are carrying a gun, you may call me a liar."

"I did not say that. I did not call you a liar."

"Then what I have said is the truth? You have been offering ten thousand dollars for my scalp?"

Avery Simpson was frightened, but he hesitated. There were at least seven witnesses in the room, and all of them were listening. The man across the table was cool, even casual, but suddenly, desperately, Simpson wished himself far away.

"Well, I—"

"If I am not a liar, Mr. Simpson, you have offered ten thousand dollars for my death. Am I a liar, Mr. Simpson?"

"No. No, no."

"Then you have offered that sum?"

"Yes."

Never in his wildest imaginings had Avery Simpson expected to be confronted with such a situation. From all he had heard, this man across the table had killed other men, and was quite capable of killing him. He waited, his mouth dry, cold sweat beading his forehead.

"Mr. Simpson, as of this moment I want you to revoke your offer. I want an item published in the press in Denver, El Paso, Tucson, and in other papers in a list I shall submit to you, revoking your offers. You need not mention what offer, just that any offers you have made are revoked and no money is to be paid to anyone for any offer previously made. When you have written those letters in my presence, and mailed them, you may leave town. You may go back to where you came from, and if you appear in the West at any future time, for whatever reason, I shall shoot you on sight."

Avery Simpson pushed back his chair. "I will. I will write the letters now."

"That is correct. However, you will not need to leave the table. I will see that paper is brought, and you may write the letters here and now. At this table."

Simpson licked his dry lips and was about to protest, but thought better of it.

"You know, of course, that I could shoot you right now and no western jury would ever convict me. You have tried to buy my death." Will Reilly smiled pleasantly.

Avery Simpson watched as Peck brought paper and pen to the table. Slowly, carefully, he wrote as Reilly dictated, and when he was finished with the last letter, Will Reilly said, "There is one more thing. As you did not know me, and have no reason for wishing me dead, I take it that you have been acting for someone else? Am I right?"

Simpson nodded.

"I want the name of that person. And I want it now."

Some of Simpson's courage was returning. During the process of writing the dictated letters he had been slowly growing more angry. Now, suddenly, the anger burst out. "I'll be damned if I will!"

Almost casually, Will Reilly backhanded him across the mouth. In that room only Val and Simpson knew the jolting force of that blow, Val because he had seen it used before, on other occasions. A slow trickle of blood started from Simpson's mouth.

"The name, Mr. Simpson."

Avery Simpson looked wildly about the room, but those present either seemed to be ignoring what was happening, or they looked at him with cold, unfriendly eyes. The men who hired their killing done were not respected men in Colorado.

"Prince Pavel Pavelovitch."

It was Will Reilly who was surprised. "Him? After all this time?"

"You horsewhipped him. He still carries the scars, and the story follows him wherever he goes. Or so I have been told."

"What else were you told?"

"That the Princess Louise will no longer have anything to do with him."

"She is married?"

"I do not believe so."

Will Reilly was silent, then after a pause he said, "You will leave in the morning, Mr. Simpson, and keep going until you reach wherever you came from."

Deliberately, he stood up and walked back to his table. After a moment, Avery Simpson got up and left the room. Val watched him go, wondering what the man must be thinking.

Will Reilly seemed uninterested in his food. Slowly he took a cigar from his case and bit off the end, and then sat for several minutes holding the cigar in his fingers and staring into space.

"She isn't married," Val said.

"We don't know . . . but I could find out. She's a well-known person."

"You would be going where he is."

Will gestured impatiently, as one brushes away a fly. "It doesn't matter." He put the cigar in his teeth, and lit it. "I am thinking of her." He looked at Val. "I am a gambler, Val, and a gambler is not simply a nobody, he is worse."

"Many of the people she knows gamble."

"Of course. But there is a difference between a man who gambles and a gambler. I have never quite been able to persuade myself of the difference but others have . . . long since."

"She loved you."

He looked at Val. "Did she? I wonder."

"You don't have to gamble. You could invest some money. Right now," Val lowered his voice—"you have money, and you own mining stock. You could—"

Will Reilly got up suddenly, almost overturning his chair. "We will, Val. We will go in the morning. I will speak to them at the stable about having our horses ready."

Filled with his plans, he opened the front door and stepped out.

They must have been afraid of him, for they used shotguns—at any rate two of them did. The other used a Spencer .56 that fires a slug as big as a man's thumb.

He stepped out the door and it swung to behind him and he had no warning. Even so, in his reflex he cleared his gun from its holster.

The blasting roar of the shotguns shook the room. Val left his chair running, and burst out the door.

There were three of them leaving, and one looked back over his shoulder. It was Henry Sonnenberg.

EIGHT

W ill Reilly had drilled Val in the procedure so many times that he acted now without even thinking. He glanced once at Will; he had seen dead men before, and he knew that Will could never have known what hit him.

He went back inside and up the stairs to their room. He was not thinking, he was as yet only feeling the terrible shock, but he did what Will had taught him to do. He went to Will's trunk and got out their stake money. It was a considerable sum.

Unbuttoning his shirt, he stuffed the gold coins into the money belt with those already there. Then he got out the three letters that had been delivered by hand from Louise to Will, back in Innsbruck, and he put them in his pocket. Only then did he go back downstairs.

He was shaking now, and he was suddenly afraid. Already the sense of loss was beginning. Will was gone, and Will Reilly had been his world. He had been father, uncle, brother, friend, all these in one; he had been his partner against the world, and it was considering that which made Val Darrant realize that he was suddenly without anyone—he was all alone.

Valentine Darrant was nearly fifteen, and he had been traveling most of his life. Not only that, but he had often made all the arrangements himself for both of them. Will might be in a game where it was unsafe to win; a signal to Val, and Val would make the arrangements. And so he made them now.

People were still gathered on the hotel steps, talking, when he went to the livery stable. He saddled their horses and led them out back of the corral, where he tied them in a concealed place. Then he went back to the hotel.

"Mr. Peck," he said when he found him, "I want a decent burial for my uncle." He produced two gold pieces. "Will you see to it? They will pay attention to you."

"Of course, son, but you don't need to think of that now. You're welcome to stay right here at the hotel until everything is settled. Everything will have to be impounded until we find his next of kin."

"He was an orphan," Val said. "He had no kinfolk, except me."

"Well, we will have to see about that. In the meantime, don't you worry. We will attend to everything."

They had taken Will to a dark shed that housed the materials for coffins, a place where bodies were kept until buried. The burial would be the following morning.

Val went to the shed and talked to the man at the door, a pleasant, middle-aged man who had two boys of his own. "May I see him?" Val asked.

The man studied him a moment. "I reckon so, boy. You an' him seemed mighty close."

"We hadn't anybody else."

"How come they killed him? Gambling fight?"

So Val told it to him there by the door, very briefly but clearly, about Will and Louise, and the horsewhipping Will had given Prince Pavel.

"Served him right," the man said. "I'd like to have seen that. You go ahead on in there, boy, an' take your time."

So Val went in.

A lantern was standing on a table and it shone on Will, who was lying there as if he were asleep.

Val stood beside him, knowing what he had to do, but dreading it. This, too, had been a part of it, and from the time Val was six years old, Will had drilled it into him.

"Remember, Val, these home guards are mostly good folks . . . but there's larceny in some of them. You know where I carry my money—in that secret pocket inside my vest. No matter what happens, you get it. And get the money hidden in the hotel, and then you get out.

"You've been around enough—stay in the best hotels if you can. Tell them you're expecting to meet your uncle, or any story they can believe, Val. Don't let anybody know you've got more than a few dollars, but money can be your friend, and your best protection."

Val hesitated a moment now, and then put his hand on Will's body, felt for the vest buttons. They were caked with dried blood, but he unbuttoned them. Sure enough, it was there, a small packet of greenbacks, and something else . . . a locket, it felt like, and a small square of paper.

Quickly he put them into his pocket, buttoned up the vest, and rearranged the blanket.

"Thanks, Will," he said softly. There was a lump in his throat and he could feel the tears coming, and fought to keep them back. "Thanks for everything. I . . . I guess you know how it was . . . you an' me. I love you, Will, and I never had anybody else, and may never have again.

"I'm going to get out, Will. I'm going to take off the way you said I should, but I'll see that you're buried, with a marker and all. Then I'll come back, you can count on it. And that isn't all. One of these days I'll find them, Henry Sonnenberg and the others, and when I do, I'll make them remember you, Will."

He went outside, and the man at the door put his hand on his shoulder. "That's a good boy. I know how you feel."

"He was all I had. We were all either one of us had."

"Sure, now." The man's voice was husky. "Boy, if you're of a mind to, you can come out to our place. We ain't got much, but you're welcome."

"Thanks. Will Reilly told me what to do if this ever happened."

Val walked away in the darkness and back to the hotel. There were people standing in the parlor talking about what had happened, but they stopped talking when he came up.

"Mr. Peck, can I speak to you?" Val said.

When they had gone into another room, Val took the small packet of money from his pocket. "Uncle Will always told me you were honest, and this here is mine. I don't know what is going to happen, but I wish you would be my banker. Take this, keep it for me, or invest it . . . whatever you think best."

Peck hesitated, studying the boy. "Where did you get this, son?"

"It's mine. He wanted me to have everything he had, but he always left this money with me in case we were separated. You know, sometimes folks did not take kindly to his winning."

"I guess not." Peck took the money. "All right, boy. I'll take care of it. I haven't had much luck with money these past years, but it has been the times. I'll care for it like you were my own son."

"He wanted a round stone," Val said, "like a rolling stone. All he wanted on it were the dates, and the words, *Here's where Will Reilly stopped last.*"

Val went up to the room, and closed the door behind him. He looked at Will's clothes . . . all those handsome, beautiful clothes.

He worked quickly, making a small pack of his own belongings, including the six-shooter Will had bought for him. He took down Will's Winchester, checked the load, and placed it ready on the bed, changed into range garb, and went to the window.

After a quick look around he slipped out, went down the slanting roof and dropped his stuff to the ground, then lowered himself to arm's length and dropped. Gathering up his gear he went through the alley and across a dark vacant lot to the back of the corral where the horses waited. There he stopped long enough to belt on the six-shooter.

Somewhere, not too far away, was Henry Sonnenberg. Val considered that. He was good with a gun. Will had seen to that. He had been shooting alongside Will for almost ten years, but he did not think he was ready for Henry. Nor for the others . . . but there was time. Will had always advised patience.

He mounted his horse, and with Will's horse on a lead rope, he took the trail out of town. He rode at an easy lope for a short time, and then walked his horse. Just short of daybreak he stopped and rested the horses; after that he mounted Will's horse and rode on.

He kept to the back country, riding west and south. He avoided people, sometimes by turning off the trail, returning to it only when the people had gone by. He knew where he was headed.

It was a small remote log cabin, high in the mountains north of

Durango. On two occasions, when drifting through the country, Will and he had spent the night there, and one other time they had stayed a week. At that time they had done some work on the cabin and had explored the country around.

The cabin stood at the edge of a grove of aspens. A spring was nearby, and there were a few acres of meadow for grazing. There were fish in a nearby stream, and plenty of game.

Riding the wild country gives a man time to think, and Will Reilly had encouraged thinking. "You have to be objective, Val," he had said. "That is the first thing a gambler learns. Each problem must be taken by itself, and you have to leave emotion out of it. Be stern with yourself. Don't pamper yourself."

Well, he no longer had Will to guide him, but he had what Will had taught him, and that teaching had been of a kind to give him strength within himself. Will rarely had positive answers, but he always offered the means to arrive at answers.

Val Darrant considered what lay before him. Henry Sonnenberg must not go unpunished. The law would hardly try very hard to find the killer of a dead gambler, and the law in the West was, in most places, still merely local law. If Henry Sonnenberg was to pay for his crime, it was Val's job to see that he did.

Three men had been involved, and Val knew their first effort would be to find Avery Simpson and collect their blood money. With Will Reilly dead, Simpson's misson was accomplished, but some rendezvous must have been arranged for the payoff.

But what was to prevent Simpson returning east by the fastest means possible, and keeping all the money for himself?

Many men had a streak of larceny in their makeup, and it was unlikely that Avery Simpson was free of it. He might simply return to his usual habitat. But he was a shrewd man, and would be cautious, so he would start in the direction of the rendezvous, wherever it had been.

Hickok had seen him in Wichita, but he had left for Hays . . . it was likely that contact had been made there, and that might be the rendezvous point. In any event, he had nothing else to go on.

That night, after he made camp, Val practiced his draw, then fixed himself something to eat, and practiced again. He had a natural speed of hand and eye, developed over the years by handling cards and guns, and by juggling several small balls, a practice started by Will.

Each night he practiced drawing, but he did no firing, for he was not anxious to attract attention to himself, and had no idea who might be in that part of the country.

In Durango he got a newspaper and found the item Will had made Simpson write. Val himself mailed those letters the first morning after the killing. He smiled at the thought of Henry Sonnenberg meeting Simpson after seeing that item.

Val folded the paper and placed it on the table beside his plate. Then he reached in his pocket for money, and found he had none there. But there was gold in his money belt—in both money belts, for he was carrying several thousand dollars.

He hesitated a moment, then took up the paper and opened it. Using it as a shield, he slipped a hand inside his shirt and took out three gold coins. As he started to place them in his pocket one slipped from his fingers and rolled on the floor.

Several heads turned. Embarrassed, Val got up to retrieve the coin, which had stopped rolling near a heavy boot, stained with red earth. As Val reached for it, the boot moved and came down hard on the coin.

Val stepped back and straightened up, his heart pounding. He had seen Will Reilly face such situations, but he had never faced one himself.

There were three men at the bar, and the foot of the man on the end was on the coin.

"You've got your foot on my money," Val said. "Would you move it, please?"

The man made no move, but he glanced at the others, chuckling. "Listen to that talk. Real gent, ain't he? Now look here, boy. That coin dropped out of my pocket. It ain't yours, it's mine."

A dozen men were watching, their eyes on Val. He was only a boy, but he was wearing a gun, and any man who carries a gun must be prepared to use it.

"There's a twenty-dollar gold piece on the floor, and it belongs to me," Val tried to keep his voice from shaking. "Take your foot off it."

"It ain't yourn," the man said, "but if you can get it, you can have it."

Deliberately, he moved his foot and Val stepped forward to pick up the coin. Instantly, he saw his mistake. As he bent over he saw the man's boot swing for a kick, only inches from his face.

His reaction was instantaneous, from long training. He struck the boot aside even as it swung toward him, and the slap threw the man at the bar off balance and he started to fall, catching himself by his right hand on the bar just in time.

Val stepped back quickly, gun in hand. "Pick it up mister," he said quietly, "and put it on my table."

Slowly the man pulled himself up. The other two had spread out a little. "Put that gun up, kid. We were only funnin'."

"Pick up the money and put it on my table." Val's voice was suddenly cold and steady. He did not want to kill, but he didn't believe he would have to. These were bad men, but dangerous only when the odds were with them. "I'm not funnin'," he added.

The big man stooped for the coin, and then he lunged in a long dive. Val did a boxer's near side-step and brought the barrel of the Smith & Wesson down on the back of the man's head. He went to the floor, out cold.

Without removing his eyes from the others, Val picked up the coin and backed off. Then he went to the bar and paid for his meal. He took up his change and pocketed it.

"You won't get away with this, kid," one of the other men said. "He'll kill you."

Val knew what a good bluff could do. He holstered his gun and faced them. "How about you? You want to try?"

The gesture worked, for the man very carefully put both hands on the bar, away from his gun. "It ain't my fight," he said hoarsely. "I'm just with him."

Val backed to the door, aware of the quiet-faced man at a table near his own, who had sat watching him. Had he seen that man before? Who was he?

Val stepped out and let the doors swing to. His horses were right down the street. He turned and walked swiftly toward them.

When he glanced back the man with the quiet face was standing outside the saloon, lighting a cigar. Val mounted, and swung his horse.

He reached the cabin on the mountain near dusk, and drawing his horses into the shadow of the aspens, he watched it for some time. There was no smoke from the chimney, no sign of life. When half an hour had passed and it was nearly dark, he rode forward.

There was no horse in the corral, no fresh manure on the ground. He tied his horses and went to the cabin, taking the thong off his six-shooter. He was almost at the door when he noticed it was slightly ajar, and there were dark spots on the split logs that formed the steps. He touched one of them, and it seemed to be damp.

Whoever was in there must have heard him at the corral, and he spoke quietly. "I am friendly. You want to strike a light?"

There was silence.

All was darkness within. For several minutes Val waited, then moved closer. He heard breathing, and stepped up to the door. The breathing was uneven, the breathing of someone injured, he was sure.

With his left hand he pushed the door wide, but nothing happened.

Then deliberately, he stepped in and to the right against the wall. There was no reaction.

"Who's there?" he asked. "Who is it? I am a friend."

There was still no response, and taking a chance, he struck a match.

Beyond the table which occupied the center of the room a man lay sprawled on the floor. A gun lay not far from his hand. The bunk from which he had fallen was bloody.

The match burned down, and Val struck another and lit the coal-oil lantern on the table. Then he went around the table and stared down at the man. The back of his buckskin jacket was bloody, and torn by a bullet. Carefully, Val turned the man over. It was Tensleep.

There was a cut on his scalp that looked to be several days old, and the blood from the bullet wound had dried.

Val straightened up and looked around the room. Tensleep, several years before, had been riding with Henry Sonnenberg, and despite what Val had heard about Sonnenberg, Thurston Peck, and Hardesty, Tensleep might have been one of them.

Never before had Val been faced with anything of this kind, although more than once he and Will had taken care of wounded people. But it had always been Will, decisive and sure, who had taken command and had known what to do.

The first thing was to take care of Tensleep. He straightened the bed, then slid one arm under Tensleep's hips and put the other around his body under the arms, and he picked him up.

Val was strong, but the wounded man was limp, and like a dead weight. Maybe moving him was the wrong thing, but Val got him on the bed, and unbuttoned the bloody shirt. The sight of the wound turned him sick at his stomach.

Turning from it, he put sticks together in the fireplace, started a fire, and put water on to boil.

Then he went outside, stripped the saddles from the horses, and turned them into the corral. He found a stack of hay, scarcely enough for two days, and pitched some to the horses. After that, he carried his gear into the cabin and dumped it on the floor.

The water was boiling, and he carried some of it to the table and with a clean handkerchief he bathed the dried blood away and cleansed the wound as best he could. He made a pad of another of his handkerchiefs and bound it in place over the wound. He did the same at the point of exit, and then washed the blood from the wound on the scalp.

He shaved some jerked beef into a tin and, adding water, made a thin broth. He didn't know whether he was doing the right thing, but Tensleep had been without food at least a day or two, so he tried him with a little of the broth. The wounded man swallowed it, and then accepted more.

At midnight Val prepared his own bed and went to sleep.

NINE

He awoke suddenly, starting from a sound sleep into sharp attention. He stared up at the cabin roof for a moment. Where was he? The cabin in the mountains . . . Tensleep . . .

He swung his feet to the floor. Tensleep was awake, and was watching him. "I ain't sure who you are, *amigo*, but it looks to me like you come along at the right time. I'm hit hard, ain't I?"

"Yes."

"You think I'll make it?"

"I'm not a doctor, but Will used to say that he'd seen men with guts pull through injuries where by all accounts they should have died. He used to say two-thirds of it was in the mind."

"Will? Ah, now I got you! You're that kid of Will's . . . from ten years back. Sure, an' I'd heard you were still with him. What d' you know about that?"

"Will's dead. They got him."

Tensleep lay quiet, staring at the ceiling. "I'd have staked my life they couldn't do it, not even the three of them."

"He was coming out of a doorway, and they gave him no warning. They used shotguns."

Val pulled on his clothes and got a fire started. He didn't know what to do except to make some more of the broth. There were

77

herbs that might help, and Will had taught him a little about them, but he remembered no herbs that grew around where they were now. With what he had, he would have to try to build some strength back into the man.

"What happened to you?" he asked.

"It was them, Hank and the others. They wanted me with them, but I wouldn't go against Will. First place, I knew he was faster and a better shot, but mostly it was because I always liked his style. He was my kind of man—the kind I'd like to have been. . . . I never was anything but a wild kind of hombre with no more sense than the law allows. . . ."

His voice trailed off, and in another minute Val saw that he was asleep. While the water was getting hot he went outside and led the horses from the corral and picketed them on the grass. Tensleep's horse had evidently been taken away, for there was neither horse nor saddle, and they must have taken his weapons too.

Val gathered fuel, and considered the situation. If he was going to catch Simpson or Sonnenberg he had to be riding, but Tensleep would never make it here alone. There was not one chance in ten for Tensleep to make it anyway, but without Val's help there was not even that chance.

The cabin stood on a gentle slope with a thick grove of aspen behind it, the trees climbing the mountainside in a solid mass. Still higher up were stands of Engelmann spruce and balsam fir. Below and to the east were slopes covered with yellow pine. Here under the aspen columbine was growing, with its lovely lavender, purple, or sometimes almost white flowers, and mingled with them some tiny yellow flowers he did not recognize. Near the cabin a stream came down the slope in a steep fall, supplying water for whoever lived in the cabin and for their horses.

As night came on, Tensleep grew feverish, and sometimes he was wandering in his mind. "Save me, kid," he cried out, "for God's sake save me long enough to find Hank!

"Watch out for him! He's mean, poison mean! He'll hate you, kid, like he hated Will! He was afraid of Will—I told him he was afraid. That's why they used shotguns out of the dark. That's why he hated Will, because he was scared of him."

After that a pause, and then he spoke more calmly. "He shot me under the table, kid, sneaked a gun out and shot me. Never gave me a chance. He gut-shot me an' left me to die—told me he was takin' my horse and outfit."

"You get well," Val said, "and I'll give you Will's horse and outfit. I brought it along."

Tensleep slept then for almost an hour, and woke up begging a drink.

"Val," he said hoarsely, "I seen men gut-shot afore this. Mostly they die in less than a half-hour, at least the ones I've seen. Some of them take a while, but if they live as long as I have, they usually have a chance. You know, boy, that bullet might have gone clean through me and never clipped a thing. Seen it happen. But I'll have a bad time tonight, I'm figurin'.

"Val, there's a plant grows down on the slope below here. I seen it a time or two over east of the stream. It has a purple flower—called cinquefoil. You find it, pick some of the leaves, and make me some tea. It's good for fever, boy. It'll help me."

Val got up. "I'd better go then. There isn't much light left."

"East of the stream, nigh that big gray boulder with the moss on it. There's a lightning-struck tree close alongside, and sumac on beyond it, higher up."

Val went out quickly, taking his rifle. The sun had set, but it was still light enough to see. He checked landmarks, choosing those useful after dark when everything looked different, and he crossed the stream and hurried down the slope, making the best time he could. He found the plants where Tensleep had said they would be, and gathered a hatful of leaves.

Tensleep was sleeping restlessly, his face already hot from fever. He threw his head from side to side and muttered unintelligibly.

Val steeped some of the leaves in hot water, and then held the wounded outlaw up so that he could sip some of the tea. Again and again he repeated the proceeding, though he was afraid he might be doing the wrong thing. If the man really was cut up inside, he certainly was; but in such a case Tensleep would die, anyway. The nearest doctor was at least sixty miles away, and Tensleep might be wanted in Durango.

At last Val slept, and when morning came he saw that Tensleep was resting easily. He fed the horses and busied himself outside, but still the outlaw slept.

Val cleaned his guns, washed out the handkerchiefs he had

used on the wounds, and cut some wood and laid it ready for a fresh fire. Then he went outside again and practiced with his six-shooter.

He was fast . . . maybe as fast as Will, who had always said Val had a gift for it. And he could shoot straight. He felt no desire to shoot anyone, yet he knew that if he could find Sonnenberg he would kill him, for there was no evidence to convict him of the murder of Will Reilly. He would do the same for Hardesty and Peck . . . if there was no other way.

He came back to the cabin to find Tensleep awake. The outlaw had been watching him through the open door. "Pretty handy with that thing, ain't you, kid? Well, you'll need to be."

"I don't intend to stay in the West. After I've had a go at Sonnenberg, I'm going back east. I'll stay there, I think."

"Maybe. But this here country has a pull on a man. You get to looking at the mountains, and at the stretches of wide-open, empty land . . . and it gets to you.

"I never had no chance to live no place else. When I was growin' up the thing I wanted most was to be a mountain man, but by the time I'd got some years on me, it was punchin' cows. I was a fair hand . . . and one of the best bronc riders around. An' then one night some of the boys were broke and we wanted to throw a wing-ding so we rounded up ten or twelve head of cows and sold them . . . and the law got wind of it, and they was after us for rustlin'."

Tensleep had gained a little strength, and he wanted to talk. So Val listened.

"I never figured to be an outlaw. I'd known too many as a boy . . . on the dodge all the time, and never anything in sight but prison or a rope. But one careless evenin' an' there I was . . . runnin' from the law.

"I never was a hired gunman, though. Fact is, the first time I killed a man it was over that. He was always hirin' out for rough work like burnin' out nesters, or killin', and he wanted me to he'p him. I told him what I thought of that and he grabbed iron. I never had any thought of bein' fast at that time, an' wore a gun because ever'body did—out on the range from time to time a body needed it."

"You killed him?"

"I got off two shots before he cleared leather, and I been outlawin' it ever since."

He was suddenly tired, and he lay back on the bed while Val rolled a smoke for him and put it between his lips. When he had the cigarette drawing he said, "You do that, kid—you get shut of this country and go east."

In the days that followed, Val was restless. Sonnenberg and Simpson would be meeting, and parting. After that there would be small chance of finding them. But he stayed on. And Tensleep gained strength every day.

Val remembered hearing an Army doctor talking to Will about western men. "They're made of rawhide and iron, and they don't die easy. It's what meat and beans and a lot of hard work and fresh air will do for you."

The day that Tensleep got up Val told him he was leaving. "All right, Val," Tensleep said. "You light out. I can manage all right now."

"Like I promised, I am giving you Will's horse and saddle, his six-shooter, and my rifle. I am going to hang onto Will's rifle myself."

Tensleep turned away abruptly. "Kid, you'll do all right," he said. "If ever I get the chance to make it up to you, I will."

Val Darrant hesitated for a moment over what he was about to say—that door to the past was closed so long ago.

"Tensleep, you knew my mother. You knew Myra Cord."

Tensleep turned to look at him. "That's a closed book, Val. You forget her."

"What was she like?"

"You've forgotten?" Tensleep's tone was rough. "She was no good, Val. She turned you out, she would have had you left to freeze. She was heartless and mean."

"Where is she now?"

Tensleep sat down and rolled another cigarette. "Look, kid, nobody knows anything about that. Me, and maybe Hank recalls it. So leave it lay. Go build yourself a good life and forget her. Will Reilly was born on the wrong side of the tracks and became a gentleman, Myra was born on the right side and became a—a shady lady and a thief. Yes, an' folks suspected her of murder, a time or two."

"Did you know my father?"

"Better than Will Reilly did. I packed for him one time, into the mountains not far from here. He was a well-off man, Val, and that's how you came to be."

"Me?"

"Myra set her cap for him. She was a tramp, workin' down on the line like the rest of 'em, but she had eyes for a good thing. She latched onto Darrant, and when she knew you were going to come along, she tried to get him to make a will in her favor.

"Darrant was no fool. He didn't believe she was going to have a child, and he could read women better than most, so he told her to forget it and she got mad and threatened him.

"Well, he laughed at her, and then she got all soft and weepy and said how she never meant it. Me, I couldn't keep my nose out of it. I'd spent time in the mountains with him and liked him, so when she bought that rat poison, I told him about it.

"He just looked at me, and said, 'There are rats in that old hotel. I've heard them.'

" 'Uh-huh. And they been there ten years, and nobody made any fuss about 'em, so how come all of a sudden she buys enough rat poison to kill half the rats in Colorado?'

"The next day he was gone out of there . . . just like that.

"Oh, you should have seen her! She was fit to be tied! Somehow she'd learned that he was well fixed, and she hated to lose."

"Did you ever see him again?"

"No. He went back east, I think, or maybe to Canada."

"And Myra?"

Tensleep shrugged evasively. "You stay away from her, boy. Forget her. That there's a downright bad woman."

"What about Van?"

"He's with her, wherever she is, unless she's got tired of him and kicked him out—or poisoned him."

The next morning Val rode out of the mountains. He followed the trail to Hays, and lost it there. Then he rode south into Texas.

The gold in the twin money belts rode heavily on his hips, but he used it sparingly. One night, camped in a sheltered draw near some mesquite, he fed his fire. A feeling of loneliness possessed him. He was missing Will's companionship, and the talks they'd had about people and books and cards. He was realizing that he wanted to leave all this behind and go somewhere very different . . . he wanted to go east.

For some time he had been conscious of a growing sound in the distance, and now there was the rattle of trace chains, and the creak of a heavy wagon. A voice called out, "Halloo, the fire!"

Val stepped back into the shadows. "Come in if you're friendly. If you're not, just come a-shootin'!"

He heard a chuckle from the darkness. "Now, there's an invite if ever I heard one! Come on, Betsy, looks like we're to home!"

TEN

The wagon rolled up to the edge of the firelight and a tall old man got down, peering toward the fire. "It's all right, stranger," he said. "We ain't meanin' no harm. Seems like Betsy an' me, we got lost out here."

He walked into the light, carrying a rifle in his right hand, muzzle down.

Val studied him. He seemed like any drifting landhunter. Val's eyes went to the wagon. Whoever Betsy was, she was not in sight. The muzzles of four rifles were.

He was still deep in the shadow and he was sure they could not see him, but he was in no position to fire. If he did shoot, they would sweep his position with rifle fire in the next instant.

"If you're friendly, why the rifles?" Val kept his tone pleasant. "And don't count on them being any help. They might get me afterward, but I'd nail your hide before they did."

"Looks like a Mexican standoff, don't it, son?"

The old man walked up to the fire. He was shabbily dressed, but he looked as if he made a try at cleanliness, at least. "You all alone, boy?" he said.

"No, I'm not alone. I've got a six-shooter and a Winchester," Val said. "They're all the company I need."

The old man chuckled. "See? I tol' you he was our kind of folks. 'Light an' set, Betsy."

The wagon curtains parted and a girl swung down lightly and easily, then she turned and faced the fire. Her hair was black, and her eyes were the same. Her skin was clear and creamy. She was beautiful.

"I am Betsy," she said simply.

"Why don't you have the rest of your outfit get down, too?" Val said. "I'd feel a lot easier in my mind if you just gathered around."

Two young men, not much older than Val himself, got down from the wagon, and Val stepped into the open. He held out his hand. "I am Val Darrant," he said, "and I am hunting a place to light."

"Same here." The taller of the boys said, "I am Tardy Bucklin. This here's Cody, an' Pa you've met." Then he turned to the girl. "And this here is Western Bucklin, our sister. We call her Betsy."

"There's coffee," Val said, "but I haven't enough grub for you all."

"Never you mind," Cody said, "I'll get a bait from the wagon."

The old man turned toward the wagon and called out, "All right, Dube, you can come out now."

Another tall boy got down from the wagon and walked toward them, grinning.

Val was annoyed with himself. He had been a fool to gamble, and they had acted wisely, keeping their ace in the hole hidden until sure of him. "Is that all of you?" he asked. "Or do you still have another rifleman somewhere?"

The old man smiled, his eyes twinkling. "Matter of fact, Boston's out yonder checkin' your sign to see if more than one of you came in."

Then Val saw the dog, a big rough-haired one, part airedale and part mastiff, or Great Dane perhaps. He was not unfriendly, but watchful.

Boston walked into the firelight then, and this was another beautiful girl, younger than Betsy.

"You'll have to watch your step, young feller," Pa Bucklin said. "These here girls ain't seen a likely young man since they left home. You'll be lucky if you get away without them catchin' onto you."

"*Pa!*" Western said indignantly. "What will he think of us?"

"Just a-warnin' of him, same's I would if I seen a rattler. An' he'll need it, won't he, boys?"

"Gals do beat all when it comes to takin' after a man," Cody said dryly. "Not," he added "that they ain't good gals. I wouldn't have you get any wrong ideas about 'em."

One of the boys took his rifle and moved out into the darkness, and the girls began putting on some food. "You set up, son," Bucklin said. "These girls cook up mighty able vittles, and no matter how much you et, they'll git you to have more."

Val did sit up, and the food was all Pa Bucklin had said.

While they ate, the old man explained. "We're like the rest of 'em, son. We're huntin' a fresh start in the western lands. We got nothin' but a little grub, some good horses, a cow, and a lot of hands used to work, but we aim to make good."

For the first time in many days, Val relaxed. They were pleasant, easy-going people. They had come from the mountains in Virginia, and they were headed west to try ranching. Pa Bucklin had been a horse trader, and occasionally had driven stock to the eastern cities for sale. Cody and Dube had been west before; they had hunted buffalo, and had taken part in two of the early cattle drives.

"They tell me there's good land in Colorado," Pa Bucklin said. "Me and the boys figured to git ourselves some while the gittin's good."

"Holding it is harder than getting it," Val said.

Tardy Bucklin smiled at him. "We get it, we hold it," he said, "don't you worry your mind about that. We got to get cattle, too, and horses. We figured to round up some wild horses to start off with. Cody says it can be done."

"Fact is," the old man said, "we got ourselves a claim staked out. We got ourselves a place. Cody an' Dube, they scouted the country when they were buffalo huntin', and they found us a spring with a good flow of water. We're a-headin' for it now."

"Mind if I ride along?" said Val. "Might lend a hand in case of Indians."

"Welcome," Pa Bucklin said, and that began it.

For three slow days they traveled down-country, three wonderful days. The Bucklins were good-humored and hard-working. Val did his part of the work, and tried to do a little more, and in the meanwhile he was thinking.

"This water hole now," he said. "Is it just sitting there?"

"It's Comanche country," Dube said, "and not many will hanker for it, but we built ourselves a soddy and Uncle Joe stayed on to sort of see after it."

They rode up to the springs on the late afternoon of an overcast day. Dust devils were stirring among the short grass, and worrying the trees around the spring—a small but sturdy grove of cottonwoods and willows. Cody and Dube started ahead to scout the layout. Val swung alongside them.

"Uncle Joe, now," Dube said. "He should be expectin' of us, I reckon."

There was no sign of smoke, no sound of axe. They spread out a little and, rifles in hand, rode closer. Then they saw the body, a dark patch on the slope of the hill, away from the trees.

Cody swung wide, circled warily, and approached the body. Then he rode back to them quickly, his face white with anger. "It's Uncle Joe. He was shot, drug, an' left to die."

They closed in swiftly on the soddy. It was a low but solidly built sod house with a pole corral next to it. As they approached the door they could see a sign on the door.

THIS LAND CLAIMED BY DIAMOND BAR
STAY OFF!!

"Well," Dube spat. "He might have talked us out of it, but he began the shootin'."

"Maybe your uncle shot first," Val suggested mildly.

"Uncle Joe? Not him. He was half blind. He couldn't see well enough to shoot at anything that wasn't close up to him, and he didn't hold with shootin', unless set upon."

"His rifle is gone," Cody said.

"We'll know the rifle," Dube said. "One time or another we'll come upon it."

The sod house was empty, but it had been rifled, the food thrown in the dirt for the wild animals and the ants to eat.

"You tell Pa, Dube. Val an' me, we'll sort of set tight."

When Dube had gone, Cody said, "Pa will be upset. Uncle Joe

was the only kin of my mother, an' Pa and him thought a lot of one another. I reckon we'll have some huntin' to do."

"You may be outnumbered."

Cody turned cold eyes on Val. "No Bucklin is ever outnumbered, young feller."

The wagon rolled in, and the girls began to make the little house comfortable. They slept in the soddy, the men slept outside.

The next day they began work on enlarging the house. They also dug rifle pits on the hills close around, and a man stayed on watch all the time. At night there was another on watch—the dog, a powerful beast, friendly as a puppy among the family, but deep-voiced and ready to be fierce to anyone who approached from the outside.

"We got to round us up some horses," Bucklin said the first day, "and hunt us some meat."

"You ought to run cattle," Val suggested. "You can't sell many horses, except to the Army, and the Indians will steal them."

"A body does what he can," Bucklin said grimly. "We got nothing but our milk cow."

Val threw his saddle into place, cinched up, and stood staring at the rolling hills. These were good people, poor but solid, and they were workers. Maybe he was a fool, but Will had always taught him that character was the most important element in judging horses, dogs, or men. And women, too, he supposed.

"Mr. Bucklin," he said, "I am of a mind to talk business."

Pa looked at him, surprised at the sudden change of tone. Cody looked at him, too.

"Are the boys all here?" Val said. "Let's sit down together."

They came in, those tall, quiet young men, Dube, Cody, and Tardy, and the two girls.

"You don't know me any better than I know you," Val said, "but I like the way you work together and the way you handle yourselves. I can feel you're honest people, and I think you're going to make a success of ranching." He hesitated, then took the plunge. "I want to buy in. I want a partnership. I won't be here much of the time—I've got to go east, and I've got some looking around to do. In fact, I've got to find a couple of men . . . three, in fact. That's why I can't work with you much of the time."

"What you figurin' on?"

"You need cattle. I will put up the money for six hundred head if you can get them for ten dollars a head."

"We can buy cows for four to five dollars in Texas," Cody said. "You got that kind of money?"

"Yes," Val said. "I inherited it from my uncle, and I can get more."

They looked at one another, and Val could see they were doubtful. He opened his shirt and took out one of the money belts. Opening the pockets he took out two thousand dollars in gold and greenbacks. "There you are. When you're ready, we can ride south and east and buy cattle."

Cody heaved a great sigh. "Well, Pa, there she is. More'n we ever hoped for. I say we go partners with him."

Bucklin rubbed his jaw. "You want half?"

"One-third . . . you do the work, I put up the money for the cattle. You take that, buy what you can. I'll come in with more later."

"Don't see's we could do better, nohow," Bucklin said. "We're with you, son."

After that several days passed, during which they scouted the range in every direction, riding in pairs for self-protection, with always one man on watch at home. The grass was good, and despite the claims of the Diamond Bar, they saw no cattle wearing any brand at all.

They did see a small herd of buffalo, numbering not over sixty head. One, grazing off to one side, they shot for meat. There were numerous antelope, and once, far off, they glimpsed a wolf.

Water holes were scarce. The one by which they had settled had a strong flow, but it was the only water hole in several miles. Its value was immediately apparent. Whoever controlled that water would control about forty square miles of range. A longhorn steer would walk three days to get to water, though cattle weren't going to fatten up much unless water was easier of access.

About a hundred yards from the soddy, they dug out a low place, shaping the sides and lining three sides with stones, to form a crude tank. Into this they directed the runoff from the spring.

"Pa," Cody said, "I don't like it much, about Uncle Joe. He was a kindly man."

"Maybe we ought to fetch it to them," Dube suggested.

"No," Pa Bucklin said, "we'll wait. We settled in this country of our ownselves. We aim to stay here, so we ain't goin' to push no fight. They started it, an' they'll come a-huntin' us soon or late. Meanwhile, we got to think about cattle, mostly about breedin' stock."

He glanced at Val. "You know anything about beef cattle, boy?"

"A little. I've worked on the range a mite, and I've sat and listened to the cattle buyers talk deals by the hour. I've waited a lot in hotel lobbies and I'd hear them talking the fine points. When Will and I punched cows a little, we worked with a very canny cattleman who used to tell us what was wrong with this one or that one. Yes, I know a little."

"None of us knows too much, when it comes to that. No more than a sight of others who are choosing land in this western country. Son, you, Cody, and me, we'll ride up to town."

"How about us?" Boston asked. "Western and me, we'd like to see the lights."

"Ain't many lights where we're a-goin'," Cody said. "You all saw that town. It's a one-street town of weather-beaten shacks, mostly saloons."

"You stay," Pa said. "There might be trouble. There might also be trouble here too, but you two can handle rifles good as any man."

Before the light came the next morning they were riding the short-grass plains toward town, startling the rabbits, which ran off a ways and then sat up, ears pricked. They rode with their Winchesters in the saddle boots, and spurs jingling.

They came into Cross-Timbers, and the first thing they saw was a Diamond Bar wagon and two Diamond Bar ponies standing three-legged at the hitch rail in front of the Cap-Rock Saloon.

The street was lined with eight buildings and a corral—there were four saloons, two general stores, a blacksmith shop, and an eating place.

They tied their horses and went into the saloon, letting the batwing doors swing behind them. Pa and Cody, they walked up to the bar, but Val did what Will Reilly had always done, and stayed inside the door, looking into the darkest corner to get his eyes accustomed after the glare. He did not drink, anyway, so he sat down at an empty table near the door.

There were four cowhands and a teamster in the saloon, as well as a couple of men in broadcloth suits at the bar. With them was a man who looked as if he might be the blacksmith.

Pa ordered a drink and then looked over at these men. "Beggin' your pardon gents," he said, "but I am in the market to buy cattle."

For a long moment no one spoke, although all turned to look at him. Then one of the cowhands at the table spoke up. "You picked the wrong country, friend. There's no range around here, not for miles. This here is Diamond Bar country."

"Seems a mighty spread-out place for one outfit." Pa spoke mildly. "Anyway, we've settled in on a nice water hole over west of here. We like it there."

"That water hole was posted by the Diamond Bar."

"I noticed that," Cody said quietly, "and they murdered an almost blind old man to mark their sign."

For a moment there was dead silence, and then the cowhand said, "That old man was armed."

"That old man was not armed," Cody said flatly. "He was my ma's oldest brother, and he couldn't see across this here saloon."

The cowhand's face tightened. "You callin' me a liar?"

"If you were there, and shot that man, I am callin' you a liar and a murderer," Cody said coolly. "If you just heard the story told, I am tellin' you whoever told you that story was a liar and a murderer."

One of the others spoke up. "You'd better say that easy, cowboy. The man who told us that was Chip Hardesty."

Val interrupted. "Cody, sorry to butt in like this, but Chip Hardesty belongs to me."

They all looked at him, and the teamster snorted.

"Kid, you keep your mouth shut. Hardesty is a mean man, and the fastest one around."

"You can tell him for me that he is a murdering skunk. He killed that old man. He also killed another man, he and two others, with shotguns, without warning as he came out of a door in the dark." Val sat facing the men at the table, and he fixed his eyes on the teamster. "And you, mister, you take a long time thinking before you tell me to shut my mouth again."

"Don't you talk to me." The teamster was shaking with anger. "You ain't dry behind the ears yet."

"This gun is," Val said, "and it speaks plain language. You just put a hand on that gun you've got and I'll write my initials in your belly."

The teamster's fury was suddenly penetrated by a cold arrow of caution. The boy was young, but the gun could be just as deadly, and the distance between them was less than fifteen feet. In any event, it wasn't his fight unless he was foolish enough to make it so. Let Hardesty do it. That was what he was getting paid for.

"You settle it with Hardesty," he said. "Like you said, he belongs to you. And I'll tell him," he added, with deep satisfaction. "He'll be huntin' you before sundown."

Val looked at him. "Mister, you get on your feet right now. You ride right to where Hardesty is, and you tell him to come on in. I'll be waiting . . . right here."

The teamster got to his feet, very carefully.

"You go with them," Val said to the cowboys, "just in case they don't believe him. And you tell the boss of the Diamond Bar he can stay in this country just as long as he's willing to stay off our backs. We want no trouble, and we aren't going to cause him any."

"Except for them that killed Uncle Joe," Pa Bucklin said. "You tell your boss to hang them before night falls or we will hang him within thirty days."

"You're crazy!" the teamster cried. "Plain crazy!"

"You tell him that," Bucklin said. Then he turned to the others. "Let's go eat. Be an hour or more before he can get here."

ELEVEN

It was a quiet meal. Nobody felt much like talking, Val Darrant least of all. He had said what he wanted to say, but now he would have to back it up. He had never met any man in a show-down gun battle, least of all a veteran killer like Hardesty, but Hardesty was one of those who had killed Will Reilly.

Pa and Cody were quiet, too. Only toward the end did Cody speak up. "They may bring an army, Pa."

"Then we'll have to take care of an army," Pa said shortly. "Let's stay under cover until we see what they look like."

"I'll go out," Val said, "I've got this to do."

They were silent for a few minutes, and then Cody said quietly, "Val, you're a good friend or I wouldn't say this, but you bein' a boy and all, I—"

"Thanks, but I told him what I could do. I've got to put up or shut up. This is my proposition."

"You ever been in a gun fight before?"

"I've fought a couple of times," Val said, "but never man to man, like this."

"Then you make the first shot count. Don't give no worry to being fast. If he shoots first, you got to face it, but take your time and put that first one where it can be the last one."

"Thanks."

There was nothing elaborate about the saloon. It had a bar fifteen feet long at one side. There were four square tables, each surrounded by four chairs, the kind called captain's chairs. The bar had obviously been shipped in, as had the chairs; the tables had been made in the town.

The stock of liquor was not large, but was adequate for men who liked strong drink and cared little about age or flavor. Several dog-eared decks of cards were on tables, and idly riffling one, Val noticed that somebody had been marking them with a thumbnail—clumsily, too.

One of the men at the bar, dressed like a western man who had been east more than a few times, came over, drink in hand. "Mind if I sit down?" He smiled. "I promise to get out of the way before the shooting starts."

There was something familiar about the man, and Val, who had been taught to remember, recognized him as the quiet-faced man who had been present when he had the showdown over the twenty-dollar gold piece.

"You travel a lot," Val commented, and the man smiled at him. "Sit down," he added.

"You mentioned buying cattle. Do you plan to start ranching?"

"We have the ranch," Val said; "now we need cattle."

"I might be interested in investing a little, if you come out of this all right."

"Thanks, but we have all we need."

"My friend over there," the man said, "is a cattle buyer. He occasionally sells, too. And sometimes we grubstake a good outfit."

Val made no comment, but he was curious. Will Reilly had taught him never to accept men at face value, and he did not. He knew that there are all kinds of men appearing in all kinds of guises.

"I am Steve Kettering," the man went on. "My friend over there is Paul Branch."

Val introduced Pa and Cody, and waited. This man was building up to something, and it might be interesting to know what it was. "What's the matter with your friend?" he asked. "Isn't he the sociable type?"

Kettering turned. "Paul, come on over and meet these gentlemen."

Branch came over and sat down. "I am sorry, gentlemen," he said, "I'm not in the best of moods. I came into town for a poker game and Kettering promised me one. If I am a bit restless, please forgive me."

"What do you play for?"

They looked at him. "I mean," Val said, "do you gentlemen play for money, or for cigar coupons?"

Branch reached down in his jeans and pulled out a thick roll of bills. "I play for that," he said, "and there's more where that comes from."

It looked to Val like what was known as a Kansas City bankroll, a couple of tens wrapped around a thick wad of ones, or even around brown paper.

This man Kettering had seen him before, seen him drop a gold coin on the floor, and now he heard him trying to buy cattle, and needing no backing. Which Val knew would be evidence enough that he had money.

"Would you boys be interested in a little game?" Branch asked. "I mean, you have some time to kill, and I thought—"

How many times had Val watched the routine? Reilly was an honest gambler, and roped nobody into a game, but he had often pointed out such developments to Val, who was amused at how clear the pattern was.

"We've got business," Pa Bucklin said. "If you've cattle to sell, we'll talk. We got no time for cards."

"I might have a little time," Val said. "I might just have enough. A man standing in my shoes can afford to take a chance. But these cards look pretty used up—"

"I am sure the bartender has a fresh deck around," Branch said. "Shall I call him?"

Val smiled. "Now there's a gamble, right there. I'll lay you three to one he does have a fresh deck. Is it a bet?"

Kettering's eyes had grown suddenly wary. He looked at Val thoughtfully, but Branch shrugged it off. "That's no bet. Most bartenders have a deck of cards for sale."

The bartender brought a deck of cards and Branch broke the seal, and shuffled the cards. "Shall we cut for deal?" he said, and promptly cut the cards. Val saw the finger tap the stack gently as Branch reached to make his cut and knew he had a slick ace, its face treated with shellac to slide easily.

Branch turned up the ace of hearts. "You can't beat that. Shall I deal?"

"But I might do just as well. Mind if I shuffle them first?"

He did . . . and promptly cut an ace.

Branch's face stiffened, but Kettering only bit the end from a fresh cigar and lit it.

"Let's just put these aces aside." Val had picked up the cards again, and was shuffling them idly as he talked. "And try again. Maybe you can beat me this time."

"It's getting to be a warm day," Kettering got to his feet. "You boys play if you like. I'm too restless." He walked to the bar and ordered a drink.

Branch started to reply, his irritation showing, but Cody interrupted. "You ain't goin' to have time. I think I hear horses a-comin'."

"One hand," Val said. "Just you and me, Branch, and we play what's dealt . . . no draw."

Branch hesitated only a minute. The deck was marked to indicate face cards and he had two aces in a sleeve holdout, so there was little to worry about.

Val dealt the hands, and Branch saw the five cards Val dealt to himself had not a face card among them. Branch picked up his hand. Two eights, two queens and an ace.

Val was studying his cards, Pa Bucklin had walked to the bar again where he could watch the street, and Cody's eyes were on the door. Branch made the shift without trouble, replacing the eights with the aces.

Branch put five gold eagles in the center of the table.

"You're a piker, Branch," Val said, "I'm just a greenhorn kid, but I'll go five hundred." And he put the money on the table.

"Forget it, Paul," Kettering's voice held an edge. "Throw in your hand and I'll buy you a drink."

Branch considered his cards. He now had a full house, aces and queens, and the chances that this boy could better it were small. He glanced at his cards and at the five hundred dollars in the middle of the table. There was a good chance this kid would be shot full of holes in the next few minutes, and somebody would steal the money from his pockets. . . .

"I'll see you," he said. The horses were stopping now in front of the saloon. Branch placed five hundred on the table, and spread his cards . . . three aces and two queens. He started to reach for the pot, but Val spread his own hand . . . four tens and a trey.

Paul Branch felt himself suddenly go empty. Val reached over and swept the money to him with his left hand.

"Paul"—Kettering's voice broke through the fury that was mounting within him—"I'll still buy that drink. Come here!"

Branch started to rise. Through a red haze of anger he remembered how Kettering had suddenly pulled out, how Kettering had tried to get him away. Kettering had seen something, sensed something, but he himself had been rooked—and good—by a mere boy.

It was in his mind to kill. He was opening his hand to reach for his gun when the doors smashed open behind him.

"I'm Chip Hardesty!" The tone was hard with challenge. "Where's that kid?"

Val Darrant stood up. His mouth was dry and his heart was pounding. "Will Reilly was my uncle," he said quietly, holding his voice down for fear it might become shrill. "You murdered him. You never gave him a chance."

"I don't fight kids!" Hardesty sneered.

"But you murdered a blind old man," Val said, "and don't worry about this kid. You were afraid to tackle Will Reilly when he had an even chance, and Will often said I was faster than he was."

Hardesty laughed, but the laugh broke off. *Faster than Will Reilly?* It couldn't be. He never knew when his hand started to move. He could not remember thinking that he was going to draw, only that his hand almost of its own volition was dropping, grasping the butt, lifting . . .

He never heard the sound of the gun, although it must have been loud in the room. He felt himself taking a step backward, and then he was sitting on the floor, and he was rolling over, and the last thing he saw were the gray slivers in the planks of the floor, and then a gray mist that crept over them.

Paul Branch was looking at the sprawled body of the gunman, feeling the icy chill at what he had almost done. He had been about to draw on this kid, and if he had done so he would now be dead.

Pa Bucklin stepped into the door. The teamster and two cowhands were outside. "You'd better come in and pick up your man.

Take him back to your boss and tell him we Bucklins and Mr. Val Darrant are staying on at the Springs."

Paul Branch said to Kettering, "If you are still in the mood to buy it, I'll have that drink."

Kettering ordered, and then spoke to Val. "You said Will Reilly was your uncle? Did he teach you about cards?"

Val put his palm down to holster level. "From the time I was that high," he said, and he walked out.

He did not want to look at Hardesty. He did not want to think about what he had done. He wanted to be out in the air, and away from people. He no longer wanted to kill Thurston Pike or Henry Sonnenberg.

He did not want to be a gambler or a gunfighter. He did not want to die as Hardesty had, or Will Reilly, or as Tensleep almost had. For a long time he had wanted to go east . . . now was the time.

He was going to keep five hundred dollars and he was going to leave the rest of it with the Bucklins to buy cattle and operate the ranch.

If he ever needed to come back, he could come back there, to the ranch. . . .

TWELVE

B ut he did not go . . . not quite yet. He rode with them to round up their cattle buy on the plains west of the Neuces, and started the long drive overland to the ranch, mostly young stuff with a few older steers to steady the herd. They wanted breeding stock, for they were not thinking of next year, but of the years to come.

After the first two days the cattle strung out, and for two weeks they moved the herd, first through dry country, and then across swollen streams and land that was soggy from the sudden rains.

At last Val pulled off to one side and said to Pa Bucklin, "I am leaving it to you. You will hear from me, and one day I will come back. In the meantime, build the herd, and when there is money for me, bank it in my name."

They shook hands, and Pa said, "The womenfolk are going to miss you mighty. My girls set store by you, boy."

"I will come back."

Cody rounded the herd and rode up to him. "If you ever need help, you send out a call and we'll come a-runnin'. We reckon you're kin of ourn now."

"I never had a family. Only Uncle Will, who wasn't rightly my uncle."

"You've got one now. From grass roots to cloud."

The day was threatening rain when he turned his horse away from the herd and pointed north for Kansas and the railroad. He held to low ground because of lightning, but he kept a steady course. When night came there was nothing around him but dampness, the clouds, and the dark. He camped several times before he saw the lights of Dodge, and when he came up to the town he was wearing sodden clothing, several days of whiskers, and a bedraggled look.

He rode past a cheap saloon and did not see the man who suddenly gave him a second look, then spoke over his shoulder into the saloon.

He drew up opposite a restaurant and leaned over to stare in the rain-wet window, trying to see how inviting it looked inside. He swung down and was about to tie his horse when two men in boots and spurs came up the boardwalk.

"Shed right back yonder in the alley," one said, "where you can put your horse out of the rain."

"Thanks," Val said, and followed the man into the alley. They were scarcely within its darkness when he heard the man behind him take a quick step. Val started to turn, but not in time. The gun barrel caught him a sweeping blow over the ear and he went down.

He heard a voice saying, "He's wearing a money belt an' packing about three thousand dollars."

He felt hands fumbling at his shirt, but he could neither move nor speak. A voice was muttering, "Hell, there ain't that much here!"

He felt rough hands seize him, and then he lost consciousness. He remembered nothing after that. When he opened his eyes it was daytime, and he was sprawled on his back.

He heard a whistle, and he realized he was on a train, lying on the floor of an empty freight car. His head was throbbing.

He tried to sit up, and finally made it. The car door was open and he saw that it was still raining—the rain, slanting across the opening, was like a steel mesh. He felt at his waist—the money belts were gone.

His gun was gone, too. He searched his pockets, but he found nothing, not so much as a two-bit piece.

The car was empty except for himself, and he had no idea how long he had been lying there. Through the night and most of the day, no doubt, for, judging by the light, it was already getting on toward evening. Several times he saw the lights of houses, so they must be in eastern Kansas or Missouri. He lay back, rested his head on his arm, and went to sleep.

A boot in the ribs awakened him, and a voice spoke. "Come on! Get up!"

The train was standing still on the outskirts of a village. The voice came again. "Get out of here, now! An' don't let me catch you on one of our trains again!"

He ducked a blow, stood up, and dropped to the ground, but his legs were weak and he fell, rolling. Slowly, he pulled himself up. The train was starting, with jerks and a rumble.

He stood watching it vanish into the town. His head was throbbing, and when he put his fingers to his skull he found lacerations.

His mind fumbled over the sound of that voice. It belonged to somebody he had known or heard once before, and obviously it was somebody who knew he was carrying money—for he had known exactly where to look, and even how much had been there.

Val shivered with cold and wetness. Hunching his shoulders against the rain, he looked around. He stood at the bottom of the embankment. Ahead of him in a shallow valley, was a small stream, which the railroad crossed on a trestle. Clumps of willows grew along the stream, with here and there a cottonwood.

He saw a thin trail of smoke rising from a point downstream. Beyond the hollow he could see a house painted white, a red barn with a weather vane, and a windmill. Sitting down on a rock, he took off his spurs and dropped them into his pocket, then he started toward the trail of smoke.

A path led to an open place among the willows where three men were sitting around a fire. Two were older men, the other in his early twenties, Val judged.

They looked at him. "Man, you look as if you really got it rough," the younger man said. "They throw you off that rattler?"

"They sure did." Val touched his scalp. "But they didn't do this. I got pistol-whipped in Dodge City."

They looked at his outfit, and his boots. "You been punchin' cows?"

It was simpler to put it that way, so he agreed. He dropped

down on a log across the fire from them. "Somebody rolled me and dumped me into a boxcar. Where are we, anyway?"

"Missouri." The younger man leaned over and filled a tin cup. "Have some coffee. Do you good."

Neither one of the older men, both of whom looked capable and tough, had spoken.

"Which way you headed?" Val asked.

"East. I got an uncle in Pennsylvania. I'm going there."

One of the older men leaned back under the makeshift shelter and said, "New Orleans for me. I can make it good, down south."

"Ain't much to do," the other one said, "and they don't pay nothing, Fred."

"I'll make out. I always have."

The coffee was hot and strong, and it was just what Val needed. He felt the warmth of it go through him. "I got to find work," he said. "They took all I had."

"You got anything to sell?"

Val thought of his spurs. They were large-roweled, California-type spurs, not too common in this area. "I've got some spurs." He showed them. "That's about all."

"You might get a dollar for them—maybe two if you hit the right fellow. Say, there's a boy about your age up at that farm" —he pointed—"who might fancy those spurs. I seen him trying to rope a post up there. Fancies himself a cowhand."

"You got to be careful," Fred offered. "You can get six months for putting the bum—" At Val's blank expression Fred explained. "I mean, for begging. You ask for grub or money, and they'll put you on a work gang."

"And it don't make any difference that you're huntin' work," the other man said. "I'm a millwright, and a good one, if I do say it. There just ain't any work to be had." The fire as well as the coffee had warmed Val, and he grew sleepy. All of the others dozed, but when a train whistle blew the three ran for the train and left him sitting there.

He stared into the ashes of the fire. The rain had stopped, and he should be getting on. He was fiercely hungry, his head still ached, and he was unbelievably tired. He got to his feet, kicked dirt over the fire, and took the path that led toward the farm where the boy lived who might buy the spurs.

The road was muddy, but he kept to the grassy border. Cows

stared at him across the fence, and at the ranch a dog barked. He walked more slowly as he neared the farm, not wanting to enter. He had never sold any of his personal possessions, and did not feel sure how to go about it. He dared not ask for food—not if he could get six months in jail for it. And he knew that some jails hired their prisoners out as laborers and collected a fee from whoever hired them.

He hesitated, then turned in at the gate. A big yellow dog barked fiercely, but he talked softly and held out his hand to it. The dog backed away, growling.

A woman in a blue apron came to the door and looked at him suspiciously. "Yes? What do you want?"

"I was wondering if you had some work I could do? I can split wood, dig . . . I guess I can do anything."

"No." Her voice was sharp. "We don't need any help, and you're the fourth man who has been here this morning."

A tall boy had come into the doorway behind her, and the contempt vanished from his eyes as he glimpsed Val's cowboy boots. They had been made by the best maker of cowboy boots, and were hand-tooled, with fancy stitching.

"Are you a cowboy?" he asked.

"I was," Val said. "I was robbed in Dodge City. Somebody put me on a train and here I am."

"Tom, you stay in the house!" the woman ordered. "You don't know who this man is."

"He ain't no older than me. Look at his beard—it's only fuzz!"

Val was irritated by the comment, but he kept his peace. "Are you a cowpuncher?" he asked, knowing well enough that the boy was not.

"Well, not really." The boy had come outside. He was about Val's age but somehow seemed much younger. "I plan to be. Only my folks, they don't cotton to the idea."

He walked out and leaned on the top rail of the fence. Val sat on the rail beside him. "It's hard work," he said, "and some of those old mossy-horn steers get mighty ornery."

They talked for a time while Val's stomach gnawed with hunger. Finally he said, "I got to go. I want to find somebody who'll buy my spurs."

"Spurs? Let's see them!"

Val took the spurs from his pocket. The Californios liked their spurs fancy, and these were an elaborate job, each with two tiny bells. He could see from the way the boy's eyes shone that he wanted them.

"You can see," Val said, "these are no ordinary spurs. Fact is, they were a gift to me. From Wild Bill Hickok."

"You knew *him*?"

"He was a friend of my uncle's. He warned my uncle that some men were looking for him. To shoot him," he added.

The boy handled the spurs. "I'd like to have them," he said, "but I've only got two dollars."

"Well," Val said, "if you could rustle me a meal, or some meat and bread or something, I'd sell them to you for two dollars."

"You just wait right here."

In a few minutes he was back with a paper sack and the two dollars. Val took the money and the sack. "You'd better go now," the boy said. "Pa's coming home and he's dead set against tramps."

"All right . . . and thanks."

He started for the gate, then hesitated. "Look, if you ever get into west Texas, you hunt up the Bucklin outfit. They're this side of the cap-rock—you ask at Fort Griffin. You tell them Val Darrant sent you."

He walked out of the gate, and when well down the road he sat down under a tree. There was a big hunk of meat and cheese in the sack, and several slices of homemade bread, as well as an apple. Val took his time, eating a piece of the bread, most of the meat, and the apple. Then he walked on.

Two days later he was in St. Louis. He rode the last few miles on the seat of a wagon beside a farmer who was carrying a mixed lot of hides, vegetables, and fruit. "Work's mighty scarce, boy," the farmer told him, "and you will do yourself no good in St. Louis. Ever since the depression hit, there's been three men for every job."

Idle men stood about the streets of the city, and Val paused on a corner, considering. He had nothing to sell. Nor was he in any position to look up any of Will Reilly's friends, for he lacked the one thing Will had always insisted he keep. He must have a "front," he must have the clothing, the neatly trimmed hair, the polished boots, even if he did not have a cent in his pockets.

Standing on the corner watching the traffic, he tried to gauge his talents and abilities. He had great card skill, but he did not want to be a gambler. He had skill with guns, but he did not want to use it. He had received from Will an education in literary and historical matters. But to do anything with any of these abilities he needed money.

All day he walked the streets, and wherever men were working he asked for a job. In every place it was the same. "We don't have enough work to keep our own men busy."

When night came, he wandered back to the river front and sat down on the dock. For the first time he realized that Will Reilly, while showing him much of life, had also shielded him from much. To be with Will Reilly had given him a position, and as Will was treated with respect everywhere, Val had also received respect. Suddenly now it was gone, and he stood alone, and unknown.

There were friends of Will's in St. Louis. They had stayed at the Southern Hotel, and Will had been accorded the best treatment that hostelry had to offer, but he could not walk into that lobby looking as he did now. He might write to the ranch for money, but the postal service was uncertain, and it might be weeks before anybody from the ranch went into town, or to Fort Griffin.

Before, even during periods of separation, Will had always been not too far away, and Val had always known there was somebody, somewhere, who cared. Now there was nobody.

That night he slept on a bale of cotton under the overhang of a warehouse. He put a newspaper under his coat for protection against the cold, huddled in a ball, and shivered the whole night through. Several times he awoke, turned over, and fought to get back to sleep again. Always there were places where the cold reached him.

At last he got up and walked down to the edge of the wharf. The river was running through the piles, sucking around them. Further up a river boat was tied, lights showing, but the lights were obscured by the falling rain.

It was still dark; he was hungry, and his eyes heavy with weariness. After a while he walked back to his cotton bale, tucked the newspaper more firmly into place, and went back to sleep.

He awoke in the cold gray of dawn. The rain had stopped, but the clouds hung low. The river rolled by, and he sat staring at it, wondering which way to turn.

An old man, puffing on a meerschaum pipe, was plodding along the dock, carrying a lunch box. He glanced at Val over his steel-rimmed spectacles. "Mornin', son," he said. "You're up mighty early."

Val grinned at him. Hungry, stiff, and cold, he still felt a streak of whimsy. "Mister," he said seriously, "you have just walked into my bedroom unannounced. I did not wish to be disturbed."

The old man chuckled. "Well, now that you're disturbed you might's well come along and have some coffee."

Val dropped off the bale. "That's the best invitation I've had for a whole day. In fact, it's the best invitation I've had in several days."

They walked along to an old steamer that lay alongside the dock, and the old man led the way over the gangplank, and along the deck to the cabin. He unlocked the padlock and they went inside.

"Sit down, boy. I'll rustle around and make some coffee." He set the lunch box on the table. "Ain't seen you around before, have I?"

"No, sir. I'm hunting work."

"What's your line?"

"Well, I've never worked much. I've punched cows a little, and I've hunted buffalo. But I'm strong—I can do anything."

"That's like saying you can do nothing. Folks who do the hirin' want carpenters and such-like. You got to have a trade, son. Ain't there anything special you can do?"

"Nothing that I want to do."

"What's that mean?"

"I can deal cards, and shoot a gun."

The old man eyed him over his glasses. "Hmm. You a gambler, son?"

"No, sir. My uncle was, and he taught me. He said it was self-defense, like boxing. Only he didn't want me to be a gambler."

"Smart man. What do you aim to do, son? I mean, a man ought to be going somewhere. You're young, boy, but you'd best be thinking of where you're going to be at my age. When I was a boy I drifted, too. Always aimed to settle down and make something of myself, but somehow that was always going to be next year—so here I am."

He had bacon frying, and the coffee water was boiling. "I bring my lunch, most times. I can stand my own cooking just so long, then I have to go out and buy something somebody else has fixed."

"You're not married?"

"Was . . . one time. Fine woman. Had a son, too."

"What happened to him?"

"Went west . . . never seen hide nor hair of him since. He was a good boy." The old man paused. "Can't complain. I done the same thing as a boy. Went west with a keel boat and spent my years trapping fur."

He glanced at Val. "You ever see the Tetons, son? Or the Big Horns? Or the Wind River Mountains? That's country, son! That's *real* country!"

"I've seen them."

The old man put slices of the bacon on a plate, and then poured coffee. Got some bread from a bread box, "It ain't much, son, but you fall to."

Val took off his coat and sat down at the table. "You don't need a deck hand, do you? I'll work cheap."

The old man chuckled, with dry humor. "Son, I'm lucky to feed myself. Ain't had a job of towing to do in five months now, and only a little work then. There was a mite of salvage I was countin' on, but there wasn't much in the cargo . . . only flour. And water-soaked flour won't do anybody any good." Val put down his coffee cup. "Where was it sunk?"

"Bend of the river—maybe thirty mile downstream. She hit a snag and tore the bottom out. It ain't in deep water. A body can land on the Texas."

"You want to try for it? I could help. I'm a good swimmer and diver."

"No use. That flour's ruined."

"Not necessarily. I saw some sacks of flour out west that had been in the water, and only the flour on the outside was ruined. It soaked up water and turned hard as plaster."

"This flour was in barrels."

"All the better. You want to try for it?"

"That water's almighty cold this time of year." The old man hesitated, but Val could see that he was turning it over in his mind.

"We'd better keep it under our hats," he said finally. "That cargo is worth something, and there's some might want to take it from us."

"Do you have a gun?" Val asked.

"An old shotgun, that's all."

They talked it over, and Val went out on deck with the old man to examine the gear. It was in good shape, and the steam winch was usable. The steamer had operated on the Missouri River and on some of its branches. It had been used to push flatboats up the river and log rafts down the river, and to tow disabled steamers. It was a real workhorse of the river.

"The water's muddy," the old man said. "You'll have to locate a hatch, and if one ain't open, you'll have to open it."

"I'll make out."

Val had never done anything of this sort, but he was right in saying he was a strong swimmer and a good diver, and he had read stories of salvage; and in San Francisco he had heard talk in the hotel lobbies about such things. There is no better place than a hotel lobby in a boom town for picking up information . . . at least, he reflected, he would be sure of some good meals.

The old man studied him with shrewd attention. "You're an educated boy."

"No, not with schooling. I never went to school. But I've read a lot, and I've discussed what I've read."

The old man shrugged. "It could be the best way maybe. You think quickly, and you seem to have a good mind. Why don't you study law?"

"I hadn't thought of it."

"Well, think of it. Even if you don't want to practice the law you can use it in many ways. And just knowing it can be important."

They talked a good part of the day, returning again and again to their project. They looked over the gear once more.

One thing disturbed Val. "We should both be armed," he said. "There are too many drifters in town. Most of them are probably good men out of work, but there will be some bad ones among them. Such men can smell money, and if we get the flour up . . . How many barrels are there?"

"On the manifest, five hundred. Some will be damaged—maybe all of them."

"It will take us a while, and somebody is sure to be curious, so we had better be prepared."

"I have no money," the old man said. "The shotgun is all I have, and not many shells for it."

Val thought of something suddenly. He and Will had stayed at the Southern. Perhaps the manager there might loan him money. They had been very attentive to Will Reilly, and there was just a chance.

He borrowed old man Peterson's razor and shaved. He had now been shaving for two years, although even now he rarely needed to shave more than once every few days. And the old man had a black dress coat that did not fit him too badly.

Night had come before he started up the street toward the hotel. He felt ill at ease, knowing that he did not look right; nevertheless, this was a chance he had to take.

The Southern's lobby was spacious, and it was busy. At the desk the clerk glanced at him, then ignored him, but Val said, "May I speak to the manager please?"

The clerk studied him with cool eyes. "The manager? What do you want to see him about?"

"Just tell him I am Will Reilly's nephew."

There was a change in the clerk's manner. "Oh? Just a minute."

He was back in a moment to show Val through a door into an inner office, where the manager sat at a roll-top desk.

"I am Valentine Darrant, Will Reilly's nephew."

"Yes, I remember you. How is Mr. Reilly?"

"He's dead. He was killed."

"Oh?" There was ever so slight a change in the manager's manner. "So what can I do for you?"

"I arrived in town a few days ago, and I am broke. I have a job but I need a little cash. I was wondering if you—"

The manager got to his feet. "I am sorry, Darrant. We do not lend money. Mr. Reilly was a valued client of our hotel, but as you have said, he is no longer with us. Now, if you will excuse me—?"

A moment later Val was standing in the street. Well, he had no right to expect a loan. It had been a foolish idea. Still, how different it had been when Uncle Will was here!

He started to turn away when he heard a voice. "Val?"

He turned. It was Bill Hickok. "This is a long way from the buffalo ranges, sir," Val said.

"It surely is." Hickok came closer. "I wasn't sure it was you, at first." Then he added, "I heard about Will. That was too bad, Val."

"Thanks, sir."

"Are you staying here?" Hickok gestured toward the hotel.

"No, sir. As a matter of fact, I'm broke. I don't have anything at all." He told Hickok all about it: the ranch, the blow on the head, the arrival in St. Louis, the old river boat. "So I need a gun," he added.

"Boy, I'd like to help you. As a matter of fact, I haven't been doing too well. I have no stomach for acting, boy. All that make-believe goes against the grain. So I am going back west to guide a couple of hunting parties."

He reached into his pocket. "Val, I don't have much, but here's a twenty-dollar gold piece, and if you'll come upstairs with me, I've got a spare gun you can have."

They went into the hotel. The manager came forward and spoke to Val. "I don't think you have a room here, young man. I would rather—"

"I do have a room here," Hickok said sharply, "and this boy is a friend of mine—a very good friend. Treat him as such," he said, "or hold yourself accountable to me."

"Yes, sir. I am sorry sir. I only thought—"

"On the contrary, you did not think." Hickok brushed by him.

Upstairs he opened his valise and came up with a new Smith & Wesson Russian. "This was given to me, Val, and I think it may be the best of all the guns of the frontier, but I like the feel of the guns I've always carried." He dug out a handful of cartridges. "Here, take these. You'd better get more, though, if you're expecting trouble."

Hickok stood before the mirror, combing his hair, which fell to his shoulders. "It was Sonnenberg, Hardesty, and Thurston Pike who got him, wasn't it?"

"They ambushed him with shotguns when he was coming out of a door. He never had a chance."

"They never could have gotten him any other way. I knew Will Reilly, a good man with a gun. Well, they'll get theirs. That kind always does."

"Chip Hardesty is dead."

"Hardesty? I hadn't heard that."

"It was down in Texas, sir. Just west of Fort Griffin. He was a hired gunhand with a cattle outfit."

Hickok's eyes met Val's in the mirror. "And you said your ranch was down that way?"

"I killed him, sir. He brought it to me."

"Good boy. Anybody who would dry-gulch Will had it coming." He straightened his tie. "Will told me you were one of the best shots he had ever seen, and the fastest."

"He liked me, sir. I think he exaggerated."

"Not to me. Will never exaggerate on a thing like that in his life." Hickok dipped a washcloth in cold water and held it to his eyes. "Makes them feel better," he commented. "Too many nights sitting over a card table, I guess. I am better off when I'm on the hunt."

Val got up. "I've got to go, sir." He paused. "Thank you very much. I'll pay you back one of these days."

"And I may need it. Luck to you, boy. If you come out around Cheyenne or the Black Hills country, look me up."

When Val was out in the street, the weight of the gun in his waistband felt good. Along the river front it was cold and foggy. His footsteps echoed as he walked along the wharf toward the "Idle Hour."

Tomorrow they would be on their way, and in a few weeks, more or less, he would have money. He could go east.

THIRTEEN

T he night was overcast, the wharf was damp, the black waters
of the river glistened where the few lights reached it. There
was a somber stillness over everything.

At the last minute they had taken on another man, a broken-
nosed Irishman with a glint of tough humor in his eyes, and an
easy way of moving and talking. Both Val and Old Man Peterson
had passed the time of day with him along the river front. He was
broke, like themselves, and he was ready to take a chance, so
they hired him on as a deck hand.

Paddy Lahey had been a tracklayer, a rough carpenter, a tie-
cutter, and a miner. Somewhere, back in the years before he left
the old country, he had been a fair-to-middling prize fighter.

"It's up to you," Val told him. "You'll come in for a fifth of what
we make. Peterson gets two-fifths because the boat belongs to
him. I am getting two-fifths because of my knowing the flour
could be saved, and because if there's trouble I will take the
brunt of it."

"You're young for that," Lahey commented, studying him doubt-
fully. "Better let me handle the trouble. I'm an old roughneck,
and used to the ways of fighting and brawling."

"You'll be needed, I'm thinking," Peterson said, "but I've confidence in Val."

"Have you done any fist-fighting?" Lahey asked.

"Not to speak of. Will Reilly taught me a little, and we boxed some."

"Then we'll spar some. You're a well-setup lad, and it could be you've got the makings. Will Reilly, was it? It's a good Irish name he has."

They cast off their lines and eased the small steamer into the current. She would sleep six, but she was short on cargo space. If they were lucky enough to get the flour up, they would have to make more than one trip to get it all to the docks in St. Louis.

They slid silently past the boats moored along the river, edged into the current, and headed south.

Just around a bend of the river they saw the steamboat they hoped to salvage lying in shallow water. After hitting the snag, the pilot had made a run for the shore to try to save his boat and his cargo, and he had almost made it.

"What we got to watch for," Captain Peterson said, "is river rats. They try to get all they can lay hands on, and you can be sure they've been down there, looking around. They're a pack of cut throats."

"That they are," Paddy agreed. "You can't trust 'em an inch."

They watched the shore, but they saw no one before they neared the wreck. The shores there were heavily wooded right down to the water, with cottonwood, box elder, elm, and willow.

After they had tied up to the wreck itself, Val stripped to dive. This would be the first time he had ever swum for any reason other than for pleasure. His activities would be shielded from the shore by the bulk of their own small steamer.

The Texas, with its pilot house, was visible above the water. A quick examination of the pilot house told Val that it had been looted of everything valuable. Even the wheel had been ripped out and taken away, as well as the brass lamps and other fixtures.

The Texas, where the officers as well as the boat's crew had their quarters, came next. This too, had been thoroughly looted.

Peterson got out a fishing pole and after lighting his pipe, dropped his line over the side. Beside him on a hatch he had his shotgun. "Let 'em figure I'm just fishing," he said. "It mayn't fool 'em for long, or at all, but it might."

Val belted on a crudely made canvas belt with large pockets attached, into which he had placed stones to weight him down. He climbed over the side to the hurricane deck, and from there he climbed down a stanchion to the saloon deck. Here, ranged around the saloon, were the first-class cabins—staterooms that on Mississippi River boats were named for the states of the Union.

The water was murky, but there was still light enough to see, and if there had been a search down there Val realized that it had been a hurried one. On the fourth dive he found a long wooden case in one of the cabins. It was an elegant, highly polished box. Tying it to the end of a line, Val signaled for it to be hoisted.

Later, on deck, they examined it. On it was the name Steven Bricker, which Val had seen before.

"Let's bust it open," Lahey suggested.

"No, let's not. The man that owns this box is at the Southern Hotel. I saw his name on the register there when I was waiting to see the manager. He might pay us for it. Anyway, I think I know what it is."

It was a gun case, Val felt sure. He had seen such cases before, and they usually held guns treasured by sportsmen, weapons often inlaid with gold, and sometimes covered with ornamentation.

The following morning he dived deep, going at once to the main deck. This was littered with boxes and crates, and on the foredeck he found some heavy lines, evidently used in mooring the boat. These could easily be sold along the river front, or used by Captain Peterson himself, and they were hoisted aloft.

Lahey made two quick dives after that. He could not stay down as long as Val, but he went directly to the hatch on the main deck and knocked out a couple of wedges and removed a batten. By mid-morning when they stopped for coffee they had the forward hatch opened and had exposed the barrels. Peterson had steam up and had turned on the power so they could use it in hoisting the barrels.

"There's a cargo net down there," Lahey said. "We've only got to roll the barrels into it. They weigh nothing much under water."

Huddled under a blanket, Val sipped coffee. He had never been in the water so much before, and had not gone so deep more than once or twice. But he was excited by the search, and there were still several cabins to be examined.

It was hard work, but by nightfall they had fifty barrels of flour aboard their own steamer. They were covered with tarpaulins, some of which had been salvaged from the wreck. So far they had seen no sign of anybody about.

They examined one barrel of flour, and found that the flour next to the outside of the barrel had settled into a hard crust for about three inches, while that in the center of the barrel was still as good as ever. This flour they kept for their own use.

Reluctantly, they cast off, leaving Paddy Lahey aboard to watch their cargo. They steamed back up the river, and when they reached the water front at St. Louis Val went ashore and headed for the Southern Hotel with Steven Bricker's gun case under his arm.

This time there was no interference. He was given Bricker's room number, and went up.

The man who answered the door was short and stocky, with graying hair and beard. He had sharp blue eyes, that went from Val's face to the case. "Well," he said, "you'd better come in." He added, "I never expected to see that again."

"I was in the hotel the other night and saw your name on the register, so when we found this . . . well, I imagine they are favorite weapons of yours, and that can be important to a man."

"They are important," Bricker said. "They were the last gifts to me from my father. What do I owe you?"

"Nothing, sir. I am merely returning your property."

Bricker looked at him shrewdly. "If you'll permit me to say so, you look as if you could use the money."

"I could," Val admitted frankly, "but I'll not take money for returning your property."

"How did you come by it? I thought the 'Gypsy Belle' was a total loss."

Val explained. He told about how he had learned about the flour, and what they had done so far. Captain Peterson, he added, had even now gone to the insurers to make a deal for recovery of the flour.

Bricker listened, lighting a fresh cigar. "Had you ever thought they might just take over and continue the salvage themselves, allowing you nothing?"

"We did think of that. I hope they will be decent about it, sir."

Bricker got up and took his coat from the wardrobe. "Let's just walk over and see how Captain Peterson is doing. He might be able to use some help."

Captain Peterson, cap in hand, was just being shown through the gate at the office of the insurers. His face was red with anger. "Boy, they've threatened us with arrest. They've said—"

Steven Bricker stepped past him and opened the door of the inner office. "Danforth, I think we had better discuss this matter of salvage," he said. "Come in, Darrant. You, too, Peterson."

"Now, see here! What's your part in this, Bricker?"

"These gentlemen are friends of mine, Danforth. And, I might add, they will be represented by my attorneys."

Danforth sat down and took up a cigar. "You can't mean that, Bricker. I've known of Peterson for years. He's nothing but a water-front bum, scavenging along the river for whatever he can pick up."

"And now he has picked up a beauty," Bricker replied, "and you're going to pay him for it. I happen to know that after the initial survey you abandoned that wreck. As it happens, if you remember, I was a passenger on the 'Gypsy Belle.' I had personal effects of considerable value aboard.

"You can buy out the interests of Peterson and Darrant," he went on, "or they will proceed to salvage it themselves. I happen to know that you have offered to settle with some of the shippers at a very modest price."

"That is none of your business, Bricker."

"I shall make it my business." Bricker got up. "You have been notified. I shall instruct my attorneys to proceed at once."

When they were outside, Bricker turned to the others. "Are you gentlemen willing to fight? I mean, can you fight?"

"We can, sir," Val answered.

"Then you get back down to that steamboat and tie up to her. Unless I'm wrong, they will make an effort to drive you off. I will get help to you as soon as possible. When my men come, they will be carrying a blue flag."

Val Darrant had grown up in a hard school, in which one often moved fast, or not at all. There was no time for contemplation, and he knew it. Peterson would arrive at the right decision but he would take too long, and Lahey was content to abide by whatever they decided.

"Captain," Val said, "you and Paddy unload the cargo. I'm going to take a boat and go back to the wreck."

He wasted no time. There was a skiff on the "Idle Hour" which he quickly launched, and then without delay he shoved off. He had a small packet of food, a keg of water, and the Smith & Wesson pistol. There was a good current in the river, and he was a strong hand with the oars.

He had not gone many miles when suddenly he heard the chug-chug of a steam engine and the thrash of paddles. Glancing back, he saw a small steamer, not much larger than the "Idle Hour," steaming toward him. At once he was sure this was a boat sent by Danforth to take possession of the wreck.

For a moment he was swept by dismay, but almost immediately he had an idea. Taking up a line from the bow of the boat, he fashioned a hasty slip knot. He had learned roping long ago while herding cattle, and although no great shakes as a roper, he knew the roping of a bollard would not be too difficult a trick. She was a side-wheeler running at no more than half-speed, but he was going to get no more than one cast and it had to be good. Still, the bollard would be as large as a calf's head, and certainly wouldn't be bobbing as much.

He coiled his line, giving himself as much slack as he could after making the other end fast, and as the steamer swept past he made his throw. It shot straight and true, and instantly he dropped into place and grabbed his oars and managed to get in a couple of good strokes to ease the jerk as the slack came to an end.

Despite that, it gave him quite a jolt, but the line held fast and the next thing he knew he was proceeding downriver at a good clip. He sat back and relaxed. It was night, no one was on deck aft, and probably the only man awake was in the pilot house.

They made good time, but he knew that when they rounded the bend they must slow down because of the risk of running upon the wreck. That would be his chance.

He was waiting for the moment, and when they swept into the cove and cut the speed to slow, he waited until the steamer swung around broadside to the wreck. Instantly he slashed the line and caught up his oars. He made two sweeping strokes before he was seen; there was a shout from the steamer's deck, but he kept on.

Suddenly there was another shout, this time a command to

halt. He pulled hard on his right oar, easing on the left, swung out of line, continued on.

A shot rang out and struck the water to his right, and then with one more strong pull he turned quickly, caught hold of the Texas and pulled himself hand over hand around it to the sheltering side. Then he tied up his skiff and climbed aboard, taking his food and water.

By now it was almost light. He climbed into the pilot house. There seemed to have been no one aboard since they had left. There were ladders on both sides of the pilot house to the hurricane deck, where the Texas was. The hurricane deck was under water, but if necessary he could retreat to that more sheltered area.

These were tough men, sent to do a job, and no doubt had been well chosen for it. They would shoot to frighten him, and when he did not frighten they would shoot to kill.

Some of the hatch covers they had taken out when opening the hatch had floated against the Texas and lay there among the other driftwood. They were about six feet long and three inches thick, so he carried several of them up and used them to thicken the pilot-house bulkhead, an added protection against bullets.

Then he made coffee on the little pilot-house stove, ate a piece of cheese and some crackers and sat back to keep watch, and to wait. And he knew he had very little time to wait.

There were at least a dozen men on that steamboat, and he could see them gathering near the rail—evidently a boat was to be lowered.

A heavily built man came near the rail. The steamer was not more than thirty yards off, and his voice was loud and clear. "You, aboard there! We're from the owners! We're comin' aboard to take possession. You can get off of your own free will, or you can be thrown off!"

"Nothing doing!" Val shouted. "I am in possession, and I intend to stay here. I am armed, and if necessary I will shoot."

There was a moment of hesitation, then the big man shouted back, "All right, boy, you're askin' for it!"

A boat was brought around to the side and men started to descend a rope to get into the boat. The Smith & Wesson Russian was a powerful gun. He aimed the .44 at the water line of the rowboat and fired. Then he fired again.

A man on the rope ladder scrambled back aboard, and there was a shout from the boat. "Hey! He's put a hole in us!"

Another man yelled, "She's leakin'!"

"Bail her out!" the big man ordered. "An' row over there! You can make it before she sinks."

Val Darrant loaded the empty chambers of his gun. He had no doubt that by plugging the holes and bailing they could make it. He was no kind of a show-off, but sometimes a demonstration of what could be done was enough to prevent having to do it.

On the ledge by the pilot house window was a bottle. He took it in his hand and stepped to the door.

"Just so you gentlemen will understand that I can do what I say," he called, and tossed the bottle into the air. Lifting the gun, he fired, breaking the bottle; fired twice more, smashing the largest of the two falling fragments, and then smashing it again. The three shots sounded like one solid roll of thunder in the small cove.

When the sound died, he said, "I hope I won't have to demonstrate on any of you."

The rest of the men, despite the protests of the big man giving the orders, climbed back aboard, and Val could hear loud argument. Meanwhile he waited, desperately anxious, for the arrival of his friends. The trouble was, these men might seize the "Idle Hour" and force Val to give up his position to save his friends.

The steamer had drifted closer now. "All right, you can shoot. So we just set here and wait. When night comes you ain't goin' to see very good. We'll come then."

Despite his doubts, Val kept his voice confident. "Fine! You can just wait out there until the United States marshals arrive. They'll be glad to see you, with all of those John Doe warrants they'll be carrying. And I imagine they will know some of you boys very well! You just stick around. I've got a thousand rounds of ammunition and grub enough for two weeks."

He had nothing of the sort, nor did he have any idea that United States marshals would be coming, but it gave them something to think about.

As Will Reilly had often said, "Let them use their imagination, Val. Nine times out of ten they will think you are holding more than you are. So just wait them out."

He was not tired, the morning was dawning bright and beautiful, birds sang in the trees along the river bank, and his gun was loaded again.

It was a bird that warned him. A mud hen was swimming near the stern of the steamboat carrying the attackers. It had flown up briefly at the shots, then settled back. Now, suddenly, with a startled squawk, the mud hen took off.

Val sat up quickly. Instantly he knew what they were doing. They were coming now, swimming underneath the water. There might be one or two, there might be a dozen, but they were coming, and he was one against them all.

FOURTEEN

H e could feel the softness of the air, see the sunlight and cloud shadows on the trees and water. He could see the men along the rail yonder, and four of them now had rifles.

The men swimming to attack him were probably coming from around both the bow and the stern to take him from both sides. He did not want to kill anyone, both because killing was no solution to one's problems and because he had an idea the courts might be more inclined to hang him than not. And he had no witnesses . . . or none that he knew of.

"Call them back," he said, shouting to the big man who watched from the pilot house. "Call them back or I'll have to shoot."

"You fire that gun," the big man shouted, "and we'll riddle you with bullets!"

There is a time for all things. He had offered not to kill, the men were closing in, and he was alone. The attackers were thugs paid to do their work, but the director of it all was that big man yonder.

"Call them back," he said again, knowing they were almost at the wreck. Incongruously, he noticed that the mud hen was back again, swimming complacently, and would still be there when all of them were gone.

There was no answer, so he lifted the Smith & Wesson and shot the big man through the shoulder.

He saw the man knocked backward, heard his cry of shock and astonishment, and Val yelled at him. "Call them back. It's you I'm going to get if you don't."

The man dropped from sight, but unless they had reinforced their walls as he had done, that pilot house was no more protection than cardboard. Yet even as the man dropped from sight, the four riflemen opened up on him. He heard the ugly smash of the bullets into the bulkheads, the whine of ricochets. From the door, flat on his belly, he fired and saw one of the riflemen spin around and drop his rifle.

He fired again, and one of the others stumbled. All of them were running now. Hastily, he fed a couple of shells into his gun, and heard a splash in the water down below. At least one of the men was now inside the Texas, and right below him.

When he had tied up his skiff alongside the wreck, he had carried his oars up to the pilot house so they might not steal the boat. Now he caught up one of the oars. He thrust his pistol into his waistband and stepped quickly out on the shore side of the pilot house. A man was just scrambling up the ladder and catching the oar in both hands, above shoulder height, Val smashed the butt end of the oar into the man's chest, knocking him back into the water.

Even as he splashed, Val heard running boots on the other side and wheeled around, drawing as he turned.

The man held a knife, an Arkansas toothpick, and he held it low down for thrusting.

Val held the gun on him. "You can drop that thing and dive off, or I'll kill you," he said. "I've already shot the big fellow."

"Him? You wouldn't dare, that's—"

"I shot him. You boys better look at your hole card. Who's going to pay you now?"

The momentary flicker of doubt in the man's face told Val that he had struck a nerve. He tried again. "Look at it—nobody else is going to do it. Do you suppose the company will admit it had anything to do with what you're doing here? If that big fellow doesn't live, you can't collect a quarter. Not a lousy two-bits."

Nobody was trying to shoot from the steamer now, for their

own men were aboard and they awaited the outcome. "See?" Val said. "They've stopped shooting. They know the show is over."
The man hesitated, in doubt. Val knew his every urge was to come on, to finish the job if he could, but the gun muzzle was pointed at his belly, and no doubt Val's argument undermined his resolution.

At that moment he heard a whistle, and around the bend came the "Idle Hour," Paddy Lahey standing in the bow with a shotgun in his hands. Moments later another boat rounded into the cove, this one with four armed men standing in the bow.

"There you are," Val said. "Now you just swim back to your boat—or swim to shore, for all I care."

"You ain't heard the last of this," the knife man declared. "We'll find you in St. Louis."

The second boat, flying a blue flag, drew alongside the wreck. The man in the bow looked up at Val. "Are you all right?"

"No complaints," Val said, "but you got here just at the right time."

Seven days and nine trips later they had emptied the wreck of its cargo of flour as well as nearly a ton of lead, and odds and ends of salvage from the staterooms. The latter would be returned, wherever possible, to the original owners.

The flour, which was currently selling for twelve dollars a hundred pounds, brought them a good return, although several barrels had been completely destroyed and others had been a total loss from water damage. When they settled up, Val found himself with something more than four thousand dollars.

Steven Bricker was in his room when Val called on him to settle up for the four men he had hired.

Bricker accepted the money, but waved away any suggestion of payment for legal fees. "Danforth was bluffing," he said. "He thought you didn't know what you were doing and he'd scare you off. It has been done before."

He studied Val. "You've a lot of nerve for a youngster," he said, "but they raise them that way out west." He bit off the end of a cigar. "I can use a lad like you. My business is building railroads, and I can give you a chance for a lot of hard work, wild country, and education."

Val shook his head. "I think I'll go east for a while. I want to study law."

"Good idea. You do that. When you decide to go to work, you write to me." Bricker scribbled an address on a piece of paper. "I will make a place for you. We can use your kind."

He got up and held out his hand. "Good luck, boy. We will meet again, I am sure."

Outside in the street it was raining again, but Val had proper clothes now, and wore a good raincoat. Earlier, he had said good-bye to Captain Peterson and Paddy Lahey. Now he walked down the street to the railroad station. He had checked his bags there earlier.

He was going east. He was going to New York.

The next few years went by so swiftly that he was only vaguely aware of the time passing. They were years spent in hard work, in study, in learning. For a year he stayed in New York, reading law in an attorney's office, and reading almost everything else he could find. He went to the opera whenever he could.

He grew taller and heavier. He became friendly with several prize fighters and spent hours in the gymnasiums boxing with them, or out on the roads when they did their road work. He wrestled, punched the bag, and skipped rope. At twenty he weighed a hundred and ninety pounds, and was six feet two inches tall.

After New York he spent a year in Minnesota, and later in Montana. He was first an assistant and secretary to Steven Bricker, who was building branch-line railroads, opening mines, dealing in mining and railroad stocks, as an associate of James J. Hill.

From time to time he had letters from Pa Bucklin, always written by one or the other of the girls. They had drilled four wells, they had bought more stock. They were now running three thousand head of cattle and planned to make their first real sale. There had been small sales from time to time, the money defraying expenses or being used to purchase more breeding stock.

It was in the autumn of his twentieth year when he was in New York that he left the gymnasium where he had been working out and walked up the street to the corner. He stopped on the Bowery, watching the faces of the people as they passed. Suddenly a hand touched his sleeve. "Sir? If you could manage it, sir, I haven't eaten today."

It was a moment before Val turned, for he knew that voice, would have known it anywhere. When he did turn, the man had already started away. "Just a minute, please," Val said.

The man turned, and Val was right—it was Van . . . Myra's man, who had left him with Will Reilly, fifteen years back.

Van's hair was grayer, his face thinner, his cheeks more hollow, he seemed not much changed. His clothes still looked neat, although he had perhaps slept in them.

"Yes?"

"Would you dine with me, sir? I should take it as a pleasure."

Van's eyes searched his face, his expression almost pleading. "You are serious, sir? If you are, I accept, most sincerely."

Val's heart was pounding strangely. He had always liked this lonely, weak man, this man who had been kind to him. He had told him stories, he had been gentle when no one else seemed to care.

"If you don't mind, we'll walk up the street. There is a good restaurant where I occasionally eat."

They walked along together, neither speaking, until they reached the restaurant, which was one with notable food.

"You are sure—? I do not look as presentable as I might," Van said.

"Come along."

Only when they were seated did Van look at him. A faint frown showed on his face. "Do I know you? I can't place you, but there is something familiar about you."

Val ignored the question until they had ordered, and then he said, "Tell me about yourself. You seem to be a gentleman."

Van shrugged. "I would have claimed so once, but no more. I am nothing."

"What became of Myra?"

Van stiffened, and stared at him. "What do you know about Myra?" He scowled. "You have known me then . . . but where?"

"What about Myra? Where is she?"

"If I had done what I should have done she'd be burning in hell. A dozen times I planned to kill her—"

"You weren't much inclined toward killing, Van."

"Damn it all! *Who are you?*"

"You haven't answered my question. Where is Myra?"

"Right where she planned to be, one way or another. Myra

Cord is a rich woman, rich and dangerous. If you plan any dealings with her, forget it. She would eat you alive."

"She must have altered her profession."

"I don't know whether she did or not. Myra is a vicious woman, who used prostitution as you might use a stepladder. Where she is now she doesn't need it, although I haven't a doubt she'd use it if it was to her advantage. She's come a long way, but she hasn't changed." Van continued to stare at him. "What's your interest in her, anyway?"

The food was served, the waiter left, and Val said, "She was my mother."

Van dropped his fork. His face turned white.

Slowly the color came back. He pulled at his tie, loosening it. "You're Val? Valentine Darrant?" he said.

"Yes."

"I'll be damned!" The words came slowly.

"I don't think you will be, Van. You kept me alive, you know. You saved my life, and did me the greatest favor a man ever did for another."

"What was that?"

"You left me with Will Reilly. He kept me, Van. He raised me. He taught me a way of life for which I owe him, and you, more than I can say."

"So? Maybe that was why we never saw him again. I was always expecting to have to meet him, and I was afraid—not of what he would do, but of the way he would have looked at me. I liked the man, damn it. I respected him. And then I had to abandon a kid on him."

"You think he avoided you and Myra?"

"He must have. You know the West. It's a small community, after all. The men of the mining camps were known in them all. They followed every boom. The same in the cattle towns. And Will Reilly was a known man. I had run into him fifty times before, but never after I left you with him."

They talked the meal through, and much of the night.

"What about you?" Van asked at last. "Where are you going? What are you going to do?"

"I'm going West. Not for long, I think, but I want to see some people out there and look at a ranch. And I made an investment a long time back, and I want to see what became of it."

He went on: "I passed my bar exam, Van. I can practice law if I want to. In fact, I have had some experience along that line. And I told you I worked with Bricker."

"It's a wonder you didn't run into Myra. She's done business with him. Knows him well, in fact."

"Myra Cord? If she had done business with him, I would know of it."

Van smiled wryly. "You don't think she would keep the old name, do you? She's too shrewd for that. She dropped that name a long while ago. She's Mrs. Everett Fossett now."

Val stared at him. Myra Cord . . . his mother . . . *Mrs. Everett Fossett?*

"You must be joking."

"No," Van said grimly, "I am dead serious. She married Old Man Fossett, married him for his name and his money. He was a respected man, you know, and a well-liked man, but he was no match for her. She tricked him and married him, and then murdered him in her own way. Oh, I know! It wasn't anything the law could call murder, but it was that, just as much as if she had used poison."

"She's worth millions."

"Yes, and not an honest dollar in the lot. She wasn't a pauper when she married Fossett. She had robbed every man she knew, I expect, and she had spent very little of it. Fossett was only another stepping stone."

"Have you seen her lately?"

"Not over two weeks ago, right here in New York. She didn't see me. I took care that she didn't, because I am one page she forgot to turn under; or rather, I got up nerve enough to run before she could do me in. She didn't see me, but I saw her." He was silent for several minutes. "She's a beautiful woman, Val, even yet. She's not much over forty, and even in the early days, mean as she was, she had good looks."

"I have seen her. I just never dreamed . . . I mean, I had heard talk of her, but the idea that she was Myra Cord never entered my mind."

"Now that it has, don't go near her, Val—she'd kill you. Don't look at me like that. She wanted you killed when you were a helpless child, didn't she? And you'd open up a whole bag of tricks she wants forgotten. She's an important woman now, socially and financially. And she's completely ruthless. Once she sets her mind on something, there's nothing in God's world can stop her."

"I wonder."

"Don't wonder—don't even think about it."

Val pushed back from the table. "Van, what can I do for you?"

"Maybe a ten-dollar gold piece. Any more would be a waste."

"Van, why don't you go home? I mean back to your own people? Your own world."

"You're crazy." He chewed on his mustache. "Oh, I'll not deny I'd like to. They know I'm alive, but almost nothing else. But I couldn't. I've no money, no clothes, no way to make a living."

"Would five hundred dollars help? I mean, five hundred dollars and clothes? I'll stake you, Van. I think it's a good gamble."

"Damn it, Val, I couldn't. I just couldn't. And what would I say to them? My parents are alive. I have two sisters. I—"

"Just go back and don't say anything. They will make up better stories than you ever could. You've been traveling, seeing the West . . . you've come home to settle down. I'll give you the money. I've done well, Van. I can afford it."

Actually he could not—not that much. But he was young, and the way looked bright ahead.

"All right," Van said at last, "I'll take it. If you will let me pay it back."

"Whenever you can . . . but go home. Go back to your own people."

FIFTEEN

The butler paused before the portly man in the dark suit. "Mrs. Fossett will see you now, Mr. Pinkerton."

He got up and followed the butler over the deep carpets, through the tall oak doors, and into the library. He rarely entered this room, and was always astonished when he did. As the guiding hand of the largest and most successful detective agency in the United States, if not in the world, he had met all manner of men, and women. This was the only one who made him uneasy, and a little frightened.

Yes, that was the word. There was something about her cold, matter-of-fact mind that disturbed him. He had the sensation that she was always at least one jump ahead of him, and that whatever he said she already knew.

She sat behind the long desk, only a few papers before her, including, he noticed, several newspapers that he recognized as coming from various cities.

"You said you had news for me?"

"Yes." He paused. "I have found him."

"Well . . . that's something, at least. Where is he? On the Bowery?"

"No, ma'am. He has gone home. He is with his family."

129

Myra Fossett felt a cold thrill of anger go through her. Was it, as Van himself had once said, that she never liked to have anyone to escape her?

"You have made a mistake. He is a proud man, whatever else he may be. I am sure he would not go home without money."

"He has money. A little, at least. He paid his bills. He bought new clothes—an excellent wardrobe, by the way—and he went home in some style."

"There must be some mistake. How could he get the money? Nobody would lend him money any longer, and he was always a rotten gambler."

"That we do not know, except that—"

"What?"

"Well, he was seen to meet a man—a young man—and they dined together. They talked for several hours. It was after that that he bought clothes and returned home."

She pondered, considering all the possibilities. Van knew too much; and a sober, serious Van who had gone home to his family might prove more dangerous than a casual drifter and drunk whom nobody would believe. Moreover, he had run away from her, and that she could not forgive.

"What sort of young man?"

"A gentleman, ma'am. Handsome, athletic, well-dressed, well-groomed. He was young . . . perhaps twenty-five. . . ."

"What was he doing on the Bowery? Is he a bum?"

"No. Nothing like that," he said. "We made inquiries . . . nobody would tell us anything, if they knew. He comes to the Bowery to train. To box and to wrestle. Incidentally, he is very good, they say."

"A professional?"

"No. I do not believe so. He is a gentleman."

Myra Fossett gave him a glacial look. "Sometime you must define the term for me, Mr. Pinkerton. I am not sure I know what a gentleman is, or how one becomes one. I doubt if I have ever met one."

"Present company excepted?"

"No," she replied shortly. "A man in your business, Mr. Pinkerton, is certainly no gentleman. In any event, I am not paying you for your moral standards. Rather," she added, "for your lack of them."

He got to his feet. "I resent that, madam—"

"Resent it and be damned," she said. "Now sit down and listen, or get out of here and send me your bill."

He hesitated, his face flushed. He knew suddenly that he hated this woman, hated everything about her, but she paid him well, and she seemed to have an unlimited amount of work to be done. He stifled his anger and sat down.

"You do not have a name for this young man? They must call him something around that gymnasium."

"Well, we do have a first name, but that is all. One of my men heard him called Val."

Val . . .

Myra Fossett sat very still. Pinkerton, who had watched the emotions of many people, had the sensation that the name had struck her a body blow.

After a moment she said, "Mr. Pinkerton, if Van Clevern has returned to his people I am no longer interested in his actions. As of this moment, you may recall your investigators.

"However, I am interested in this young man. This Val, as you say he was called—I shall want a full report on him, his associates, his actions."

"It is going to be very difficult—"

"If that means you will want more money, the answer is no. If you believe the task will be beyond your scope, Mr. Pinkerton, I believe I can find somebody who will find it less difficult. Surely, the investigation of one unsuspecting young man cannot be such a problem."

"We have no idea who he is, or where he lives."

"But he goes to the gymnasium to box, doesn't he? Have him followed. Ask questions of those with whom he boxes. . . . I do not need to tell you your business, I hope."

"If I had some idea—"

"Of why I wanted the information?" Myra Fossett smiled. "Mr. Pinkerton, I have known for some time that you are eaten with curiosity as to the reason for my investigations. You might just tell yourself that in business matters I find the human element is always important. I like to know the manner of man with whom I deal, and what his associations are. You are valuable to me for that reason. Do your work and keep your mouth shut, and you will have a valuable client; make trouble for me, and I will ruin you. . . . I believe we understand each other, Mr. Pinkerton."

He got to his feet, his features set and hard. "We do, Mrs. Fossett. I shall have a report for you within the week."

When he had gone, Myra Fossett sat staring straight before her into the darkening room. She had told the truth and she had lied, at one and the same time. Information she wanted, but only in part for business reasons, and in part only for the malicious satisfaction of knowing the secret lives of her associates. Knowledge was indeed power, but it was for her more than a weapon, for it fed her contempt for the men with whom she associated and for the sheep who were their wives.

The information she required about Van was for an altogether different reason. For twenty years he had been a part of her life, and there was little in those twenty years that he did not know or suspect. When he had suddenly broken with her and run away, she had been furious, both with him and with herself for not recognizing the signs. The trouble was that he had threatened to leave so many times that she no longer believed him.

He had become necessary to her, for exactly what reasons she did not venture to ask herself. He was, even yet, a fine-looking man, acceptable in any company; and although a drinker, he had never yet allowed it to show in company to any degree more than dozens of others whom they met at one time or another. She had no intention of letting him leave when he wished, but she had already recognized the fact that a time was coming when he would be more of a handicap than an asset. To be realistic, that time had arrived.

Had he guessed her intentions? He might have suspected. Certainly, he knew enough about others who had gotten in her way. She remembered a day long ago when he had been just drunk enough to speak out, and he had told her in that curiously speculative way he had of talking when drunk, "Myra, you are a moral cripple. I mean it. Just as some people are born with physical defects, you were born with a moral defect. You have no conception of right and wrong. Things are good or bad as they serve your purpose or do not serve it."

Val? It was impossible, of course. Val was dead. He had died out there in the night and the cold after Van had abandoned him . . .

She had never believed Van would have the guts for it. She had been surprised when he returned without the boy, but when he had suggested they leave at once, she thought that he might really have done it. And Van had never referred to Val again, never mentioned him even once, so he must have left him to die.

But suppose he had not? Where could he have taken the boy? Where might he have left him? All she had now was that twenty years later Van met somebody who might be twenty-five years old and called him Val . . . or perhaps something that sounded like that. This person, whoever he was, might have given Van money; might have talked him into going home.

If so, what did it mean to her? It could mean everything, or nothing. Van close to her, under her thumb, frightened of her, was one thing. Van free of her, back with his own family . . . would he want to forget all that lay behind? Or would he have an attack of conscience?

Myra Fossett, who now had wealth and power and was close to the position she craved, could not afford Van's conscience. He simply knew too much. A Van Clevern who seemed to be headed down into the gutter was no danger, but a Van Clevern back with his family, that self-righteous family of which she had heard so much, was a very real danger. One minute or two of talking on his part could destroy everything she had so carefully built.

He even knew about Everett Fossett, or suspected. And Everett had friends and perhaps relatives of whom she knew nothing who might start an investigation.

She considered the question coolly and made her decision about Van Clevern. Of course, she admitted, that decision had really been made a long time ago, but then he had been useful to her.

It would have to be an accident. There would be no chance for poison in this case.

She considered the others. It had worked well with them. Seven men and two women, and each one had been a step toward the success she wanted. It had been poison with all but one, and that one was knocked on the head when he started to wake up, and was left out in the mule corral. Van still believed he was covering something that could be called an accident, that she had hit harder than she wished.

Val . . . Could it be that she had a son still alive?

She had never wanted the child, had planned it merely as a trap for Darrant, and he had gotten away from her before she could spring the trap. And then she was saddled with a child.

But now she was curious . . . did he look like her? Or like . . . what was his name?

Andy . . . that was it. For Andrew, she supposed, or possibly André, considering the fact that he was partly French.

Val . . . suppose he really was alive? What then? What difference could it make?

Van had always had a weakness for the child, and Van might talk too much . . . no, he wouldn't. Not to Val. Yet Van might tell him where she was, who she was, and Val might come to her for money.

Scarcely a week had gone by when Pinkerton's report was on her desk.

The young man's name was Valentine Darrant . . . *so her son was alive* . . . he had read law with the firm of Lawton, Bryce & Kelly . . . *a good firm* . . . had been admitted to the bar. Seemed to have come from the West. Had worked for Steven Bricker . . . *that tall young man she had passed in the doorway* . . . a young man of very definite ability who seemed to know many people of doubtful reputation . . . *maybe he did take after her* . . . spent much time in shooting galleries, never played cards, rarely gambled except an occasional friendly wager on some fact of sports or history. Went often to the theater and the opera, well-educated, but nothing known as to his academic background.

It was little enough, and left a number of questions unanswered. Where had he been during the intervening years? Who had reared him? Who had given him his education? How long had Van known him?

Myra glanced at the report again. The last line told her that Val had left town. He had bought a ticket for St. Louis.

Well, enough of that. Now there was the problem of what to do about Van Clevern.

Nevertheless, she found herself beset by a nagging curiosity: What was her son like? Was he like her? Or like Darrant?

For Darrant she had a grudging respect. He had had sense enough to get away while the getting was good, and not many had done that, not before she had bled them dry.

Some people said a child took after his grandparents. She had no idea what Darrant's family had been like, but for her own she had only contempt. They had been good, God-fearing people by contemporary standards, and her father had done well in a limited way. Well, no matter.

Van Clevern had indeed returned home. He had taken a little while to get himself looking presentable. He had stopped drinking, had eaten regular meals, had caught up on his sleep. And as Val had said, his family were glad to see him, and they asked few questions. If they did ask he had a story to tell them. He had been involved in mining deals out west. He had made money, lost it, and now was planning to find a local connection and stay home. . . . Only at times did he think of Myra, and uneasily wondered what she would do.

He shook off his doubts, doubts brought on by an all too clear memory of her fury at being thwarted, of her ruthless, relentless nature. But then, he told himself, she would be glad to be rid of him.

Slowly, his manner changed. He became more confident, and began to pick up old associations. It was discovered that he had acquired a lot of information about mining and railroad stocks, and possessed a good deal of on-the-spot information. Three weeks after his return he was hired as a consultant by an investment house in which his father was a partner.

By the time two months had gone by he had proved himself worthwhile to the firm. He met people easily, and his knowledge—much of it acquired from Myra—was proving of value.

Another month passed, and Van Clevern had obtained several new accounts for the firm, so it was with a distinct shock and sorrow that they heard of his death.

He had been riding in the park on a Sunday morning, and had evidently been thrown from his horse. His skull was badly shattered and he had been dead for at least an hour when they found him.

Val Darrant, stopping at Knight's ranch, in New Mexico, read a brief notice of the death in a newspaper somebody had left at the ranch. It was a Chicago paper, several weeks old, and the item was a small one, on an inside page; it gave only the barest details.

Val put the paper down and sat back in his chair, a curious emptiness within him. Of all those whom he had known, next to Will Reilly himself, he had loved Van Clevern the most.

A weak man, but one who had been kind, who had taken time to talk to a small boy when nobody else so much as noticed him, and who had saved him from death.

And now he was dead. An accident, they said.

As to that, Val was not so sure. Van had been an excellent horseman, often riding the half-broken mustangs of the western country. It seemed unlikely he would be thrown by any rented-out horse in an eastern state. It could be, but it was unlikely.

SIXTEEN

Val Darrant had no liking for open country, and a good stretch of it lay before him. Beyond it the Burro Mountains bulked strong against the sky. He drew rein at the mouth of an arroyo and studied the terrain before him.

He had a feeling that he had glimpsed a faint cloud of dust only minutes before, but now, with a full view of the plain, he saw nothing. He touched his Winchester to be sure it was not jammed too deeply into the scabbard, and then touched his heels to the buckskin.

The gelding was a good horse with black mane and tail and just a suggestion of black spots on the left shoulder, as if there might have been some appaloosa strain somewhere in the buckskin's past. It was a strong horse with a good gait, mountain- and desert-bred.

The country ahead looked innocent enough, but he stayed where he was, knowing that to trust innocence too much could lead to trouble.

He had ridden the stage from the little village of Los Angeles to Yuma and thence to Tucson.

He had believed he'd had enough of the West, but now he was singing a different song. He now knew this was the country for

137

him. No matter how far he might travel, he would always come back here. He was riding now for Silver City, then across country to Tascosa and to the ranch below the cap-rock.

Suddenly, he heard the soft beat of horse's hoofs behind him.

He turned his mount and waited. It was one rider, on a shod horse. This ride from Tucson had been enough to get his eyes and ears tuned to the western lands again. He waited. . . .

The horse was gray, with a black mane and tail, the rider a slender young man wearing a battered black hat, his hair down to his shoulders.

"If you're riding east," Val said, "I'd be glad of the company."

He was a good-looking young man, almost too good-looking, except for two prominent teeth. They did not disfigure him, but did mark his appearance. He weighed not more than a compact one-fifty, and he was probably about five-eight. His hair was blond, his eyes gray.

"Ridin' east myself," he said. "You alone?"

"Yes."

Val looked at him. "Say, now I know you. You're Billy Antrim."

The rider rolled a smoke and glanced at him quizzically. "It's been a while since I been called that, but come to think of it, you do look familiar."

"Your mother ran the boarding house in Silver City. I came into town traveling with Will Reilly. Remember? You, Dobie, and I took a ride into the hills a couple of times. We swapped yarns, too."

"Sure, I recall. Where you been all the time?"

"Drifting," Val said. "Will's dead. He was killed up in Colorado a few years ago."

"Heard about it. The way I heard it he was shot from the dark. Never had a chance."

"That's right. It was Henry Sonnenberg, Hardesty, and Thurston Pike."

"I heard that, too. Sonnenberg was in Fort Sumner a couple of years ago. Hardesty's dead."

"I know."

Billy looked at him quickly. "Say! You were the one who got him! Over at some ranch in Texas."

"In town. He wasn't much."

They rode for several miles, both watching the country, and

suddenly Val said, "You mentioned that nobody ever called you Billy Antrim any more. Knight's Ranch is up ahead, and maybe I should know what to call you."

Billy looked at him. "My name's Bonney," he said. "They call me the Kid."

It was a name on everybody's lips. Even the eastern newspapers knew about Billy the Kid and the Lincoln County War.

"Are you all right at Knight's? If you aren't, I'll ride in and buy whatever you need."

"They're good people. They know I am wanted, but I never trouble them and they don't trouble me. Anyway," Billy added, "so far as I know, only Pat Garrett is hunting me. The rest of them either don't care, or they don't want to borrow trouble."

Shadows were growing long, reaching out from the Burro Mountains ahead. The ranch lay in the mouth of the canyon of the same name, and had become a regular stop on the stage line. Richard S. Knight had built the fortlike adobe in 1874, and sold out a few years later to John Parks, who now operated the ranch.

Val led the way into the ranch yard and Parks came out to meet them with two of his seven children. He glanced at Val.

"Valentine Darrant, sir. I think you know Mr. Bonney."

"Yes, I do. How are you, Billy?"

"Middlin', Mr. Parks, just middlin'. But I'm shaping up to feel better when I've eaten some of your good grub."

"Too much of your own cooking, Billy?"

The Kid laughed. "I'm not much of a hand at cookin', Mr. Parks, not even when I have it to cook. I ain't been close to food in three days."

"Go on inside. Ma will put something on for you."

Val swung down. "I'll look after your horse, Billy. Go ahead."

He led the two horses to the water trough and let them drink, then to the corral, where he stripped the gear from them. Parks was pitching hay to his own stock.

"You know Billy pretty well?" he asked.

"We met a long time back. When his mother was boarding people over at Silver City. We played some together as boys."

"A lot has happened since then."

"I've heard some of it." Val rested his hands on his buckskin's back. "I like him. So far as I've heard, he's done nothing his enemies weren't doing, only he ended up by being outlawed and they didn't."

"He's stopped by here several times, and he's always been a gentleman. Shall we go in?"

After supper Val went outside and sat down on the steps. He felt a growing irritation with himself. He had a right to practice law, but he had done little of it, and then merely as an employee. He owned a part of a ranch which he would soon visit, but he had no taste for ranching. He had a good deal of experience with railroads and investments, but not enough to qualify him for the kind of a job he wanted, nor was he very interested in business.

Here he felt at home. He liked the West, and he liked the drifting, but it was no use. Beyond every trail there were only more trails, and no man could ride them all. He had known a few girls in passing, but had never been in love. Within himself he felt a vast longing, a yearning for something more . . . he did not know what.

He did not believe that anything was to be solved by killing, yet the memory that Thurston Pike and Henry Sonnenberg were still at large, and undoubtedly still involved in killing, nagged at his mind.

Was he hoping that something would intervene? That somebody would do his job for him? When he remembered Sonnenberg he felt a kind of chill. He was a great brute of a man . . . he seemed invulnerable. Was he, Val Darrant, afraid of Sonnenberg?

Yet Sonnenberg's hand had only held the gun and squeezed the trigger. Equally to blame were Avery Simpson, who had traveled the West offering a price for a man's life, and Prince Pavel, who had hired the killing done.

Will Reilly would have known what to do, and Will Reilly would have done it.

Was that why he could settle down to nothing else? Was that what subconsciously worried him? Was it the feeling that he had left the murderers of his best friend, Will Reilly, unpunished?

And what about his mother? What about the woman who now called herself Myra Fossett? Should he go to her and identify himself? To what purpose? He wanted nothing from her, and she had never shown any interest in him except to be rid of him.

Billy came out and sat on the stoop beside him. "Nothing like a desert night," he said. "I always liked riding at night."

"Where's Sonnenberg now?"

Billy turned his head and looked at him. "Don't mess with him, Val. Not even if you're good with a gun. He's poison mean, and he's fast—real fast. I wouldn't want to tackle him myself."

"He was one of them."

"Forget it. Look where followin' up an idea like that got me. After Tunstall was shot, well, I figured to get everyone of that crowd that done it. Well, we got several of them, and now the war's over an' everybody else is out of it but me."

"You didn't tell me where Sonnenberg was."

"Reason is, I don't know. Somebody said he was up Montana way." Billy paused. "I know where Pike is, though."

"Where?"

"If you're goin' back to that ranch of yours you'll be pointing right at him. Last I heard he was in Tascosa. He's got him a woman there."

"You going that way?"

"No," Billy said after a minute, "I think I'll set for a spell. This here's good grub, they're nice folks, and I just think I'll rest up a few days. It ain't often I get a chance to rest these days."

"I'm pulling out, come daylight." Val stood up. "So long, Billy, and good luck."

He went inside, and to bed. Before he got into bed, however, he checked his gun. It was the Smith & Wesson .44 Russian that Hickok had given him. He liked the balance of it, liked the feel. Val Darrant rode away from Knight's Ranch before daylight, curving around the mountains, over a spur, and down across the rolling country beyond. This was still Apache country, and he had had his fill of them as a boy in the bitter fight when they had attacked the stage on which he'd ridden with Will, so he kept off the skyline and was wary of the route he chose. He avoided possible ambushes, studied the ground for tracks, watched the flight of birds. All of these could be indications of the presence of people.

At night he chose a hidden spot, built a small fire, and prepared his coffee and whatever he chose to eat. Then he put out his fire and rode on for several miles, masking his trail as much as possible.

The country he was passing through after the first day or so was the area touched by the Lincoln County War, and many of the hard characters connected with that fight were still in the area. He stopped in Lincoln itself and tied up at the hitching rail in front of a small eating place.

Inside there was a short bar and half a dozen tables. He sat down and a plate of beef stew was placed before him. In many such places there was no question of giving your order. You simply ate what was prepared and were glad to get it. The coffee was good.

There were half a dozen people in the place, and two of them he recognized at once as toughs—or would-be toughs. One of them glanced several times at Val, whispered to the other, and then they both looked at him and laughed.

Val ignored them. He had been in so many towns as a stranger, and he knew the pattern. Most people were friendly enough, but there were always a few who were trouble-hunters, choosing any stranger as fair game.

"I figure he pulled his stakes," one of the men was saying. "All the Mexicans liked him, so I figure he just pulled out for Mexico."

"Naw, he's got him a girl up at Fort Sumner. He'll go thataway. He'll never leave the country 'less she goes with him."

A hard-looking young man with reddish hair, turned to him, leaning his elbows on the bar. Val knew they were about to start something and he was prepared.

"You, over there! Where d' you think Billy the Kid will go?"

Whatever he said they were prepared to make an issue of it. So he merely shrugged. "You can tell by looking at his horse's nose."

"His horse's *nose*? What's that got to do with it?"

"You just look at his horse's nose. Whichever way it's pointing, that's the way he's going."

The waitress giggled, and some of the men chuckled. Val merely looked innocent. The red-haired man's face flushed. "You think you're almighty clever, stranger. Well, maybe we'll see how clever you are. What d'you do for a livin'?"

"I'm an actor," Val said.

The man stared at him. The others in the room seemed to be paying no attention, but Val knew all of them were listening. He wanted to finish his meal in peace.

"You don't look like no actor to me," the redhead declared. "Let's see you act. Get up an' show us."

Here it was . . . well, he intended to finish his meal. Val put down his fork. "Actually," he said, "I'm a magician. I can make things disappear, but you boys will have to help me."

He turned to the waitress. "Have you two buckets? I'd like them full of water, please."

"You goin' to make them disappear?"

"If you boys will help me." A Mexican boy was coming from the back door with two buckets of water. "And two brooms," he added, "or a broom and a mop handle."

He took a broom and handed it to the redhead. "You take this broom and stand right here. And you," he said to the other tough, "stand over here with this broom."

He got up on a chair with a bucket of water and held it against the ceiling, then guided the redhead's broomstick to the exact middle of the bottom of the bucket. "Now hold it tight against the ceiling, tight as you can or it will fall.

"You," he said to the second man, "you hold this one." He placed the second bucket against the ceiling, and the man's broomstick was held against it.

"Now as long as you boys hold those sticks tight, the buckets won't fall. If they fall you'll get mighty wet."

"Hurry up with this disappearin' act," the redhead said, "this is a tirin' position."

Then coolly Val reached over and flipped their guns from their holsters and stepped back to his table.

"What the—"

"No," Val said quietly, gesturing at them with a pistol, "you boys just hold those broomsticks tight unless you want to get wet . . . or shot."

Placing the pistols on the table beside his plate Val calmly returned to eating. He finished the stew, then asked for his coffee cup to be refilled.

"Hey, what is this!" the red-headed man demanded. "Take this bucket off here!"

"Be still," Val said; "these gentlemen want to eat quietly . . . without any trouble from you."

He sat back, sipping his coffee and contemplating them with no expression on his face. The story had already got out, probably from the Mexican boy who had brought the water, and quite a crowd gathered outside. Some even came into the restaurant.

The two would-be toughs stood in the middle of the room, the buckets of water above their heads. If they let go of the broom-handles the heavy buckets would fall, dowsing them with water and probably hitting them a rap on the skull.

"Don't be nervous, boys," Val said. "You wanted to see something disappear. I've made my stew disappear, and three cups of coffee. And now"—he got up and placed a silver dollar on the table—"*I* am going to disappear."

He turned to the others in the room. "They'll get pretty tired after a while, so when you boys get around to it, just take down the buckets for them, will you? . . . but only if you're in the mood."

He stepped to the door. "Good-bye, gentlemen," he said. "I regret leaving such good company, but you understand how it is."

He paused just long enough to shuck the cartridges from their guns, then he dropped the guns on the walk outside. Mounting up, he cantered out of town.

The land lay wide before him, and overhead was the vast arch of the sky. This was what he had missed, the unbelievable distance wherever he looked, the marvelous sweep of rolling hills, the sudden depths of unexpected canyons, the cloud shadows on the desert or the grassland.

Now, topping out on a rise, he could see for sixty or seventy miles across land that shimmered in the sun. He was alone with himself, and he heard only the hoof-falls of his horse, the occasional creak of the saddle, or jingle of a spur.

As he rode, he thought how impossible it was to live in such a land without being aware of it at all times. Even within the narrowed scope of barroom, hotel lobby, bunkhouse, or campfire, much of the talk was of water holes, grass conditions, and Indians.

The Indian was part of the terrain, and travel could not be planned without considering the Indian. Few of them had anything like a permanent home, and they might be expected anywhere. Waterholes were the essentials of all travel, important to wild game, and as important to the Indian as to the white man. Any approach to a waterhole must be undertaken with caution.

In regard to waterholes Val had adopted the practice he had heard Tensleep mention . . . Tensleep, that curious gunman, half an outlaw, half a good citizen, an ignorant man in the way of books, but with a mind crowded with knowledge of which he was scarcely aware, it was so much a part of him and his way of living.

Tensleep would never camp at a water hole, even in country safe from Indians.

"Ain't rightly fair," he had told Val. "Other folks have to get water, too. And if you crowd up a water hole, what about the animals and the birds that have to drink? They're goin' to set out there dry-throated whilst you crowd the water. Get what you need, then make room."

He had learned, too, that it was never safe to drain a canteen until one had actually seen the water hole with water in it, for often there was only cracked mud where water had once been. And he knew that the ancient Indian trails were the safest, for they followed the easy contours of the land, and always led from one water hole to another.

Twice Val stopped at lonely ranches, exchanging news for meals, and listening to the gossip of the country. At the second ranch the rancher offered to sell him a handsome bay mare.

The man leaned on the corral bars, extolling the animal, and Val asked, "What about a bill of sale?"

"Why not?" The rancher grinned at him. "Write it up and I'll sign it."

"But will it be good?"

The rancher chewed his mustache, and then said, "Now, mister, I won't lie to you. If you're riding east I'd say that bill of sale was good; riding west I'd say it wasn't."

"I think one horse is enough," Val said, "but she's a good mare."

He swam the Rio Grande, and pointed across country toward the Pecos, riding easy in the saddle.

SEVENTEEN

Tascosa was born of a river crossing. It thrived on trail herds; and died, strangled with barbed wire. Its life was brief and bloody, and when it died there were left behind only a few crumbling adobes, the ghosts of dead gunmen slain in its streets, and Frenchy McCormick, the once beautiful girl who had promised never to leave her gambler husband, and who never did, even in death.

But in the 1870's and '80's Tascosa was wild and rough and hard to curry below the knees. The cattle outfits and the rustlers were drifting in, and the ranchers who drove in the big herds wanted the toughest fighting hands they could find.

Billy the Kid was a frequent visitor. The town had its tough ones, and its shady ladies, and some of these were as tough as the men to whom they catered.

Valentine Darrant was headed for Tascosa. He told himself he was not hunting Thurston Pike—he was riding to his ranch, and Tascosa was the only town within a hundred miles or more in any direction. He had stopped one night in Fort Sumner, spending it in a bedroom turned over to him by Pete Maxwell. Pete and his father had been friends to Will Reilly, and Pete remembered Val.

"Quiet around here now," Pete told him. "Pat Garrett comes in hunting Billy the Kid, but the Kid won't come back this way again. If my guess is right, he's headed for Old Mexico. The Mexicans swear by that boy—he's one American who has always treated them right."

"I know Billy," Val said, "I knew him in Silver City when we were boys."

"He's all right," Pete said, "just so's you don't push him. He don't back up worth a damn."

"I saw him a while back," Val commented. "He's riding some rough trails."

Pete Maxwell knew better than to ask where he had seen the Kid, and he knew that Val would not have told him. They parted with a hand-shake after breakfast the next morning.

Now Val was riding into Tascosa toward sunset. He was older, tougher, and stronger than when he had last seen Thurston Pike. He had been a boy then—he was a man now.

Cottonwoods grew along the streets and back of the town. The Canadian River ran close by, and a creek ran right down Water Street. Val rode part way around the town to scout the approaches before actually riding in on the Dodge Trail, which took him in on Main Street. He turned left and rode to Mickey McCormick's livery stable.

After putting up his horse he walked to the corner and went into a saloon. It was near four o'clock and the saloon was nearly empty.

A glance told him he knew nobody there, and he went to the bar, a tall young man in fringed shotgun chaps, boots with Mexican spurs, one tied-down gun, and a spare in his waistband under the edge of his coat. He wore a checkered black and white shirt, and a black hat. His coat was also black, but dusty now.

"Is there a good place around to eat?" he asked, after ordering a beer.

"Yonder," the bartender pointed; "Scotty Wilson's place. It's likely he won't be there himself, but the food's good. Scotty always sets a good table . . . no matter whose beef it is."

Val smiled. "Those might be fighting words in some places."

"Not with Scotty. He's the Justice of the Peace, and I guess he figures the easiest way to settle an argument over beef is for the court to take it. But he won't charge the parties of the first part if they come in his restaurant to eat their beef."

"Sounds like a man I'd like," Val said. After a moment he asked, "What's going on around town? Any excitement?"

"Here? Ain't been a shooting in a week. Or a cutting."

Val idled at the bar. He had not wanted the drink, but he did want the talk, and the western saloon was always a clearing house for trail information—about water holes, Indian troubles, rustlers, and range conditions generally.

A few men drifted in and ranged themselves along the bar. Val listened to the talk, aware of his own vague discontent. What was he doing here, anyway? Why didn't he eat, go to bed early, and be ready for a hard ride the following day? But he did not move, and his soul-searching went on. What did he intend to do with his life? He could hang out a shingle in any of these western towns and gradually build a law practice. He was short of money, and desperately needed some means of income. The ranch had prospered, but the income had been put back into the place.

The thought of Thurston Pike and Henry Sonnenberg lurked in the recesses of his mind, and he felt guilty. He should hunt them down, and do what the law could not do . . . what everyone would expect him to do. But he had no taste for killing.

"Young feller?"

"Yes?" It had been a moment before he realized one of the men was speaking to him.

"Like to take a hand? We're figurin' on a little poker."

He was about to refuse, then said, "All right, but I'm not staying in. I've got some miles to ride tomorrow."

He was a fool, he knew. He hadn't that much money in his pocket, and a man needed money to play well. Two hours later he checked out of the game, a winner by sixteen dollars.

A small, slender man left the game at the same time. "Had supper?" he asked. "I'm going over to Scotty's for a bite."

"All right."

They walked across the street, talking idly. "Win much?" the man asked.

"No."

"Neither did I. About twenty dollars."

The steaks were good at Scotty's. Val had not realized how hungry he was.

Suddenly the other man said, "I think we know each other."

Val studied him. "Where?" he asked. "I've been west and I've been east."

"So have I, but I can't place you. My name is Cates, if that helps. Egen Cates."

Val grinned at him. "You have a bullet scar on your arm, and another one somewhere about you. You got them from the Apaches one time, down Arizona way."

"And you?"

"I was the kid who gave you my seat on the stage. I loaded rifles for you and the others. My name is Valentine Darrant."

"Darrant? Have you been to Colorado lately?"

"No."

"Better go up there. They've been looking for you up at Empire . . . and some of the country around. I think they have news for you."

Val searched his face. "What does that mean?"

"I was a miner . . . remember? Now I'm a mining man. The major difference is that I don't collect wages, I pay them." He grinned. "Although it isn't always as easy as it sounds." He was serious again. "Seems you invested some money up there, some years back. You'd better go see what happened to it."

Colorado . . . he had always liked Colorado. "I knew a pretty little girl up there once, when I was a kid," he said, remembering. "She said she was an actress. Her name was Maude Kiskadden, and she was some relation to Jack Slade."

Cates smiled. "I know the story. She was no blood relation. Her father had been married to Slade's widow after Slade was hung by the Vigilantes . . . which never should have happened."

Cates called for more coffee. "You say you've been east. Did you ever hear of Maude Adams?"

"Who hasn't?"

"Maude Adams, who is about the best-known actress in the country right now, was your little Maude Kiskadden. Her mother used the stage name of Annie Adams."

They were still talking half an hour later when the door opened and Thurston Pike came in.

Val Darrant looked at Pike and then said to Cates, "Mr. Cates, we've known each other quite a spell, but do you remember my uncle?" He had purposely raised his voice a little.

"Your uncle? You mean Will Reilly? Of course I remember him."

Thurston Pike looked across the room at them. He was a tall, thin man with rounded shoulders and a lantern jaw. He had a grizzled beard, and looked dirty and unkempt.

Val returned his look, a faint smile on his lips, and Pike lowered his eyes. He seemed uncertain what to do.

"He was murdered, you know. Shot down from the dark by three men who were afraid to meet him face to face."

Val saw the slow red of anger creeping up Pike's neck. He could think of him only as a killer for hire, undeserving of any consideration or pity.

Cates was unaware of the impending drama. "What happened to them?" he asked.

"One of them is dead," Val replied, "and the others have not long to live."

Egan Cates was looking at him now. "What is it, Val? What's happening?"

"I don't think anything is going to happen," Val replied. "Thurston Pike wouldn't think of shooting a man who is looking at him."

Cates glanced around quickly and got up abruptly. He shifted his chair to one side and sat down again. All eyes were on Pike.

He stared at his plate, knife and fork clutched in his hands. Suddenly, with an oath, he put them down on the table, got up, and lurched to the door, knocking over a chair as he went.

"You might have warned me," Cates said.

"I wasn't expecting him, although I knew he was in Tascosa."

"Well, if he's like you say, you'd best be careful. He'll try to kill you now." Egan Cates ordered fresh coffee. "I'll say this for you. You've got nerve. You had nerve even as a kid."

"I had a good teacher," Val said. "Nobody had more nerve than Will."

"You said one of them was dead. Pike was another . . . who is the third?"

"Henry Sonnenberg."

Cates let out a low whistle. "Leave him alone, Val. You can't get him. Nothing can touch him."

"Maybe."

"Are you going to hunt Pike down now?"

Val thought about that a moment. "No, I'll let him hunt me. He'll do it, because he's worried now. Will had a lot of friends, and some night they might decide to hang Pike."

Cates put his hands on the table. "I have to be getting back to the hotel. Val, why don't you forget this? I like the cut of your jib, and I wish you'd come in with me. I have some excellent properties that need developing, and I have access to the cash . . . come in with me. I think we'd make a team."

"I'll give it some thought."

When Val was alone he sat there considering what he had done, and when he finished his coffee he did not go out the front door. He paid for his supper and went through the kitchen. The cook turned to protest, but Val waved, went on through the storeroom, and out the back door into an alley.

He circled around, moving warily, but he saw no sign of Pike. At the corner he studied the street, then returned to the alley and entered the Exchange Hotel from the back.

Once in his room, he put a chair under the doorknob and drew the curtain down. Then, with water poured into the wash bowl, he took a quick sponge bath. After that he was soon in bed and asleep.

He awoke about daybreak and lay still, listening to the town as it came alive. A rooster crowed, somewhere a door slammed, a pump creaked, water gushed into a bucket. Somebody walked by on the boardwalk, and he heard a low murmur of voices.

Presently he got up, and shaved in front of the flawed mirror, which gave his face a twisted look. After he had dressed he glanced around the room to be sure he was not leaving anything behind. He went out of the room, and moved quietly through the hotel corridor.

The sun was not yet up in the streets of Tascosa. He stepped outside, breathing the fresh morning air, his eyes in one quick glance sweeping the street, then the rooftops and the windows and doors. Such observation had been drilled into him by Will Reilly, and his brief examination now missed nothing.

Scotty Wilson's restaurant was open, and he went in. Two sour-looking cowpunchers, still unshaven and red-eyed from the night before, drank coffee at the counter. They were obviously in no mood to talk. Taking the table at the back of the room, Val ordered breakfast.

He thought of the ride before him. It was unlikely that for some time to come he would have another meal he did not prepare himself. The route he was taking was somewhat roundabout, but water was scarce on the Staked Plains.

Actually, the Palo Duro Canyon offered the best route, but there he would be a sitting duck for anyone shooting from the bluffs. Out on the cap-rock he could see for miles and it would be impossible for anyone to come upon him without warning.

As he sat there, the door from the street suddenly opened and a tall, lean man with frosty eyes came in. He looked at Val, and crossed to his table. "Mind if I sit down?"

"It would be my pleasure," Val said. "What can I do for you?"

"You could leave town." The man smiled as he spoke. "Darrant, your name is?" He held out a hand. "I am Sheriff Willingham. There's a rumor around that you had some words with Thursty Pike last night."

"No, I can't say I did. I was talking with Egan Cates, and Pike was in the room. He got up and left."

"All right. Have it your way. No offense, my friend, but we've had too much shooting here already, and if you and Pike have something to settle, do it outside of town."

"That's agreeable to me, Sheriff. I haven't spoken to Pike, and do not intend to if I can avoid it."

"He's a bad actor, son. He'll give you no fair chance if he can manage it."

Willingham studied him. "Are you planning on locating around here?"

"Not exactly, but I'm a third owner of a ranch southeast of here. Do you know the Bucklin outfit?"

"Yes—good people. I hunted buffalo with the Bucklin boys when they first came west." He gave Val an amused glance. "You a single man?"

"Yes."

Willingham chuckled. "You'll have yourself a time. Pa Bucklin's got two of the prettiest daughters you ever did see, and that Betsy . . . the one they call Western . . . she's something to look at."

"What about Boston?"

"A ring-tailed terror. Beautiful and wild, and she can ride as good as any puncher on the cap-rock. She can shoot and she can rope. At the roundup we had a while back she beat every hand we had at roping and tying calves."

"They aren't married then?"

"No, and they won't be if they stay around here. They scare the boys. Who wants to marry a girl who can do everything you can, and better?"

The wind was picking up when Val Darrant rode from Tascosa, south and a little east. The tumbleweeds rolled along with him, rolled toward a ranch he could call home. Thunder rumbled in the clouds, and when the first drops fell he dug out his slicker. It was going to be a wet ride.

EIGHTEEN

There was no question of shelter. So far as Val was aware there was nothing nearer than his own ranch, which lay miles away. The country was flat as a billiard table, and it was only after he had ridden several hours in a driving rain that he saw the edge of an arroyo. It was the first break in the level of the cap-rock in all that distance, and he judged it to be a branch of the Palo Duro, long a hide-out for the Comanches.

The rain rattled on his slicker and ran from the brim of his hat. Thunder rolled and lightning stabbed through the sky. His one consolation was that if Thurston Pike was riding in this weather he was doing no better than Val. He figured now that it might be best to ride to the Palo Duro and see if there was some kind of shelter in the canyon. He turned abruptly and headed that way. Riding out here on the cap-rock would make him a target for lightning.

The rain drew a steel curtain across the day. His horse slipped once in the mud, and then he reached the rim of the canyon, but saw no route by which he could descend. He followed along the rim, searching for a way.

Lightning flashed again, and the time between the flash and the roll of thunder was much shorter. Suddenly he saw where the rim was broken and a trail led down to the bottom of the canyon. It was a buffalo trail, and an easy ride.

He started down, but in a moment something struck him a wicked blow on the shoulder. In the moment when he started to turn, believing he had been hit from behind, he heard the report of a rifle and his horse leaped. Val lost his grip and toppled into the mud, while his horse, frightened and perhaps hurt, went racing away down the slope. He realized he ought to move, and lifted his head to look around. He lay on a steep part of the trail. Crawling off it, he found a place under the rim where he would be somewhat protected. He struggled to pull himself to his feet, managed it, and caught hold of a crack in the rock face and worked along it, hunting for a larger crack.

He had been shot, and whoever had shot him had been lying in wait. The chances were good that the unseen marksman, who might be Pike, or might be an Indian or an outlaw, was even now coming closer.

He clung to the rock face, his boots on the steep talus slope that fell away behind him. The rain still hammered against his slicker. He could hold himself up, but though he had been hit he did not believe he was seriously hurt.

His horse, as he saw when he turned his head and looked down, had reached the bottom of the canyon and was cropping grass near the stream, almost half a mile away. His rifle was in the scabbard on the saddle.

He listened, but heard no sound except the rain. Vaguely, he thought he smelled smoke, the smoke of a campfire.

He edged his way along the rock, knowing he had to get himself out of this spot. If the unknown marksman was within sight of him, he would certainly have fired again, but he must be working himself around to get in that final shot.

The rim-rock along here was perhaps fifteen feet high, and was topped by a thin layer of soil and sparse grass. Below him the slope fell away steeply to the bottom, several hundred feet away.

The rim-rock was split in many places, and suddenly he found a crack and eased himself into it. There was no overhang here, but there was a flat sheet of broken-off rock that lay canted across the split, and he backed under it, dried his hands on his shirt under the slicker, and drew his gun.

It was a long wait. Several times he thought he caught the smell of damp wood burning, but a fire in such a place was unlikely; and it was unlikely the killer, whoever he might be, would have a fire.

A slow hour passed, marked by Val's watch. More than once he shifted the gun; at times he was on the verge of crawling out, but the memory of that rifle shot restrained him. There was no chance to check his wound. The shock had worn off, and now it hurt like blazes, but the bleeding seemed to have stopped.

He had almost decided to move out of his shelter when he heard footsteps. He tilted the gun and waited. He had never shot at anything he could not see, and he was not about to begin, but if that was Thurston Pike . . .

"Mister," said a girl's voice, "I can see your tracks and I know you're in there. The geezer who shot you is gone. If you'll let me help you, I will."

"Step out where I can see you," he said.

She hesitated a moment. "That voice is familiar, mister, and I think we know each other. I am stepping out."

She came suddenly into full view, a tall girl in boots and a beaded and fringed buckskin skirt reaching to below her knees. She wore a slicker that was hanging open, giving her hand free access to the belt gun she wore. In her right hand she carried a Winchester. Her blouse was open at the neck and she wore over it, beneath the slicker, a man's coat, cut down to fit her.

He saw that in a glance, but he saw much more. She was young and she was beautiful, with a wild, colorful beauty of dark hair, flashing eyes, bright red lips, and a figure that not even the rough clothes could conceal.

He eased out of his cramped position and stood up. "I thought so," she said. "Val Darrant, isn't it? I'm Boston Bucklin."

"You couldn't be anybody else," he said. "I've heard it said that you were the wildest, most beautiful thing on the Plains. I believe it."

She blushed, but stared back at him. "It won't do, your making up to me. Besides, you've been shot."

"Was that your fire I smelled?"

"Yes."

"You didn't shoot at me?"

"If I'd shot at you, you'd be dead. No, it was a man on a big dapple-gray horse. When he saw me he rode off, mighty fast. He didn't guess that I was alone."

She looked at him as he came away from the crack, watching him move. "You can walk all right. My fire's about two hundred yards down canyon. If you can get yourself to it, I'll round up your horse."

"Thanks," he said.

Her camp, when he reached it, was almost perfect. The rim-rock had caved in underneath, leaving a shelf that overhung a small area within the rim-rock itself. There was room enough for the fire and a bed under the rim shelf, and a place for three or four horses in a sort of pocket not under the shelf. The camp was hidden, with no way it could be seen from above or below until one rode right up to it. Obviously the girl had spent the night here.

She rode back shortly, leading his horse, and when she had tied it, she joined him under the rim, throwing off her slicker. Her wet black hair hung down over her shoulders.

"We've been expectin' you, Val," she said. "Pa, he said you'd be along soon. We've been hopin' you'd come."

"How is your pa?"

"Fair to middlin'. He's packin' a Kiowa bullet picked up last spring. Ails him some when it's wet or cold."

"And the others?"

"They're all right. Cody had him a mite of shootin' over to Fort Griffin. Some fancy gent in a flowered vest had words with him."

"But Cody's all right?"

"Sure."

She had put the coffeepot on, and now she turned to him. "You'd better let me look at that wound. You tenderfeet sicken up almighty fast, seems to me."

"I'm no tenderfoot. I was born in this country."

"I know, but you've been living it high and handsome back east." She helped him off with his coat and shirt. She looked at his powerful muscles with approval. "Well, all that beef hasn't gone soft, anyway."

The wound was not serious. The bullet had struck the top of his shoulder and glanced off, tearing the muscle some, and he had lost blood.

"In those fancy stories a girl always tears her white petticoat and makes a bandage. Well, I haven't got a white petticoat—never had one—and if I did I wouldn't tear it up for no man. Not unless he was in dyin' shape."

"There are a couple of clean white handkerchiefs in the pack behind my saddle," Val suggested.

She got them out. "My, aren't we the fancy one!" She looked critically at the handkerchiefs. "You've become a real dude, I see."

Val watched her. He had never, anywhere, seen so beautiful a girl. She was wild, free, and uninhibited as an animal. "Aren't you a ways from home?" he asked.

"It isn't so far, not across country. I like to ride. I like to see a lot of country, and I'm not worried. I can ride and shoot as good as any man, and better than most. I can also use a knife."

"Pretty dangerous. I'll bet all the men are scared to death of you."

She flushed. "Maybe," she said, lifting her eyes to him, "but it wouldn't do them any good if they weren't. I'm spoken for."

He felt a twinge of disappointment that startled him. "I'm surprised," he said.

Her head came up from the coffee she was pouring. "Oh? You don't think I'm good enough?"

"Oh, you're good enough, all right. Maybe too good. You've got a streak of broncho in you, I think, and you'd need a man who'd bridle you with a Spanish bit."

She gave him another of those straight glances. "I'd handle with a hackamore for the right man," she said, "and no other could do it, Spanish bit or no."

When he had finished his coffee she broke camp quickly and efficiently, brushing aside his efforts to help. "Save it, tenderfoot, you'll need all your strength."

"Not if you're spoken for," he said. She turned on him sharply and seemed about to speak, then swung astride her horse. Only then did he notice that she wore a divided skirt. He had heard of them, but had never seen one. All the women he had known rode sidesaddle. It was considered the only ladylike way.

"If you can sit your saddle," she said, "we can make it tonight . . . late."

"I'll be with you," he said, and she led off at a lope.

The sky was heavily overcast, although the rain had stopped and there was no more thunder and lightning. The ground was soggy and slippery, but they made good time, with Boston leading the way.

So far as he could see, there were no landmarks. The cap-rock was level and seemed to reach to the horizon on all sides. By the time they were a few hundred yards from the canyon they could no longer tell that it was there. Val studied the ground for tracks that might have been left by the would-be-killer, but there were none.

The ranch lay in a hollow among the hills, the spring at the back, a little higher in the notch. That notch was lined with trees, and other trees were growing about the place.

There was a good-sized, two-story ranch house with a balcony, and with a wide veranda all around. There were two large barns for the best riding stock, some milk cows, and the storage of feed, and there were several corrals and a bunkhouse.

Boston drew up on the slope and swept a wide gesture toward the valley. "Well, there she lays. Did we do right by you?"

"You surely did. It's beautiful."

She glanced at him. "I think so. Pa said we'd have to make it so. He said you were the kind of man who would want it to look nice."

Cody Bucklin came up from the corral as they neared the house. "Pa will be pleased," he said. "I knowed it was you when you topped out on the rise. It's the way you set a horse," he said.

Pa rode in with the last light, Tardy and Duke beside him. "We've been makin' a tally," he said. "We'll drive a herd to Kansas this year."

He studied Val thoughtfully. "You've taken on some size, boy, and some beef in the shoulders."

His eyes went to Boston. "So she found you, did she? Boston allowed as how if you didn't come back, she was a-going after you. Be careful, boy."

"Pa!" Boston said. "You're just a-makin' that up!"

When suppertime came they seated themselves about the table, and Pa Bucklin said grace. Val looked around at their faces, and suddenly he felt at home. At home with these people he had known so slightly, yet with whom he had made a business pact that had proved itself, and with whom he felt strangely warm and comfortable.

He felt their easy understanding, their friendship, their sympathy. They were strong, honest people, hard-working, hard-fighting, but simple in their ways.

They knew that not all men are men of good will; they knew there was evil in the world, and stood strong against it. They knew that there were some who would take by force what they would not work to acquire. They knew, as Val did, that outside their windows waited hunger, thirst, and cold; that beyond their doors there were savage men, held in restraint only by a realization of another force ready to oppose them, to preserve the world they had built from savagery into order and peace, where each man might work and build and create without the threat of destruction.

Betsy came into the room, bringing a platter of steak. She was tall, as Boston was, almost queenly. Val glanced again at Pa. How had such women come from this gnarled and hard-shelled man? Yet they were here, slender, shapely, and beautiful.

"We've got four workin' cowhands now, Val," Pa said, "and a grub-line rider who drifted in a few days ago huntin' you."

"Me?"

"Calls himself Tensleep. Said he had word for you." Pa Bucklin paused to chew on his steak, and then added, "Looks like a right tough man."

"He's an outlaw, Pa, but he's been a good friend to me. I met him when I was five," he added, "and I've seen him around since. After supper I'd better hear what he has to say. He isn't given to talking through his hat."

"He's a good hand. He's turned out for work every day since he came, and he works fast and steady. I'd say he's as good a man with stock as I ever did see."

"Does he want a job?"

"Ain't said. I'd say he's been up the trail and over the mountain, and he'd like to light an' keep his feet under the table for a spell."

Then Bucklin looked sharply at him. "You figurin' on stayin' a while? We've made provision. You've got a separate wing of the house for your ownself. The girls furnished it, so if you have complaint, speak to them."

"I . . . I'm not sure." Val looked over at Boston, then turned his eyes away. "I would like to stay, but there is much I have to do. And I don't know yet what I want my life to be. Or where I want to live."

"You got call to be restless, never staying put all your born days."

Val told them then of the places he'd seen, of the men and the women, of the gowns and the wine and the music, and the world beyond the rim of the hills out there, beyond the cap-rock and beyond the Brazos. He told of the work he had done, of the loneliness, and of Van Clevern; and then, of Myra.

After talking a long time he got up from the table, and the girls cleared the dishes away. He said to Pa, "I'd better go see Tensleep."

It was cool out on the dark veranda. He went down the steps to the yard, and he could see the rectangles of light from the bunkhouse windows and the glow of a cigarette from the stoop. He started across the hard-packed earth, listening to the pleasant sound of the horses feeding in the corral, and when he turned once to look back at the big house and its windows, he heard the sound of male voices, then laughter from the girls.

He strolled toward the bunkhouse and said, "Tensleep?"

"He's in yonder, a-waitin' for you. He spotted you the minute you skylined yourself up on the ridge." Then he added, "I'm Waco."

"Val Darrant. Glad to meet you, Waco."

He opened the door and stepped into the bunkhouse. There were bunks for eight men, three of them empty of bedclothes. The men inside looked up, and two of them then returned to their checker game, while another watched. Tensleep was lying on his bunk, but he sat up and swung his boots to the floor.

"Howdy, Val. I come a fur piece, a-huntin' you." He took up his hat, and they went outside, walking to the corral.

Val was thinking: *He's thinner . . . older . . . and if anything, tougher.*

At the corral, Tensleep turned to him. "Boy, you in any kinda trouble? Anything I can take off your back?"

"No. Nothing."

"You sure?" He could feel Tensleep's eyes on him.

"Somebody shot at me. I'm carrying a scratch on my shoulder. Either he figured me for dead, or was scared off when Boston Bucklin rode up. Anyway he ran off. I think it was Thursty Pike."

"Him? He'd be likely to do that. I heard he was in Tascosa."

"I saw him there. He left town."

Tensleep chuckled. "He did if he was smart. Boy, you made yourself a name with Chip Hardesty. They're still talkin' about it."

"I don't want the name. What's on your mind, Tensleep?"

"The Pinks," he said, "they're huntin' you. And when they hunt you they find you."

"The Pinks?" Val's mind was a momentary blank, then it came to him: the Pinkertons. But why would they be hunting *him*?

"Well," he said, "it's not for anything I've done. But somebody must want to find me." He studied the idea, and could think of no one. He had been in touch with Bricker. Van Clevern was dead. There was no one . . . no one at all. He said as much, but Tensleep snorted.

"Don't you believe it. Somebody wants you almighty bad. They've had men a-huntin' you up and down the country, and that costs money. I never knew even Wells Fargo to spend so much. I got wind of it, and put some feelers out." He looked up at Val. "I got friends, you know—I hear things. You done wrong to some woman?"

"No."

"Well, the way the story goes, it's a woman huntin' you."

Myra . . .

She had the money, and she might know of him. She might want to find him . . . but for what?

"It might be Myra," he said.

Tensleep stiffened. "Boy, you watch your step. That ain't no woman, that's a rattler. She's pure poison."

He was silent for a moment. "Myra! I never gave a thought to her. I ain't seen or heard of her in years."

"She's been back east," Val said. "She's made a mint of money and a name for herself."

"I bet you," Tensleep muttered. "Watch yourself, boy. I wouldn't trust her a foot." He paused. "Whatever became of that fancy man of hers?"

"He's dead . . . accident."

"I'll bet," Tensleep said cynically. "He knew where the body was buried—all the bodies. If she's big, she can't afford him." Tensleep dug in his pocket for the makings and built himself a smoke. "And she can't afford you, neither. Look, boy, if you saw anything of Van, she'll figure he told you some things about her.

"Van was always a pretty good man," he went on. "He hadn't no more backbone than so much spaghetti, but he always had a ready hand if a man was on his uppers. I figured him for a straight one . . . there was no thief in him . . . trouble was, she had him wrapped around her little finger. He was roped and hog-tied by that woman."

Long after Val was back in the wing of the house the girls had prepared for him, he lay in bed staring at the ceiling.

Of course, Tensleep was right. Van had been murdered. It was all too pat. And now she—or somebody—had the Pinkertons looking for him. The Pinks might be strikebreakers, they might be strong-arm men, but so far as he knew they weren't killers. However, once he was located, there were other men who could handle that.

Perhaps that shot today? No . . . that was Pike. He was sure of that in his own mind. He also knew that Pike would still be around.

His thoughts went back to Tensleep, and the end of their conversation. The old outlaw had said, "Boy, I like this place. I'm riding the grub-line here, but—well—I sure enough care for it. If they'd take me on, I'd hang up my saddle."

"They like you, Tensleep," Val had said, "and they like your work. I'll speak to Pa Bucklin."

"Thanks." Tensleep had thrust out his hand. "Boy, that there cabin in the snow is a long time back, ain't it? An' Will Reilly, and all?"

"And Henry Sonnenberg," Val added.

"Yeah—there's him, all right," Tensleep said. "Boy, you want I should go get him? I could find him. I was never afraid of Henry—he was never up to taking me on. My hand may not be as steady, but if you want—"

"Forget it. He killed Will Reilly . . . he and Thursty Pike are still left. I want them myself. And I want Sonnenberg most of all."

At last his eyes closed, and he slept. On the far ridge above the ranch a lone rider stopped and looked down at the spread below him. He sat there a long time before he rode away . . . but his day would come.

NINETEEN

At daybreak Boston rode away from the ranch and headed south. It was a sixteen-mile ride she had ahead of her, but when she made up her mind to do something she was not one to waste time.

She was crossing the creek below the ranch when she saw the tracks, and drew up. This was not one of the ranch horses, for she knew every hoof on the place. This was a strange horse, with a long, swinging gait, and the tracks were fresh, probably not more than four or five hours old. She thought of the man who had shot at Val, but at present she would not consider this—she had to go ahead with her errand.

She reached the Winslow place well before noon, and rode into the ranch yard and swung down. Melissa Winslow came out on the porch to greet her. "Boston! Of all people! Do come in!"

Boston went up the steps, spurs jingling. "Mel, I need your help."

"*My* help? *You*?" Melissa smiled. "I would have believed you were the one person in the world who would never need help from anyone."

"I want to be a lady."

Melissa glanced at her again. "I never knew you when you weren't. What's all this about?"

"Valentine Darrant. I'm in love with him."

"You mean he's come back? After all this time?"

"He has, and he's . . . he's just wonderful."

"I never thought I'd hear you say that about any man. But do you mean he has complained? He doesn't like you? The man's obviously a fool."

"I think he likes me. I really believe he does; but Mel, I'm too rough. He didn't say that, I'm saying it. I want to know how to act like a lady, how to talk, how to eat the proper way. . . . I want to know it all."

"You *must* be in love," Mel said. "All that for just one man?"

"Yes." Boston sat up eagerly. "Mel, it's got to be fast. I'll work at it. You know I can. He'll be going east again and I wouldn't want him to think he had to be ashamed of me. You've lived in the East. You grew up there. I've never lived anywhere except on a ranch, and Ma died when I was so young. Will you help me?"

"Of course." She looked at Boston again. "But I hate to spoil you. There are a lot of ladies, but I never knew anyone like you. You're the only one of your kind, Boston. I shudder to think what you'd do to the men if you weren't a good girl."

"Don't call me that. It sounds so . . . so prissy."

Before the long day was over, Melissa was sure of two things: Boston was instinctively a lady, and she was also a natural actress, graceful and easy, with an ear attuned to the proper usage of words.

Val had slept late that morning, awakening to a painful shoulder, and a stiffness, especially in his right leg, that hampered his movements. Breakfast time was long past, but Betsy brought his and sat down with him.

"Where's Boston?" he asked.

"She left a note. She rode off this morning before daylight and she'll be gone overnight and tomorrow."

Val had a distinct feeling of disappointment, but he only said, "I hope she hasn't gone far. I think the man who shot at me may still be around."

"She went to Melissa Winslow's place. They have a small outfit about a few hours' ride from here. He's English." She added,

"Mel is a Virginia girl who went to school in London. That was where she met David."

He was in no mood for riding, nor for looking over the ranch. After breakfast he sat on the veranda and looked out over the valley, mentally reviewing his situation. Nothing about it looked particularly favorable.

He should have faced Pike in Tascosa. He should have forced him to draw, and killed him. As it was, the man was free to shoot whenever he chose, and Val must be on guard every hour of the day and night. That Pike would ride on out of the country he did not believe for one moment. The man was vindictive, and dangerous. He would wait. . . . The worst of it was, he might be trapped by one of the Bucklins, forcing them into a shoot-out.

Throughout the day, Val worked the fingers of his right hand. They were limber enough, but the shoulder was stiff, and there was no ease in his movements, and no speed. Meanwhile, he could not help but notice how well kept the ranch was. The buildings had been painted, the gates all worked easily, and what stock he could see was in good shape.

A third of this was his, but though he had provided the money that made the difference, there was here no work of his hands, no planning of his brain. This was the work of others, for which he could take no credit.

He shifted in his chair. He was nothing but an aimless drifter; he was not even as much as Will had been, who was a gambler, admitted it, and enjoyed it—enjoyed it, at least, until he met Princess Louise.

What had become of her? And of Prince Pavel? At the thought of Pavel he felt coldness take hold of him. He would never forget that day on the outskirts of Innsbruck when Pavel had tried to whip Will Reilly.

Yet in the end it was Pavel who had triumphed. His money and his hatred had reached where he could not, dared not. Henry Sonnenberg was only the tool. The killer was Pavel.

"I think I will go to Europe," he said aloud.

"Boston will be disappointed, Val," Betsy said. She had come up to him quietly. "Why to Europe?"

"I've some unfinished business over there," he said. "There's a man I must see."

"You haven't told me how you liked your part of the house," she said. "We spent a lot of time planning it, thinking about it."

He was ashamed. "I've been preoccupied," he said. "Will you show me through?"

He struggled to his feet, swung his stiff leg around and limped after her.

There were three rooms in the east wing of the house—a small but comfortable living room, a bedroom, and a bath. The walls of the living room, which he had not entered until now, were lined with books. He crossed the room to look at them.

"You were always reading," Betsy said, "and you mentioned several of the books you liked, and sometimes when you wrote to us you mentioned what you were doing, so we asked Mel and David to help us."

He saw there Scott's *Marmion*, Volney's *Ruins of Empire*, *The Life of Sir Walter Scott,* by Lockhart, *Hypatia,* by Kingsley . . . and there were works by Plato, Hume, Locke, Berkeley, Spinoza, and Voltaire, and a shelf of the poets.

"You must thank Mrs. Winslow for me," he said. "And I want to thank you and Boston."

It was an easy, comfortable room, unlike the crowded, over-done rooms of so many eastern homes he had seen. It was closer in style to the rather bare rooms of the Spanish ranchos in California.

When Betsy had gone into the other part of the house, Val browsed through the books, taking them one by one from the shelves. A few of them he had read, most of them he had not, but all were books he had wanted to read.

He heard the door from the veranda open, and took a book from the shelf, turning as he did so.

Thurston Pike was standing there, gun in hand. "Got my horse right here," he said, "an' I'm goin' to kill you, mister, an' nobody the wiser."

As he finished speaking, he fired, and the impact of the bullet, fired at a distance of not more than a dozen feet, knocked Val back against the bookshelves, but he drew from his waistband as he fell back, and fired as his shoulders braced against the book-shelves. He felt the impact of another bullet, but Pike was going down as Val shot the second time.

The door burst open and Betsy stood there, a rifle in her

hands. Thurston Pike was on his back in the doorway, half in, and half out.

Val was staring at the book in his hand. He had taken it from a shelf, had turned, and the thick, leather-bound book had taken both bullets, aimed directly at his heart. Neither bullet had gone more than two-thirds of the way through the book.

He glanced at the title. It was Burton's *Anatomy of Melancholy*. "You know, Bets," he said, "I was never able to get through this book myself."

TWENTY

Myra Fossett sat behind her desk and looked across at Mr. Pinkerton. "You have news for me?"

"Yes . . . from several sources. First, the young man, Mr. Valentine Darrant. He is now in Texas, and we discover he is part owner of a ranch there. It comprises some sixty thousand acres of range land."

"They own this land?"

"No, ma'am, actually it is government land, but they own the water holes. You understand this gives them—"

"I do understand. I know all about water holes and water rights, Mr. Pinkerton. What else?"

"There was an attempt to kill him by a gunman, a notorious killer named Thurston Pike. He did not succeed."

"What happened? Get to the point, please."

"Young Mr. Darrant was surprised in his library by the killer. Pike seems to have fired twice, Mr. Darrant also. Mr. Darrant's bullets found their mark."

Pike, was it? She remembered him, remembered him as a customer of one of her girls far away in Idaho. He had been a tough, dangerous man even then. Evidently her son could take care of himself.

"What led to the fight?"

"We checked into that. It seems Mr. Darrant was reared by a gambler, a man named Will Reilly."

Of course. Will Reilly had been a friend of Van's, but no friend of hers. She felt a little pang when she thought of him, for Will Reilly was the one man who had really interested her. As a matter of fact, she hated men; she used them and got rid of them, but Will had never so much as given her the time of day.

Pinkerton had turned a leaf in his notebook. "This Reilly was the target of a reward offer . . . not by the law, by some private party." Pinkerton looked up at her as he said this, and she smiled cynically.

"Don't worry yourself. I know nothing of that."

"Of course. I did not for the moment—"

"You're a damned liar, Pinkerton. Now get on with it."

"There were three men—Thurston Pike, Chip Hardesty, and Henry Sonnenberg. They ambushed him, caught him coming out of a lighted door."

He paused. "The first two are no longer with us. Mr. Darrant seems to have killed them both."

"And Sonnenberg?"

"I know a good deal of him in another connection, and we have him on our wanted list. He killed a Wells Fargo guard a year or two ago, and there have been other—"

"I know about him. He is an outlaw, a paid killer. Who hired him?"

"That's the odd part. Some jack-leg lawyer from here in town named Avery Simpson offered the money. I don't know who it was who wanted Reilly killed. I suppose it was some gambling trouble. Men who live like that—"

"You have talked to Simpson?"

"No, but—"

"Leave him to me." She stood up, indicating the interview was over.

"There's one thing more . . ."

She waited, impatient to be rid of him.

"That man, Van Clevern. He was killed in a fall from a horse."

"Too bad."

She turned away sharply, her irritation showing, but he remained where he was, his eyes on her face. "I know you told us

you were no longer interested in him, but one of my operatives
. . . well, it tied in with Mr. Darrant—"

"Yes?"

"Van Clevern, shortly before he was killed, directed his family
to mail a certain box—without opening it—to Valentine Darrant."

Myra took up a pen and turned it in her fingers. She was aware
that Pinkerton was watching her, but she had to think. Such a box
would certainly contain papers . . . what else could it be? And
what papers would he be likely to be sending to Val? Something
about Val's mother.

He might have written it all down, there at the last, leaving it
up to Val to do with it as he wished.

"This box . . . Val Darrant has it?"

"No. It has been forwarded to a bank in Colorado to hold for
him. Apparently they expect him soon because of some investments they have been handling for him."

There was still time then. She took the report from Pinkerton
and watched him leave, but her mind was working swiftly. That
box, described as a small metal chest or bond box, undoubtedly
contained Van Clevern's signed statement. With that statement
they would have no trouble finding the evidence needed for a
conviction, and Myra Fossett would be on trial for murder.

Even if, by some chance, she was able to gain an acquittal, her
whole life would have been exposed. She would be ruined. . . .

She picked up the report. The box had been shipped, but only
just now. If she wanted to get the box she must act at once.

A train holdup was too difficult to arrange, but after the train
there would be the stage, and then the bank. She knew a dozen
men who could handle either affair, but the name that came to
her mind at once was Sonnenberg.

Sonnenberg would have reason to want to get Val out of the
way. He was a tough man, and as she knew from the old days, he
was an experienced yeggman who knew all the tricks of cracking
safes.

For a long time she sat at her desk, considering the problem,
but her thoughts returned again and again to Val.

She had a son. What, after all, did that mean? She had given
birth to a child she had never wanted, by a man she had never
loved, and the child had failed to serve its purpose. At the time it
had seemed the quickest road to money, a lot of money. Now she

had the money, from another source, and the child had turned up again and might deprive her of it.

What was he like? She had, of course, no feeling of love for him. Love was not only a matter of blood and flesh, it developed from holding a child, caring for it, answering its need for protection. There had never been any of that. He would have different ideas from hers, different feelings . . . he might even be a weakling, like Van.

She had passed him that day in Bricker's outer office, or so she believed. If that was indeed Val, he was a handsome young man, and anybody who could take Hardesty and Thurston Pike in gun battles was certainly no weakling.

Myra got up and went to the window. It was raining, and she watched a hansom cab go by the door, the lamps thrusting narrow beams of light before them. She remembered nights like this when she was a child . . . remembered her father lighting the carriage lamps and carrying her out so she would not get her slippers wet, nor the hem of her long skirt. How old was she then? Twelve?

She had never gone back, and she had not written. No doubt they believed she was dead, and surely they would never dream that she was *the* Myra Fossett who controlled mills, mines, and railroads.

Of course, if her son got that box and chose to expose her, they would know . . . everyone would know. No doubt he hated her, and once the box was in his hands he could blackmail her for every cent she possessed. That he might not choose to do so never entered her mind.

Avery Simpson had never met Myra Fossett, but he had heard of her, and he smelled money. But he was cautious. He knew who her attorneys were, and he also knew they would not want any dealings with him.

She received him in the library, seated behind her desk. He had grown fat, and was almost unkempt. The woman he saw was not what he expected.

She was very handsome, slender, with a splendid figure, and if there was gray in her hair, he could not see it. She motioned him to a chair and took up a single sheet of paper that lay on the desk.

"You are Avery Simpson. You were involved in the Carnes-Wales business."

He was startled. His connection with that, his hiring of thugs for the company, had never appeared in the papers or the trial proceedings.

Before he could protest, she continued. "You were also concerned with the payoff in the Sterling case."

He jumped up. "Now see here!"

"Sit down!" Her tone was sharp. "You're a cheap, blackleg lawyer, and I could list a dozen cases which, if they were known, could get you disbarred. Now listen to me. If you give me honest answers I will pay you for your time, not as much as you think it is worth, but more than I think it's worth. Are you going to listen, or do I have you thrown out of here and then give all this to the press?"

He sat there, shaking and frightened. Nobody could know all that . . . yet she did. He had best play this very easy.

"You hired the murder of Will Reilly."

He started to protest, but she brushed him aside impatiently. "I suppose you know that Hardesty and Pike are dead?"

He had not known. He dabbed at his face with a handkerchief. Hardesty and Pike dead! "How—?"

"They were killed in gun battles by Reilly's nephew. Do you remember him?"

"But he was only a boy!"

"They grow up very fast out west, they tell me," she said grimly. "He knows about you, doesn't he?"

The boy had been in the room when Will Reilly had forced him to write those letters. Simpson shifted uncomfortably. That was far away in the West. It was true he sometimes worried about Sonnenberg, but—

"That boy was back east a few weeks ago," Myra said, "and he has been asking questions."

Avery Simpson felt as if he was going to be sick. He tried to sit up straighter, his jowls quivering. Back east? Then he was not safe, not even here.

"Who paid for Reilly's murder?" The question was shot at him, suddenly, without warning.

"It was Prince—" He stopped. "I can't tell you that."

Myra Fossett had dealt with men too long and on too intimate terms not to know about such men as Avery Simpson. "Simpson," she said coldly, "and even as I say it I know it is not your true name"—she saw him cringe a little at that—"I did not ask you here to make conversation. You tell me what you know, and no damned nonsense. If you don't," she smiled at him, "I will tell Henry Sonnenberg where to find you."

He stared at her. *Who was she?* How could she know about *him?*

After a moment she said, "Now tell me. And tell me all about it."

Avery Simpson dug into his pocket for a cigar. "Mind if I smoke?"

"Not if it will help your memory," she said; "but get on with it. I have better things to do than sit here talking to you."

Prince Pavel had not told anyone his reasons for wanting Will Reilly killed. He had told neither the go-between who put him in touch with Simpson, nor had he told Simpson; but Avery Simpson, drinking in a pub one night, had mentioned the scars on the face of Prince Pavel, and was told the story of the man he had tried to horsewhip.

After Simpson had gone, Myra Fossett found herself smiling. *The idea, she said to herself, of anybody trying to horsewhip Will Reilly!*

She was grimly amused, but her thoughts began to toy with the information she had acquired, and what it might do for her.

Her business was doing well, but there were many doors which were still closed to her, doors that could be opened by such a name as Prince Pavel . . . or by any other prince, she told herself cynically.

He had wanted to make a rich marriage for Princess Louise. Had he succeeded? What, exactly, was his financial situation at the moment? He might be someone she could use.

He was obviously a good hater, and she liked that, but he was also a fool, for no man in his right mind could look into those cool green eyes of Will Reilly's and still fancy they could have him whipped. Killed, perhaps, but not whipped. She had known other men of his kind, men you had to shoot to stop, for their pride and their courage was such that they could not be broken.

She considered the several plans that had been lying in the dark and secret drawers of her mind, plans that awaited the right knowledge of the right people, or their assistance, but all of those people lay beyond walls she had not been able to breach. But with a captive prince . . .

Her thoughts returned to her son. It was with a feeling of irritation that she realized she had thought of him thus. He was a stranger, by accident her son, with whom she had nothing in common. And at this juncture he was an outright danger to her, and to all she had planned and accomplished.

Avery Simpson had provided her with a handle for the manipulation of a prince, or the possibility of it. The first thing was to ascertain the financial standing of Prince Pavel, and of the Princess Louise, if she was still around. If the prince was gambling, as Simpson had implied, he would probably need money.

She glanced at her watch. She had been invited to dinner at the Harcort's, and there was just time to make it. At such times she missed Van.

Though she had no use for men, yet there were times when a woman needed an escort, and Van had always been there; and even when drinking his manners had been perfect. She could have used him now.

At the Harcort's there would be a number of fashionable people, including men with far-reaching business connections. It was at such parties that she had made most of the contacts she had developed and used. Men who were drinking often explained things to a beautiful woman who was a good listener, telling her of stock deals and financial arrangements in which their wives were rarely interested. It was true that some of them had grown cautious after their casual boasting had cost them money. For Myra not only knew how to get information, she knew how to use it.

She rarely worried about meeting anyone who might have known her in the past. The men she had entertained in the mining and cattle towns rarely came east; and she had changed the color of her hair, wore higher heels, and presented a very different appearance. She had never returned to the West, and had no desire to do so. But there remained the chance of encountering some former client, so she restricted her social activities to private parties, rarely going to large hotels or restaurants, or to watering places.

She called for one of her runners and before she left for dinner she had started the movement of events that would have Henry

Sonnenberg checking the arrival of a certain box, and would bring her information as to the financial status of Prince Pavel Pavelovitch.

In a saloon, not more than a dozen blocks away, Avery Simpson stood at the bar and nursed a drink. He needed that drink and those that would follow, for Myra Fossett had scared the daylights out of him.

She knew too much for comfort, but what puzzled him was her familiarity with the identities of Will Reilly, Henry Sonnenberg, and some others. All of which gave rise to the question: Who was Myra Fossett?

TWENTY-ONE

A few weeks later Prince Pavel was asking himself the same question. He had received through his bank a note written in a small but beautiful hand a suggestion that if he were in a position to come to America on a brief visit it might prove financially interesting to him.

He put the note aside, a bit curious as to this Myra Fossett who had written it. When he went to dinner he noticed an old friend across the room, a man known for his international business affairs, and for his unusual success. It was Robert Fleury. Prince Pavel went over to his table.

"Robert," he said, "do you by any chance know anything of an American woman named Fossett?"

Fleury turned sharply. "*Myra* Fossett? How do you know anything about her?"

"Shouldn't I?"

Fleury shrugged. "It is simply that she is a business woman . . . beautiful, but very shrewd, also."

"A woman? In business?"

Fleury shrugged again. "There are more than you think, but none of them like Madame Fossett."

"She is wealthy?"

"Rolling in it." Fleury studied his friend. "But what do you know of her?"

Pavel's explanation solved nothing. "I do not know what she has in mind," Fleury said, "but be assured there is money in it. She thinks of nothing but money, that one. Be careful, my friend. When she makes any such proposal you can be sure it is for her benefit alone—that much I know of her. She is not only shrewd, she is utterly ruthless, and without a scruple."

Pavel was not impressed. He had no scruples himself; and a woman, a beautiful woman, and very wealthy . . . "I have no idea what she has in mind," he said.

Robert Fleury, whose interests in America were many, was puzzled, because so far as he was aware Madame Fossett had shown no interest in any man that was not casual, nor did she seem very active in a social way. She was not a party-giver, and seemed to ignore most of the social highlights of the season.

"Just be warned," he said again, "but you can be sure whatever it is has money in it."

Prince Pavel, ten years before, had come into a good-sized inheritance which had since dwindled because of his enthusiasm for gambling. It was growing increasingly difficult to borrow, and although he had a small reserve he had kept untouched, it was too small for comfort.

His cousin, the Princess Louise, was single again. Her husband—Pavel had finally been successful in that matter—had died, leaving her a considerable estate, but so far Pavel had been unable to touch it. Louise was careful, and she knew him well enough to distrust him. Nevertheless, they were on friendly terms.

Louise had beauty, she had presence, and there were a lot of millionaires in America, he had heard. If he handled it wisely . . . he did not like the idea of Louise marrying an American, but if the man was rich enough . . .

Prince Pavel was no longer handsome—the scars took care of that—but he had found that scars seemed the utmost in masculinity to some women, and his he represented, without actually saying so, as dueling scars.

He had an idea it would not be difficult to persuade Louise to accompany him. She had always had an interest in everything American . . . at least since she met that damned Reilly.

A few days later he replied to Myra Fossett. *My cousin, the*

Princess Louise, and I, have been considering a visit to New York. Am I to assume you wish us to come as your guests?

The response was immediate. Passage was arranged, everything paid for, and there remained nothing but to go.

For three weeks Val Darrant had been working harder than he had ever worked in his life. He had branded calves, cleaned out water holes, repaired corral fences, trapped wolves, pulled steers out of bogs, and helped in the breaking of horses. He had been getting out of bed before daylight, and rarely coming in off the range until well after dark. He had worked as hard as any hand on the ranch, and he had worked with Tensleep beside him, learning from him as they worked.

His shoulder wound had healed rapidly, and he was not one to pamper himself when there was so much to be done. But always, in the back of his mind, there remained the thought that soon he must catch the stage for Colorado.

He was thinking of it now as he topped out on a rise and looked over the wide basin below.

Cody rode up to join him, a lean, wide-shouldered young man with cool eyes and an easy way of moving and talking.

"How you comin' boy? Shoulder botherin' any?"

"No, it's all right now, though I find myself favoring it a little. I just don't like to think about leaving."

"We'll miss you," Cody built a cigarette, touched the paper with his tongue. "You've been doin' more'n your share."

"We need rain," Val commented. "The grass on the high range looks bad."

"Heel flies are gettin' worse, too," Cody said, and he added, "boy, you better let one of us ride along with you. Dube, he's a-rarin' to go."

"It would be company," Val admitted. "How's the work stack up?"

"We got it whupped. You take Dube. I'd admire to go myself, but if trouble shapes up, me an' Tardy ought to be here. Dube is dead fast with a gun, a better than usual tracker, and maybe the best rifle shot amongst us."

"Why all this concern?"

Cody grinned. "Boston said there'd be no foolin' you. Fact is,

Tardy picked up a story. Boston heard talk of it over to Wins-lows', too. Henry Sonnenberg was in Mobeetie, roundin' up two or three tough ones."

"So?"

"They taken off, night before last . . . headin' for Colorado."

Far down the valley some cattle were walking toward the creek, and a thin plume of dust told of a lone rider coming across the flat. That would be Boston, returning from the Winslows'.

"I can handle Sonnenberg."

"Yeah, I think maybe you can, although there's nobody more dangerous than him, but what about the others? He's got himself some tough men."

"You think he's gunning for me?"

"No. I figure there's something else in the wind. So does Pa. You see, a body don't live long in this country unless he keeps track of folks, so we got us a little bird over to Mobeetie. Pa, he gives him eatin' money and this little bird keeps us alive as to who's comin' and goin'. Seems like one of these men he picked up, one he asked for special, is just out of prison for blowing the safe in a bank."

Val turned his horse toward the ranch house, angling across country to intercept Boston. Cody rode along beside him, and suddenly he spoke up. "Didn't you tell me one time that you knew Billy the Kid?"

"Yes."

"He's dead. One of the Turkeytrack boys told me. I met him yonder, huntin' strays. He was shot by Pat Garrett at Pete Maxwell's place."

So he had gone there, after all. And now he was dead. He had known Billy only a short time, but it had been one of the first times he had been around boys of his own age. He and . . . what was his name? Dodie . . . Dodie Grant. They had ridden out with Billy.

Hickok was gone, too, shot in the back up in Deadwood a few years ago.

He and Cody rode on in silence. Suddenly he felt lost and lonely . . . old ties were being cut, and so much of the country seemed to be changing. He said as much to Cody.

"You ain't heard the most of it. This cowhand was tellin' me they've passed a prohibition law up in Kansas. You can't buy a drink nowhere in the state."

"I had heard they were talking of it."

Val stared at the horizon, thinking. He had to belong somewhere, he had to put down some roots. He could not forever be moving. He wanted a *home*.

After all, why should he feel any urge to kill Sonnenberg? Hardesty and Pike were dead, and they had paid their debt for Will. Avery Simpson was somewhere in the East, and Prince Pavel was far away in Europe. Let the course of natural events take care of Sonnenberg.

This was where he belonged, somewhere here in the West. He would marry Boston, if she would have him, and hang out his shingle in some lively western town, in Texas, New Mexico, or Colorado.

Boston came wheeling up then, flashing him a quick smile, her black hair blowing in the wind.

"Do you know what I am going to do, Val? I am going to Denver with you!"

"What?"

"I mean it! We made it up between us this afternoon! Dube, Tensleep, and me. We're all going with you!"

"What is this going to be—a gypsy caravan?"

"I need some clothes, some girl clothes. Dube has never seen a big town and he wants to go, and Tensleep figures he should go along and look after all of us. So there! It's settled!"

The land lay wide before them, under a wider sky—long, slow swells of the grass sea, a grass now tawny with the dryness of a parching summer, streams now scarcely a trickle lost in the width of sandy bed.

A few tracks of buffalo, here and there the trail left by a drifting band of mustangs, and always, lost against the brassy sky, the slow swinging loops of the buzzards. Men may plan, they may dream and struggle, but the buzzard has only to wait, for all things come to him in the end.

They rode due north toward the railroad, coming once upon a covered wagon, standing desolate in a small hollow, its cover blown to shreds, one of the bows broken, and several stacks of buffalo hides standing nearby. The wagon had been looted and left, but there were two grave mounds close by, no marker on either.

"Happened to a man I knew," Tensleep said. "He come upon a trailside grave and rode over to read the marker. It was his brother buried there, alongside the Chisholm Trail, a brother he hadn't seen in ten years because they left home separate. You ever stop to think the number of men who come west and nobody ever hears of again?"

They camped that night near a seep where a tiny trickle of water made a pool the size of your hat and a small area of damp grass where the horses ate and breathed up what little water they could get.

The next creek bed was dry, with cracked mud for a bottom, and digging brought nothing but dust.

They heard the long whistle of the train before they could see the station, four lone buildings huddled together on a flat valley with no trees. Four buildings and a water tank—the station with a few feet of platform, a saloon with a postoffice sign on it, and a general store next to it where the bartender sold supplies between drinks. There was also a stable and some stock corrals.

Several men with drinks in their hands came to the door of the saloon to stare at them as they rode in, and when they reached the stable two of the men in the saloon followed. One was only a boy of seventeen, the other a few years older.

They took sidelong glances at Boston, and approached Val. "Mister," the oldest one said, "meanin' no offense, but is that a woman yonder?"

"Yes, it is. It's his sister." He indicated Dube.

"You reckon I could speak at her? An' maybe look a little closer? Mister, Willie an' me, we ain't seen a woman in nigh onto a year. Nine, ten months, I'd put it."

Val turned. "Boston, these young men haven't looked at a girl in some time. They would like to talk to you."

"Sure!" She walked over. "How are you, boys?"

They stood grinning, the red creeping around their ears.

"Are you ranching out here?" she asked.

The older one nodded. "We went to work for a gent up at Newton, Kansas, and drove some cows down here for him. We been here quite a spell, and a man sure gets hongry to even look at womenfolks."

The hostler came to take their horses. "I'll buy 'em if you're sellin," he said, "or keep 'em for you if you're comin' back."

"We're comin' back," Dube replied, "an' we want these same horses waitin' when we come. I'm Dube Bucklin," he said, "an' you may have heard of our outfit."

"I surely have. That reminds me. Got a letter over to the post office for a gent named Darrant—one of your outfit, I reckon."

Val turned. "I am Val Darrant."

"Pleased . . . This letter, it was misdirected here. Guess those folks back in Boston don't know much about west Texas."

"Are you the postmaster?"

"You could say that. Rightly I am only half of him. Smith Johnson is postmaster and I'm Johnson. Smith is over to the saloon. You see, we couldn't decide which was to be postmaster, so we decided we both would, and we made application for the job as Smith Johnson. You walk over yonder and Smith will give you that letter. Been settin' here nigh onto two weeks."

The saloon-post office was a bare room with a short bar and four or five bottles on the back bar. Smith was a fat, unshaven man in his undershirt, who leaned massive forearms on the bar. A cowhand lounged at the end of the bar, nursing a beer. At a table in the corner two men sat drinking beer.

"Quite a town you've got here," Val said.

"Yep! She's a lollapalooza! Biggest town between here and the next place. Was that really a flesh-and-blood woman you had with you?"

"Yes. That was Miss Bucklin, from down south a ways. Her brother is with her, and we're catching the train for Denver."

"Won't be much trouble, catchin' it. We got a signal here that we hang out and she stops ever' time. You just order yourself a beer, and—"

"I'll have the beer, and the letter for Val Darrant. The other half of the postmaster said you had one for me. Incidentally, which are you? Post or Master?"

Smith chuckled. "First time anybody asked me *that*. Now if I said I was Master I'd have to lick Johnson, and he's a tough old coot, but I wouldn't want to say I was Post, not with all those stray dogs runnin' loose hereabouts."

He drew a beer from the barrel, then took down a letter from a high shelf. "And there's your letter. As for the train, that old busted-down bronc-stomper yonder at the table is what passes for a stationmaster. He'll sell you a ticket. If you ain't got the money he'll trust you for it if you'll buy him a beer."

"Seems like a man can get almost anything around here if he can buy a beer," Val said, smiling.

"Mister, you already have," Smith said. "In this here town when you've put up your horse, bought yourself a ticket and a beer, you've just had about all there is to offer!"

"We pitch horseshoes," the stationmaster said, "and toward evenin' we shoot at jack rabbits or coyotes. Ever' oncet in a while, somebody hits one."

Val drank his beer and waited for the others to come over. The board at one end of the saloon showed a timetable, and the train was due about sundown.

On all sides the brown and slightly rolling plains stretched away to the sky. Nothing changed here but the seasons, and occasionally the cloud formations. Not long ago this had been Comanche country, and some miles away to the south was the site of Adobe Walls, scene of several great Indian fights.

Smith went to the door when Boston crossed the street toward the saloon, accompanied by Tensleep and Dube. "Ma'am," he said, "would you like to come into the post office an' set? It ain't often we have a lady in town."

"Thank you." Boston entered, and went to a table with Val and Dube. Tensleep strolled to the bar.

Smith gave him a sharp glance. "Tensleep, what are you up to? These here folks shape up to mighty nice people."

"I ride for Darrant and Bucklin," Tensleep said. "I'm a *ree*formed man, Smith."

At the table, Val opened his letter. It was from Van's sister.

Dear Mr. Darrant:

As you may know, my brother was killed in a fall from a horse. He had left word that if anything happened to him, this box was to be forwarded to you, unopened. Being unsure of your exact address, we have forwarded the box to Mr. Peck, at his home in Empire, Colorado.

Van said Mr. Peck had handled some business matters for you, and would deposit the box at the bank, to await your pleasure.

A few words followed to say that Van had often talked of him, and asking him to call on them if he came to Boston. He read the note twice; then, after reading it to Boston and Dube, put it down on the table.

When it came right down to it, he knew very little about his mother, and what he knew he did not like, but Van Clevern had been with her throughout her bad days, and if anyone knew the whole story it would be Van.

Now Van was dead, and unless Val was much mistaken, his death had been anything but accidental. Did Myra know about this box? He did not see how she could know, but little escaped her attention if it concerned her. The thought made him uneasy. Too many had suffered because of her, and if she had the idea that Mr. Peck or anyone else had a box that contained incriminating evidence, whoever had the box was in danger.

Suddenly he remembered the account of Henry Sonnenberg recruiting a safe-cracker . . . and hadn't Will told him that Henry himself had been a yeggman?

Could there be a connection? Even as he asked himself that question he realized there easily could be. If Myra knew of the box, and if it worried her, she would try to gain possession of it.

All right, he told himself, it was a pretty flimsy case, filled with ifs, but the wise thing to do was to act as if it were a positive fact. In any event, he was going to Colorado, and this would be part of the business he would do there.

Sonnenberg . . . Henry Sonnenberg! Val had thought of putting all that out of his mind, of avoiding the man and letting him come to his own bad end in his own time, but now they were pointed in the same direction just as if some fate was pulling the strings.

He thought of Sonnenberg as he remembered him, heavy, powerful, a man who seemed a composite of rawhide and iron, a man who seemed indomitable. Even Billy the Kid had looked a bit wary when he mentioned him. Somewhere ahead he might meet Henry Sonnenberg, and when they met it would be the last meeting for one or both of them.

Val Darrant had never wanted a gun battle. He had learned to use a gun just as he had learned to handle cards, or ride a horse, or swim. That he happened to be good with a gun was due to some natural dexterity, some inborn skill, and of course to practice.

He listened to the long drawn-out whistle of the train, and got up with the others and went across to the railroad platform to pick up their tickets. The entire population—all six of them—was there to see them off.

Val escorted Boston to one of the red-plush seats. "Val," she said, "I'm kind of scared. I've never ridden the steam cars before."

"It isn't that hard," Val said. "You just hook your spurs in the bellyband, grab the horn with both hands, and hang on."

He sat down in the seat beside her, while Dube sat across the aisle, facing them. Tensleep, who had held up more trains than most people had ridden on, pulled his hat down over his eyes and went to sleep.

The sun set over the prairie far ahead of them, the night came down, the stars appeared, the whistle echoed across the lonely buffalo lands. The coach rocked pleasantly, and they slept.

TWENTY-TWO

P rince Pavel was tall and straight, and the scars served to add a somewhat romantic and piratical aspect to his otherwise cold features. Born in St. Petersburg, he had visited the estate from which he drew his income on only three occasions, all of which he remembered with distaste.

His father had been involved in the reform movement of Tsar Alexander II, but father and son had little in common, and disagreed violently on the subject. Pavel had spent most of his life outside of Russia, and like many other Russians of this period who were of the nobility, he spoke French almost exclusively.

Prince Pavel's inheritance was sufficient had he been content to devote part of his time to his estates, and had he not become an obsessive gambler. Unfortunately for him, he had utmost belief in his skill with cards, a faith that was unwarranted.

Moreover, the reform movements of Alexander II had left the nobility politically emasculated; and Pavel, although he served briefly in the cavalry, had no taste for the military life. By one means or another he contrived to maintain himself in the style he preferred, but this had grown increasingly difficult, and nothing remained but to obtain an income somehow, or return to his estates to live the life of a provincial, and to Prince Pavel this was a fate worse than death.

Myra Fossett had opened a way. Where it might lead he had no idea, but a still young woman, worth millions, was a chance not be missed. And for the other barrel of his gun, there was the possibility of a rich marriage for Louise.

Pavel's belief in his own ability with women was equaled only by his contempt for them. Robert Fleury had warned him about Myra Fossett, but the warning merely amused him. If she had that much money, and needed him for some purpose, he intended to have some of that money. Americans, he had heard, were awed by titles, and he was prepared to awe them some more.

"Be careful, cousin," Louise warned him. "This Myra Fossett may cost you more than you can afford to pay."

For the meeting Prince Pavel wore his dress uniform, and the orders on his chest presented an impressive array, especially to someone who did not know what they meant. Confident as he was, he was embarrassed by his position. He needed money, and in a very real way this might be his last chance.

The library was dimly lit, which irritated him. One cannot make a dramatic entrance into a darkened room.

He was announced, and he strode in. Myra Fossett looked at him, asked him to be seated, and returned to the papers on her desk.

He was coldly furious, and was tempted to rise and walk out, but he restrained himself. "Madame—" he began.

She looked up. "I am not called that. I am called Mrs. Fossett."

"You have invited me here to discuss business, I believe. I am here." He glanced at his watch. "I have other engagements."

Myra sat back in her chair and studied him. "Prince Pavel," she said, "you are an attractive man. If you are also intelligent you can be of assistance to me. By being of assistance to me you can make yourself a lot of money, but first we have to understand each other." Suddenly her voice changed. "*So don't give me any God-damned nonsense about other engagements!*"

He could only stare at her. Nobody had ever spoken to him like that in his life; nobody had dared to. But before he could reply, or even rise to walk out, she was speaking again.

"I said you can be useful to me. When I talk about being

useful, I mean, if you will do what I ask, useful to the tune of fifty or perhaps a hundred thousand dollars."

He looked at her. Fifty thousand . . . one hundred thousand dollars! What was that in rubles? In francs?

She moved a sheet of paper under the light on her desk. "Prince Pavel, I have here a list of your debts."

"*What!*" He started to rise. "What kind of impertinence is this?"

"Sit down," she said coldly, "and shut up, or I'll have you thrown out of here, and I'll file charges against you for attempted assault. And"—she smiled—"I will produce witnesses."

He was appalled. He moved again to stand up, then sank back. She had to be joking! This could not be happening to him.

"You are an amazing woman," he said. "Just what was it you had in mind?"

Even as he spoke, he was playing for time. He had to get out of here, he had to go somewhere and have a drink, he had to think this over.

She took up the sheet from her desk and handed it to him. It was, indeed, what she had said—a list of his debts. And they were all there, some even that he had forgotten about, and it came to a very ugly sum. In fact, there were the names of a dozen men there who would sue him immediately if they dreamed he owed as much as this list showed.

"It is rather complete," he admitted, "but I still do not understand what you want of me."

"We are short of princes this season," Myra said, "and the last one was pot-bellied, and his beard smelled of tobacco . . . cheap tobacco. There are a lot of people in this town, people otherwise quite intelligent, who are impressed by titles. I brought you over here to impress them."

Before he could speak, she shook her head. "I am not a social climber, Prince Pavel. Not, at least, in the sense you might think. I am interested in money. Many of the men who own industries or businesses with whom I have no contact are people I do not meet socially. I need to know those people, and I know which ones I want to know, and I know what to do about it when I know them. And that is where you come in."

"Yes?"

"I shall give a party to introduce you. I shall see that there is much in the public press about you, and everyone will come, including the men I wish to meet. Their wives are to come also, and we will in turn be invited to their homes. You can open doors for me that I cannot open by myself."

"And you will pay me for this?"

There was contempt in his tone, but Myra ignored it. She could afford to ignore it because she knew so much more of what was going to happen than he did.

"I will provide expense money," she said quietly, "up to a point. Beyond that point you will have your commissions. I shall require your services for ninety days, no more, no less. If I have not done what I wish to do in that length of time it would be of no use to try any longer. I am prepared to give you five per cent on every deal I make through the meetings I arrange at the affairs where we go in company, or to which your name gives me access. And I will give you my word that such commissions will total not less than fifty thousand dollars, and perhaps several times that."

He searched for the flaw, and could see none. He had merely to pose as this woman's friend . . . the only flaw he could see was the woman herself. She was too cold, too hard—and, he told himself, she was not a lady.

"I might decide to leave," he said. "I might decide simply to take your expense money and go back to Europe."

He looked at her to see what effect that had, but she merely shrugged. "Don't be a fool. If you try that with me you'll carry worse scars then you got from Will Reilly."

His face went white. He felt as if he had been struck in the stomach.

"You were lucky that he only whipped you," Myra said, "obviously you had no idea what kind of a man he was. Will Reilly had killed seven men in gun battles before he ever went to Europe. And they were tough men.

"Of course," she added, "that doesn't count Indians. He survived a dozen Indian fights. I know of some very tough men who would sooner tackle a she grizzly with cubs than Will Reilly."

He was silent at first, hating every word she had said, but then he had his triumph. "You are right. I did know nothing of him." He paused, then added ever so gently, "He is dead now, I believe?"

"You should know. You arranged for his killing. Of course, you had more money then than now. Avery Simpson found the right men for you, didn't he? I wonder if you know the sequel?"

"What sequel?"

"Two of the men who killed Will Reilly are dead . . . There were three."

He stared at her. This woman must be the devil in person. Did she know everything?

"That's another reason," she said, smiling slightly, "why you had better be a nice boy. Avery Simpson, in turn for a lighter sentence, could give evidence against you. And they hang men for murder in this country."

"I think," he said, "you do not understand my position. In my own country—"

"But you are not in your country," Myra interrupted, "and you will find little sympathy here. On the other hand, since we like titles over here, and with those scars and all those medals—oh, don't worry! I'll not tell anybody how you got the scars—that you were horsewhipped by a gambler."

She looked at him, still smiling. "And you may even find it amusing here. The women will idolize you, especially the older ones, or those with daughters who are single. You can make a lot of money; and if you are interested you might marry one of the daughters and get a substantial settlement."

Pavel's mind was reaching for a solution that would save him, but he was realizing that there was none. From now on, until he had money enough to escape from this situation, he was practically a prisoner.

She was hard—he admired her for that even while resenting it that any woman could outgeneral him. He was, he admitted, a little afraid of her. She had told him a good deal. She had, as these Americans would say, "laid it on the line," but what worried him were the things she had not told him, the further plans she preferred to keep to herself.

"I shall need money," he said, "as long as we are talking money. If this is to be your operation, it is only correct that you should finance it."

"Of course." She opened a drawer and took out a packet of bills. "There are five thousand dollars."

Then she said, "There is to be a performance at the opera tonight. We will go . . . You and your cousin are to be house guests of mine. You are to accept no invitations that do not include me; however, I doubt if anyone would go to that extreme.

"If anyone inquires as to how we met, say simply that we have mutual friends." She took another list from a desk drawer. "I want you to memorize these names. The three men on the left are the men with whom I wish to do business. They operate on a very large scale, they make excellent profits, and no outsider has ever participated in their operations.

"The names on the right are those of men who belong to clubs to which the men on the left also belong. They are occasional associates of yachting, gambling, hunting, and at social events. Any one of those on the right might introduce you to those on the left.

"Don't gamble with them. They are very shrewd, tough gamblers, and any one of them can win or lose enough in an evening to support you for a year—I mean that—and there is no sentiment in their gambling. It is all-out war.

"If I succeed in what I have planned," she added, "your share might even come to a quarter of a million dollars. You could return to Europe a modestly wealthy man."

"It seems simple enough," he said at last. "Those people will be at the opera?"

"They will. They will see you, and they will be curious. I shall see that they know who you are. The rest will follow."

He stood up now. "And my cousin, the Princess Louise?" he asked.

Myra got to her feet also. She was almost as tall as he. "She need know nothing of all this. You have some land in Siberia, I believe?"

He was no longer surprised, but he had almost forgotten that land himself.

"You can tell her I am interested in hydraulic mining, and wanted to discuss a deal whereby one of my companies would dredge for gold there. In fact, you can mention this to anyone, if you like. The people with whom we are concerned know that I am a business woman."

"These arrangements . . . they will be here? In New York?"

"Yes." She hesitated. "There is a possibility we may have to travel to San Francisco. One of the men in whom I am most interested lives there."

When Prince Pavel was out on the street he stood on the curb for a moment, waiting for the carriage to come around.

Ninety days, she had said. Three months—and then a rich man. He doubted many things about Myra Fossett, but he did not doubt the genuineness of her intentions. She wanted to make money and she would; and after all, was not that what he came over for?

TWENTY-THREE

The Windsor, in Denver, opened in June of 1880, was the height of elegance, with three hundred rooms and sixty bathtubs, gaslights, and Brussels carpets. The backbone of its business was furnished by mining men and cattlemen, the latter coming from half a dozen states, for Denver was considered by many to be the only city worth visiting between Chicago and San Francisco.

Denver had the name of being a wide-open sporting town, but Valentine Darrant had no desire to gamble or to visit any of the tough joints on Blake or Holliday streets. He was in town on business, and he was wary of trouble.

It was a gun-toting town, but the guns were usually kept out of sight, worn in the waistband or elsewhere not visible to the immediate glance. Bat Masterson was in town, and so was Doc Holliday. They were only two of the best-known of the forty or fifty known gun-handlers in town.

Val was in his room, dressed in a gray suit, with black tie. His black hat lay on the bed. Dube came in, uneasy in his store-bought clothes.

"Where you goin' to meet this gent?" he asked.

"Peck? He should be here now . . . In Denver, I mean. He was coming down from Empire to meet me here."

195

"He the man you left your money with?"

"His father, actually."

"Lot of eastern folks down in the lobby. Seems like some big mining deal is about to be pulled off. You know anything about it?"

"No."

"Well, those eastern folks do. Come up all of a sudden, they say, and there's a scramble on."

Val was concerned only with Peck. Once their business was completed, he could relax and show Boston some of the town. Dube and Tensleep probably had plans of their own, but there were several places in Denver noted for their good food. Although he had not been in the city for several years, he remembered the City Hotel where Charles Geleichman was chef, he who had been chef for the King of Denmark, or so it was said. There was also Charpiot's.

He was combing his hair before the mirror and debating whether he should wake Boston, if she was not awake, when there was a sudden tap on his door.

His pistol lay on the table, and habit made him pick it up as he moved to the door. Opening it, the gun concealed but ready, he was surprised to see Stephen Bricker standing there.

"Val!" Bricker stepped in quickly and closed the door. "Have you heard the news?"

"What news?"

Bricker glanced at the pistol. "Thank God, you're armed!"

Bricker was older, a little heavier, but still a fine-looking man. He looked at the lean, powerful-shouldered young man before him with pleasure. The boy he had known had become a man.

"Val, we've been trying to get hold of you for weeks! Peck told me what he believed was happening, and I did a little discreet investigating, and whether you like it or not you are right in the middle of one of the biggest railroad-mining fights this country has ever seen!"

"How could that be?"

"Look," Bricker explained, "when you were a youngster you left some money with Peck, senior, to be invested. Am I right?"

"Of course. It wasn't much, but—"

"Val, Peck turned that money over to a banker and he and his son have since acted in a sort of unofficial supervisory capacity.

Right at the beginning they bought a piece of some mining claims—the discoverer needed money—and then because there seemed to be an effort developing to close off access to the upper end of the canyon, they went down below and bought about half a mile of the canyon right where it opened out. Today that half-mile of canyon is worth almost any price you want to ask for it."

"What's happened?"

"The railroads want it. They want a branch line in there to bring out coal. Nobody dreamed that stretch was anything but government or state land, because it was just about useless for anything but a right-of-way. We hoped to let you know what was happening before anyone talked you into signing anything."

Val chuckled. "Me? Mr. Bricker, you know I never sign anything. Will Reilly was a born skeptic, and I guess I developed into one."

Steve Bricker lit the cigar he had in his fingers. "Forgive me, Val, if I talk like a Dutch uncle. We've been friends for a good long time now, and I tell you you are going to have to move fast, very fast."

"Why? There seems to be something going on here that I don't know about."

"Val, if anything should happen to you, who would inherit?"

Val realized, with a kind of startled wonder, that he had never given the idea a moment's thought. Will Reilly had been his family, and they had been uniquely close, drifting continually as they had, and having no one but themselves to consider.

"I haven't given the idea much thought. Of course I'd want it to go to Boston."

"But you have not made a will? Is that right?"

"No, but—"

"Then who would inherit, Val? Have you stopped to think of that? Who would suddenly find herself the owner of the hottest piece of property in the country? And believe me, Val, it is worth millions."

"Myra . . ."

Myra was next of kin. If anything happened to him, whatever he had at the time would be hers.

"Does she know about this?" he asked.

"*Know* about it? Why do you think she's coming to Colorado?"

"Myra is coming out here? She told Van once she would never come west again . . . never as long as she lived!"

Bricker brushed the idea away with a gesture. "When she said that she didn't know how much returning could mean; and after all, she won't be here more than a day or two. If the Sante Fe doesn't get that stretch, the Denver & Rio Grande will. She and that prince of hers can arrive here one day and go back the next if she likes."

Val thrust his pistol into his waistband and put on his coat. "Have you had breakfast?" he asked.

"I had some coffee. I can't spare the time now, Val, but promise me you'll keep your eyes open."

They went down to the lobby together and Val went in to breakfast. His thoughts were confused, and he needed to think clearly, to decide what he wanted to do. If Myra was coming west, the chances were good that they would meet. The idea of meeting her after so many years was disturbing. Yet, why should it be? To him she was a stranger, a woman whose wish it had been to have him left to die in the snow.

What Bricker had said was right, of course, and he should have a will drawn up at the earliest possible moment. He wanted nothing of his ever to fall into the greedy hands of Myra Fossett.

He ordered breakfast and sat staring out of the window, wondering what his next move should be. He should prepare a list of his assets, and then find a reputable attorney. He might draw up the will himself, but he was not experienced in such things, and he wanted a will that was fool-proof.

He considered his situation. If possible, he wished to avoid trouble. Nothing was to be gained by meeting Myra. What he ought to do was to get the best offers of the companies concerned and settle quickly.

Once the deal was made, the reason for Myra's presence here would be gone, and he himself need stay no longer. He should have asked Bricker just who the men were with whom he should deal; it was likely that some were living right here in the hotel.

Of course, even if Myra were kept out of the right-of-way deal she would still be his heir, in the event of his death. There was a solution to that which would not require the writing of a will. He could marry Boston.

As he sat there the door of the dining room suddenly opened

and Dube came in. He looked exactly what he was, a cowhand in off the range, and Denver knew that a cowhand in run-down heels and faded Levis might be a grub-line rider, but that on the other hand he might own five thousand head of stock.

Dube glanced around the room, where only a few people were eating at this early hour. Then he went across to Val and dropped into the chair opposite him. "You packin' iron, boy?" he asked.

"Yes."

"Well, watch yourself. Sonnenberg is in town. I run into him down on Blake Street, and he's walkin' wide and mean. He's a big one, ain't he?"

"He's pretty big, all right. Weighs about two-fifty, I'd say, and he carries no more fat than a jay-bird."

Val let the waiter fill his cup again, and then he said, "Dube, I want to marry Boston."

Dube grinned at him. "You figger that's news? If it's news to you, it sure ain't to Boston."

"I haven't said a word to her. Not exactly, that is. I think she understands, all right, but the point is, it may have to be here . . . now . . . if she'll have me."

"Why so sudden? Pa an' them would sure be put out."

Val explained, as briefly as possible, and then he added, "I am going to make a will, but that won't be enough, if I know Myra Fossett. She would try every trick in the book to break the will, and as she's a blood relative she could probably do it."

"Can she prove she's your kin?"

"There may be records up north, but anyway she would find a way."

Dube was quiet, and looked his name, which was Dubious. After a while he said, "Val, why don't you just cut and run?"

When Val started to protest, Dube interrupted. "Look, you got this friend Bricker. Now, if he ain't in on the deal himself, he knows who is. Let him handle it for you, subject to your okay, and you just duck out. You don't check out of the hotel, you just walk out one evenin' in your fancy duds, but you have yourself a horse staked out, and you run. You make it to Leadville or Walsenberg, or even Durango. Then you just hide out there under another name, an' let this Bricker handle it for you. Me and Tensleep could keep an eye on 'em for you, and we could keep you in touch.

"It ain't that I'm agin' you marryin' Boston," he went on. "That's up to her, but we folks set a sight of store by marryin', and Pa an' Bets, they'd be almighty put out if you an' Boston tied the knot without them handy. I mean it."

Val stared out the window at the street, considering the idea. It appealed to him, and that disturbed him. Would he be avoiding responsibility if he ran? Did he want to dodge the issue? Would it be an act of cowardice?

Mulling over the idea, he had to admit Dube had come up with a solution. If he stayed in town there was every likelihood there would be violence. He was not prepared to guess what Myra might plan or attempt; but he was sure that sooner or later he would come face to face with Sonnenberg, which would surely mean a gun battle.

Denver was no longer the frontier town it had been, but a city with law and order, and some very definite ideas about men shooting at each other to settle personal quarrels.

To leave would seem to be the wise thing. Stephen Bricker was a trustworthy man, but there were ways in which Val could learn of the prices to be offered other than through Bricker.

"Maybe you've got the right idea," he agreed, "and if I can bring this thing to a head by nightfall, I'll do it."

"All right," Dube said, "I'll stake out a horse for you."

Dube got to his feet and Val stood up with him. He had eaten almost nothing, and his food had grown cold as he talked with Dube.

Suddenly the door opened again and Boston came in, but a different Boston, a Boston he had never seen before.

TWENTY-FOUR

Val was startled, and so was Dube. Val could only stare

Her black, wild hair had been drawn back and parted in the center; the corwn of her head was covered with curls and there were ringlets down the nape of her neck. The dress she wore was floor length, cut almost like a coat, of black wool rep over black and gray striped satin. The black skirt was draped back over a bustle to expose the pleated flounces of the silk skirt underneath. The waistcoat front was held by a strap of mother-of-pearl buttons. The sleeves were tight, with a silk facing.

She started toward them, and they stood, while Boston walked up to them and held out her hand, obviously pleased at the effect she was creating—not only on them, but on the entire room.

Val held her chair for her, and when she was seated he sat down abruptly. Dube hesitated, then sat down.

"Boss, where did you get that riggin'? I never seen the like!"

"I bought it." Her chin went up. "You aren't the only one who can maverick calves, Dube Bucklin! And this isn't all," she added. "I've got more! I've got six new dresses, just like the ones they wear in Paris and Vienna!"

"You're beautiful!" Val exclaimed. "Boston, I want to marry you! I've just been talking to Dube about it."

"Dube! What's he got to say about what I do?" She gave him a straight, frank look from her dark eyes. "When you ask me that, don't be looking at the girl in this dress. There's a lot more to a girl than clothes."

"I'm quite sure of that," Val said.

She flushed slightly. "I mean, I'm not just a girl who is wearing these clothes, nor just a girl who can rope and brand calves, either."

"At this moment," Val said honestly, "you look as if you'd stepped right out of a fashionable shop in Vienna. Where did you get the dress?"

"Mel Winslow measured me, and she sent the measurements to a lady right here in Denver. She sews for Mel. She came over from Austria about two years ago and her husband was killed in a mine accident, so she's had to sew."

Boston turned to him eagerly. "Oh, Val! Do I look all right? I mean . . . I never wore clothes like these before!"

"You look as if you had never worn anything else," he said. "If I hadn't been in love with you for a long time, I'd fall in love with you right now. I couldn't help myself."

She laughed at him. "That's blarney—I know it when I hear it. But Val! There's the most beautiful woman here! I just met her in the lobby. There she is now!"

It was Myra . . . and she was both beautiful and smartly gotten up, and the tall man beside her was an impossibly handsome man but for the three scars. . . .

Val was suddenly cold.

"Val?" Boston caught his sleeve. She looked frightened. "Val, what's the matter?"

"That's my mother," he said quietly, "and the man with her is Prince Pavel Pavelovitch."

He sat very still, looking at Myra. She was, he admitted, a very striking-looking woman. She was slender and tall, and looked not within ten years of what her age must be. When she looked across the room at them, her eyes met his.

This was his mother, but she was also the woman who had him taken out to be left to die in the snow. This was a woman that even such a man as Tensleep feared. If all he had heard was true, men had died at her hand, yet looking at her now as she came toward them it was hard to believe.

For only a moment she hesitated. Then she walked straight to him and held out her hand. "Val! You've grown into a very handsome man."

She turned slightly. "Val, I want you to meet Prince Pavel Pavelovitch. Pavel, this is my son, Valentine Darrant."

"How do you do?" Val's tone was cold, and the Prince looked at him in surprise.

Val turned and introduced Boston . . . Dube had disappeared.

"May we join you?" Myra asked, and she seated herself without waiting for any word from Val.

Myra ordered tea, as did Prince Pavel. As he was still hungry, Val ordered something more, wondering how he could escape from this situation. Only Boston seemed completely at ease. She chatted gaily with the Prince about Denver, the mountains, and the hotel. When the tea arrived she poured for them all.

During a momentary lull Myra said, "You're in a very fortunate position, Valentine. They tell me that you own the land needed for the right-of-way."

He shrugged. "It isn't important."

"But it is. If the situation is handled correctly, it can make you independent . . . even a wealthy young man."

"I really don't need very much. I prefer the simple life, except" —he paused—"that I do like to play cards occasionally."

Boston gave him a quick glance. This was something new.

"We all like to risk a little something occasionally," Prince Pavel said.

"And in doing so, sometimes one risks too much," Val replied. "Sometimes one underestimates those with whom he plays."

"I dare say," Pavel said, and he looked thoughtfully at Val. Why did the fellow look so damned familiar? And what had he meant by that, exactly?

"You have a chance for a real coup, Valentine," Myra said, "and if you'd like, I'd enjoy helping you. After all, you are my son."

"It must be nice," Boston said brightly, "to discover that you have a son."

Myra glanced at Boston without expression, then she said to Val, "Or if you don't want to bother with the details, I would buy you out for a hundred thousand dollars—in cash."

"It is a nice sum," Val agreed.

"Then it is a deal?"

"I only said it was a nice sum, and don't worry about the business part of it, Myra." He discovered he could not call her mother. "I served an apprenticeship with Stephen Bricker."

"I heard you had been admitted to the bar," she commented.

Myra was searching for an opening. She had not believed it would be easy, but she would have expected her son to react in a rather different way. Val seemed in no way impressed.

"I might be able to make a better price," she suggested.

Val gave her a direct look. "You would have to, Myra. Many times better. I haven't discovered yet what that property is worth, but I do know it is worth in excess of a million dollars."

Before she could reply, Val turned his attention to Pavel. "Are you staying with us long, Prince Pavel? The hunting in Colorado is excellent."

"Mrs. Fossett and I have some business to take care of," he said. "I doubt if I shall remain longer than necessary. In any event, I am not a hunter."

"But there are times when hunting can be quite interesting, especially when circumstances contrive to bring the game to the hunter."

Pavel was puzzled. What exactly did he mean, this American? He asked the question.

Val shrugged. "With deer, it is a bit of cloth on a stick that will bring them near. With men, I suspect that money would do it. Have you ever played poker, Prince?"

"Very often. In fact, it is a favorite game of mine. I learned at Salzburg from an Englishman who had lived in America. It is an exciting game."

"Then you should enjoy Colorado. They play an exciting brand of poker here."

Myra was puzzled even more than Pavel. The conversation seemed to have no point, yet she seemed to detect an undercurrent of hidden meanings. But that was absurd. It would have been directed at her, not at Pavel.

There had been little chance to utilize the Prince's name in New York. They had appeared at the opera, and they had attracted attention, just as she wished. Several invitations had arrived, at least one of them from one of the men close to those with whom she wished to do business. It was from this man that she received the first inkling of something impending in Colorado.

To travel in the West was the last thing she wanted, but when she discovered that it was her own son who held the property needed for the right-of-way, she decided to accept the risk of recognition in that part of the country. After all, years had passed, and she knew that she had changed. When she had worked on the Line she had been considerably plumper. Men who paid for their women liked them well rounded and full. She was fifteen pounds lighter now . . . everything was different.

It would be only a few days—a meeting with Val, a quick deal, and then a return to the East. The Prince would serve as wonderful window-dressing, and there was also the possibility that he would prove valuable in any subsequent negotiations. Ostensibly, she would be showing the West to the Prince and his cousin.

She had no doubts about success. Even if Val was skeptical of her good wishes, she could always appeal to sentiment. And if all else failed there was always the other way, and whatever he had would automatically become hers.

She was not without contacts in the Rocky Mountain area, though none of them knew who she was, but she had arranged to gather information on mines, railroads, and cattle through them, and to make it worth their whole.

Myra studied Val's face as he talked to Pavel. Was there any of her in him? If so, she could not see it. He looked like a taller, more handsome version of his father; and something, she had to admit it, of her own father was in his jawline and nose.

She supposed she should feel proud of him, but she did not. Suddenly she felt a pang of jealousy. It was Will Reilly who could feel proud, for after all, Will had raised him, and he seemed to have done quite a job of it.

Val had mentioned poker . . . was he a gambler, too? But her Pinkerton reports had made no mention of that, and it was something they would not have missed. So if he gambled at all, it was very little. No doubt Will had tried to keep him away from all that.

"If we could talk alone, Val," she suggested.

"He has promised to go shopping with me," Boston said.

Myra was growing irritated. The girl annoyed her, and she sensed a like feeling from Boston. "Please"—there was just an edge of sarcasm in her tone—"he can buy you pretty dresses any time. This is business. It is important."

"You misunderstand," Boston said very politely. "I buy my own dresses, with my own money. Some girls do, you know."

Myra stiffened as if she had been slapped. For an instant everything within her was still. Then she felt a shock of cold anger. She started to retort, but cut the words off and forced herself to speak with care.

"That's very nice, I'm sure." Then she added, "I suppose you have your own ways of earning money."

"Yes," Boston said, smiling, "I mavericked calves, if you want to know, out on the range with a branding iron and a rope."

Myra looked at her in frank disbelief, and Pavel said, "I don't understand . . . what is it . . . maverick?"

"It's a Texas name for an unbranded calf, or whatever," Val said. "It got its name from a Texan who didn't take the time to have his cattle branded, and when he sold the herd, riders moved in and branded every one as one of Maverick's.

"There are a lot of loose, unbranded cattle around, and although the practice is beginning to be frowned on, it is still the fastest way to build an outfit of your own. Boston is one of the best riders, male or female, I've ever seen, and she's good with a rope and fast with a branding iron, so she has done very well."

"It is difficult to believe," the Prince said. "You do not seem the type, somehow."

"We all work in this country," Val replied, "and Boston rides like one of your Cossacks."

Myra sat waiting, fighting down her impatience. The conversation kept wandering away from the subject, and this room would be filling with people at any moment now. Already a few had come in, and she was expecting Masters and Cope.

"We must settle this, Val. If you are going to sell the property, why not sell it to me, your mother?"

Val stifled the sharp answer that came to his lips. "I shall have to think about it. In the meantime, you might decide what is your best offer and make it to Bricker. . . . But don't waste time returning to the fact that you are my mother. I haven't had much of an example of that, Myra."

He got to his feet. "Prince Pavel, if you are interested, there are usually some good poker games around. Don't bother with Blake Street. You can find a good one right here in the hotel."

Myra sat very still as he walked out, but her mind was working rapidly. She was going to lose this deal unless she acted swiftly. There was also the matter of the box . . . she had forgotten about the box temporarily.

Had Val received it? If not, he must be prevented from receiving it. His room must be searched, and then she must get word to Sonnenberg. She had come west so quickly there had been no chance of waiting to learn if they had obtained the box.

"Your son," Pavel asked, "has he ever been to Europe?"

Her thoughts were elsewhere. "Europe? Of course not. How could he have been in Europe?"

Myra was frustrated and bitter. The breakfast conversation had been inconclusive, to say the least. Valentine seemed in no mood to do business with her, and she dreaded his receiving an offer from Cope or Masters.

First the box. She must have it, or at least examine its contents. . . . And then Val. For Myra Cord, now Fossett, killing had come to be simply a solution to a problem.

She got up, waited for Pavel to receive his change, and then left him in the lobby, and went to her room.

She had already taken care to find out which room was occupied by her son

TWENTY-FIVE

In the lobby, Val paused and took Boston's hand. "I was proud of you, but be careful. She's not like ordinary people, and she has been pretty successful in what she has done. By now she probably believes that she cannot make a mistake.

"Her entire life has been a struggle for money, for power. She doesn't have to have a reason for killing other than that you are in the way, and I am sure she feels you are, as I am."

"I'm not afraid of her, Val. I think she is more afraid of me."

"I've got to find Bricker, and tonight I must have a meeting with Pavel."

"What are you going to do?"

He hesitated. "Boston, I am going to play poker. I am going to play for blood, using everything I have except the ranch. I am going to twist him and break him."

"Can you do it?"

"I've got to try. He had Uncle Will murdered, but there is no way I can prove that here and now, so this will be my way to make him pay."

"All right, Val. Only be careful. I do not like him."

Dube met him outside. "Val, you better do as we planned. You grab yourself a horse and light a shuck."

"I've got to see Bricker, then Pavel."

"I looked him over. I don't care for that Russky. I've known some good ones, but he's got a mean look under all of that polish."

"I can't go now. I've got to stay in town."

"Val, don't you do it. Light out for Durango. You've got business there, anyway. Make 'em follow you—I mean those gents who want you to sell to 'em. But you get away from that woman . . . and from Sonnenberg. I meant to tell you about him. He ain't alone. He's got three men trailin' him around. One's a kind of crazy galoot they call Tom, then there's—"

"Tom?" His thoughts went back to the cold winter day when Will and he had driven up to that lonely hide-out in the snow, the hide-out where Tensleep, Sonnenberg, and . . . wasn't the other one named Tom?

"That's what they called him. Odd-lookin' crittur. Eyes never stop, one shoulder hangin' lower than the other, sunken chest, hollow cheeks."

"Who are the others?"

"There's a brood called Pagosa, and a long, lean slat of a man named Marcus Kiley. They're bad ones."

Dube was silent for a moment. "Well, I told you. That's all I can do except to have that horse where I planned. It will be there, come midnight, but you do whatever you're of a mind to."

By noon Val had located Stephen Bricker, and had made arrangements with him to open negotiations with Cope, Masters, or anyone else interested in the right-of-way.

When Val emerged on the street he paused to take stock of the street and of the windows all around before moving on. He was wary, and he liked the feel of the Smith & Wesson in his waistband. Every bit of common sense he had told him he should do just what Dube had wanted him to do . . . leave town, leave fast, and by back trails.

He had never been a man who hunted trouble, and as he had not faced Sonnenberg, nobody could ever call him a coward for quietly dropping out of sight. Moreover, he had business in Durango and the vicinity. But the memory of Pavel and how he had bought the death of Will Reilly held him in Denver.

There would be a big poker game in the Windsor that night, and if Pavel entered, Val would. And from that moment on, it would be war.

Myra had wasted no time. Val's room was not far from her own. And she had long possessed five skeleton keys that would open almost any lock. If seen by anyone in the hotel, she had only to say what was true—that she was going to her son's room.

She opened the door and stepped inside quickly. She stood still for a moment, sweeping the room with her eyes.

There were half a dozen suits in the closet, shirts and underwear in the drawers. Her son, she decided, after a glance at the clothes, had good taste. She went through the room working with the skill of a professional. If the box was in the room at all, she was quite sure it would be hidden, and she knew the places where things are usually hidden. She had hidden things many times herself, and she had a devious mind, given to quick apprehension of trick or device. Within a matter of minutes, she was sure the box was not in the room.

Where, then, was it?

She had had no word from Sonnenberg; if he had the box he had not notified her. If he had not been able to get it, the box must be at the bank, in which case the bank must be entered and the box obtained. This part of the affair was in Sonnenberg's hands.

But what if Val already had the box? If not in his room, where was it likely to be?

In the room of Boston Bucklin.

Myra paused, considering that. To enter the girl's room was dangerous, too dangerous unless she definitely knew the box was there and the girl was out.

The solution; then, was to get into the room by invitation, and then look around. If she could not see the box, she could, at least, eliminate all but a few hiding places, which could be examined later.

What her son would do with that box and its contents she had no idea, but without it nobody could do anything. Men had died, and by now worms had eaten them, and only Van could name dates and places. Only Van could know or guess where the bodies were buried.

She was positive, judging by his attitude, that he had not yet obtained the box—at least, he had not opened it and studied the contents. She must move quickly.

She listened a moment at the door, heard nothing, then slipped out. As she pulled the door shut behind her she thought she heard the click of a closing door an instant before Val's closed.

Quickly, she glanced around, but the hall was empty. She walked back to her room, fumbled with the lock long enough for a quick look around again, then stepped inside.

There were five doors along that hall. Surely, Boston's room was one of them. Had she been watching? Had Boston seen her leaving Val's room? Or was it that cowhand brother of hers who had come to Denver with them?

For several minutes she watched from a crack of her door, wondering if anyone would come to check Val's room, but no one did. Whoever had opened and closed the door might have been a stranger . . . or it might have been her imagination.

After a few minutes she went down to the lobby, inquired for Miss Bucklin, and learned that she was in her room. From a writing desk in the lobby Myra sent out several notes, one to Stephen Bricker, others to Cope and Masters. Another note went to a man on Blake Street.

Cheyenne Dawson did not look the way his name sounded. He should have been a cowhand or a bad man, the "bad" used in the western sense, meaning a bad man to tangle with. Cheyenne was all of that, only he made no show of being tough or mean, or good with a gun.

Cheyenne Dawson held forth in a saloon or two along Blake Street, and was known in all the less savory spots in Denver. He was a huge, sloppy man, wide in the hips, narrow in the shoulders, the tail of his shirt nearly always hanging out on one side or the other.

He had large, soulful blue eyes, was partly bald, and wore a coat that was too big, even for him. He was five inches over six feet, and was said to weigh three hundred pounds.

The years that lay behind him had covered about everything

dishonest that a man could do, but his activities usually were those that demanded the least activity. After a spell of smuggling over the border and of rustling cattle, he had decided it was easier to make a living by selling whiskey and guns to the Indians. As the country built up and the Army became more active, he decided there was too much risk in that, so he opened a saloon with a couple of barrels of "Indian" whiskey.

One day he was approached by a cattleman who was having nester trouble. Did Cheyenne know of a man who was discreet, good with a gun, and who could keep himself out of trouble?

Cheyenne did, and the man proved to be just as good as Cheyenne promised, and he also kept out of trouble. Soon Cheyenne became known as a reliable source for hired gunmen, or anyone who was needed to do anything at all, and Cheyenne got a satisfactory payment without moving more than a city block or two from one of his accustomed chairs.

For some time now Cheyenne had been getting notes, accompanied by cash, for various errands, mostly for information he acquired simply by listening, or through minor thefts.

The first time it was connected with assays on gold from a certain mining property, and after his report the property's source of eastern capital dried up. Cheyenne noted the cause and effect with considerable interest, and over the years he learned that whoever was asking for the information had considerable money, and furthermore seemed to have a wide knowledge of the West and its people.

Often when that person asked for a man to do a job, the man was asked for by name, as in the case of Henry Sonnenberg. In every case that mysterious person in the East had known exactly whom to ask for, and the person requested was the best at his job.

Cheyenne Dawson owned a part of a saloon, a part of a livery stable, and had more than a passing interest in several cribs in the red-light districts, but during the past ten years the income from that person back east had been so substantial that he had roped in, through women or drink, bookkeepers or shift bosses from various mining and railroad ventures to keep him supplied with the information he needed.

The notes that came to him were invariably written on a

typewriter, until one day he received a hastily written note in long-hand.

Interrupted in the reading of it, he had started to get up when Lila Marsh, one of the older girls, indicated the note. "Haven't seen hide nor hair of her in years. What's she want . . . a job?"

Cheyenne's scalp prickled, but he merely folded the note. "Who? Who ya talkin' about?"

"Myra Cord. I'd know that handwriting anywhere. We worked in the same house in Pioche one time . . . and again in Ogalala."

Cheyenne fished the stub of a cigar from his capacious coat pocket and lit it. "How was she?" he asked.

"Good . . . maybe the best I ever saw at taking them for money, but cold . . . all she ever cared about was money. Even her man—Van Clevern, his name was—didn't seem to mean a whole lot to her. She owned her own place in Deadwood for a while, then she sold out and I haven't heard a thing of her since."

"How old would she be then?"

Lila hesitated. That was cutting closer to her own age than she liked. "Oh, she was older than most of us! I guess she'd be forty odd now, but she'd look good. She always kept herself well."

Cheyenne started for the door. "Are you going to bring her down here?" she asked.

"I'll think on it. I doubt it," he said.

Outside on the street, he rolled the cigar in his fat lips and considered. Of course, Lila had had only a glimpse of the handwriting and she could be wrong. On the other hand, a woman who'd been on the line would know the people she had mentioned. Cheyenne went on up the street, stuffing in his shirt-tail.

During the year that followed he had pieced together quite a dossier on Myra Cord, without any idea of how he expected to use it . . . or if he intended to.

There were a couple of rumors . . . a trail-drive foreman had sold a large herd, paid off his men and headed for the station with the bulk of the cash, some sixty thousand dollars. He dropped the comment to one of the hands that he had found himself a girl and was going to stop in Kansas City for a wild time.

He had disappeared, and investigation brought nothing to light except that he was said to have visited Myra at least twice after the herd arrived in town.

Now, nearly five years after he had received that first hand-written note he received another. Only this one was written on Windsor Hotel stationery. Not that the printed heading had been left on, for in fact it had been neatly creased and torn off, but Cheyenne Dawson knew that paper, and knew the watermark. Nobody else in town used it.

This woman then, Myra Cord or whoever, was in Denver and staying at the Windsor.

Cheyenne Dawson, like a lot of people before him, had tired of the petty day-to-day deals he was making. He wanted a big killing and retirement. This looked like it. He tucked his shirt-tail into his pants, rubbed out his cigar and put it in his coat pocket, donned his narrow-brimmed hat, and walked to the Windsor.

He leaned his heavy forearms on the desk and stared at the desk clerk from watery blue eyes. "Woman here . . . stayin' here. Wanted to buy a horse. Forgot her last name . . . Myra . . . Myra something-or-other."

"You must mean Mrs. Fossett. However, I did not know she wished to buy a horse. If you would leave your name, Mr.—?"

He shook his head. "I'll come back," he said, and padded away through the lobby. He was just going out of the door when Myra Fossett came in from the dining room.

She caught a glimpse of him, and then the clerk said, "Oh, Mrs. Fossett, I didn't know you were in the dining room. There was a man here . . . said you wished to buy a horse."

"I had thought of it," she replied. "Did he ask for me by name?"

"Well, as a matter of fact, no. He wasn't sure about your last name."

"I see. Well, thank you very much."

In her room Myra Fossett sat down quickly, for suddenly her legs were trembling. She had been a fool to come west! A triple-dyed fool!

Yet how could he have traced her? Even if she had written from here in the city . . .

Now she was in trouble, in real trouble.

TWENTY-SIX

Val knotted his tie before the mirror. It was time to leave. He should not be going to the game, but to that horse that Dube had for him. He should be riding out of here, for his every instinct told him he was heading for trouble.

His room was somehow different. Not that anything was disturbed, but there was a vague, troubling suspicion of perfume in the air, as though a woman had been here. It was the perfume his mother wore, but no, that could not have been.

He looked at himself. It was for the first time, it seemed, that he truly saw himself as he was. He was two inches over six feet, and he weighed a hundred and ninety pounds, though he looked less. His clothes were well tailored, his general appearance perfect. Even the pistol under his waistband made no bulge.

He knew what it was—he looked like Will Reilly.

He was as tall as Will, a little heavier, and perhaps broader and heavier in the shoulders. He looked like Will and he could do a lot worse, for Will had been a handsome man. And tonight, if all went well, he could pay Will's debt to Pavel.

For it was Pavel, after all, who was to blame. Avery Simpson and Henry Sonnenberg were only tools. The man who had pointed the gun was Pavel.

Once free of that burden, he would marry Boston and they could make a life for themselves here in the West. But first there was Pavel.

Suddenly he was uneasy. He had that cold chill, that quick shudder that comes when, as the saying is, somebody has stepped on your grave.

He had the feeling that he was caught fast in a web, and the strings were drawing tighter and tighter. For an instant he felt panic, the desire to get away. He did not want to be killed, and he did not want to kill.

It was all very well to have faith in himself, and he had it. He knew he was good with a gun, but many men had died who were good with their guns. Billy was dead, and Hickok was dead . . . it could happen to anyone. There was no divine providence that would watch over him.

Yet while he was thinking these things, he was straightening his tie, buttoning his vest, and drawing it down . . . but not over his gun.

He checked the room one last time, then stepped out into the hall.

Before him, not fifty feet away along the passage walked a woman alone. He felt his mouth go dry . . . he knew that back, those shoulders, that carriage. He started to speak, then turned and went back. He unlocked his door, entered the room and rummaged among his things. He found the book where he kept it, at the bottom of his trunk. He had stored it there after he repacked his clothes in the trunk after his arrival in Denver.

Then he turned and went down to the lobby. It was early, but dinner time still. He walked into the dining room.

She sat across the room, her back toward him. He motioned to a waiter, handed him the book and a coin. "Take it to the lady," he said.

He waited, his heart pounding. He saw her take the book, and he was walking toward her when she turned.

"*Val!*" She held out both her hands to him. She was a beautiful, a truly beautiful woman. "Val!" she said again. "Can it be!"

For a moment she looked at him. "Val, you have become quite a man. Will would have been proud of you."

"I hope so." He seated her, then rounded the table and sat

down opposite her. "He loved you, you know. You were the only woman he ever loved."

"Thank you, Val. I believe that. I always wanted to believe that. And I loved him . . . I still do, I think."

"He was not a man it was easy to forget."

"Val, how did he die? I heard it was a shooting of some sort."

"You don't know then?" Val hesitated, but this was no time to hesitate. "He was murdered, shot down in cold blood as he walked out of a door in a town not very far from here. There were three men . . . they were paid to do it."

"*Paid?*" There was something like fear in her eyes.

"Paid through an American attorney, a cheap lawyer called Simpson . . . it wasn't even his real name."

"Who paid him, Val?"

"Who could it have been but Pavel? Avery Simpson confessed that. I am sorry, for your sake."

"You needn't be, Val. For a long time I felt sorry for him. He was always borrowing money from me, but his mother had been good to me, and I always liked her, and Pavel seemed harmless enough. When I began to see that he was using me, that he was interfering in my life . . . I tried to get rid of him, and for a few years I did.

"That was when he had money. He inherited a little, won some gambling, then lost it all. I had not seen him in a long time when he came to suggest this trip to America. I don't know why I came. Maybe I was hoping just to see where Will had lived, what his country was like."

Suddenly, she looked at him. "Val, you're not going to—"

"In a way. He is gambling tonight, I think. I am going to play in the game. I play very well. I am going to bring up the question of Will Reilly."

"Val! He will kill you—in those rages of his he is terrible!"

"I have a debt to pay. I must pay it the way Will would have done. I do not want to kill him, only to face him with it."

"Don't do it. Please."

"One of the men who actually killed him is here in town, too."

"You said there were three."

"Two of them are dead . . . I killed them in gun battles. I did not really look for them. They came to me."

He changed the subject deliberately. After a few moments, he got to his feet. "I will keep my *Faust*, if you do not mind. I have treasured it. You were very kind to a boy who was often lonely. I never saw much of women in those days, and it meant a lot to me."

"I am glad."

"Will is buried at Empire. It is a little town not far from here. When this is over I will take you there, if you wish."

The game had been in progress for at least an hour when Val arrived. Pavel was winning. He was flushed and excited, and he was pushing. Val watched the game for a few minutes. Stephen Bricker was one of the men, the only one except Pavel whom he knew.

Bricker nodded when he entered, and continued playing. After a while he looked up. "Would you like to sit in, Val? That is, if these gentlemen do not mind."

Bricker introduced them. "Valentine Darrant—Jim Cope, Quentin Masters, Clyde Murray. I believe you know Prince Pavel."

Val seated himself and received his cards. Cope glanced at him. "Darrant? Are you the man we're looking for?"

Val smiled. "That's a dangerous way to put it, out here, but I guess I am if you're referring to the right-of-way business."

They played, and did not talk then about the right-of-way. Val's cards were nothing to speak of, but he passed or went along for the sake of staying in the game and seeing how the others played.

He lost fifty . . . a hundred . . . thirty . . . He won a little, lost a little more. Then bucking Pavel, he drew two pair and on a hunch stayed with it and added a third queen for a full house. He won sixty dollars, then won again.

"You have been doing all right," he commented to Pavel. "You're a lucky man."

Pavel shrugged. "Sometimes."

An hour later Pavel was sweating. His run of luck had failed him and he lost three hands running, at least two of them when he was obviously beaten.

Bricker had been losing, Masters had won a little. Murray cashed in and left the game. Cope was watching Val with some curiosity and a little puzzlement. He had become aware that Val was playing against Pavel, that it was only when Pavel was raising that Val pushed his luck.

Val was taking his time. He had played poker since he was a child, and he had been coached by a master, and had watched many games. Moreover, he knew that Pavel was a compulsive gambler as well as a complete egotist.

He picked up his hand to find three nines. Pavel was staring at his hand, trying to compose himself. Pavel took one card, Cope threw in his hand, and Masters took two cards. Val hesitated, seemed uncertain, then asked for two cards. He drew a trey and a nine . . . four nines.

Pavel was raising, Masters stayed, and Val saw Pavel's raise and boosted it five hundred dollars. Masters threw in his cards, Pavel saw the five hundred and raised another five.

"It's been a long time, Pavel," Val said, "but for old times' sake I am going to raise you one thousand dollars . . . if you aren't afraid."

Pavel stared at him, his irritation obvious. "What do you mean . . . afraid?" He counted one thousand dollars from the stack before him and shoved it to the middle of the table.

Val glanced at him. "Are you going to boost the price a little bit? You must have six or seven hundred on the table."

Pavel stared at him. "All right, if you have money to lose." He shoved the money to the middle of the table. When Pavel spread out his cards he had a full house—aces and kings.

Val took his time placing his four nines on the table; then he reached for the pot.

Pavel flushed as he watched the money drawn in and stacked. "I have had enough," he said lurching to his feet.

Val remained where he was. "As I said a few minutes ago, it has been a long time."

"What does that mean?"

"You don't lose well," Val said, "but you never did." Val tucked a sheaf of bills into his inside coat pocket, and gathered the coins into a sack. "I think you had better get on the train and go back to New York, and from there back to Russia, and be glad you're getting there alive."

"I don't know what you mean," Pavel said. "Are you trying to quarrel with me?"

"You aren't a man with whom one quarrels," Val replied. "You hire your killing done."

Several other men had come into the room, and all were standing about, watching.

Pavel's face had turned pale. "That's a lie!"

"I could kill you for that," Val said, "but I don't intend to. I think you will suffer more from staying alive."

He pushed back in his chair. "You gentlemen deserve an explanation," he said. "The Prince here does not remember me. I was only a child then." Coolly, in a quiet voice he told them the story. The attempted whipping, the escape over the mountains, the final murder of Will Reilly.

"Three men performed that killing, using shotguns on an unsuspecting man. I should kill him, but I decided that taking his money would cause him more grief."

He stood up. "Gentlemen, I understand that you may wish to talk business with me. Tomorrow morning I am leaving for the new town of Durango. If you still wish to talk business, I can see you there."

Deliberately they walked out, and no one looked back at Pavel. He stood there for several minutes, his face gray and sick-looking. Then he went out into the night and started for the hotel. Why had he been such a fool? He might have known he would lose, lose to that, that . . .

He stumbled once, then walked on. When he reached the hotel he went at once to his room. He had six dollars and a handful of rubles.

Myra was not in, and he went to Louise's room. There was no one there, but a maid walking along the hall paused and said, "The lady that was in that room left about an hour ago. She said she was going to Empire or Georgetown or somewhere."

Louise *gone?* He couldn't believe it, but at the desk they confirmed what the maid had said.

There was nothing to do but wait for Myra. After a few minutes Masters entered and walked past him, ignoring him completely. Pavel swore, but he remained where he was.

He had to get out of this town. He had to get back east. He began to pace back and forth, then went outside. If only Myra . . . but suddenly he became uneasy. If Myra knew, if she even guessed, he would no longer have any bargaining position with her at all. The first moment he could get he had best cable for some cash . . . cable to whom? He owed everybody.

Cheyenne Dawson was sitting at his usual table when Henry Sonnenberg strode through the door. "Hi, Henry! Come an' set!"

Sonnenberg strolled across the room and dropped down at the table. "Where's the bar-keep?"

"I let him off. Things're slack today. Here"—Dawson pushed the bottle toward him—"this here's better'n bar whiskey."

When Sonnenberg had filled a glass, Dawson spoke up. "Hank, I been keepin' an ear to the ground. There's more goin' on around here than a body would figure. Me, I got me an idee how we can make some money."

"I got a job."

"Now, see here. You been gettin' work through me. Don't you figure you should ought to split with me?"

Sonnenberg chuckled, without humor. "Now that would be somethin', wouldn't it? No, I got me two jobs, Cheyenne—one of them right here in town, the other one in Durango."

He paused for a drink. "Cheyenne, this here's a job I'm going to like. I'm going after Val Darrant."

Dawson sat up slowly. Val Darrant was living at the same hotel as Myra Fossett, and he was the one they said owned all that property.

"Ain't he the one who got Hardesty?"

"Uh-huh . . . and Pike, later. I never figured that kid would get old Thursty."

Cheyenne was drawing wet circles on the table top with his glass. He was scarcely listening to what Henry was saying. "You know," he said, "there's money in this. Not just a few dollars . . . there's real money in it, but we got to act fast."

"I told you I got a job. I got one right here in town."

"In town?" Cheyenne looked at him. "Who is it, Hank?"

Henry Sonnenberg wiped his mustache. He smiled suddenly, his small eyes almost closing.

"It was this woman," he said. "She gave me five thousand for Darrant's scalp, and a thousand for the other job."

"Who is it? You can tell me, Henry."

Henry grinned at him. "Sure I can, Cheyenne. It's you."

Cheyenne Dawson stared at Sonnenberg, not grasping what he had said. Then slowly the idea got through to him, but even then it was not real. It could not happen to him, not to Cheyenne Dawson.

"You got to be joking," he said. "That ain't funny."

"This woman, she gave me a thousand for you. I never figured to make that much so easy, but she wants you done in, Cheyenne, and tonight. So I taken the money."

"Why, that don't make sense. Look at all the money we made together."

"After I done the work," Sonnenberg said. "No, she paid me for the job. That Val, he might be good with a gun. He might give me trouble, but not you. Seems you've been getting nosey in the wrong places, Cheyenne. You've been askin' questions."

"Look, Henry, this is real money. You forget this deal and work with me. You'll make twice as much—"

The gun sound was muffled by the table, but it still seemed loud. Cheyenne felt the blow in his stomach, and he tried to cling to the table as he slid off his chair and fell to the floor.

For a moment he was there on his knees, his fingers on the edge of the table as he stared across at Henry, who picked up the bottle, took a long drink, and got to his feet. Cheyenne slid down from the table and sprawled on the floor.

Henry Sonnenberg nudged him with his foot, then taking the bottle with him, he went out the back door into the alley, through the stable, and out on the street on the other side where his horse waited.

Within twenty minutes he was out of town and riding west.

TWENTY-SEVEN

Nobody slept in Durango unless lulled to sleep by the sound of pistol shots. The town was not quite two years old and was still celebrating. The grand opening of the West End Hotel had to be postponed when it was badly shot up by the Stockton-Simmons bands of outlaws and gunmen.

The Stockton gang, from the Durango area, had a going feud with the Simmons outfit of Farmington, down in New Mexico. The West End Hotel happened to be caught in the middle.

Some of the pistol shots in Durango were fired in sheer exuberance of spirits, others were fired with intent to kill, and a good many of them were fired erratically, and often as not it was the bystanders who suffered.

Val Darrant rode into town, coming up the trail from Pagosa Springs. Purposely he had chosen the longest and less traveled route from Denver, for he had a hunch that somewhere along the way he was supposed to be met by Henry Sonnenberg, or somebody like him.

Dube caught up with him thirty miles out, and Boston, not to be left out, had taken the stage.

Animas City had been the town of the locality until the railroad came . . . but did not come to Animas; so the bulk of the population promptly packed up bag and baggage and moved to Durango, two miles or so to the south. Animas City had been alive for twenty years, and it died in the space of a day.

Val Darrant was riding a line-back dun when he came into Durango, Dube Bucklin beside him on a dapple gray. They rode to the livery stable and left their horses, and packing their Winchesters they walked along the street to the West End Hotel.

Boston met them in the door. "Val, there's a man here named Cates. He knows you, and has a box for you."

"Thanks." He paused before the hotel, sweeping the street with sharp attention. He saw nobody with the bulky body of a Sonnenberg.

He did not know the men who had been reported to be traveling with Sonnenberg, except by name. The half-breed Pagosa, Marcus Kiley, and Tom . . . he might know Tom.

He would surely know him. Tall, lank, ill-smelling because he rarely bathed, a strange, mentally disturbed man. As Will had said so long ago, nobody ever knew about Tom . . . and it was something to remember.

He said as much to Dube. "Don't worry," Dube replied. "Tensleep is in town. He rode west right behind Boston's stage, sort of keepin' an eye on her. She'd throw a fit if she knew . . . says she can care for herself, and likely she can, but a body never knows. But Tensleep knows them all, especially Tom."

"I remember him," Val said. "As a matter of fact, I remember that he knew my grandparents—Myra's folks. He came from the same town, or somewhere near. He said they were good people."

It was cool and pleasant here. A few thunderheads showed in the north, over Animas Mountain.

Val went into the hotel, and looked down the street from the lobby window. A man had gotten up from a seat on the edge of the boardwalk and gone into the saloon.

"Val," Boston said, close behind him, "be careful."

They heard a door close, and turned to see a man coming up the dark hall from the back of the hotel. It was Tensleep.

Suddenly Val realized that Tensleep was an old man. He had never thought of him that way, for the outlaw-cowhand-gunfighter had never seemed to change.

"They're all here, Val. I don't think they saw me, but I seen

ever' last one of them. And they're loaded for bear. Pagosa's got
him a buffalo gun, and Kiley is packin' a double-barrel shotgun."

"Thanks. Stay out of the way, Tensleep."

"You kiddin'? This here's my party as much as yours. I never
did like that Sonnenberg, and he knows it."

"How about Tom?"

Tensleep shrugged. "He's with them, ain't he?"

Egan Cates came into the room. "Val, we've got to talk. There's
this box—"

"I know about it."

"Yes," said Cates, "and so does everybody else. I've had two
flat cash offers for it in the last twenty-four hours. Masters wants
to buy it because of what he could do to Myra if she starts
trouble. Myra herself wants it . . . and Lord knows who else."

"Where is it?"

"Under my bed . . . and it isn't easy to sleep with it there."

"I'll take it off your hands. Tensleep"—he turned to him—"you
go with Cates. Move that box to my room and you sit on it, do
you hear?"

"And miss out on the fight?"

"No, just until Boston can get there. She will take care of it."

Dube had been leaning on the door jamb, watching down the
street. "It's quiet," he said, "but that's normal, this time of day.
This here's a Saturday-night town, and by day most folks are
about their business, whatever it is."

"Your canyon is right out of town," Cates said, "if you want to
look at it."

"I'm selling it," Val said, "that's all." He was cold inside, and
he felt oddly on edge, and did not want to talk.

Boston was quiet, and he liked it that way. Just having her here
was important. They moved into the dining room. The waitress
was apologetic. "They hadn't really planned to serve meals, and
they may not continue the practice, so we're really not set up for
it."

"Just anything," Val said. He was not hungry, but he wanted to
be busy.

"You hadn't better eat," Cates said. "It makes it worse if you
get shot in the stomach."

But they ate, and Val gradually began to simmer down, some of
the tenseness going out of him as he drank the coffee.

"Boston," he said then, "you go back and stay in my room or yours, but watch that box."

"Is it so important?"

"To me it isn't important at all, but it is important to her. Everything she's done goes right down the drain if that box is opened and the contents get known."

"What about you? And her people?" Boston said. "Val, her people probably believe she's dead. It would ruin them if all this came out now. Don't do it, Val."

"Why should I? She hasn't anything I want. The one thing she could have given me was just to be a mother to me, but that's long ago and far away."

The street was empty except for a dark man who leaned on a horse as if he were sick. He had just come from a saloon and he had his head down against the saddle, one hand gripping the horn as he stood there.

It was quiet in the room. Somebody had put a grandfather's clock in the lobby when they began fitting the hotel for operation, and they could hear its ticking. Val pushed back from the table and stood up. "I never was much for waiting," he said. "I'm going down there."

"That's taking too much of a chance," Dube said. "You might get drilled when you walk out on the street."

"I don't think so. I think Henry would like to let me have it close up."

"Even so," Cates protested, "you're forted up here. Make them bring it to you."

Val was wearing a holster, had been wearing one since riding out of Denver. He eased it into position on his leg, dropped his hand to the butt. "You can do me a favor, Cates, by keeping an eye on Boston and that box."

"All right." Cates hesitated a moment, started to speak, and then went out.

"Well," Dube said, "there's three of us, and four o' them . . . so far as we know."

"That Sonnenberg," Tensleep said, "is an army all by himself. I've seen him work."

The sick man leaning against the horse was no longer visible, for the horse had turned broadside to the door of the hotel, and the man was behind it now. How old had he been when Will

taught him that trick? If he walked out of the hotel there would
be a rifle peering at him from over that saddle.

"Sonnenberg is the one I want," Val said, "I don't care about
the others."

The rifle muzzle had appeared over the horse's back now.

Val took up his rifle, and then put it down. He did not want
anybody to get hurt helping him. "Dube, there's a man behind
that horse down there with a rifle trained on this door. I can't
take a step if he's there. Why don't you go upstairs where you'll
have a better view of him. Just give him a shot to get him out of
there . . . shoot at his feet or whatever you like, but move him."

Val poised at the door, waiting. Suddenly a rifle's sharp crack
cut the stillness of the afternoon. The horse sprang away, and the
suddenly exposed rifleman raced for the door. He had taken no
more than two steps when a second shot ripped splinters from the
boardwalk. He fell, got up, and a second bullet struck his boot
heel and knocked him sprawling.

Val left the door running, reached the back of the buildings,
raced along them to the saloon, stopped suddenly, and stepped
inside.

At the sound of his step Sonnenberg, Kiley, and Tom turned as
one man. They were spread out badly, but that could not be
helped.

"Well, Henry," Val said quietly, "it's been a long time since
that time on the mountain in the snow. I never figured you'd live
this long."

Sonnenberg was smiling. He looked huge, invulnerable. His
body seemed like the side of a battleship. "You come to get it, kid?
We're goin' to kill you, you know."

Val was smiling and easy. All the tenseness seemed gone from
him. He heard himself talking as if he were another person.

"Howdy, Tom. You're the one I'm not likely to forget. You
knew my grandparents once, Tom."

"They were good people," Tom said, "not like their daughter."

"But she's the one who is paying to have me killed—or did
Henry tell you?"

"No, sir, he never told us that. You never told us any of that,
Hank."

"Hell, who cares?" Kiley said. "Her money's as good as
anybody's."

"But she's his mother! She's blood kin to 'im! Why, I used to deliver milk to that house when I was a boy, I—"

"Shut up, old man!" Kiley said. "We got us a job to do."

"I remember you, Tom," Val said. "I was a mighty lonely, frightened kid then, and when I left in the sleigh with Will Reilly, it was you who tucked the blanket in."

"What is this?" Sonnenberg said. "Old home week?"

"No," Val said, "I just wanted Tom to know I wasn't going to shoot at him," and he drew.

Henry Sonnenberg was fast and sure, but that split second of reaction time cost him his speed. Val's gun slid out as if it was greased.

The speed of it shocked Sonnenberg, and something clicked in his brain. *I couldn't have beaten him anyway!* it said.

The bullet slammed into him, but he never moved his body, only his gun came up like the arm of a well-oiled machine. The gun muzzle dropped into line and the hammer slid off his thumb just as the second and third bullets jolted him. He took a step back then, his arm swinging wide.

Guns were hammering in the room, but Val Darrant knew the man he had to kill was Henry Sonnenberg. He took a step to one side, so that Sonnenberg would have to swing his gun into line, and he shot the big man again.

Four bullets . . . one more.

Sonnenberg turned and shot and the bullet knocked Val around and to his knees. He felt another bullet cut through the hair at the side of his head, a sure hit had he not been knocked down.

He lunged up and dived into Sonnenberg, who took a cut at his skull with his gun barrel, but Val had ducked in close and stabbed the muzzle of his gun into the big man's belly. He held it tight and squeezed the trigger and felt the man's body jolt into his arms. Their faces were only inches apart.

"Hello, Henry," he said, and then, "Good-bye, Henry."

The man sagged against him, his gun going off into the floor, and Val stepped back, letting him fall heavily as Tensleep and Dube came bursting through the door.

Marcus Kiley was down, shot to doll rags by Tom, who was sitting wide-legged, his back against the bar.

"They were good folks," Tom said. "Used to let me warm

before their fire on cold mornings. They never deserved a girl like Myra . . . even then she was a mean one."

Blood was staining his shirt. "You got him, boy. You killed ol' Henry. He never believed the bullet was made that could kill him."

Val dropped to his knee beside him. "Thanks, Tom. Will Reilly always said you were a good man."

"But a little crazy. Just a little crazy in the head, that was what they always said about me—but Myra's folks, Will Reilly, and you . . . it never made no difference to you all."

"Tom, I—"

"Val," Tensleep said, "he's dead. He died right there."

Val was feeding shells into his empty gun. "What about the breed?"

"He was dead before we got to him. One of those bullets of mine or Dube's must have ricocheted into him—we were both shootin'."

They started back up the street together, walking side by side.

Boston came out of the door to meet him, running into his arms.

"There's a train through here tomorrow," Val said. "Let's go home on the Denver & Rio Grande."

The stage came in just before sundown, and with the crimson and pink of the sunset coloring the sky and the rims of the mountains around, Val closed his deal with Cope, a clear sale for cash and stock.

"Myra's gone east," Cope told him. "She could only make money with the right-of-way if she sold to one of us, and we wouldn't do business with her."

Cope glanced around at Dube, Tensleep, and Cates. "Son," he said, "it looks to me as if you've made some friends, some really good friends."

"I hope I can always be as good a friend to them as they have been to me," Val said, "and I think I can. I had a man who taught me how."

Over on the Dry Side

To
Don Demarest,
companion
of the
High Country

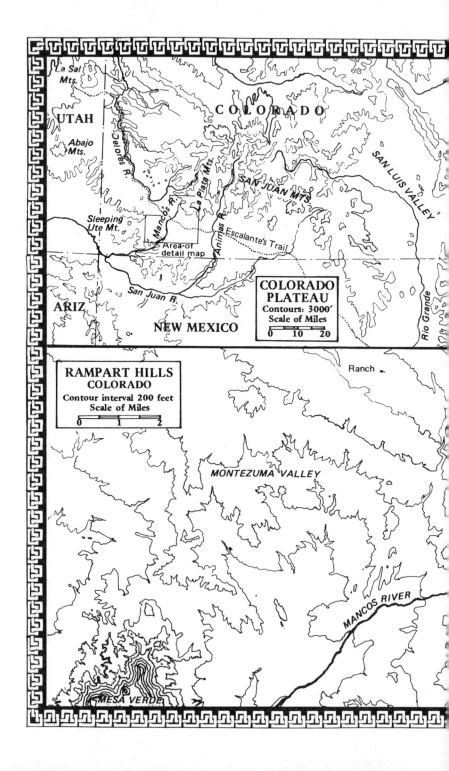

La Sal Mts.

UTAH

Abajo Mts.

COLORADO

Dolores R.

La Plata Mts.

San Juan Mts.

SAN JUAN MTS

SAN LUIS VALLEY

Mancos R.

Sleeping Ute Mt.

Animas R.

Escalante's Trail

Area of detail map

COLORADO PLATEAU

Contours: 3000'
Scale of Miles
0   10   20

ARIZ

San Juan R.

NEW MEXICO

Rio Grande

RAMPART HILLS
COLORADO

Contour interval 200 feet
Scale of Miles
0   1   2

Ranch

MONTEZUMA VALLEY

MANCOS RIVER

MESA VERDE

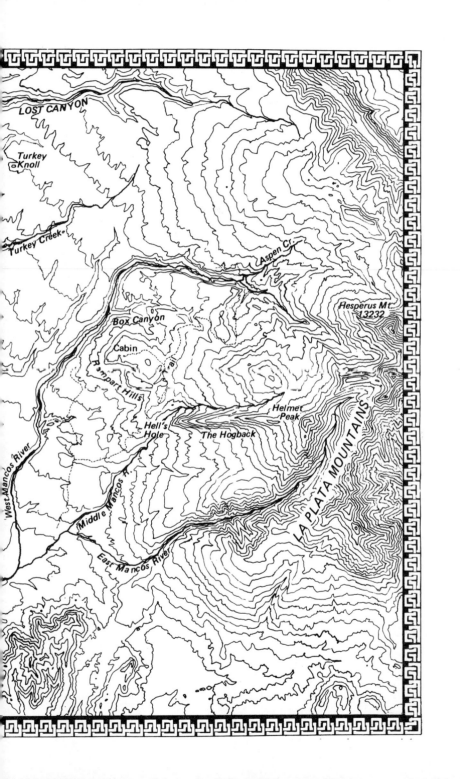

ONE

All that spring, I was scared. Why Pa ever took a notion to stop on that old Chantry place I never did know. Maybe it was because he was just tired and wishful of stopping someplace . . . anyplace.

There'd been a dead man on the steps by the door when we drove up. He'd been a long time dead, and nobody around to bury him, and I was scared.

The cabin was strong. It was built mighty solid like whoever had shaped it up and put it together had planned to stay. That was before the Indians come.

There was nobody inside and the place was all tore up . . . of course. It had been vacant for weeks, prob'ly. Maybe even months. That man had been dead a long time.

There wasn't much left but torn skin, dried out like old leather, and bones. His clothes was some tore up and all bloody.

Pa, he stood there looking down at him a long time. "Don't seem logical," he said, at last.

"What's that, Pa?"

1

"Indians most usually take a body's clothes. They ain't taken nothin' from him."

"His pockets is inside out."

"I was seein' that, boy. It do make a body think." He turned. "Boy, you run out to the wagon an' git my shovel. We got a buryin' to see to."

He stepped around the body and pushed wide the cabin door. That door had been half-open, and Pa looked in like he feared what he might see, but like I said, there wasn't nothin' to fear.

When I come in later I saw just what he saw. A bed with two sides nailed to the outside wall, a table, two chairs . . . all mighty well made by a man with lovin' hands for wood.

Pa always said you could tell a man who loved wood by the way things were fitted and dressed, nothing halfway, but smooth and nicely done. Pa couldn't do that sort of work himself, but he had admiration for it, and it made me feel like working at it until I was good. If fine work impressed Pa so much there must be something to it.

"I never had no craft, boy. I worked hard all my life but never had no craft. Just a few slights I picked up handling heavy things and the like. I do admire a man who does fine work. It is a pleasure to look upon."

We taken that dead man out to the hill back of the house and we dug us a grave. When we'd dug it down, we laid that body in a blanket, covered it around him sweet an' neat, and then we lowered him easy into the ground and Pa said a few words from the Book.

I never did know how Pa come to so much knowing of the Book, because I never did see him reading much in it.

We filled in the grave an' Pa said, "Come tomorrow we'll make him a marker."

"How'll you know what to say? We ain't sure who he is."

"No, we ain't. But they do call this the Chantry place, so I reckon his name must be that." Pa stopped there, leaning on his shovel, like.

"What'll we do now, Pa? It's late to be startin' on."

"This here's it, son. This place here. We ain't goin' no

further. You know, son, I ain't been much of a success in my time. Fire burned me out back to home, and we lost everything. In Missouri the grasshoppers et it all up, and in Kansas it was hail. But you know, I never was much hand at pickin' land.

"Your grandpap, now he knowed land. He could look at what growed there, and he knew. He could ride over land at a gallop and tell you which was best, but me, I was a all-fired smart youngster and no old man was going to tell me anything. I just knowed it all already. So I never learned.

"Son, I got to admit it. Ever' piece of land I picked was poor. Sure, we lost out to grasshoppers, hail, and the like, but those places never would have made it no way.

"Now this here . . . some other man picked this. I heard talk of Chantrys and they were knowing folk. The man who built this house, he was a knowing man. He had a craft. So I reckon maybe he picked himself a right good piece of land.

"So this here is it. We just ain't a-goin' no further."

We cleaned out the cabin. We mopped an' we dusted like a couple of women, but she was spic an' span when we finished.

The shed and the stable were solid-built, and there were good tools in the shed, leaning just like that dead man must have left them.

Right close to the house was a spring, not more'n thirty feet away. Good cold water, too. Never tasted no better.

There was a fieldstone wall around that spring, maybe eight, ten foot back from it, so a body could get water and go back to the cabin, leaving himself open to fire only in front. Even that was partly protected by a swell of the ground.

Cabin had a good field all around, and a corral joined the house to the barn. The horses had been run off, and whatever other stock he might have had, but we pulled our wagon close and we unloaded.

Not that I liked it much. Fact was, I didn't like it at all. Ever' time we stepped out of that cabin we stepped over where that dead man had lain. I never liked that.

Pa said, "Pay it no mind, son. That man would admire to

see folks usin' what he built. No man with a craft builds to throw away. He builds to use, and to last, and it would be a shameful thing to leave it die here, all alone."

"Ain't no neighbors, Pa."

"We don't need neighbors right now. We need time an' hard work. If this here land's rich as I think, neighbors will come. Only when they do they'll find a fair piece of it staked out an' marked for we 'uns."

"Maybe those Indians will come back."

He just looked at me. "Boy, your pa ain't as smart as some, but I'm smart enough to know that Indians take the clothes off a dead man because they need 'em."

"His clothes wasn't taken," I said, wanting to argue with him.

"You bet. His clothes wasn't taken, but somethin' else was. You notice his pockets, boy?"

"They were inside out."

"They surely were. Now, boy, somebody wanted what was in that man's pockets. Money and the like. Indians this part of the country don't set much store by money. They want *goods*. They want *things*. Ain't no money in them wigwams."

"You mean, it wasn't Indians?"

"Seen no moccasin tracks, boy. But I seen boot tracks a-plenty. Those who killed that man weren't Indians. They was white men."

We were eatin' supper when Pa said that, and it give me a chill. If it wasn't no Indian, then we were in trouble, 'cause a man can tell an Indian. He can spot him right off. But a bad white man? How you goin' to tell until he's bad?

I said as much. Pa, he just looked at me and said, "Boy, you see strangers around, you come tell me, you hear? But you see 'em first, an' when you do you get clean out of sight."

Wasn't much time for thinkin' about things, because we worked. Seemed like Pa felt he owed something to the dead man, because he worked a sight harder than I ever seen him before. It was work from can see to cain't see, for Pa an' me.

We measured out four sections of land . . . four square miles of it, field, forest, meadow, and stream.

We had seed corn and some vegetable seeds. We planted forty acres to corn, and of an acre we made a vegetable garden. One reason we taken that corner because there was berries in it.

But I never did forget that dead man.

The stranger, when he came was alone. He was one man riding.

He was a slim, tall man with a lean, dark face and high cheekbones. He wore a black store-bought suit and a bandanna tied over his head like in the old pirate pictures. He had polished black boots, almighty dusty, and a fine black horse with a white and pink nose.

He stopped afar off, and that was when I first seen him. He stood in his saddle and shaded his eyes at us, seeing me first and then Pa, who was working with a hoe in the cornfield.

"Pa?" I said, just loud enough.

"All right, boy. I seen him."

Pa had his rifle in a scabbard set next to a bush close by. I seen him start to usin' his hoe over thataway, but this man on the black horse came right along, an' when I looked again I seen he was leading a spare . . . a packhorse. I guess it had been hidden behind him before, and I'd missed seeing it.

He come on toward the house settin' easy in the saddle, and then I seen he carried a rifle in a scabbard, too. Close to his hand. From under his coat I could see the tip end of a holster.

Pa wasn't far from the house but he moved over to stand where his rifle was, and he waited there. The man rode up, and called out, "Is it all right to get a drink? We've come far and we're almighty thirsty."

Pa taken up his rifle and walked toward the house, leaving the hoe where the rifle had been. "He'p yourself," Pa said. "It's a dusty road you've traveled."

The man's features relaxed a little, almost like he was going to smile, only I thought he didn't smile very much, by the look of him. "Yes, it is. Most of my roads are dusty, it seems like." He glanced around. "Is this the Chantry place?"

"They call it that."

"Are you a Chantry?"

"No. I'm not. We found the place deserted. Found a dead man on the doorstep. We buried the man, and we moved in. Seemed too fine a place to lay idle."

Pa paused a moment, and then he said, "Even if the land weren't so good, I'd have hesitated to go on. That man Chantry, if he was the one built this place, had a feelin' for good work. I just couldn't bear to see it left run down."

The man looked at Pa a long minute. "I like that," he said, then, "I think Chantry would want you here."

He drank from our gourd dipper. The water was cold an' sweet. We both knew how welcome that kind of water was to a long-ridin' man.

Pa taken to him. I seen that right off. There was somethin' lonely and standoffish about that man, yet there was warmth in 'im, too. Like he had a lot of friendship in him that hadn't been used.

"Might's well stay the night," Pa said. "It's a fur piece to anywhere from here. Beyond, there's the wild country."

"Well," the man hesitated. "My horses could stand the rest. Thank you, and we will."

"You he'p him, boy," Pa said. "I'll start some bacon in the pan."

We went to the stable. I always liked that stable. In the hottest weather it was always shadowy and cool. The walls was thick, the roof was high, and there was a loft in one end for the hay we'd mow come autumn time. I like the smell of fresh-mowed hay, of horses and harness, saddles and such.

"You got some fine horses, mister," I said.

He nodded, putting a gentle hand on the black's shoulder. "Yes, I have. You can always put your trust in a good horse, son. Treat them right and they'll always stay by you."

We took the rig from his riding horse and then from the buckskin packhorse. It was a heavy load—lots of grub and a blanket roll. From the feel of the blanket roll I near 'bout decided he had another rifle or a shotgun hidden there. . . . One or t'other.

Then he commenced to work on his horses. He taken out a currycomb and he done a good job, first one, then the other.

"Been here long, son?"

"Got here early spring. We put in a crop soon as we cleaned up."

"Cleaned up? Was the place a mess?"

"Nossir. It was in mighty good shape, 'cept dusty and all. Course, it was tore up a mite inside by them men searchin'."

"Searching?"

"Them men that killed him. They tore things up like they was huntin' for somethin'." I paused, not sure how much I should say. "Pa don't think it was Indians."

"No?"

"That dead man . . . his clothes wasn't took, and his pockets was turned inside out. Pa says Indians would take his clothes . . . an' maybe burned the place."

"Your pa is right." He paused, his hands resting on the horse's back. "I like your pa, son. He seems like a right-thinking man. And I think he's correct. Chantry would have wanted a man like him on the place."

Then he taken his saddlebags and rifle, an' we walked to the house with the smell of wood smoke and bacon frying. He paused there on the stoop, and looked out an' around. You could see a far piece from the door, 'cross meadows and past stands of timber. It was a pretty view, and the man just stood there, lookin' at the rose color in the clouds where the sun was leaving a memory on the sky.

"Yes," he said, "this would be the place. This was what he would have wanted."

The floor inside was clean-swept and mopped. He glanced about, and I could see approval in his eyes. Pa saw it, too.

"I never had much," he said, "but I've got sense enough to know that a place doesn't stay nice without you keep it so. It takes a deal of work to build a place, and a deal of work to keep it up."

The food was good, and Pa always made a good cup of

coffee. I knew that from what folks said, for Pa never let me have coffee 'cept a couple times on mighty cold mornin's.

"Too bad about that dead man," the stranger suddenly said. "Anybody know who he was?"

"I ain't been to town but once't and never talked to nobody 'bout it more'n to just report I'd found a body and buried it. I guess nobody knew Chantry well, or much about his place.

"There ain't no sheriff. Just a marshal, and he pays no mind to nothin' outside the town. I 'spect the dead man was the Chantry the place was named for, but I got no way of knowin'. There wasn't nothin' in his pockets."

"Nothing inside the house either?"

"Only books. A lot of them books, thirty or forty. Never look at 'em m'self. I don't find much time for readin', nor the boy, either. Though he seems to have a leanin' toward it . . . like his ma. She was a reader."

Pa hesitated, then said quietly, "My wife's friends figured she married beneath her. That was one reason we come on west. Only she never made it. She died in Westport of the cholera."

"Was there anything else of his?"

"In that desk yonder. There's papers and things. They was scattered all over when we come in the place. Dust over the papers. Some blood."

Pa paused. "Y'know, mister, I never said this even to my son, but I b'lieve there was somebody here with Chantry. Somebody who either went away with whoever come and killed him. Or who was taken away or maybe left before his killer come."

The stranger looked at Pa. "You are an observing man."

Pa shrugged his thin shoulders and refilled the stranger's cup. "See that alcove yonder? With the bed in it? Well, there was another bed in t'other room, and that alcove had a curtain before it.

"The curtain was tore down when we come, but it ain't likely there'd be a curtain lest there was a woman in the house. I figger that woman either run away or was took away, and if she run away I figger she'd come back to bury her man."

"So the mystery deepens," the stranger smiled, showing even white teeth under his black mustache. "You've done some thinking."

"I have. There's a deal of time for it, with the work and all to keep a man's hands busy. But not his mind. It's by way of protection, too, for there's two ways to think if they were white men. Either they come to rob him of what he had, and robbed him, or they come lookin'. For something else.

"Now if they came lookin' for something else and didn't find it, they'll be comin' back." Pa glanced at me. "I think the boy's been thinkin' of that, and it worries him."

"It is a thing to consider," the stranger said. "I think your son is wise."

"It ain't only them," I burst out of a sudden. "It's *her*!"

"Her?" The stranger looked at me.

"That girl . . . that . . . woman! If she comes back, this place is hers. All Pa's work'll be for nothin'."

"If she returns," the stranger replied, "I think she would be pleased that her friend had been buried and the place cared for. I should believe she would be very grateful, indeed.

"I cannot presume to speak for her, but do you stay on without fear and, if she returns, you will find you have lost nothing and perhaps gained much."

"They didn't get her," I said then. "She got away."

Pa looked at me, surprised. The stranger stopped with his fork halfway to his mouth. Slowly, he lowered it. "How can you know that?"

"I seen tracks out back. They were old tracks, but a body could read 'em. Somebody came up, ridin' easy . . . cantering. Of a sudden that horse was pulled up awful sharp, his hoofs dug in an' he reared, then that horse turned in his own tracks and took off like lightnin' for the hills."

"Did you see any other tracks?"

"Yessir. They taken out after her. There was two, three of

'em . . . maybe four. But she had a good horse an' a good lead."

"They still might have caught her."

"They never done it. She got into them hills, and she knowed them hills like her own hands. She . . ."

"How d'you know that?" Pa said.

"The way she taken to them hills, no stoppin', no hesitatin' like. She rode right into them hills and she got to the little valley yonder an' when she got there she drove a bunch of cattle—"

"What cattle?" Pa said. "I ain't seen no cattle!"

"There's cattle," I insisted. "She drove 'em up and then she started 'em back the way they come, wiping out her trail. Then she went into soft sand where she wouldn't leave no tracks."

"Still, they might have found her."

"Nossir, they didn't. They followed her into them hills, but they lost her trail under the hoofs of them cattle, like she figured they would. They hunted a long time, then they come back."

"Are those tracks still there?"

"Nossir. There ain't no tracks of any kind. On'y rains before that was soft and gentle, not enough to wipe out good tracks."

"Doby," Pa never called me by name an awful lot, so he was almighty serious, "Doby, why didn't you ever tell me?"

I could feel my neck gettin' red. "Pa, you was so set on this place. You takin' to it like no other an' all. An' me, I liked it, too. I was afeared if you knowed you might pull out an' leave. You might just give up an' we'd be ridin' the wagon agin, goin' nowhere much. I want to stay, Pa. I want to stay right here. I want to see our work come to somethin', an' I want a place I know is home."

"Stay on," the stranger said. "I think I can safely say it will be all right."

"But how?" Pa asked. "How can anybody?"

"I can," the stranger said, "I can say it. My name is Chantry. The dead man you buried was my brother."

Well, we just looked at him. Pa was surprised, and maybe I was, too, a little. I'd had a funny feelin' all along, only mostly I was afraid he was one of *them*.

"Even so," Pa said, "what about his daughter? An' his wife or whoever she was? Don't she have first claim?"

"That's just it," Chantry said quietly, "my brother was a widower, with neither wife nor child. He was a lot older than me. If there was a woman, then I have no idea who she was or what she was doing here."

TWO

Pa cut himself a piece of work when he decided to farm that place, and it taken some doing for the two of us. And from time to time I headed for them hills, Pa liking fresh meat and there being no game close by 'cept an occasional deer in the meadow.

Come daybreak, it bein' Sunday, I taken Pa's old rifle and saddled up the dapple. Saying nothing to Pa or Chantry, I just taken off.

They were low, rolling hills that broke into sharp bluffs, kind of a bench, and then the high-up mountains lyin' behind 'em. So far, I'd never been so far as the mountains, but there they lay, a-waitin' for me. They knew and I knew that one day I'd ride those trails.

Right now I had me an idea, and huntin' meat was second to that. Because that girl or woman, or whichever she was, headed right into them hills like she knew where she was going, and neither me nor them other folks found her. Least, I didn't believe they had. For certain, they never found her that first day.

If she knew where she was goin', it stood to reason she'd rode the hills before, many times maybe, and if there was any kind of a hideout, she'd know where it was.

It wasn't worryin' me much who she was. She'd either been close by when the killin' took place, or she knew somethin' about it. She surely didn't waste any time askin' questions when the shootin' started.

By now any sign she left would be washed away, 'less she was still back yonder and had cut fresh sign for somebody to follow. Any way you looked at it, she was headin' for some place and I wanted to find out where. Whatever it was, or wherever she was, she figured she'd be safe when she got there. Or that's how it looked to me.

It was cool an' pleasant. My horse had a liking for far-flung trails as well as me, and he pointed for the hills like he already known where he was going. The grass was bound to be thick up yonder, and the water cold and fresh.

I never had but just the rifle. I'd always wanted me one of them pistols, but we never had the money for it. I had me a rifle and it was a good one too—a Henry. I also carried me a bowie a man could shave with, it was that sharp.

The dapple pointed us into a fold of the hills, climbed a little bit, and we topped out on a grass knoll with the wind stirring his mane and all the world spread out before and behind.

The ranch land lay spread behind me, but I wasn't looking back. I was sixteen year old, and somewhere in the mountains there was a girl. Now in all my sixteen years I never stood up right close to not more than three or four girls of her age, and ever' single time I was skeered. They just look like they knowed it all, and I didn't know nothin'.

That woman who rode off on that horse might be fourteen, forty, or ninety-three for all I knew, but in my mind's eye she was young, gold-haired, and pretty. She was every princess I'd ever heard stories about, and I was goin' to meet her.

For three, four years now I'd been rescuing beautiful girls from Indians, bears, and buffaloes. In my dreams. But it never got down to where I had to talk to 'em. I kind of fought shy of that, even in my dreams, for I had no notion what you said to a girl.

Settin' there lookin' at the mountains I kind of sized 'em up. Now mountains just ain't all that easy to ride through or cross over. There has to be ways, and if you give study to a situation you can surely come up with one of the ways.

Looked to me like I saw a faint trail goin' up through the grass along the slope of a certain hill, so I taken a chance and moved out and that dapple taken that trail and held to it.

I thought the trail seemed to peter out, but not for the dapple. He seen or smelled it, and just kept a-goin' and we dipped down off that slope across a meadow so green it hurt your eyes, and then across a rough and randy little mountain stream that boiled along over the rocks like it was going somewhere a-purpose, and then into the trees.

We skirted the aspens, and I seen an elk. It was a bull elk, maybe half-grown, and fat as a tick. That was meat for a coupla weeks plus jerked meat for winter, and my rifle came halfway up before I stopped it.

That shot would go echoing off up that canyon and warn anybody, friend or enemy, that I was on my way. Unhappy and feeling bad, I let that elk go. But it was too soon to shoot. I had a sight of country to see before I started telling ever'body I was there.

At the edge of the aspen stand, I drew up the dapple and sat and listened. The elk kinda moved off, paying me no mind. I let him walk away, then looked up at the great swell of the mountain. It was rounded green, with a battalion of aspens marching down the slope in a solid rank till it came to a halt. Like a troupe of soldiers. From there on, it was only grass with a few dips and hollers here and there with tufts of brush showing. That trail I was following, or one kin to it, made just a little thread across that slope.

Now trails in the mountains can be game trails, but you usually don't see them from afar unless a body is above 'em. Trails can also be Indian trails, or they can be where some prospector has staked him a claim . . . or maybe even built him a cabin.

Chantry had said his brother had no wife nor daughter. Who, then, could that mysterious girl or woman be?

She might be some woman Chantry taken up with. Or just somebody he'd met or found who needed help.

The dapple walked along easy-like. We dipped down into a draw, waded a branch, and had started up the opposite slope through the aspen when all of a sudden there were two men setting their horses right slam in front of me, barring the trail.

One of them was a stocky, barrel-chested man with a broad, hard face and tiny eyes. The other man was much like him, only a mite bigger.

"Where d'you think you're going?" the smaller one asked me.

"Huntin' meat," I said, kind of careless-like. "Figured I might scare up a elk."

"This here trail's closed, boy," the other man said. "We got us a claim back yonder. We wouldn't want to get hit by no stray bullets. So you just hunt down below or off to the other direction."

A grin broke his hard face like somebody had cracked a rock. "Why, somebody was to shoot up here we might take it wrong. We might just figure he was a-shootin' at us an' shoot back. You wouldn't like that, now would you, boy?"

He wasn't runnin' no bluff on me. I didn't cotton to him, nohow, and didn't believe he had a claim back yonder. "Nossir," I said, "I wouldn't like that. I wouldn't want nobody thinkin' I actually shot at 'im an' missed. Thing like that," I said, "can ruin a man's reputation."

Well, they just looked at me. They'd took me for some kid they could scare, not dry behind the ears, but I never was much of a one to scare.

Back yonder to home I'd heard a fussin' in the pigpen one night when Pa was gone, and I'd taken down his shotgun loaded with buckshot an' gone with a lantern to see what for. Well, I opened the door of the pigshed an' they was all backed into a corner with a full-growed cougar lookin' 'em straight in the eye. When that door opened he turned on me, ears back an' tail a-lashin'. Now nobody in his right mind corners a cougar, 'cause cornered they'll fight. But I wasn't of no mind to let that cougar make a bait of one of our pigs, so I ups with the shotgun and let him have a blast just as he leapt at me.

That cougar knocked me a-rollin', tail over teakettle back out the door, an' my head smacked up agin a rock and laid me out cold. But when Pa got home I had me a cougar skinned and the hide nailed up to dry out on the outside cabin wall.

"Look, kid," the bigger man said. "You're a mite sassy for a boy your size. Somebody'll take you off that horse an' give you a whuppin', if you don't watch out."

"Mebbe," I said. "But he'd be doin' it with a chunk of lead in his belly. An' if there was two of them, two chunks of lead.

"This here's a free country, wide open for all, and if you're worried about gettin' shot at, you just hightail it back to your claim, because I reckon I could see a claim and men workin' and I'd put no bullet near 'em . . . 'less they asked for it.

"I come up this mountain for meat, an' when I go back down, I'll have it." I had that Henry right across my saddle. Both men was pistol-armed and one of them had a rifle in his boot, but it was in the boot and them handguns was in their holsters. My Henry was lookin' right at them.

"You get your meat," the stocky one said again. "But make sure you stay shy of this mountainside or you'll get all the shootin' you want and then some."

They turned their horses then and went back up the trail, and soon as they were out of sight, I reined my dapple over and whisked through the trees, myself. No tellin' when they might try to circle around an' take a shot at me.

Followin' that trail that day didn't look like good business, so I angled off through the trees, just getting myself out of harm's way. I wasn't no way eager for a shootin' over anything like that, but I didn't figure to back up, neither. So I worked my way up a slope, turned north and then west with the lay of the land and the trees, and suddenly I come out atop a mesa, riding down amongst some all-fired big ponderosas, scattered spruce and aspen. Coming down through some big old trees I come upon a cabin.

It set on a slab of solid rock with a big wide view of the whole country spread out in front. A body could see the Sleeping Ute, the great juttin' prow of Mesa Verde, and way afar off, the Abajo and La Sal mountains of Utah. Some trees growin' on the edge of the cliff kind of screened the cabin off, but a man with a good glass could of picked up ridin' men some distance away.

The builder had cut grooves in the solid rock and put in fitted squared-off timbers that were nigh two-foot through. They'd been fitted like they'd growed that way, and the roof was strongly built and solid.

I knocked on the door, expectin' no answer, and none came. So I lifted the latch and stepped in.

I got a surprise.

The place was empty. But the floor was swept clean, the hearth dusted, and everything spic an' span. There was a faint smell in the room that wasn't the smell of a closed-up place. It was a fresh, woodsy smell. And then I seen on a shelf behind me a pot with flowers in it and some sprigs of juniper.

The flowers wasn't two days old, and when I looked in the pot there was water for 'em.

There was no bedding. There were no clothes hung on the pegs along the wall, and no dishes for cookin' 'cept for a coffeepot.

Outside, there was a bench by the door, and the grass below it looked like somebody had been settin' there, time to time. That somebody could see our ranch right easy. It was miles away but the air was mountain clear, and you could see the ranch plain as day.

By now I was three miles or more from where I'd come up against the two trouble-hunters, and I'd followed no trail to get here. Yet I knew there must be a trail. Maybe more than one.

I scouted around the place, around the clearing. Now nobody ever said I couldn't read sign, and by the time I'd finished and set down on that bench I knowed a thing or two.

It was a girl or woman who come here, and she didn't come often, but when she did she set awhile. I found no tracks but hers . . . not even horse tracks.

She must have come by horse. She'd likely left it back in the brush somewheres. This was a deserted, lonely place, and it looked to me like the girl who come here liked to be alone.

Was it the selfsame girl who'd been to Chantry's place? I had me a feelin' it was. From here she could see the Chantry place clear.

Maybe, when she came here, she watched and got curious to see who was living on the Chantry place.

Maybe.

Whoever built this cabin had known what he was doin', anyway. The land sloped gently away in front of the cabin for a hundred yards, and where the grass ended against the trees there were some tall old pines that make it unlikely anybody could see the cabin from way down below, even with powerful glasses.

There was water. And beyond the pines the mountain fell clean away down through timber where no horse could go, nor a man climb up without a good struggle. Behind, there was forest that swelled up into the mountain. A trail could lead off somewhere right or left of that swell.

Suddenly I had me a idea. That woman had cleared up this place and left flowers. She liked the place and she liked it neat. I figgered to let her know somebody was about who liked what she had done. Who liked what she liked.

Under one eave of the house I found a small Indian pot. I taken it, rinsed it good, and half-filled it with water. Then I went down the slope and picked some flowers and put them in the water. This I left on the table where she'd be sure to see it.

Then I scouted for a trail to go back down and found one. It was a faint trail, but it had seen some use, time to time. First off, I looked for sign. Whatever there was seemed to be maybe a week old. I followed along, studying tracks. It was a horse that weighed no more than eight hundred pound, but with a nice, even pace. And the woman who rode that horse was small, 'cause I saw the hoof tracks when the horse was unmounted and after, and her weight didn't make hardly a single bit of difference.

Now I knew that trail led somewhere, and I had me a idea it led right to where those two men had come from, who braced me on the trail. So once I spotted the direction the trail taken, I moved into the timber and hightailed it for the Chantry place. To home.

Pa was out near the barn and he looked up when I come in. "First time you ever come home without meat, boy. What's the matter? Didn't you see nothin'?"

"Never got a good shot," I said. "Next time it'll be different."

"We got to have meat, son. I'll take a walk down the meadow, come sundown. Sometimes there's a deer feedin' down thataway."

Chantry come out on the steps. He threw me a quick, hard look. He'd dusted off his black suit and polished his boots with a rag. He stood there on the steps, looking toward the mountains while I filled a bucket of water for the house. We all kept busy for a while, even Chantry, with his thoughts.

It was coming up to sundown now, and when Pa took his rifle and started off, Chantry just stood there watching him go. "He's a good man, your father is," he said. "A real good man."

"Yessir. We've had us some hard luck."

"This is rough country," Chantry replied. "I like what he's doing here."

"He just plain fell in love with the place. . . . All the work that somebody else had done. He couldn't just go off an' leave it be."

"I know." Chantry looked at me again. "Now, boy, tell me what you saw today."

"What I saw? I . . . ." Well, I started to lie, but he was looking right straight into my eyes and smiling a little, and suddenly I didn't want to lie to him. So I told him the whole business from the start. Leaving out the flowers.

"You think she and those men came from the same outfit?"

"There ain't too many outfits around I know of. I think

maybe it's the same outfit. She bein' a woman. . . . Maybe she's got different feelings."

"That might be the reason. And sometimes an honest person gets roped into a setup they don't rightly know how to get clear of. What about that cabin? Anything strike you odd about it?"

"Yessir. I believe it was built by the same man who built this. The same kind of work. . . . Only that place up there is older. I think maybe he lived up there first and kept lookin' down on this flat country and decided to come down here and settle."

"Might be right. Or maybe he just wanted two homes. One up high, one down below." He looked at me again. "What's your name, boy?"

"Doban Kernohan. They call me Doby."

"Irish. . . . Well, we come of the same stock, Doby. I'm Irish, too. . . . Mostly Irish. My family left the old country a long time ago, and an ancestor of mine went to Newfoundland, then to the Gaspé Peninsula. From there to here, it's a long story."

"You got a first name, mister?"

"Owen. A name that is sometimes Irish, and sometimes Welsh, they tell me. Well, there's been a sight of changing of names, Doby, especially among the Irish.

"There was a time long ago when Irishmen were ordered by law to take an English name, and around about fourteen sixty-five, a time later, all those in four counties were to take the name of a town, a color, or a skill. Such as Sutton, Chester, Cork, or Kinsale for the town. Or the colors—any one they'd happen to choose. Or a trade, such as carpenter, smith, cook, or butler, to name just a few.

"And some of the Irish changed their names because there was a move against us. Many in my family were killed, and when my great-grandfather escaped to England he was advised never to tell his true name, but to take another . . . or he'd be hunted down. So he took the name Chantry, although how he came by it I do not know, unless he happened to see and like the name, invented it, or took it from

some man he admired. In any event, the name has served us
well, and we, I trust, have brought it no dishonor."

"I know little Irish history," I said.

"That's likely, Doby, but the thing to remember is that
this is your country now. It's well to know about the land
from which you came. There's pride in a heritage, but it's
here you live. This is the land that gives you bread.

"Yet it's a good thing to know the ways of the old countries,
too, and there's no shame in remembering. There's some as
would have it a disgrace to be Irish. . . . You'll find places in
eastern cities where they'll hire no man with an Irish look or
an Irish name. A good many of those who come here are
poor when they land, and nobody knows what lays behind
them.

"Some are from families among the noblest on earth, and
there's many another who's put a 'Mac' or an 'O' to his name
to which he's not entitled. But a man is what he makes
himself, no matter what the blood or barony that lays behind
him."

"What was your family name, Mr. Chantry, sir?"

"We'll not be talking of that, Doby. Three hundred years
gone by and every child of the family has known the name.
But not one has spoken it aloud. And so we shall not. Chantry
is the name we've taken, and Chantry is the name we'll
keep."

"Did you come here to claim your brother's ranch? Pa says
it's yours by right."

"No, lad, I came not for that. There was another thought
in my mind, though t'was my brother I wished to see. The
ranch will be your Pa's and after him yours—but only to
keep, and not to sell. I'll make a deed that way. . . . But I'll
want living quarters here when I pass by, and I think I'll
claim the cabin up there the mountains are holding for me."

Something in my face drew his notice, for I was right
worried, thinking of the girl. "What is it, boy? What's troubling you?" he asked.

"It's just the girl . . . the woman, sir. I believe she likes
the mountain place. I believe she goes there to be alone.
She left some flowers there . . ." I said.

"If she loves the place she can come when she wills, but give it up, I'll not." Owen tapped his breast pocket. "I've a deed here to all the land you've claimed and more. Even the slope of the mountain is mine, and a bit beyond it, here and there.

"Four sections your father has claimed, and those four sections he can have. There's thirty more I'll keep for myself, for I've a love for this western land, and here I may stop one day after I've done some things that need doing."

It was the most I'd heard him talk, and the most he did talk for many another day.

At daybreak my eyes opened to hear the echo of a rifle, and I came bolt upright and scared. Pa was puttin' on his pants and reaching for his gun.

But we couldn't see aught. Only that Chantry was gone and his horse was gone, too. But an hour later when he came in he had some nice cuts of venison wrapped in its own hide.

"Here's some meat," he said. "I'll not be a drone, Kernohan."

Chantry did his share of the woodcuttin' too, and he was a better than fair hand with an ax, cuttin' clean and sure and wasting no effort. Yet he stayed close to the house, spending most of his time on the porch with his glass in his hand to study the rise of the mountains.

Once I asked if I could look through it. "Yes," he said, "but handle it gentle. There's not its like in the world, I'm thinking. It was made some time ago by a man in a country far from here. He was the greatest master of his craft, and the lenses of this scope he ground himself."

It was astonishing the way the mountains leaped up at you. Far away as we were, you could almost reach out and touch the trees. I could even make out the cabin behind its trees, the bench at the door.

Was it that he was watching? I felt a pang of jealousy, then. Was he watching for her?

THREE

It was lonely country. When Chantry come along he brought some news. We'd heard nothing of what went on. Here and there a prospector worked in the hills, but they were shy of Indians and so kept out of sight, just comin' and goin' on the run.

South of us, in New Mexico, folks had told us there wasn't no white men at all, that those who come before us had just gone on through or left their hair in some Indian's wickiup.

Some had come, all right, as we had, but they'd not stayed and there was no record of their comings and goings. Pa found a rusted Patterson Colt once, down on a wash to the south of us. An' a couple of bones an' a few metal buttons, all that was left to show for somebody who tried to move into that country.

But there was Indians a-plenty, though a body saw mighty few of 'em. There were Utes to the north and around us, Navajos to the west and south, and Apaches east. Some friendly, some almighty mean and evil. Some just plain standoffish, wantin' to stay to themselves and not be bothered. Well, we didn't aim to bother them none.

"I never give 'em much thought," Pa said. "No more'n I would a white stranger. They're folks. They got their ways, we got ours. If we cross, we'll talk it over or fight, whichever way they want it to be."

Chantry agreed. "You can't talk about all Indians the same way, boy. Any time a man comes along and says 'Indians' or 'Mexicans' or 'Englishmen' he's bound to be wrong. Each man is a person unto himself, and you'll find good, bad, and indifferent wherever you go."

Didn't seem to me that Owen Chantry was taking any chances, though. When he put his pants on in the morning he also put on his gun belt and his gun. Most men put their hat on first. He put on that gun belt 'fore he drew on his boots.

"You figurin' on trouble?" I asked him once.

He threw me a hard look. "Boy," he said, "when a man comes at me shooting I figure he wants a fight. I surely wouldn't want him to go away disappointed.

"I don't want trouble or expect trouble, but I don't want to be found dead because I was optimistic. I'll wear the gun, use my own good judgment, be careful of what I say, and perhaps there won't be trouble."

He still didn't tell us why he'd come to start with, and it was a question you didn't ask. He was more than welcome. In them days you could ride a hundred miles in any direction and not see a soul.

Once Chantry got started he was a natural-born storyteller. Of a nighttime, when the fire burned down on the hearth and the shadows made witches on the walls. He'd been a sight of places and he'd read the stories of ancient times, the old stories of Ireland, of the sea and some folks called the Trojans who lived somewheres beyond the mountains and did a lot of fighting with the Greeks over a woman. And stories of Richard the Lion-Hearted, who was a great fighter but a poor king.

An' stories of Jean Ango, whose ships had been to America before Columbus. And of Ben Jonson, a poet, who could lift a cask of canary wine over his head and drink from the bunghole. He told of Gessar Khan, stories that happened in the black tents of nomads in haunted deserts on the flanks of a land called Tibet.

An' so our world became a bigger place. He had him a way with words, did Owen Chantry, but he was a hard man, and dangerous.

We found that out on the cold, still morning when the strangers come down the hills.

I'd gone to put hay down the chutes to the mangers for the stock, an' I was in the loft with a hayfork when they come.

Pa was in the yard, puttin' a harness on the mules for the plowing.

They come ridin' up the trail, five rough men ridin' in one tight bunch, astride better horses than we could afford, and carryin' their guns.

They drew up at the gate. And one of the men outs with his rope, tosses a noose over the gatepost, and starts to pull it down.

"Hey!" Pa yelled. "What d'you think you're doin'? Leave that be!"

"We're tearin' it down so you'll have less to leave behind. When you go." The speaker was a big brawny man with a gray hat.

"We're not goin' nowhere," Pa said quietly. He dropped the harness where he stood and faced them. "We come to stay."

The two men I'd met on the trail were in the bunch, but my rifle was inside the house. Pa's was too.

We might just as well have had no weapons for the good they could do us now.

"You're goin'," the brawny man said. "You're ridin' out of here before sundown, and we'll burn this here place so nobody else will come back."

"Burn it? This fine house, built by a man with skill? You'd burn it?"

"We'll burn any house and you in it if you don't leave. We didn't invite you here."

"This here is open land," Pa said. "I'm only the first. There'll be many more along this way 'for long."

"There'll be nobody. Now I'm through talkin'. I want you out of here." He looked around. "Where's that loud-mouthed boy of yours? One of my men wants to give him a whippin'."

I'd dropped from the loft and stood just inside the barn. "I'm here, and your man ain't goin' to give me any kind of a whippin' . . . not if it's a fair fight."

"It'll be a fair fight."

The words come from the steps, and we all looked. Owen Chantry stood there in his black pants, his polished boots, a white shirt, and a black string tie.

"Who in hell are you?" The brawny man was angry some, but not too worried.

"The name is Owen Chantry," he replied quietly.

The stocky man I'd met on the trail got down from his horse and come forward. He stood there, a-waiting the outcome.

"Means nothing to me," the brawny man said.

"It will," Chantry said. "Now take your rope off that post."

"Like hell I will!" It was the man with the rope who shouted at him.

In the year of 1866, the fast draw was an unheard of thing out west of the Rockies. In Texas (so Chantry told me later), Cullen Baker and Bill Longley had been usin' it, but that was about the extent of it 'til that moment.

Nobody saw him move, but we all heard the gun. And we seen that man with the rope drop it like something burned him, and something had.

The rope lay on the ground and that man was shy two fingers.

I don't know whether Chantry aimed for two fingers, one finger, or his whole hand, but two fingers was what he got.

Then Owen Chantry come one foot down the steps and then the other. He stood there, his polished boots a-shinin' and that gun in his hand. First time I'd ever seen that gun out'n the scabbard.

"The name," he said, "is Owen Chantry. My brother lived

on this place. He was killed. These folks are living here now, and they're going to stay.

"I, too, am going to stay, and if you have among you the men who killed my brother, your only chance to live is to hang them. You have two weeks in which to find and hang those men. . . . Two weeks."

"You're slick with that gun," the brawny man said, "but we'll be back."

Owen Chantry come down another step, and then another. A stir of wind caught the hair on his brow and ruffled it a mite and flattened the fine material of his white shirt against the muscles of his arms and shoulders.

"Why come back, Mr. Fenelon?" Chantry said pleasantly. "You're here now."

"You know my name?"

"Of course. And a good deal more about you, none of it good. You may have run away from your sins, Mr. Fenelon, but you can't escape the memory of them. . . . Others have the same memories."

Chantry walked out a step toward him, still with that gun in his hand. "You're here already, Mr. Fenelon. Would you like to choose your weapon?"

"I can wait," Fenelon said. He was staring at Chantry, hard-eyed, but wary. He didn't like nothin' he saw.

"And you?" Chantry looked at the stocky man who was settin' to whip me. "Can you wait too?"

"No, by the Lord, I can't! I come to slap some sense into that young'un, and I aim to do it!"

Chantry never moved his eyes from them. "Doby, do you want to take care of this chore right now, or would you rather wait?"

"I'll take him right now," I said, and I walked out there and he come for me, low an' hard.

My Pa come from the old country as a boy and settled in Boston, where there was a lot of Irish and some good fightin' men amongst 'em. He learned fightin' there, and when I was growing up he taught me a thing or two. Pa was no great fightin' man, but he was a good teacher. He taught me something about fighting and something about Cornish-style wrestling. There were a lot of Cousin Jacks in the mines, then as ever, and Pa was quick to see and learn. But he was a teacher, not a fighter.

Me, I started scrappin' the minute they took off my diapers. Most of us did, them days.

Here I was sixteen, with plenty of years already spent on an ax handle, a plow, and a pick and shovel. So when he come at me, low and hard like that, I just braced myself, dropped both hands to the back of his head, and shoved down hard with them.

I was thoughtful to jerk my knee up hard at the same time.

There's something about them two motions together that's right bad for the complexion and the shape of a nose.

He staggered back, almost went down on his knees, and then come up. And when he did his nose was a bloody smear. He had grit, I'll give him that. He come for me again and I fetched him a swing and my fist clobbered him right on the smashed-up nose.

He come in, flailing away at me with both fists, and he could hit almighty hard. He slammed me first with one fist and then with the other, but I stood in there and taken 'em and clobbered him again, this time in the belly.

He stood flatfooted then, fightin' for wind, so I just sort of set myself and swung a couple from the hip. One of them missed as he pulled back, but the other taken him on his ear and his hands come up so I belted him again in the belly.

He taken a step back and my next swing turned him halfway round and he went down to his knees.

"That's enough, Doby," Chantry said. "Let him go."

So I stepped back, but watchin' him. Fact is, I was scared. I might have got my ears pinned back, tacklin' him that-away. . . . Only he made me mad, there by the road.

"Now, gentlemen," Chantry said, "I believe you understand the situation. We are not looking for trouble here. These good people only wish to live, to work the ranch, to live quietly.

"As for myself, I've told you what I expect. I know either

you or someone you know killed my brother. I'll leave it to you. Hang them, or I shall hang you. . . . One by one.

"Now you may go. Quietly, if you please."

And they rode away, the stocky one lagging behind, dabbing at his nose and mouth with a sleeve. First one, then the other.

Pa looked at me in astonishment. "Doby, I didn't know you could fight like that!"

I looked back at him, kind of embarrassed. "I didn't either, Pa. He just gimme it to do."

Suppertime, watching the clouds hanging around the highup mountains, I thought of that girl and wondered what she was to them and would anything happen when they rode home.

"You don't really b'lieve they'll hang their own men, do you?" Pa asked.

"Not right away," Chantry said quietly. "Not right away."

We looked at him, but if he knew it he gave no sign, and I wondered just how much he believed what he said.

"You'd really hang 'em?" Pa asked him then.

Owen Chantry didn't reply for a minute, and when he did he spoke low. "This is new country, and there are few white men here. If there is to be civilization, if people are to live and make their homes here, there must be law.

"People often think of the law as restrictions, but it needn't be, unless it's carried to extremes. Laws can give us freedom, because they offer security from the cruel, the brutal, and the thieves of property.

"In every community—even in the wildest gangs and bands of outlaws—there is some kind of law, if only the fear of the leader. There has to be law, or there can be no growth, no security.

"Here there is no established law yet. We have no marshal, no sheriff, no judge. And until such things exist, the evil must be restrained. A man has been murdered, you have been warned to leave.

"This country needs men like you. You may not think of yourselves as such, but you are the forerunners of a civilization. Where you are, others will come."

"And how about you, Mr. Chantry?" I asked.

He smiled, with genuine warmth. "Doby, you've asked the key question. How about me? I am a man who's good with a gun. I'll be needed until there are enough people, and when there are enough, I shall be outmoded.

"I do not recall any other time in history when men like me existed. Usually it was a baron or a chief who brought peace to an area, but in this country it is often just a man with a gun."

"I don't put no stock in guns," Pa said suddenly. "I figger there should be a better way."

"So do I," Chantry replied. "But had there been no gun today, your son would have been beaten by not just one man but several. Your fence pulled down, your house burned.

"Civilization is a recent thing, sir. With many, it's still no more than skin deep. If you live in a busy community, you must live with the knowledge that maybe two out of every ten people are only wearing the outer skin of civilization. And if there was no law, or if there was not the restraint of public opinion, they would be utterly savage. . . . Even some people you might know well.

"Many men and women now act with restraint because they know it is the right thing to do. They know that if we are to live together we must respect the rights of those around us. Our friends in the mountains do not feel that way. They've come to this remote place because they wish to be free of restraint, to be as cruel, as harsh, as brutal as they wish."

"You talk like a schoolteacher, Mr. Chantry," I said.

He glanced at me. "I wish I was a schoolteacher. It is the most honorable profession, done well." He smiled at me. "Maybe, in a sense, that's what I am."

"You say when there're enough people you won't be needed anymore," I said boldly. "How long're you givin' yourself?"

"Ten years. Maybe twenty. Surely not more than thirty. Men become civilized by degrees. By adapting, compromising."

"A man like you, with your education, I reckon you could do anything," Pa said.

Chantry's smile was grim. "No," he said. "I've had a fine education, good opportunities, but I was trained for nothing. . . . To be a gentleman, to oversee land, to direct the work of others. To do all that one must have a business, or money to employ. . . . I have nothing.

"I have read . . . and riding long distances alone has given me time to think."

"What about that woman up yonder?" Pa asked.

"She's to be considered. Most definitely, she's to be considered."

Somethin' in the way he said it made me uneasy. I liked him . . . figured he was quite some man, but he worried me, and he knew it. Suddenly I knew. That was his trouble. He *knew* the kind of man he was. Whatever he done, one part of him stood off and watched.

He walked outside to the steps and lit one of them slim cigars he smoked. He stood there, away from the light, and after helping Pa with the dishes, I followed him.

"Have you seen her, Doby? I mean that girl up there? Have you seen her?"

"No. I ain't."

He was silent awhile. His cigar glowed in the dark. At last he said, "I'm going up there, Doby. Can you tell me how to get to that cabin?"

Then I was silent. There was a resentment in me. I had found that cabin my own self. What did he want to go there for? What was the woman to him?

"Don't know's I could," I said. "It ain't easy."

"Is it that you cannot . . . or will not?"

"Mr. Chantry, that there cabin is where she comes to be *alone*. She's got a right . . . once in a while. I figure maybe she needs to have her a place, and I don't want—"

"Doby," he was patient. I could sense his patience. And his irritation, too. "That cabin is mine. I plan to live there, to return there from wherever I go. I, too, need a place to be alone.

"I am not," he paused just for a moment, "going to interfere with her solitude. There are other places in the forest and mountains where she can be. But I must go there. I have business there. . . . And perhaps I wish to see her."

"You'll get her in trouble, Mr. Chantry."

"Doby," his patience was wearing thin. "You don't even know that girl . . . or woman. You don't even know who she is or what. You're making a thing out of this that it should not be."

"I just don't like it," I said stubbornly. "She even swept up. She dusted. She had everything to rights. She put out flowers. She loves the place like it is. . . ."

"All that may be true," Chantry said quietly. "But it's my place, and I must go there."

A thought came to me at a sudden, a chance to get the better of him. "How about your brother? Maybe he give her the right to go there. Maybe he even *give* the place to her."

It was a point, and he saw it. "Not that place, Doby," he said then. "Some other place, maybe, but not that one."

"What's so different about it?" I demanded.

"It's a whole lot different." His voice was harsh. "Don't mix into things you don't understand, boy. Just remember this: that cabin is mine, and there's a lot more to it than you know."

Well . . . maybe. All of a sudden, I didn't like him nearly so much.

Yet, a man had to be fair. What he said was straight-enough talk. This here ranch was his, and he was lettin' us have it. He couldn't be more decent than that. When he could have told us to load up an' git.

He done no such thing. Plus he'd stood by us in trouble.

But still it rankled.

Fair was fair. And it come to me that all I was sore over was because he was buttin' into my dream. I'd been dreamin' of a girl up there at that cabin, a girl who was *mine* somehow. When I'd never even seen her, didn't even know if she *was* a girl, an' not some growed-up grandma of a woman.

Maybe it was because I was kind of short on dreams and short of girls to think on. A body needs somethin' to build a dream with. Which was why, when I come to consider it, I'd not been too anxious to meet up with that girl. . . . Because once I seen her, and her me, the dream might be gone forever.

She might figger I was no account, or she might be nothing a man could be proud of herself. Just because a woman sweeps the floor and puts flowers in a pot don't make her a princess. Nor even a girl to walk with. . . .

She might be old and fat. She might be a married lady with babies. She might be anything.

The trouble was that all my thinkin' wouldn't shake loose my dream, of her being young and gold and beautiful.

She *had* to be. She just had to be.

FOUR

Come daylight, Owen Chantry saddled up and rode away. I watched him take a trail that went to the hills, and then I headed for the dapple.

"Doby!" Pa's tone wasn't gentle like usual. "Where d'you think you're goin'?"

"To the hills," I said. "I want to see what he's doin' up there. What he's goin' to do."

"You stay right where you are. There's work to do, boy, if we spec to make a crop and get wood laid by for winter. We ain't got no time to go gallivantin' over the mountains."

"Pa, I—"

"You leave him be. He's lettin' us have this outfit, ain't he? He stood by us, didn't he? Whose business is it what he does?"

Well, there was that girl. Only Pa wouldn't understand about her.

"Boy, don't you get no notions now. That there's a good man, but he's a hard man, too. He'll take no nonsense from nobody. If that cabin up there is all he wants, 'tis little enough."

Pa was right. Yet I didn't want him goin' up there. He'd change things. Maybe she wouldn't come there anymore. Then how would I ever find her?

But all the time I knew I was playin' the fool. Knowin' nothin' about her, and her not knowin' me. And who was I? Just a green country boy who knowed nothin' but horses and cattle. Scarce sixteen year old. How could any such girl be interested in me?

I thought no such thing, only I *wanted* to think it. And most of all I didn't want him to spoil it for me. So I went to work like Pa said and dug postholes and trimmed poles for the fence. But every now and then I'd stop and look to the mountains and wish I was up there under them aspen, ridin' the green trails like him.

Owen Chantry rode his black horse into the canyon below the hogback. He had ridden in a wide half circle since leaving the ranch, scouting the country with care, and taking his time.

It was all strange country, and the approach he was making gave him a better opportunity to locate the actual position of the cabin. Doby Kernohan had come upon it by accident and from another direction, and Doby's grasp of its actual situation had been less than accurate . . . or perhaps Doby hadn't wished to explain too well.

Chantry frowned thoughtfully. What was it that bothered Doby? Could it be the girl herself? But Doby hadn't even seen her, knew nothing about her. . . .

His brother had built the cabin on the rampart. That he knew.

Chantry's left hand held the reins. His right was never far from his gun. Nothing in his years had left him trusting of men or human situations. He never lay down at night without a built-in readiness to rise suddenly to action. He never sat down to a meal with the certain feeling that he would finish.

He rode forward slowly. Kernohan had known nothing of

the men who had tried to drive him out, nor of their connection with the girl. A lawless outfit, doubtless.

On his right the towering mass of the rampart reared up, walls of rock almost sheer, but broken and rough enough so a skillful man might climb, if need be. It was crowned with a forest of trees. . . . Pine or spruce, he couldn't make them out at that distance. It lay like a big long loaf, thrust out from the mass of the mountains behind it.

He studied the mountains before him. He must work a little more to the east, for the mesa seemed thus easy of access, and the faint trail he followed led that way.

A deer walked into the trail before him, unawares. It stepped slowly along, then suddenly caught a glimpse of him, ducked into the trees, and was gone. Overhead the sky was impossibly blue, with puffballs of white cloud. Toward afternoon they would bunch together, turn gray, and rain would fall. Every afternoon the rains came, never lasting for long. Sometimes the showers were intermittent.

There were no tracks in the trail he followed except the tracks of deer. This trail was possibly unknown. Yet Chantry was cautious. It never paid to underrate an enemy, to assume they knew less than they did.

Were they southern renegades, come west after the war? Some of the old Quantrill or Bloody Bill Andersen crowd?

He drew up in the dappled shadow of a clump of aspens and studied the trail ahead of him, watching the trees, the ground, the birds . . . listening.

Did they know of the cabin on the rampart? Possibly only the girl did, if she came there to be alone, as Doby believed. Doby had seen no other tracks, no other signs.

He slid his Henry from its scabbard and rode forward along the trail.

It was very still. He turned off the trail and went into the trees. When he had gone a short distance, he paused again. Through a break in the trees he could see all the land to the west, a magnificent sweep of country with the vast bulk of the Sleeping Ute topping the horizon.

He was high up, with a sheer drop of two hundred feet or so a few rods away, with trees all the way to the edge. This was the vast rampart visible from the ranch. He must be close to the cabin.

He stepped down from the black and stood listening. Far off he saw several elks come from the brush to feed. There was much ponderosa here. He walked slowly forward, crossing a wide area of bare rock swept by runoff water. He saw several old stumps from trees cut down long ago, no doubt to build the cabin he was looking for.

Suddenly he saw it, partially screened by ponderosa and spruce. He knew it had been built by his brother, who understood the use of broadax and adz, of squared logs. He liked its solid look, yet he was puzzled by the chimney, which might have belonged to a still older structure. But like the cabin, it was set deep into the native stone.

Owen Chantry, in a lifetime of drifting, had looked upon many constructions with a critical eye, and this one presented some interesting aspects. At first glance it was but another log house, yet it gave evidence of care in its framing and fitting, and the choice of its site. Concealed, it nonetheless offered a magnificent view to the west, with almost equally fine views to the south and north. To the east the view was cut off by trees and beyond them the vast bulk of the La Platas, with their bare peaks, slide-rock slopes and forested flanks.

Chantry could detect no movement near the cabin. Tying his mount under the trees and out of sight, he took his rifle and crossed the sparse grass to the doorway. The latch-string was out.

Lifting it, he opened the door. Inside all was empty and still, yet freshly swept and dusted. There were two pots of flowers. The hearth was cold, the ashes long dead.

He walked back to the open door and looked westward through the trees. Screened from view, the cabin was nevertheless a perfect observation point for all that moved in the valley below—and the vast spread of land that reached out in all directions.

The air was cool with the scent of spruce. A pleasant place, certainly, and a place in which to be alone. Owen Chantry leaned against the doorpost.

The mountains showed blue with distance. Farther to the north, somewhat fainter, lay the La Sals. . . . Wild country, almost unknown country from here to there. And farther on lay a maze of canyons. Father Escalante had come through, and Rivera had explored some of it a hundred years ago. Seeking a route only, they probably had seen little of the country.

He looked around him again. For the first time in thirty years, he felt at home.

The winters would be cold, for the altitude was high. A man must lay in a good supply of food to last out such a winter, and he must have reserves within himself on which to draw.

He went inside the cabin. It was as trim indoors as out.

Thoughtfully, he examined the walls, the logs solid and fitted one to the other without crack or crevice. No chinking here, for the logs had been faced with an adz until each lay cheek to cheek against the other. . . . A wall two feet thick or more, and a handsome stone-flagged floor.

There was a ceiling and hence at the back, at least, a small loft. The hewn planks of the ceiling lay from beam to beam, fitted tightly. There seemed to be no—

He distinctly heard the sound. . . . A horse walking, a horse that came slowly forward, then paused . . . just outside.

Owen Chantry turned swiftly, rifle in hand.

FIVE

The horse stopped, blew slightly, and a saddle creaked. Owen Chantry stepped into the doorway.

The girl was facing him, wide-eyed. For a moment they stared at each other.

"You're more beautiful than I expected," he said.

"Who are you?"

"You cannot guess? You knew my brother, I think, and he was not unlike me."

"You are Owen Chantry, then? Yes, I see his face in yours. I knew Clive. He was a good man. A silent, mysterious man, but good. Too good a man for what happened to him."

"That needs to be talked about," Chantry said quietly. "I noticed a coffeepot inside, but no coffee. Did you bring some? I notice you have a lunch."

Her eyes searched his face. He was tall, leaner than she had seen at first, but wide-shouldered. There was a deceptive stillness in his face, deceptive because she already knew much of this man.

A strange, morose man, Clive had said. Too good with a gun at too early an age. In the War Between the States, Owen had at first been a wild and reckless leader in the cavalry, a man whom the war had changed. The war, and other things.

She took the pack from the horse and walked past him into the cabin. She turned. "Will you build a fire? I think there's enough here for two, if we eat lightly."

"Eating lightly has become a way of life for me," he said wryly. "Yet there have been good times."

He went out to the edge of the woods and broke the small dry twigs off the lower trunks of several trees, the little branches that start to grow, then die. From a fallen tree he peeled bark, and then he walked back into the house.

There he knelt, crushing the dry bark in his hand, placing it on the old ashes, and then the twigs. When he had the fire going, he added the larger branches. There was a good stock of dry wood in the house, and more alongside, most of it old now, and rotting.

"You know they intend to kill you?" she asked.

"I have that impression," he said. "I met some of them but they didn't seem disposed to attempt a killing then."

"Strawn wasn't with them . . . nor Freka."

He looked around at her. "Tom Freka? And Jake Strawn?"

"Yes."

"Well, well. That, of course, changes the situation somewhat."

"You know them then?"

"We've never met, if that's what you mean. But I know them by reputation. Yes, I know them. I'd say the company you choose is not always the best."

"No? Perhaps I didn't choose them. Perhaps I was put into a situation I never wanted."

Chantry chuckled softly. "That happens to many of us. I guess the true worth of a man or woman is just how far they can rise above it." And then he added, the smile disappearing. "And I haven't risen far."

She turned and stared at him. "Do you know the whole story?"

He shrugged. "Who does? I think I know most of it. I never believed it all." He smiled wryly. "One hears so many stories. . . . Lost mines, treasures buried by outlaws. . . . The country is full of such stories, most of them pure nonsense. Most people who have gold do not bury it. Clive had no interest in gold, I think. But he had a scholar's ways, which took him to Mexico to start with. Were you close to him?"

"No, not close. He didn't confide in me." The smell of coffee reached them.

Chantry leaned back and looked out through the open door at the way the sunlight fell through the aspen leaves. "Nor me either," he said. "After he got back from Mexico, he was a silent man."

She turned around to him. "Yes, he was," she said. "And also a gentle man."

"Mac Mowatt has surmised . . . as others must have . . . that a treasure of gold was buried here, or somewhere about it. . . . But that is purely their speculation. Nothing of the kind is certain."

He smiled again, and the girl was amazed at the way his face became warm and bright. He was a man, she knew suddenly, who rarely smiled.

"Value is a matter of personal attitude," he said. "What is very valuable to one man may be utterly useless to another. Your outfit thinks it must be gems or gold."

"You don't?"

"Look," he said quietly, "none of us can know for sure. My brother was a man of letters, an explorer, a scholar, a man of inquisitive mind. To him, the most valuable thing would be a book, an ancient manuscript, a clue to some historical revelation."

"A book! Just think of that!" She was amazed. She stared at him. "Why, those men out there would go mad with disgust! They'd never believe it. They'd never accept it. All this effort for something not made of gold?"

"They have a faith," he said. "They're believers, the men of your family. They live with that one idea in mind—to find a treasure that probably doesn't exist. But you could never convince them of its nonexistence."

"You truly don't believe there's gold?"

"No."

"We'll have to drink from the same cup," she said.

"Charming!" he smiled again. "It will be a privilege."

She indicated the flowers in one of the pots. "Did you leave those?"

"No. I thought you put them there." Suddenly he chuckled. "Doby . . . I'll bet it was Doby."

"He must be the young man living with his father in Clive's house below. I've seen them from here."

"That's right. He's Kernohan's son. . . . They've moved in on Clive's place. Doby's the one who whipped one of your boys."

She made a face. "That was Wiley. I never liked him. Nor Ollie Fenelon, either."

"Are they kin of yours?"

"Wiley isn't."

"I think Doby's dreaming about you," Chantry said. "He found this place, and he wasn't at all happy I was coming up here. He wants you left alone."

"I believe I like Doby."

"He's sixteen, and lonesome. I know how he's feeling because I've felt it myself. I used to dream about a golden-haired princess I could rescue from all kinds of danger."

"But you don't anymore?"

He smiled, looking across the room into her eyes. "A man never stops dreaming. I like Doby. He's a good lad. He's got a father who works hard even when the odds are against him."

She refilled the cup and handed it to him. "They'll kill you, you know, all those men. There are too many of them."

"We all must die. Sooner or later. But I don't think I'll make it easy for them. How many are there?"

"Fifteen to twenty. Some of them come and go."

"Where do you fit in?"

"Mac Mowatt is my stepfather. My mother is dead. I am Marny Fox . . . I am told our name was Shannach until the English made us change it."

"They're a bad lot out there, you know."

"Some of them are bad," she spoke with heat, "and some of them are not. Some are simply loyal to Mac Mowatt. Oh, there's bad ones among them, but Frank is fine. He's Mac's oldest son. If it hadn't been for Frank . . ." She hesitated. "Frank is different. He'd prefer to be ranching somewhere. He's a good man, a solid man, but he's loyal to his father. . . . And he's been like a father to me."

They sat silently then, listening to the soft rustle of the aspen leaves. Chantry emptied the cup and handed it back and Marny refilled it from the coffeepot on the hearth. He knelt beside the fire and added a few sticks to the coals. The day was waning and she must leave soon. . . . There was always danger—the danger of discovery—if she stayed long.

"It's damned foolishness," he said irritably. "Nobody even knows what's actually here.

"Two men rode north out of Mexico. One Chantry. One Mowatt. They had something with them that Clive considered valuable. The two men wintered here, and then Mowatt . . . or so one story goes . . . died here. Some say he was killed.

"And some say that started the bad feeling. Some say it began when Mowatt was accused of deserting Clive. It's all long ago. Over the years the story has grown to include a vast treasure. And men have died for believing it."

"But you don't believe it?"

He shook his head. "Marny, I just simply don't know. But Clive was akin to us all in his interests, which were intellectual, historical . . . what you will.

"Some of us have done well with money—damned well in some cases—but more by accident than intention. So I simply believe that Clive found something of historical interest . . . something immensely valuable to him."

"Wouldn't Mowatt have known it?"

"Possibly . . . but possibly not. Possibly he couldn't even read. There are still many who can't. Clive was a linguist."

"So?"

"He might have been bringing back proof of some fancy of his. From Mexico. And how much could two men carry?

They were riding Apache country. How 'vast' could the treasure have been?"

Chantry stood up. "You'd best be getting back, and so had I."

She gathered up a few things and went to her horse. "You're going to move in here?"

"Soon."

"They'll find it, Mr. Chantry. And they'll also find you."

"Call me Owen." He smiled easily. "You won't tell them, then?"

"No . . . I owe them nothing. Perhaps I owe Mac Mowatt a little. And Frank. Frank's looked after me since I was a little girl."

"Your mother married Mac Mowatt?"

"Yes. He was much older than she, though she already had me. My real father was an army officer. Mac had known him. Mac met my mother when he came by the house to see my father, not knowing he was dead."

She swung into the saddle. "Be careful, Owen. There's no nonsense about them, and some are a bad, bad lot. In their minds there *is* a treasure, and in their minds they've already split it among them. They'll kill you as quickly as they killed Clive."

He watched her ride away and then walked back to his own horse. He brought the black in close to the house and then he went inside. It was dark there now, shadowed and still. He took a stick and spread the coals a bit, pouring the last of the coffee on them.

Then he stood up and looked slowly around. Something was hidden here, something he must find.

He believed in no treasure. But find it he must or he would never be free and it was freedom—and this place— that he wanted.

If he could live here, sit outside on that bench with a few books, watch the sun set over Utah and . . . he would ask for no more.

Well, he might not have to be alone. For the first time, he even considered that.

SIX

All the day long I waited for Chantry to get back. Pa seen I was restless, and a couple of times he stopped to say something but he didn't. It was away after dark before we heard his horse come clip-clopping into the yard. He hallooed the house, then he rode on to the barn to put up his black.

Pa had left some bacon an' side meat on the table, but he only ate a mite. "I had a little something in the hills," he said.

Now I knew he taken nothin' with him, so's he must have been fed. Was it her he got his food from?

"Did you find the place?" Pa asked.

"I spent most of the afternoon up there," said Chantry quietly. "And I can see why Doby was impressed. My brother had a love for this country."

"Wonder how come he got clear up there?" Pa said. "It ain't a likely place."

"Prob'ly hunting meat," I said.

"Or searching. . . ." Chantry said.

45

Well, then I looked at him, and so did Pa. "You mean he might have knowed somethin' was up there?" I asked him.

"My brother was a man who knew much about a lot of things. He had a gift for languages. Let him hear one . . . or so I was told . . . and inside a few days he'd be speaking it. I think when he came north he rode to a place he'd been told to find. I don't think it was accidental."

"But why?" I insisted.

He shrugged. "Sometimes a man just wants to know what happened and how." He paused. "You know, Doby, this is Ute country, with Navajos west and south of here. But even they never saw this country until about the year one thousand, when they came down from the north.

"They were migrants then, as we are now. They came, they conquered whoever was here, and they settled down. Just a few miles east of here the Utes will tell you there are ghost houses along the sides of the mesas.* No white man has seen them, but I believe the Indians.

"Who built those houses? Where did they come from? How long have they been there? Who was here first? Did the builders invent the structures they built? Or were they drawing on memories of other houses somewhere else?"

"You got a awful lot of questions," I grumbled, "but no answers."

He smiled. "That's the charm of such questions, Doby. Sometimes it's a joy just to try to find the answers. Whether you ever do, or not."

Pa taken the coffee to the table and I set there just itching to ask Chantry if he seen her, for he surely wasn't going to tell 'less I did ask. Made me mad, the way he set there eatin' and talking about nothin' that mattered. Finally, I couldn't wait no longer.

"Did you *see her*? That girl?"

"I did. I did even more."

"You mean you *talked* to her?"

"For an hour or so. Had a bite of lunch with her. Like a picnic."

* *Mesa Verde National Park.*

Chantry looked up at me, his eyes calm. Maybe there was just a mite of laughter in 'em, too. "Her name is Marny."

"Is she kin to *them*?"

"No blood-kin. She's old Mac Mowatt's stepdaughter."

Well, you should have seen Pa's head come up then. He turned straight round on Chantry. "You mean . . . you mean them were Mac Mowatt's men?"

"They were."

Pa looked like a ghost stepped on his grave. "Mac Mowatt. . . . That's a bloody outfit, Chantry. I'd no notion they were even in the country."

"Do you know them?"

"I know 'em. I knowed 'em years back, 'fore the war. They were a tough bunch then, but ever since the war they been a mean, man-killing crew. Ever since Strawn and Freka tied up with 'em."

"The big man was Ollie Fenelon. The fellow you whipped, Doby, is named Wiley."

"What's she like?" I asked him of a sudden. I wasn't payin' no mind to what he said about Mowatt and them. Or what Pa said. I was thinkin' of that girl.

"She isn't blonde . . . no golden hair and blue eyes, Doby. I'm afraid that part didn't pan out."

"She . . . *ugly*?" I asked, desperately.

"No. She's very beautiful. . . . Very. She's about five-foot four, with auburn hair and greenish eyes. Good complexion. Her name is Marny Fox, and she's Irish."

"How . . . how old is she?"

"She's an old woman, Doby. Why, she must be every bit of twenty!"

Twenty . . . four years older 'n me.

Four years! That was a lot, a whole lot. But I had to protest. "That ain't no old woman!" I said.

There was more talk. And finally I went to my room and turned in, but I lay there quite awhile. The outlines of my dream had already grown kind of mistylike. Twenty years old. . . . Lots of married women weren't that old. Still, she was pretty. Maybe even beautiful.

Right then I made up my mind. I was going to see for myself. I hadn't seen no woman in more'n a year.

Looked like I'd have to be mighty careful. From the way Pa acted, Mac Mowatt must be something fierce. And I'd heard talk of Strawn, myself. An' he was a killer sure enough.

When he was in Kansas there was talk of him. He'd killed a man around Abilene, and another on a cattle drive. You heard a lotta stories of such men in them days. Talk went up and down the trails. There wasn't no newspapers, but where a man stopped there was always somebody with a story to tell. There was talk of trails, gunfighters, Indians and the like, along with talk of wild horses like the famous white pacing stallion. That was a story ever'body heard, in sev'ral different accounts. And stories of mean steers, even the length of their horns, and of horseback rides men had taken.

Them western horses, mustang stock, were tough and wild. When they run the rough country on their own they'd travel days to water, graze far out from the holes they knew best, and range back to 'em ever' now and then for a drink.

Herds them days was big . . . hundreds of horses runnin' together, maybe sometimes thousands, and some fine stock among 'em. That surely couldn't last. Horse-hunters was always weedin' out the best breedin' stock for themselves.

Next day, I give some serious study to Owen Chantry. He was a hard man who'd rode some rough trails, and he shaped up like trouble. Still, the day he nailed that gent's hand he could have killed him . . . an' some would say he should.

I said it. He looked at me sharply. "I should have, Doby. I'm just a damn fool sometimes. I should have killed him. Because somebody will sure enough have it to do."

Then when we were alone outside, he said, "That was a nice thing you did, Doby. Leaving the flowers."

Well, I blushed. I never figured him knowing anything about it. "I found the pot, an' . . . well. I figured she was a lonely woman. . . ."

"It was a nice thing to do." He paused a moment, looking westward across the wild, broken land. "When you ride,

Doby, make sure you carry a gun and keep your eyes open. That's a bad outfit up there."

"Maybe," I said.

He shot me a glance. "You think otherwise?"

"Maybe they'll get friendly, like. . . . They're *her* folks."

"They're not blood-kin."

"Ain't no matter. I ain't anxious to shoot nobody."

He just looked at me again and walked away to the end of the porch. All I could think of was riding to the mountains again. I was wishful of meeting up with that woman . . . that girl. I wanted to see for myself.

We didn't have much to say, come breakfast. Chantry talked with Pa about bringin' some good cattle into the country. On the dry side of the mountains like we were, there wasn't much water, but still, there was enough so cattle could drink, and the forage was pretty good stock feed.

Same time I was thinkin' of that girl I was also thinkin' of that golden treasure Chantry had told us Mowatt believed was there. Owen Chantry took it light, but maybe he was just tryin' to talk us out of lookin'. Somebody'd gone to a whole lot of trouble if it was just a little thing. Didn't make sense to me that a growed-up man would set that much store by anything but gold or jewels, like.

Seemed to me a mighty silly thing that a man would risk his life to save a little old book, maybe nobody but a school-marm would put a value on. There just had to be gold up yonder.

A thought came to me, but I put it quick away. A thought that maybe my dream was replacing the golden-haired girl with a golden treasure of coins and such. But I paid no mind to the thought. I'd not even seen that girl yet, and I'd not believe Chantry 'til I did.

Right that minute I didn't care much for him. He was a sharp, hard man, I figgered, with reasons of his own for what he done. And seen close up that black suit of his was worn on the cuffs, and the boots he polished nigh ever' night, they were far from new.

Not that Pa and me had better. But he set himself up so high.

"What was her name?" I asked him again. I recalled her name. It was a dream name that was downright pretty.

"Marny Fox. She's Irish, Doby," he said, "or part Irish. They don't much like the Irish back east. Too many of us were poor when we came. But this is a good land and we will earn a place for ourselves."

"I heard Pa speak of how hard it was. Why do folks have to be like that, Mr. Chantry?"

"It's the way of the world. Across the sea, every man has a place he fills, and it's a hard and long thing to break free from it.

"We have to earn our place, Doby, just like all the others. There's no special sun that shines on any man, regardless of religion, philosophy, or the color of his skin. There's no reason why any man should expect a special dispensation from pope or president. In this country, more than any other, you have to make your mark. You're not going to be treated like something special until you are.

"Some men become outlaws. They can't make a living honestly, so they try to do it by force and strength. But everything is against them, and they cannot win."

"A man has to have some schoolin'," I said.

"It helps. Every book is a school in itself. Each one can teach you something. But you can learn a lot by observation. The most skillful trader I ever knew, a man who started as a pack-peddler—he was Irish, too—became a mighty big man in business, and he couldn't write his own name until he was over forty.

"By the time he was fifty he could speak four languages and write as good a letter as any man. . . . He was a wealthy man before he was able to write."

"If you know so much, why ain't you done better?" I demanded, rudely. "I don't see you sportin' no pocketful of gold, an' you're out here at the bobtail end of creation with nothin' but a horse."

He looked at me and his eyes were almighty cold. "I haven't done well, Doby, because I've been following a will-o'-the-wisp. Someday I'll find out what it really was." He paused a moment. "Your comment is just. I know what can be done, but I haven't done it. Perhaps there were too many rivers I wanted to cross, too many canyons I hadn't followed, too many towns with dusty streets down which I hadn't ridden.

"The trouble is with wandering that after a bit a man looks around and the horizons are still there. There are nameless canyons and rivers still unknown to man. But a mortal man is suddenly old. The dream is there still, but rheumatism and weakening strength rob him of the chance to go further.

"See me five years from now, Doby . . . or ten."

Well, I just looked at him. He wasn't payin' me no mind, just lookin' off across the country, thinkin' his own thoughts. Me, I had thoughts of my own.

Then Chantry walked out to his horse. Whenever he had thinkin' to do, he curried his horse, fussed over it. You'd think that black was a baby. Yet he cared for the packhorse just about as well.

I went inside. Pa was settin' by the fire. "Pa, you think he's speakin' the truth?"

"Who?" Pa was startled. "You mean Chantry? 'Course he is!"

"But maybe they had reason to kill his brother, if they done it."

"We done found the body, son. And I know 'bout Mowatt and his outfit. I heard."

"You *heard*. Ain't you always told me not to b'lieve all I heard?"

"You had trouble with 'em first, Doby."

Well, that kind of backed me up in a corner. It was true. They'd been mighty rough with me. So I just said, "That don't prove nothin'." It was a feeble answer and I knowed it.

We needed poles for fencing if we were growin' any garden, so daybreak next day I packed me a lump and taken off for the hills to cut aspens.

Aspens grow tall and slim. Just right for making a fence quick, usin' them as rails. I taken an ax and when I fetched up to the nearest grove I go down and set to.

Sixteen ain't many years, but I was strong and I'd used an ax good, and I made the blade bite deep an' fast. By noon I'd cut enough poles for the best part of a day. I looped a half hitch and a timber hitch to 'em, took a turn around the saddle horn, and dragged the poles out to where I could get at 'em when I come with the team.

I dragged the first bunch, then the second. That done, I taken my horse to the creek, and when he'd had himself a drink I picketed him on the good feed there was where I'd been cuttin' aspens, and then I set down by the stream and opened my lump.

It looked like a lump, too, the bread all squeezed up and out of shape, but it tasted almighty good.

When I finished eatin', I hunted 'round for wild raspberries but they was skimpy and small. In a good year they'd be plenty of 'em around, if a body got to them before the bears and birds. But I found a few dozen and started to turn back to my horse when I seen something move out of the tail of my eye.

My rifle was on my saddle so I just squatted down at the edge of the trees, hopin' I hadn't been seen.

By that time it'd been the best part of an hour since I'd been choppin' trees. So there'd been no sound from me that a body could hear more'n a few feet off.

Lookin' up to where I'd seen that movement, I set still an' waited.

The mountain sloped up under that cloak of aspens to the very foot of that great red wall that was the rampart below the mountain cabin. The cabin itself was across the canyon and more than a mile . . . maybe two mile off. Lookin' over a canyon that way, distance can fool a man.

Mountain air, specially over here on the dry side, is almighty clear and I could see somethin' movin' at the base of the red wall. He might be atop a rock slide. That was a place I'd never had cause to go, and I didn't know for sure . . . but he was alongside the rampart.

Now my eyesight is good, and blinkin' my eyes a couple times, I set to lookin' off to one side a little and, sure enough, I saw that movement again. Something was movin' along the base of that cliff, for sure. And while I set and watched, that somebody or something—moved along the base of the wall and finally disappeared. I set there a-awaitin', but whatever it was was gone.

Now I studied on what I'd seen. It might have been a animal, but it looked otherwise to me. I believed it was a man, or a man on a horse, and whoever it was might have been lookin' for a way to the top.

If a body could find a way up that cliff, he could save himself several miles of ridin' to and from . . . an hour or more each way. And it struck me then that whoever I'd seen was him . . . Owen Chantry.

He was huntin' a quick, easy way to the top.

Well, why not? I could just as well do that my own self. Settin' back where I was. . . . Well, I pulled back fifty yards from where I'd been an' set down on a stump. Then I gave study to that red wall.

Most places it was so sheer a man would have to be a sure-enough mountain climber to scale it. But there were a couple notches on the south side of the mesa that looked right promisin'. Chantry'd been workin' north along the west face when I seen him, and when he disappeared.

I looked at the sun. Too late. I'd have to hightail it for home to get there 'fore sundown, 'cause I had to go down to the river canyon and up the other side, and I wasn't wishful of tryin' it after dark. It was a right spooky ride down and up in the daylight. Even ridin' a good mountain horse like I had.

Tomorrow . . . tomorrow I'd have to hitch up the team and come after them poles. Once up here I'd picket the team and head for the red wall.

Right then I had a worried time. What right did I have to go traipsin' off? Pa was doin' his share, and it was up to me to do mine. He needed them poles. He needed the team, and he needed me and my time. We had our work cut out for us.

Still, how long would it take? An hour, maybe two. I picked up my ax and stuff and headed for the canyon.

What if I picketed the team an' a mountain lion come

down on 'em? Or a bear? 'Course, most times bears won't kill livestock, not unless they done it before or need to eat.

We couldn't afford to lose that team, not even one of 'em.

The bottom of the canyon was dark when I got there, but the top was still gold with sunshine. That trail was a hair-raiser. But it would've been more scary if it hadn't been for part of the slopes bein' timbered.

I fetched to the bottom. It was dark down there, only water shinin' like silver. We splashed through and started up to the crest. A third of the way up I stopped to let my horse catch wind, and I turned in the saddle and looked back.

I seen nothin', but I heard splashin' in the water, then a hoof clicked on stone.

Me, I touched a heel to my horse an' we started on. I didn't know what was back there, and I wanted to make no effort to find out. This was a plumb spooky place, and even if it was just one man, I wanted no gunfight on that hairline trail.

When I topped out on the crest, I put a spur to that gelding an' lit out for home. It wasn't far, but I let my horse go. Goin' home, that was the fastest horse. I never seen a horse had more love for home and the stable than that one. He lit out for home like he had fire under his tail.

The house light sure looked good! I rode into the yard, slid off that horse, and led him into the stable. Pa come to the door.

"Dry that horse off, boy, an' git in here. Supper's on the table."

When I taken my riggin' off, I went to throw it over the partition and there was Owen Chantry's black. I hung up my saddle and spoke soft to the black, and put a hand on it.

Wiped off, yes. Curried a mite, yes. . . . But the skin was damp. I was sure the skin was damp.

When I come through the door, Chantry was settin' at the table with Pa. He looked up and smiled, and that made me sore. Who did he think he was? And how did he beat me gettin' home? Maybe it wasn't him.

Then I was wondering. Who was it out there? Who followed me up that canyon trail?

SEVEN

Owen Chantry was restless, irritable. What he wanted was something to read, but the Kernohans were not readers. There was only a copy of the *Iliad*, which had belonged to his brother. Which was odd, for Clive had always been a reader.

"Kernohan," Owen said suddenly, "weren't there any books here when you came? Clive was a man who liked reading. I would have expected him to have some books."

"Books? Oh, sure! There's a-plenty. We boxed 'em up an' stored 'em in the loft. They was takin' up space and collectin' dust, so we just put 'em up there.

"Me, I never did learn to read much, an' Doby here, he's mostly innerested in horses an' guns."

"If you don't mind," Chantry said, "I'll look those books over. Might be something to read."

"He'p yourself. I looked through a few of 'em but there ain't much there that makes much sense to me. Books by them Greeks, histories an' such. Nothin' that would he'p a man work land."

Dawn came with a cool wind off the mountains, a smell of pine and the chill of rocky peaks where some of last year's snow still lingered from the winter, awaiting the next snow.

Owen went to the woodpile and took up the ax. For a half hour he worked, cutting wood for the cooking fires. From time to time he paused, leaning on the ax and taking time to study the country. His eyes searched out every canyon, every draw, placing them exactly in his mind.

Lost Canyon lay just north, a great, timbered gash coming down from the northeast. Only barely visible from where he stood, he had ridden to it on his first scouting of the country. A creek ran along the bottom. . . . One day he would go down there.

It was one of the last areas in the States to be settled. Rivera had reached it in 1765, and Escalante had passed through in 1776. Otherwise the vast land had remained unrecorded by any white man, yet men must have ridden through, hunted and prospected here. There was always one curious rider who went a little further, or passed through going from here to there. Discoverers were only those who called attention to what they'd seen and done.

When Owen left the woodpile he climbed to the loft and rummaged through the books. The *Odes* of Horace in the original Latin did him no good at all. Clive had been the Latin scholar of the family.

There was a two-volume edition of the poems of Alfred Tennyson—a contemporary—published in 1842. Chantry had read some of Tennyson, and enjoyed him. The rest could wait. He took up the two Tennyson books and climbed down.

He opened a book when he reached the last step and looked through it, riffling the pages and glancing at a poem here and there. One page was marked by a torn piece of newspaper. It was "Ulysses."

He closed the book and put it down for later reading.

When he walked outside again, both Kernohan and Doby had gone. The team was gone, as was Doby's gelding.

Owen had started back toward the house when he glimpsed three riders coming down the draw toward the house.

Chantry took his rifle from inside and placed it beside the door. Suddenly, he saw movement near a bush by the stable. His hand was poised for a draw when a voice called out, "Don't shoot, Owen!"

It was Kernohan, hoe in hand, unarmed.

"Stay right where you are or get into the barn," Chantry advised.

He was watching the riders. He knew that bay. It was a big horse, weighing twelve hundred or more and standing over sixteen hands. It was notoriously fast and had won many races around the country.

It was Strawn's horse, and nobody ever rode that horse but Strawn.

Freka would be with him. Freka was part Finlander, a troublemaker who had lived in a colony of Scandinavians in Utah until they drove him out. He was known to be a good man with a gun and had figured in several pointless killings in the past few years.

They turned into the yard and drew up when they saw Chantry standing in the door, waiting for them.

"Howdy, Chantry!" Strawn said casually. "It's been awhile."

"Fort Worth, wasn't it?" Chantry asked.

Freka was the thin, blond man in the checkered shirt. The third man was heavier, a barrel-chested fellow with a bull neck and a shaved head to whom Chantry couldn't yet put a name.

"You boys traveling?" Chantry asked them.

"Sort of prospectin' around. You ever been to the La Platas?"

"Time or two."

"Rough country, but mighty purty. How's for a drink?"

"Water or coffee? We haven't any whiskey."

"Coffee sounds good." Strawn swung down from his bay, and the others followed. Slowly, they walked toward the house. Halfway there, Freka suddenly turned and looked toward the barn, pausing, then saying something in a low voice to the barrel-chested man, who was nearest him.

Owen Chantry got down four cups from the shelf and then the coffeepot. They seated themselves around the table and Chantry filled their cups.

"No sugar out here," Chantry commented. "Honey all right?"

"I favor it," Strawn said.

He was a good-looking man, his face somewhat long under a high forehead, with carefully parted and combed hair. He was a man of nearly thirty but he looked younger. He was good with a gun. He had been in a couple of cattle wars and several shoot-outs.

Jake . . . that was the third man's name. He'd used other handles from time to time, but that was his real name.

"This here's a long way from somewhere for you, Chantry," Strawn said. "I figured you for a town man."

"I like wild country. The wilder the better."

"Well, you got it," Strawn said. "There just ain't hardly nobody around here. You could ride a hundred miles in any direction and find nobody. . . . Nobody."

"Except the Mowatt outfit," Chantry commented.

Strawn looked up, grinning. "You seen them?"

"They stopped by to visit. Didn't stay long."

Strawn stared at him, then smiled. "Well, well. You mean you backed him off? You backed off Mac Mowatt?"

Chantry refilled their cups. "You know how it is, Strawn. Mac didn't figure the odds were right. Maybe he wanted company to be present. He might have been waiting for somebody."

Strawn chuckled. "You know, I like you, Chantry. I really do. Hope I never have to kill you."

"Be a shame, wouldn't it, Strawn? Somebody sending you out on a job like that? And you so young, too."

Strawn's eyes glinted, but he chuckled again. "Good coffee, Owen. I'm glad we stopped by."

"You know, Jake, I was hoping to have this talk with you.

You know me better than Mowatt does, and I don't think you ever knew me to lie."

"You?" Strawn stared. "I'd shoot the man who even suggested it."

"Mowatt is after something, Jake. He's after something that isn't even there, that never was there. I don't know all the facts, but I do know there's no treasure. There's nothing here that would be valuable to anybody but a scholar."

"What's that mean?" Freka was suddenly alert.

"It means that when my brother rode up out of Mexico he brought something he valued greatly . . . and the treasure story got started."

"So?"

"What he brought . . . and I'll admit I've never seen it . . . was information. A book, a manuscript, some notes . . . perhaps a plaque of some kind. To someone trying to reconstruct history it would be valuable. But to the average person, worthless."

Freka smiled with exasperation. "You must think we're all simpleminded to believe a story like that. Why would a growed-up man risk his life for something like that?"

Jake Strawn looked thoughtful. "And if there's nothing there, we wind up empty?"

Chantry shrugged. "Did you ever hear of Mowatt giving away anything of his own? Look, Jake, you've ridden for some tough outfits, and so have I, and you know that nobody but some crazy kid, some wild youngster fights for anything but gain. . . . Not in our world. So if there's no gain in treasure, where's the payoff? You know I'm good with a gun. I know you are. I know damn well I don't want to come up against you for fun, and I don't think you want to lock horns with me for no payoff."

"And you say there's no gold?"

"I do. What I suggest is this, Jake. I suggest you and Freka talk to Mowatt. Make him lay it on the line. I know all he's doing is following a dream. Somebody told a story once, and then it was told again and again and each time it got bigger. A Chantry riding out of the desert with treasure in gold on him. With a Mowatt. How did they carry all that vast treasure?"

Strawn, Chantry could see, was half convinced. But Freka wasn't even listening. In fact, he was making a great show of ignoring the talk.

"Hot air," Freka said. "Mowatt's no fool. He knows what he's about."

"Like a hundred other foolish prospectors roaming these mountains to the east of us, hunting for gold they'll never see." Chantry emptied his cup. "Just thought I'd lay it on the line, Jake. You know me, and I know you."

"So why're you here?" Freka demanded.

"A good question, Freka. I've had a brother killed, and that's a part of it. The rest is something you'd not likely grasp.

"I've been up and down and across this country. I've gambled and fought, and I've killed men for reasons that might seem slight. I've fought in cattle wars, and town-site battles, for railroad rights of way and just about everything else. I've never had much and never expect to have, but I'd give ten years of my life to add just one little bit to the knowledge of the world.

"We Chantrys have a failing, Freka. We like to finish what we start. I know the history of my family for two hundred years the way you know the trail to Santa Fe. And we've always finished what we started, or died in the trying. It's a kind of stubbornness . . . damned foolishness, maybe.

"Look, Strawn, a million years or more ago men began to accumulate learning. Over the years more bits and pieces of knowledge have been added and all of it is building a wall to shut out ignorance.

"I think what Clive Chantry brought back from Mexico was a piece of the pattern, his brick for the wall. Maybe it was a clue to a lost civilization, maybe a treatment for some killing disease, maybe a better way to grow a crop. Maybe it's one of the books of the Mayas that didn't burn. The one thing I know is that it wasn't gold."

Freka yawned. "Jake, let's ride. This talk is puttin' me to

sleep." He got up. "You talk mighty well, Chantry, but I don't buy it, not even a piece of it."

Strawn got up. "You suggestin' I lay off, Chantry?"

"No. We're mercenaries, you and me. We're paid warriors. All I'm asking is that you make sure the payoff is there. If I go up against a man of your caliber, I want to be sure I'm getting paid for it, one way or another. And I'll be paid, that I know. But what will you get out of it?"

"If we lock horns, Jake, one of us is going to die. There's a better than even chance that both of us will. I've seen you in action, and you're good. Damned good. I believe you've seen me in action, too."

"I have."

"Well, make Mowatt come up with something more than hot air."

"Mowatt knows something. He doesn't go off half-cocked."

"No? How many times has he told of a Wells-Fargo treasure chest that was supposed to be loaded with gold and then it turned up empty?"

"Maybe you're right, Chantry. But Freka won't buy it. He wants to kill. And he's good, Chantry, damn good."

"I hope when I find out how good he is you don't have me in a cross fire, Jake."

"Hell, I fight my own battles. You and him . . . I'd kind of like to see that."

Strawn picked up his hat and followed Jake and Freka, who had gone outside. "See you, Owen." He paused. "I'll talk to the old man."

Owen Chantry stood in the door and watched them ride away.

Kernohan slowly approached the house. "What was all that about?"

"Strawn and Freka, killers working for Mac Mowatt, and dangerous men."

"Taken you long enough. I figured you was old friends."

"No . . . Jake Strawn and I know each other by sight and reputation. We've even eaten in the same bunkhouse, and he rode shotgun on a stage I drove a few times. I've never seen Freka before . . . but he's mean as a rattler, and just as deadly."

"Strawn ain't?"

"Strawn's one of the best men with a gun I ever saw, and he'll take a lot of lead before he dies. He's got six bullet wounds I know of, and he's still breathing good. The men who shot at him are dead. I was just trying to convince him there was no gold, so there couldn't be a payoff. He almost bought it, but Freka didn't. Freka doesn't care."

Kernohan was silent a minute. Then he said, "Chantry, I'm goin' to pull out. Me and the boy ain't geared for such as this, and I don't aim to get him hurt."

Chantry shrugged. "Your decision, Kernohan, but you've got a nice place here. You can run cattle and do well. You've a meadow or two where you can cut hay, and there's water. You'll have to hunt awhile to find its equal."

"Mebbe. But I don't aim to get my boy shot up for nothin'. I don't take to shootin' folks. I don't want him endin' up like Strawn or them others."

"Like me?" Chantry suggested.

"Or you. I don't know much about you, Chantry, but if your stories are true you've been mixed up in a lot of shootin'."

"Yes, I have. And you're right, Kernohan. But stay . . . I'll keep them off your back. But talk Doby out of going into the hills. He's got a kind of case on that girl."

"He's never even seen her!"

"He's a boy alone, Kernohan. Don't you recall how it was? At sixteen there's always a girl you dream about. Well, she's the only one around."

"Let 'im dream. Won't do no harm."

"Not unless he ties in with that Mowatt outfit just to be close to her."

Kernohan swore. "I wondered why he taken his ridin' horse when he went after them poles!" He paused, worried. "He'll come back. I know he will."

Chantry had a sudden thought. "Kernohan, when you first got here were those books boxed up?"

"No, they was on that shelf." He pointed.

"Was there anything else?"

"No, not's I recall." Kernohan sat down at the table. "That poor man lived a bit after he was left for dead. You could see that."

"How do you mean? He'd been dead a good while, you said."

"He had. But there was writin' on the step. That's why I figured there might be treasure. He tried to write some numbers."

"Show me?"

"Sure. It's faded now. He had a stub of pencil."

They walked outside. On the riser between the first and second step was written, in a barely legible scrawl, one word:

Ten . . .

"He was layin' there, kinda bunched up. Course, coyotes or wolves might have twisted his body round some, but I figgered he started to writin' some figgers and died 'fore he got any more wrote down."

Owen Chantry straightened up, disappointed. He had hoped for a clue . . .

Clive had been a careful man. He would have known that if Owen was alive he would come. And, being Clive, he would have tried to leave some message, some clue.

But there was nothing . . . simply nothing at all.

EIGHT

When I got back to where I'd cut the poles I picketed the team and taken my saddle horse. Right then I had my doubts. I had a sinkin' feeling in my belly, like. Pa would never've left a team like that, to be gone nobody knew how long.

There were varmints in the mountains, and a heavy team, picketed like that, wouldn't even have a fightin' chance against 'em. These were big horses, and most times they'd give a pretty good account of themselves if they had to fight.

But all I could think of was that girl. Owen Chantry might have been tellin' the truth, but I just had to see. I still didn't like him much, he was too durned sure of himself. I couldn't see where he was so high an' mighty.

So with one long look around, I taken off a horseback. Pa was back at the ranch, and so was Chantry. I had it all to myself. I'd scout around, then come back, hitch up, an' try to make it back with the poles before it come nighttime.

Sure 'nough, back in a notch of that rampart I found me a way up. It was a scramble, that was, but I had me a good mountain horse and we made it to the top of the mesa. A moment there, we stood to take a look.

Then I turned that horse of mine and started across the top of the mesa to cut into the trail to the cabin. When I come into the open, I could look off across the country. There was a box canyon in front of me, just off a little ways, and beyond it a fine roll of country, timbered heavy.

Some place off thataway was prob'ly where Mowatt was holed up. I had me a notion to ride over there, explaining that we were neighbors an' all, so why not be friendly? But I had another notion that warned me that for all my words to Chantry, I wasn't that sure. So I turned my horse toward the cabin.

Out of the corner of my eye, I thought I seen something move in the trees, so I turned quick in the saddle and looked back.

Nothing.

Maybe I was a half, or three quarters of a mile from the cabin. I walked the horse along. Here and there I could see bare spots on the trunks and limbs, high up off the ground where porcupines had eaten the bark. Give 'em time an' they'll kill a good tree.

The cabin stood silent. I saw no horse, and it was a disappointin' thing. I pulled in. I walked to the door and lifted the latch.

Inside it was cool, dim, and still. There were fresh flowers in the pot I'd put on the table. I looked around some more, then turned and went outside.

An' there sat three men on horses, an' one of 'em was that man Wiley. They just set a lookin' at me an' grinnin'.

My rifle was on my horse and my horse was away t'other side of them riders.

"Well, well!" Wiley was grinning. "This is the one I was tellin' you all about."

A redheaded man I hadn't seen before had him a rifle across his saddle. "You want I should shoot him a little?" he asked Wiley, grinning. "Maybe cut his ears back?"

"Well," Wiley scowled kinda like he was studyin' on it.

"No. I reckon not. I promised myself I'd pin his ears back my own self and if you shoot 'em off, how can I?"

"Look here, boys," I said. "No use for us to have trouble, us bein' neighbors an' all. Why don't we just set down an' get acquainted? Pa an' me we're no kin to Owen Chantry. We never seen the man 'til he showed up down there."

"What's the matter, kid? You scared? Why you so friendly of a sudden?"

Wiley had got down from his saddle, taking his time. I started to move toward my horse, and the redhead aimed his rifle. "You stand quiet, kid, unless you want your guts all over the grass."

The other one, the one who'd been on the trail that first day with Wiley, he was takin' his rope off the saddle. Suddenly, I was real scared. Here I was, all alone, and them three men was beginnin' to shape up trouble. I wished I had me a handgun, and for a minute there I wondered if I could jump back into the cabin and slam the door.

There wasn't no way I could make it to the woods without bein' run down or shot. That redhead just kept a-grinnin' at me. Then Wiley started for me, an' I started to jump for the door.

But the redhead snapped a loop over my head 'fore I'd took a step, and his horse taken off at a jump, throwin' me to the ground. I'd heard about men being dragged to death, so I grabbed for the rope. But he just jerked me again, and the rope tightened. Then Wiley walked over to me, and he had him a club about four feet long.

After startin' to get up, I had my feet jerked out from under me again. And Wiley lambasted me with that club. I saw it comin' and tried to twist away. Maybe I done so a little, but he fetched me right over the shoulder with that club. An' then he started at me again. I tried to get up but that rope jerked me down, and then all I could remember was a terrible pain from them blows. Wiley swung that club. He hit me over the head, over the shoulders, and across the back.

I come to, raised myself an' run at him, butted him with my head, knockin' him sprawlin' on the grass. Then I jumped on him with both feet. They jerked me with the rope and I fell again, but when Wiley reared up over me I doubled back my knees and kicked him on the knee with both my heels.

And down he went again, roaring with pain and anger, and I rolled around and lunged at him. I think the redhead wasn't tryin' too hard, and that he didn't truly mind Wiley gettin' knocked around, 'cause he and that other feller, they sat up there laughin'.

Wiley give me another bat over the head and I went down to my knees. I could feel the blood comin' down in my eyes, and I dove at him again. He got away from me and knocked me sprawlin'. Then he came in swingin' at me, but I fetched him a kick again, and he fell.

Dazed like I was, and hurt, I could only just try to keep goin' at him. But when he got up again he just had at me. How many times he hit me, I couldn't later recall, only he beat me somethin' fierce. When I finally tried to get up, he hit me a fearful swing and I felt a terrible pain in my side an' I just fell over and laid there. All I could feel was pain, and I bit at the grass so's they wouldn't hear me groan.

Wiley walked up on me, and I heard that redhead say, "Aw, leave him be, Wiley! You got your evens!"

"I'm gonna kill him," I heard Wiley say.

"Forget it," somebody said. "Hell, he's hurt bad. The way it is, he'll never get home. I think you busted some ribs that last time. Leave him be."

Nowhere then did I lose my thoughts. I could hear them talkin' and I didn't much care if they killed me, I hurt so bad. Finally I heard them just a-ridin' off, an' I lay there, thinkin' of night comin' on an' Pa's team with the varmints around.

Somewheres along there I kinda passed out, an' when my eyes opened again it was plumb dark, an' must've been dark for some time, because I was all over wet from dew. And cold, so cold I couldn't hardly breathe.

Diggin' my fingers into the grass, I drawed myself toward the step. I heard somethin movin' toward me and it was my horse. I spoke to him, "Brownie," I said. "Brownie . . ."

He come to me, snortin' a little because I smelled of

blood. But he stood by me and I managed to rear up enough to catch hold of a stirrup. I drawed myself up, and a pain went through my side like a knife stuck in me, so I leaned against the horse, and whispered to him.

My head throbbed an' I was sore. I wasn't goin' to get into that saddle. There wasn't no way could I make it. Best thing to do was get inside that house and get a fire a-goin'.

Somehow I got the reins up and looped them over the pommel. Then I got my rifle from the scabbard and I taken my saddlebags with my lump in 'em. Then I kinda leaned on the rifle and slapped the gelding on the hip and said, "Go home, Brownie! Go home!"

Brownie walked off a ways and stopped. That horse didn't want to leave. Then I must've passed out again, 'cause I was cold and shivering when next I opened my eyes. Somehow I crawled inside. Dragged my rifle with me, and got the door shut.

There was fuel there, and a fire fresh-laid. I managed to get it alight, fed it some sticks, and passed out again.

During the night I half woke up, sick and moaning with pain. The fire was down. I got more sticks on it and saw the coffeepot.

There was a mite of coffee left but not near as much as I wanted. I nudged it into the coals. Then I set, shiverin', feelin' that terrible throbbing in my skull and the pain in my side and a rawness and soreness all over.

At no time was I more'n half conscious, but when I come to again—woke up by a pain, I guess—there was a smell of coffee in the room. I had me a old cup in my saddlebags with my lump, and I got it out and spilled coffee into the cup. I got myself a swaller or two and spilled some over my lips. They were all swole up, but the coffee tasted good. I passed out again, all torn up with pain and sick and wishin' I'd listened to Chantry and never come up here at all, nor trusted them people.

She found me. That girl. I was almighty sick and she came across the mesa to the cabin and found me there. It was full daylight and I was conscious but I couldn't move anyway. I was just layin' there, all sick and sore and knowin' I was goin' to die.

Laying there half-dead I'd heard a horse a-comin'. At first I figured it might be Brownie, or them men comin' back, but it wasn't no wanderin' horse. That horse come right up to the cabin and I heard a saddle creak.

Somebody said somethin'—I guess it was when she seen blood on the stoop. And then the door opened and I heard a gasp. It was like in a dream, or when you're only half-awake or somethin'. I felt a hand touch my shoulder and turn me on my back, and it hurt somethin' awful and I cried out.

Next thing I knowed I heard breakin' wood and smelled the smoke and heard a fire going. I could hear the pine wood crackle and smell it, too. I knowed I was in bad shape, but there was just nothin' I could say or do.

She taken some cloth and wiped off my face, cleanin' up the cuts and dabbin' here and there at me. Then she began to work over me with her fingers, testin' for sore spots an' breaks. When she touched my ribs I gasped right out.

She went out for water and brought in some more wood. And once when my eyes were open I glimpsed her. She sure was pretty, on'y she was no blonde. She had no golden curls, but her hair was kinda dark red, like, with a little bit of gold in it, and prettier'n any gold-haired girl I ever seen.

"Pa," I whispered. "I lef' Pa's horses. . . . I was cuttin' poles. I lef' 'em."

"Don't worry 'bout it," she told me. "They'll be all right."

"Pa sets some store by that team. I got to—"

"You just lay still. We'll get word to your pa. I'll go get the team later."

She made up soup and got some of it in me and I felt her fussin' with a finger that was hurtin'. Somewhere along there I faded out again, and when next I knowed anything I heard him talkin'. Chantry.

"His horse came home," Chantry was saying, "and I made sure his father stayed to watch the place. Just like them men to burn it down if they get a chance."

"Did you come straight here?"

"Backtracked Doby to the team. They're all right. I watered them and changed the picket pins and then headed up here. He'd found a way up the face through a notch, so I followed him. I knew he'd come here."

Chantry come nearer and stood over me. I felt like I was a hundred miles off, driftin' in some dream world. The voices came through, but faintly. "He's taken quite a beating," I heard him say.

"I think some ribs are broken, and he has a broken finger."

Chantry touched my hand. "See? A rope burn. They roped him and he tried to grip the rope. That means there were at least two of them, probably more. This boy's a fighter."

He was checkin' my body. I felt his fingers at my ribs, an' winced from their pressure. After a while I heard him say, "We'll splint that finger. And we'll tear up his pants and bind them tight around him to hold those ribs in place. I've known ribs to knit with no trouble.

"The rest is mostly cuts and bruises. Whether he's hurt worse, only time will tell. He took some nasty raps on the skull."

"How can we move him?"

"A travois. The same way the Plains Indians carried their goods and their wounded. I'll cut a couple of poles and we'll rig up a travois."

They talked some more, and then he was gone. When I next figured out where I was, we was alone in the cabin, me and her. I opened my eyes. Every part of me was sore, and my head throbbed somethin' awful.

When she seen I was awake she come over and spooned more soup into me. It tasted good. "Thanks," I mumbled.

"How many of them were there?"

"Three. One of them put a rope on me, but I put Wiley down. I put him down two, three times. We fought all over the place. That redhead—"

"Thrasher Baynes."

"He left me just loose enough to fight. I figgered maybe he didn't mind all that much if Wiley got hurt."

"He wouldn't. Thrasher doesn't care much about anybody. But he appreciates nerve. If you showed grit, he'd like it."

"I marked him. I marked Wiley."

"Good for you. Now rest."

It was a mighty long trip down that mountain. The team followed behind, draggin' the poles I cut. There was times when I knew what was happenin' and times when I just passed out. And times when the joltin' down the trail hurt something fierce. But they taken me home, Chantry an' her.

Pa was there with his gun. He was standin' by the gate watchin' us come in, and he was nigh to tears when he seen me. Pa's not a cryin' man.

"He looks worse than he is," Chantry told Pa. "That's a tough son you got there, Kernohan."

"He's a good boy," Pa said. "He's always been a good boy, and a he'p to me. I figgered to take up land so's he could make a better start than me. But I don't know. All this, I might just—"

"Don't. You stay on. This is a good place." Chantry suddenly changed his tone. "This is land bought legally from the Indians. When the time is right, I'll transfer title to it."

Long after they had me inside and in bed, I heard the murmur of her voice out there with them. She wasn't blonde with golden curls and all, but she was pretty, she was almighty beautiful. And twenty wasn't so old. Why next year I'd be seventeen, and I was a man growed. . . . And she even said I had nerve.

Later, some time later, I heard Pa say, "If there's nothin' there, an' you know it, why don't you just tell 'em?"

"I tried to. They believe too hard, Kernohan. Men will give up anything rather than what they want to believe. And hate you for telling them there's nothing to believe. And even if you prove it to them, they'll continue to believe, and hate you for proving them foolish. Sometimes they give up, but they'll like you no more.

"I've seen men come to a ground where treasure was said to be buried, and with holes all over the hills, they'll dig another one, and then another.

"One thing I know, my brother was here for some time. If

there was anything of value here, he would have found it. And being a methodical man, I believe he would leave some clue."

Chantry paused. "Moreover, knowing him, he would probably leave such a clue as only I would be apt to discover."

"What kinda clue could that be?"

Chantry shrugged. "I will have to remember what passed between us, and which of my tastes he knew best. Clive was a fine man, a much better man than I in every moral way. But he had a complicated mind, and so have I, and any clue he left would be useful to no one else."

"Well," said Pa, "for the life of me I can't figger out what kinda clue, or how you'd ever guess it."

"I've got to go back," Marny said.

Chantry turned toward her. "Don't. Stay here."

"No, I've got to go back. At least one more time. I have things there. . . . Well, I want them. I'll need them."

"Will they know you've been to the cabin?"

"No. I don't think so. But they'll go there now. Mac Mowatt will be certain he can find what there is. They'll tear the place apart."

"Maybe not," Owen Chantry said. "Maybe I'll be there."

"Alone? Against them all?"

"I won't be inside. I'll keep some freedom of action." I heard Chantry walk across the room. "Yes, I think I must do that. I must be there when they come. I want to keep that cabin."

"It's lonely," Pa said. "It's a mighty lonely place. Of a wintertime a man could be snowed in. That house must be nine thousand feet up."

"I've been up high before."

I never seen her go. She just taken off and was gone when I waked up, with only the faint smell of her perfume left in the air. But I was scared for her . . . *scared*. I had a bad feeling about her going back.

I tried to sit up and got such a stab of pain in my side that I laid down quick, gasping for breath.

She was gone. There was nothin' I could do.

If I just had my old rifle and was up in them rocks . . . well, maybe I couldn't do nothin', but could surely try.

Suddenly Chantry stood over me. "You all right, Doby? I heard you cry out."

"Didn't mean to. Yeah, I'm all right. But I wish you'd bring her back. That's a bad outfit. I wish you'd fetch her, Owen Chantry."

"I'll be at the cabin. She knows that."

"If she ever gets there. Mr. Chantry, I'm scared. I'm plumb scared for her. She don't think they knew she knowed about that cabin, but they prob'ly seen the flowers there."

Chantry looked grim, and he had a face for it. He was a right handsome man, but there was a coldness in him sometimes that would frighten a man.

"I'll just go see, Doby. I'll ride up there. Right now . . . today."

He wasted no time. He got on the big black and taken his packhorse and headed for the hills. And seein' him ride out, I wondered what would happen when him and the Mowatts come together.

Maybe he was only one man and they was many, but she sure wouldn't be no one-sided fight. Not with him being the other side, no matter how many they had.

There was somethin' about that man that made you believe. Even me, who up till then hadn't wanted to believe much of anything 'bout Owen Chantry.

Somehow, busted ribs and all, I had to be there. I had to be up on that mountain when the shootin' started.

NINE

Owen Chantry was a man without illusions. Nothing in his experience had given him the idea that he was protected by any special dispensation from Providence. He had seen good men die when the evil lived on, and he was aware that he was as vulnerable as any other man.

Yet a man doesn't command a cavalry outfit, scout for the army against the Indians, drive a stage and ride shotgun without acquiring a feeling for the possibilities.

Chantry's life was due to his own skill and to a certain amount of sheer coincidence. For if he was a foot past the spot where bullets struck, it was only circumstance and the fact that he was moving faster or slower than the men the bullets found.

Owen Chantry had asked no favors of destiny. He put himself in the hands of his own skills, a good horse, and a good gun.

Crossing the canyon at a place where another canyon joined it from the east, he climbed a rough but not too difficult trail. It was timber country. There were many dams among the aspens, which were favored by beavers and elks.

He took his time. At this altitude a man did not hurry, not even with a mountain-bred horse. Mac Mowatt was a tough old renegade who knew every trick in the book and could invent more on the spur of the moment. Nor were his followers to be taken lightly, for they were all bred on the frontier. To a man.

Chantry paused near a beaver pond, letting the horses drink a little while he studied the mountainside.

Always he was careful to stop against a background where his body merged easily into the colors. From a few yards away, he was almost invisible to the casual eye.

He studied the mountainside with no sweeping glances, but with a yard by yard survey, leaving no tree, no rock, and no shadow unobserved. Occasionally, he took a quick glance back over what he had just examined.

A squirrel leaped to a branch nearby and eyed him curiously. A few yards off, another descended a tree trunk headfirst, pausing to look around. Owen Chantry spoke to his horse and turned into the aspen, weaving through the slim and graceful white trunks, around deadfalls and occasional boulders, fallen from the mountain.

The hogback, a ten-thousand-foot ridge—timbered on top, the sides rugged and almost sheer—thrust out from the mountain just below a peak called the Helmet. Before him were the towering cliffs of the Rampart Hills. He avoided the route that he had first taken around to the back of the hills, but turned toward the trail Doby Kernohan had discovered.

His problem was simple enough. He was to get Marny Fox out of there and, if there was time, to get whatever it was they were all looking for. Not for a minute did he believe it was gold.

Tracks of deer and elk were everywhere, and twice he saw the tracks of a grizzly, distinguished from other bears by the long claws on the forepaws. He noticed a log the bear had ripped open to get at the termites.

Once he paused near a small stream to watch a dipper bob up and down on a rock. He saw a school of trout lurking in a shady place where a branch hung low on the water. No amount of seeing ever made nature old to him, and he was conscious of every movement and every sound.

It was very still. Sitting his horse among the trees Chantry could look up above the towering red cliffs at the clear blue sky, tumbled with banks of fleecy white clouds.

Somewhere he was conscious of movement. It was no sound he heard, but simply some feeling, some sense that alerted his nerves. He put a hand to the stock of his rifle, then stayed it. He could feel the weight of his pistol and sat quietly, listening.

No sound. . . . Touching a heel to the ribs of the black, he started forward, holding to the thickest stand of trees. He sat up straight, weaving among them, emerging suddenly into a small clearing. He crossed it at a fast walk.

He was now almost directly under the cliffs. Again he paused to listen, studying the narrow opening before him. Chantry swore softly under his breath. He had no love for such places. A man up in those rocks with a rifle. . . .

He rode forward swiftly, trotted his horse to the gap, and then started up. It was a steep climb, but the sooner up the better.

Topping out at the head of the draw he rode swiftly into the trees, then drew up and dismounting, tied his horse with a slipknot as usual and walked back through the trees. Taking a careful look around, he then moved to the head of the draw and crouched down among the brush and rocks, waiting.

Several minutes passed with neither sound nor movement. Confident that he had not been followed, he moved back into the trees.

Mowatt now knew the cabin was there. If he hadn't already torn the place up looking for what he hoped to find, he almost surely would. Waiting where he was, Chantry sat down and considered again what he knew of his brother.

Had Clive hidden it there? Or had he hidden it elsewhere? Clive had always been a cautious man, who left no page unturned, no aspect unregarded.

What could the clue be? And where?

He and Clive had been much apart, yet there had always been understanding between them, and a taste for the same things. Clive had been more bookish and, if anything, even more of a loner than Owen.

His love for wild country had been deep and abiding. His understanding of it, also. There had been a kind of poetry in the man. He was a man who could live richly and well without money, as long as he had wild country and books.

He must try and place himself in Clive's position.

Clive had not intended to leave here, but to stay. He would have considered all aspects of what that meant—including being killed or dying. He would have planned to leave some word behind for Owen.

Mounting his horse again, Owen wove a careful way through the aspens. It was no simple thing, for the trunks stood close together, and there were many deadfalls.

The wood of the aspens broke easily and was subject to attacks from insects as well. Consequently they fell, making travel difficult. Many wild flowers that grew under the aspens sprang up quickly as a rule. It was an unexpected route he was taking, so his tracks might not likely be found.

When he drew near the cabin he dismounted and led the black into a shadowed place where the growth was thick. He tied it, leaving line enough so the gelding could crop the grass and flowers close by.

Moving out of the aspens into a thick stand of spruces, he worked his way closer to the cabin, then squatted down and watched it for several minutes. His eyes searched the grass and could discern no evidence of passage since dewfall. No smoke came from the chimney.

He must spend as little time as possible inside the cabin. He pictured it in his mind and went over each wall with a careful mental scrutiny. Then he devoted some time to the chimney, made of slabs of country rock, carefully fitted. He was mentally searching the cabin to cut down the time he must spend inside. But he found no likely hiding place there for treasure.

The walls were solid—carefully hewn logs fitted with care and precision. The windows, of which there were three, were actually little more than enlarged portholes, a little taller than wide, each closed by solid shutters that were tightly fitted and double-latched in the middle. They could thus be kept small, and the shutters could be set ajar to direct a breeze into any corner of the room. Yet the windows had been cut through solid logs and offered no hiding places.

The hearth was possible. But knowing Clive, Owen dismissed it at once. The hearth was too apparent, and whatever Clive might do he would never be so obvious.

No . . . it would have to be a clue that would be a clue to Owen alone. Some interest, some knowledge they shared; something Clive would know Owen would understand and that would be understood by no one else.

Rifle in hand, he left his cover and walked across to the cabin. Lifting the latch, he thrust open the door. It creaked on its hinges and swung slowly inward. The room was empty.

Standing just inside the door, Owen Chantry listened, but heard nothing. A quick glance around the house showed no evidence of anyone's presence there since his last visit.

Turning slowly around, he looked for anything he might have missed in his mental survey of the cabin. He found nothing. Unless one tore the cabin down, the house could reveal no hiding place. The planks of the floor were tightly fitted. The flagstones of the hearth offered no hidden crevice.

Where then?

For a moment Owen stood looking out the doorway, across the grass and into the distance. Then he looked through each window. He saw the timber from which he had come, the forest behind the house, and a rugged mass of rock, trees and brush.

If he knew what he was looking for, it might be helpful, he thought wryly. If he knew the size, the kind of thing. But he had no clue.

The number ten written on a step. . . . A clue? Or something just written there in passing . . .

Ten what? Ten feet? Yards? Miles? And in which direction?

Chantry studied the earth outside, made a circle of the cabin, ten feet out from its sides. . . . Nothing.

He tried to find ten trees, ten rocks, anything in some shape or design or line that might provide the answer to that mysterious ten. He found nothing.

He looked up. There was a loft, or at least an air space between the ceiling and the peaked roof. He saw no sign of an opening, yet it could be there.

Suddenly he heard a horse approaching. Turning quickly, he glanced through the window. One man, on a gray horse with black mane and tail—a long, rangy horse built for speed and staying power.

The man looked to be around forty-five . . . perhaps a year or two younger. He drew up outside.

"Chantry?"

Owen Chantry stepped to the door, and they studied each other.

The stranger was a quiet-seeming man with strong features and blue gray eyes. On this morning, he was unshaven. His gray handlebar mustache was shapely, however, and he was dressed neatly if roughly.

"I am Frank Mowatt."

"I've heard good things of you," Chantry said quietly "Marny Fox said them."

"She is with you?"

"With the Kernohans, I hope." The question had surprised him. He had supposed she was with them, as she was not here.

"No, I just come from them . . . near them, at least. She isn't there."

"And she's not with you? Your outfit, I mean?"

"No."

"That doesn't make sense. If she's not at one of those places, then where can she be?"

Frank Mowatt's worry was apparent. "Look, Chantry, we may shape up to be on opposite sides in whatever happens next but I'm for that girl. She's a fine girl, and her mother was a fine woman. I want you to know."

"We won't argue the point, Frank. There's no reason she should be caught in the middle. I'm with you all the way, as far as Marny is concerned. Now all we've got to do is find her."

Frank Mowatt shoved his hat back on his head. "She come to me last night. Said she was pullin' out. I told her it was the smartest thing she could do. Said she was tellin' nobody else. Well, I got to worryin' about it and went to her shack.

"She was gone, all right, and her stuff with her. All that she aimed to take. I started out to trail her, but lost her sign back yonder on Turkey Creek. I cast about but couldn't find no tracks, so I decided to ride on over to the old Chantry place. She wasn't there, so I hunted for this place."

Owen Chantry frowned. He looked up suddenly, "Frank, are any of your outfit missing? Tom Freka, for instance?"

"Why him?"

"He's had trouble before. A dance-hall girl was killed down Fort Griffin way. The murder was never pinned on Freka, but a good many figured he was guilty."

"I didn't see him around, but that don't cut no ice. I don't see much of either him or Strawn at any time."

Chantry waited, thinking. There was a kinship between himself and this man, this tired, lonely man tied by a blood relationship to men who seemed not to be his kind.

Where would Marny go? In all this vast wilderness, where *could* she go? Obviously, she'd try to ride to the Kernohans. They were close and she knew them, and she also knew Owen Chantry.

Knew him? Well, possibly not. At least, they had talked. They had seemed to share a certain unspoken understanding, a certain warmth. Was it only their loneliness? Or was it something more?

One thing was certain: She must be found; she must be protected.

It was a curse of the Chantrys—and perhaps of all the Irish—that they belabored themselves with sorrow and old sadnesses, old griefs.

"Go back, Frank. If she returns, she'll need you."

"I could do nothing for her. Among us it is my father who decides."

"Even over the will of Strawn?"

Frank Mowatt stared at him. "Can you doubt it? If you can, you know nothing of Mac Mowatt. Wherever he is, he is in charge."

"I came out today to find her, Frank. I may have to come your way."

"They'll kill you, as they did your brother."

"If they kill me, Frank, I promise you this, you'll have some dogs to bury at my feet. Don't judge me by what happened to Clive. He was more trusting than me . . . and not nearly so good with a gun."

"Strawn said you were good. Very, very good."

"I'm not proud of it. I do what has to be done when the moment comes. And no more than has to be done. I'll find her, Frank."

"Are you in love with her?"

"I would like to find out. And so, perhaps, would she. It is not an easy thing to know."

Frank nodded. "Yes. I do know. . . . There is compassion, sympathy, companionship. All are important," said Chantry.

"They are," said Frank.

"Frank?"

He turned to look at Chantry.

"Can't you talk some reason into them? I don't think there's any treasure here. Nothing they could possibly want. They don't even understand anything but gold or treasure or money of some kind."

"You don't think there's treasure buried here?"

"Why the hell would Clive bury it? If there was treasure—and if he was a man who valued such things—he wouldn't bury it. He'd take it to where he could spend it."

"But if he didn't have time to get away?"

"Think, man. He had time to build this place, and believe me, for a man working alone that took time. You've worked with tools. He had to have time; he had to have patience."

"What could it be besides gold?"

"What I've said. We Chantrys have a love of history, of knowledge. What I think was left here is some odd fragment to an unfinished piece of history, something in the way of a clue."

"You don't know that."

"No . . . I don't. But I do know my family. And although

we've sometimes had money we've never placed much store on it."

Frank chuckled, suddenly. "Be a joke on Pa . . . and them." He smiled a rare smile, then shook his head. "They'd never believe it."

"Do you?"

Frank hesitated. "I don't know . . . maybe." He looked embarrassed. "I never had no education to speak of. Most of two years of schooling and some newspaper reading here and there. I read a whole book. Never did own one though."

Owen Chantry felt the man's half-understood longing for something beyond what he knew.

"There's no end to what a man can learn if he's of a curious mind," Chantry said quietly. "And we Chantrys have been blessed, or cursed, with such minds."

"You better light out," Frank said, suddenly. "They don't aim to wait around. You're here, and they figure you know something. They'll be out to either kill you or make you talk."

"I'll be around," Owen replied coolly, "but I like you, Frank. I think you're a good man, too good for that lot. Do me a favor . . . don't stay with them."

Frank looked around at Chantry, as he turned his horse. "They're my family," he said. "I'll ride with them."

And he rode off, walking his horse, then lifting it to a trot. Owen Chantry watched him go, then turned back to the cabin.

Once more he looked quickly and carefully around. Nothing . . . not a clue. If there was anything left here it wouldn't matter. If he couldn't find it with his knowledge of Clive's thinking, they would not either.

He went outside and crossed to the trees where his horse was waiting. It was time to go.

First, before anything else, he must find Marny.

Fear mounted inside him, fear and helplessness. Where, in all this empty land, would he find her?

TEN

Owen Chantry rode his black horse north. Too much time would be lost in returning to the Kernohans to tell them of his intentions. It was better that he didn't. It would be just like Doby to try to follow, and Owen wanted no interference. Big country it was, a vast and empty country.

He rode due east as the country would allow until he struck a north-south trail, the one he had first followed to the cabin on the rampart. Now he turned north. Frank's tracks were in the trail dust, and Owen rode swiftly, noting by the tracks that Frank had also traveled fast.

Chantry was riding into enemy country, so he carried his rifle in his hand, ready for action—or, if need be, to leave the horse and take to the timber.

The tracks of another horse came off the mesa north of the box canyon and cut into the trail. This rider, whomever he was, had been just ahead of Frank.

The air was cool and very clear. During a pause to study the trail ahead, Chantry took a deep, long breath of the fresh mountain air. Judging by the growth about him, he must be almost ten thousand feet up.

High overhead, an eagle circled against the blue. In the distance thunder rumbled . . . the usual afternoon rain shower would be coming. Lightning hurled its flashing lance against the darker clouds. His black moved on, of its own volition, and Chantry let the gelding go, ears pricked, aware of its rider's alertness.

He shifted the rifle in his hands. The trail he now rode was fresh.

The trail forked suddenly, and Chantry drew up. The trail dipped down and crossed a shallow river. The water was clear and cold, running swiftly over and among the rocks. He crossed over and went up the far bank. He rode up the trail, studying the tracks.

Five horses . . . and one that held to the outside of the trail, the prints were clearly visible in the grass and wild flowers. He had seen the tracks of Marny's horse before, and he believed he was looking at them again.

He moved swiftly, deeply worried now. He was in the bottom of the canyon, which at this point was close to a half mile wide. He forded another creek coming down from the high country and went up the canyon wall through a gap where the wall had fallen back from its usual line and was somewhat lower.

Suddenly the tracks changed. For an hour, Chantry examined them. All the horses had started to run. How long ago? An hour? Two hours? Longer, surely, than that. Apparently the rider of the first horse, the outside one, which he believed had been Marny, had sighted her pursuers and broken into a run. At a dead run, she had ridden a twisted, winding trail down through the trees toward a large clearing, and here and there her horse had actually leaped over deadfalls. Then, suddenly, at the crossing of another trail that skirted the large clearing, the tracks of her horse just vanished!

The pursuers had apparently reined in, too, studying the ground. The trail that Marny had come to led east and west, but which way had she taken?

Where had she gone?

Her pursuers had turned to the west, riding hard. Owen

Chantry took his time considering, for he did not wish to make the mistake they had made. Marny's life might depend upon it.

They had made a mistake, for their own returning tracks were here and there imprinted upon their outgoing tracks.

Still Chantry had not moved. Slowly he began to cast about. She was an uncommonly shrewd girl, who knew the wild country, and she had here decided, he thought, having gained a little time, to lose them.

He had to guess. . . . He had to surmise what he could not know.

He turned west, climbed over the end of a comblike ridge that pointed north from the mountain ahead of him—a peak that looked to be thirteen thousand feet high or more. He crossed another meadow at a fast trot, watching the grass for any sign of passage, and skirted another lake.

Suddenly he was on a trail, a dim trail, long unused. It led north past some beaver ponds and some standing but stark dead trees, and into the deepening shadows of the forest.

Here it was damp and cool. He could smell the forest itself, the pine smell, the spruce smell, the smell of crushed greenery and the faint perfume of flowers.

He drew up sharply. A sound . . . something moving. His gelding snorted and tried to turn, and then he saw it.

A huge grizzly on all fours, almost as tall as his horse and weighing half again as much. The bear was in the trail before them and showed no inclination to move.

Owen spoke softly, calmly, to his horse and kept the rifle in his right hand. The horse stirred its hoofs, eager to be off.

The bear stood up, staring at them through the vague half-light. "It's all right, boy," Chantry said calmly, speaking both to his horse and the bear. Then he added, and he spoke only to the bear, and a little louder. "We're not hunting trouble. You go your way and we'll go ours."

A bear does not charge when standing on two feet, and the big grizzly was probably more curious than anything else. A bear prefers ants, grubs, berries, nuts, and roots, and only a few become consistent meat eaters.

The black gelding reared, snorting. The bear looked a

moment longer as the gelding's hoofs came down to the trail. Owen Chantry steadied the horse, talking quietly, but keeping his rifle ready.

At that distance, if the bear should elect to charge, they were in plenty of trouble. A bear can move fast for a short distance, and this one looked to be a monster, although in the dim light he probably looked larger than he was. The gelding was fast and could turn on a dime. It might be best to chance a shot and run, but the path beyond the bear was where Chantry wanted to go.

Finally, after what seemed a very long inspection and when Chantry could hear the bear sniffing to study their scent, the big bear turned calmly and walked into the woods.

Chantry waited, holding the horse steady until he heard the sounds of movement die away. Then he rode on down the trail. "No use to get spooked," he said, speaking aloud to the horse. "He was just curious."

Now it was too dark to see tracks, and Chantry trusted to the gelding. The horse would hold to the trail, and by its ears and actions Chantry would know if anything was close by that needed his attention.

He rode on, walking his horse along the uncertain trail. Night when it came was cold. A small wind crept down from the icy peaks above. Timberline was only a thousand feet above him, more or less, and a vestige of last light clung there.

He made his camp by moonlight, gathering his wood from the broken bones of fallen trees. He could hear running water from some small stream of melting snow, and where the shelter was best he built a small fire and made coffee. He chewed on a strip of jerky and looked out across the vast blackness toward the stars in that grayer blackness overhead.

How many lonely campfires? How much incense offered the gods of desolation from his nightly resting places? And how many more to come?

He smiled wryly and got out his frying pan.

He pushed a couple of pine cones into the flames to make the fire flare up. He was in a reckless mood, irritated at not finding Marny Fox and afraid he might never find her.

He shaved bacon into the pan and put it up on a couple of rocks and watched it bubble and spit.

"Hello, the fire!" A voice called from out of the night and the cold.

"Come in, if you're of a mind to. And come any way as suits you."

A horse walked up to the fire, a gray horse bearing a gray man in the saddle. A gray old man in buckskins, with young gray eyes a-twinkle in an old gray face.

"Seen your fire," the old man said. "Figured you was wishful of company."

"I was, but I wasn't expecting you. I was expecting trouble."

"Seen a mite of it myself, time to time. I don't know's I care for no trouble, but the smell of bacon an' coffee is durned near worth whatever comes."

"Get down then, and sit up to the fire." Chantry watched the old man with a careful eye. He carried a Sharps .50 and a bowie knife, at least. If he had a handgun, it was not in sight.

"These are lonely hills," said Chantry

"They was," the old man said, fussing with his saddle. "They was almighty empty for many a year. A man could live out his time 'thout bother from other folks. I seen more folks t'day then I seen all year."

"There was sign along the trail," Chantry commented.

"You betchy," the old man muttered. "They'll be blood on the rocks afore we see the last of that outfit. Blood on the rocks for sure."

"Four men?" Chantry suggested.

"Aye. Four of 'em. Mean an' miserable, too. I seen 'em an' got off into the rocks and hunkered down with old Mary here. If they'd a come at me I'd a shot 'em, I would. I never took nothin' from their likes and ain't about to. I'd of hung their hair to dry on a tall pole or a tree somewheres."

"Where are they now?"

"Four, five mile down the mountain and west. I come up the mountain to be rid of them or their breeze. Then I fetched a sight of your fire, and I looked about to see who else was up."

"Did you see anyone else?"

"Ain't that enough for one day? Mister, I been years up and down these mountains, ain't seen nobody. Didn't want to see nobody. I seen a man two year back over on the Animas, an' I reckoned that was enough. Now all to oncet they're a-comin' out of the rocks, all around. Gettin' so a man can't find no peace."

"You better ride high and camp high from now on. That's a bad outfit down yonder."

"You're a-tellin' *me*? I seen 'em."

"You didn't see anyone else? A lone rider, maybe?"

The old man walked up to the fire and speared a rasher of bacon from the pan with his bowie knife. He peered at Chantry from under gray brows. "Was you lookin' for somebody?" he asked, peering.

"I am," Chantry replied. "I'm looking for a girl. And I'd better find her before those down below do. She's who they're hunting for."

"Are they now? Well, why don't you an' me just slip down there 'fore daylight and shoot the four of 'em? Save trouble."

"Shoot them? In cold blood?"

"Cold blood? I don't know if their blood is hot or cold or lukewarm. They're varmints. *Varmints*. I could read their sign and smell their smell. Shoot 'em, says I. Shoot 'em down an' leave 'em for the buzzards. I'd a done it m'self, only one man can't noways get off four shots fast enough. You got you one o' them six-shootin' pistols an' a repeater. Hell, if I had a repeater they be dead by now."

"That's a lovely lady they're chasing," Chantry said. "I'd not want her in their hands."

"Shoot 'em. Stretch their hide. They ain't no good. Not one mother's son of 'em. Shoot 'em, I say."

He ate his bacon and speared another slice. Chantry took up the slab he had and sliced off half a dozen more.

"Seen you huntin' 'em," the old man said, past a mouthful of bacon. "Watched you from up yonder." He gestured toward the high peaks. "Had m' glass on you."

"Glass? You've got a pair of field glasses?"

"Nope. I got me a telyscope. A ginuwine telyscope." He

went to his pack and from a roll of blanket extracted a four-foot seaman's telescope of a type Owen Chantry had not seen since he was a boy, and it was an antique then. "With this thing I can see from here to yonder. I was a-watchin' you a-follerin' them. I watched them, too. I seen 'em huntin' that girl. Seen her give 'em the slip."

He demolished the rest of the bacon and wiped the blade of his bowie on his sleeve, then sheathed it. "Come daylight, you an' me an' that girl can meet up. I know a way off this mountain that'll bring us to her before they get there."

"We'd better," Owen said quietly. "That's a bad outfit."

The old man studied him. "You kin to that Chantry feller had the ranch?"

"I am. Did you know him?"

"Know him? I should smile. I knowed him. Why, I rode right up to these mountains with him and helped lay the timbers of his cabin on the rampart. I knew him. Good man."

Owen Chantry stared. This gray old man had known Clive Chantry.

ELEVEN

Owen Chantry had seen too much to doubt too much. He was intelligent. He had a healthy vein of skepticism, but he had traveled too widely and read too much not to understand that the seemingly impossible could happen.

As the old man ate and talked, Chantry watched him thoughtfully. The old man was quick and active, also very thin, wiry, and strong.

The oldest people Chantry had known all lived at relatively high altitudes, where many illnesses simply do not exist because the germs that spread them are not active in that cold, clear air. Or perhaps there were simply fewer people to harbor the germs.

"If you know a way to head them off, we'd better get going early," said Chantry.

The old man looked over his shoulder. "Worried about her, ain't you? Well, I'd be too. Them as follers her are a mighty poor lot, a sorry lot."

Chantry pushed a few heavier sticks into the fire, then stretched out. He was tired . . . he hadn't realized how tired.

90

Yet he slept, and well. It was still dark when he heard the old man breaking sticks. When Owen raised up, the old fellow glanced over. "Seen you had coffee," he said. "Ain't had much lately. Git some chicory in the woods, time to time, but it ain't the same."

Chantry sat up, shook out his boots carefully to be sure no wanderers had taken shelter there during the night, and tugged them on. He didn't know this old man and preferred to make the coffee himself.

The fire blazed up brightly. Chantry glanced around. It was a perfect camp, sheltered from the wind, partly sheltered from rain, with wood and water.

When he had made coffee and started some bacon, he rolled his bed. The old man went about his business as if alone, taking his horse to water and returning to pack up. Owen did the same, and when they had eaten he kicked earth over the fire. When Owen would have dumped out the coffee, the old man insisted on keeping the grounds, wrapping them carefully in a piece of well-tanned hide.

"Ain't tasted coffee in a spell," he said. "Might be a long time agin. Out here I don't throw nothin' away 'til it's plumb used up."

They started out. The old man led them at a good fast walk down a very steep trail for a hundred yards or so, then at a canter along a gradual slope.

The shot came from afar. A single shot, and then silence. The old man pulled up sharply. Chantry's eyes swept the country in a quick, measuring glance.

All was still. There was no movement, no further sound. The shot seemed to have come from somewhere before them, but in the clear air the sound might have carried for some distance.

Chantry started forward again, the only sound the swishing of the horses' hoofs in the grass. He held his rifle in his right hand, ready for use.

Then right before them, he saw the tracks of several hard-ridden horses. Grass was torn and earth kicked up where the hoofs had dug in. Men riding that hard were going straight to an objective, and not in doubt about it.

Suddenly, half a mile away and racing across a meadow, he saw three riders, two bay horses and a buckskin, running all out.

The old man spoke up suddenly. "Chantry, if I cut out, don't you worry none. I'll be around about."

"Just don't get in the way," Owen replied. "You do what you're of a mind to."

"What you figurin' on?"

"I'm going in and get that girl out of there."

"You see her?"

"No. . . . But look at that rocky knoll yonder? The one covered with aspens. There's been a blowdown hit that slope. See the dead trees? My guess is she's there, trying to make a stand."

"Yeah," the old man said. "They've left one man to pin her down while they try to outflank her. Don't you go gittin' yourself killed. I ain't much hand at goin' agin three, four men single-handed. If'n I was huntin' 'em, now. . . ."

"Hunt them then, but stay out of range. When I go in there I don't want to think about where else my bullets are going."

Chantry walked his horse forward, sitting straight up in the saddle, missing nothing. He was reminded of a time during the war when he was outside Chattanooga. He had led a cavalry charge against a crossroads position, and they had come out of the trees, just like this, unseen by the men in position below.

But this was war of another kind, and he commanded no company. There was only himself and one old man of whom he knew nothing.

He began to trot, his eyes searching for the fourth man.

He heard a shot and saw a puff of smoke from the knoll under the aspens. Almost instantly the hidden marksman replied, and then Chantry saw him, hunkered down behind a mound of earth and brush, lifting his rifle for another shot.

Owen wheeled his horse, the packhorse following, and went in at a dead run.

The man heard him coming too late. Wheeling around, he drew up his rifle for a shot. Yet the turn and the lift of the gun were too fast. The rifle went off before it was fairly lined up, and the next instant Owen rode in up on him, firing with his rifle downward, shooting with one hand.

The man jerked back, spun and dropped. He started to get up and Chantry reined in, turning in a small circle around him.

He'd been hit, all right. Blood stained his shirt and pants right about the beltline on the right side.

"You played hell!" he said.

The man was a rough-looking fellow, but unfrightened.

"You surely bought yourself a ticket!" he said angrily. "The old man will have your scalp for this."

"Does it take four of you to round up one little girl?" Chantry asked.

"Are you Owen Chantry?"

"I am, and that girl is to be left alone. You understand?"

The man spat. "You better tell them yonder. They ain't about to leave her alone. They done had enough of her uppity ways. Who does she think she is?"

"Why don't you ask Mowatt?" Chantry suggested.

The man spat again. "Hell, Mowatt don't know what's good for him. That girl ain't no kin."

The man was clasping his leg tightly, but even as he talked the initial shock was wearing off. The pain was growing and he squinted his eyes against it, not wanting to let Chantry see.

Out of respect for the man, Chantry turned away. But as he rode off he kept an eye on him to see that he didn't reach for a gun. But the man was wholly concerned with his wound and didn't again look up.

Chantry rode forward, and there were no shots. As he mounted a small knoll he glimpsed Marny's horse, deep inside a clump of trees.

"Marny?" he called softly.

"Come on in," she spoke just loud enough for him to hear. "Although you've come to a poor place."

He rode in through the trees and swung down. She got up from a tangle of fallen logs. There was a smudge on her cheek and the skirt she wore was rumpled.

"Are you all right?" he asked.

"So far, but there's still three more, and they'll be back."

He glanced around quickly. The clump of trees was no more than fifty or sixty feet across, any way you looked, and there were a good many deadfalls and several clumps of boulders. The field of fire in most directions was good.

"They'll come. But when they find out you're not alone, they'll pull out. Then we'll have to run for it."

She glanced at him. "You needn't, you know. I can get along."

She thought again how cold his face was. It was hardboned and strong, but there was little warmth in it until he smiled. There was loneliness in it, too, yet nothing about him invited sympathy. This was a man who had been much alone, with no experience at sharing feelings—probably because there had been nobody to share them with.

"You've always been alone, haven't you?" she asked.

He shrugged, watching the timber across the meadow. "It's better alone than with somebody you don't trust."

"You've never learned to share your feelings."

"Who wants my feelings? A man alone keeps his feelings to himself."

She saw a movement among the leaves. "There's somebody over there."

"I see."

"Are you going to shoot?"

"Not until I see what I'm shooting at. Anybody who shoots blind is a fool. Something moving in the brush may be your best friend. Whenever I squeeze a trigger I know what I'm shooting at."

"But we don't have any friends here!"

"There's Doby. And his Pa. . . . And that old man I met last night."

"Old man?"

"He knows you. He's got a telescope, and there's not much he doesn't know . . . He's also got a Sharps fifty."

"How old is he?"

"Looks like he was here first and they built the mountains around him. But he's spry . . . he's mighty spry, and canny."

There was a yell off to their right, and when Owen turned they were coming . . . all three of them. They were well scattered and coming in at a dead run.

Chantry lifted his rifle like a man shooting ducks, and he fired left, middle, and right.

There was no wasted motion, and no emotion. He just lifted the rifle and came down on his targets, held up the merest second and squeezed off his shots.

The first man veered sharply and dropped his rifle, then fell down the slope and into the bottom. The second man dropped from the saddle, hit the grass, and lay there. The third wheeled his horse wildly and tried to escape. Chantry let him have three good jumps while he held his fire. Then he shot.

"I held high," he explained, apologetically. "I might have shot through him and killed a good horse."

The horse and rider went racing away across the field, but the man rode limply, one arm dangling.

"Only the horse? Not the man?"

"The man came a-hunting trouble. He rode after a lone woman and he brought plenty of help, so whatever he gets is too good for him. The horse didn't have a choice. He was ridden into this fight, so there's no use for it to suffer." Chantry loaded his rifle again. "If you want to dance, you pay the fiddler. Only in this dance," he smiled at her, "in this dance the devil does the fiddling and you pay in blood."

He glanced around the rocky, tree-covered knoll. "I like this place. When you pick a place to make a stand, you do all right."

The last echoes of the firing had died away. Not the faintest smell of powder smoke remained. It was as if nothing had happened. Only the body lying out there in the grass said otherwise, only a dark patch against the green.

It would still be like this when they were gone. The few scars they left would be erased quietly. Even if left unburied the body would be disposed of in time, and after many years only a few buttons and perhaps a buckle would remain. Men would come, would pass, and where they walked the grass would grow again, and the forest, and there would be no signs of their passing.

"We'd better go," he said. "There's been enough of this."

"They won't stop, you know. Mac Mowatt is losing control. They will want blood now. They'll come after you, Owen, and they'll come after me. But it's the treasure they want."

"Treasure!" he was irritated. "The treasure is out there," he waved a hand. "The treasure is the country itself."

He helped her to the saddle, then mounted and picked up the leadline of his packhorse. They rode out and down across the meadow.

Suddenly the old man came down from a clump of spruces across the way. He rode up to them and reined around, staring angrily at Chantry. "Might o' left me one!" he said. "You cleaned house 'fore I got my fifty up. I d'clare, I never seen such shootin'. You an' me, we could make us a passel out on the buffalo grass."

Owen Chantry led away to the south. He was withdrawn, not wanting to talk. Fighting had been a way of life for as long as he could recall, but he wanted no more of it.

Sensing his mood, Marny said nothing. Against the far-off horizon the Sleeping Ute Mountain bulked large and, nearer, the great shelf of Mesa Verde thrust out, sharp against the sky.

"Do you know what they say?" she spoke suddenly. "We had a half-breed Navajo with us for a while. He said there were ghost cities up there . . . houses, walls, rooms, all empty and still."

Owen's eyes turned toward the bulk of the great plateau. "Could be," he said, "though it's a less favored place than the mountains we've come from."

The old man disagreed. "Depends on what you're lookin' for. If you're in a country where there's savage Indians, fighters like the 'Paches and the Navajos, then maybe you want a place you can defend."

Owen Chantry offered no comment. He had been looking far off, and now he drew up on the edge of a slight shelf that offered a good view to the west.

Far off against the sky a slim column of smoke was rising toward the sky. Chantry swore softly, bitterly.

Startled, Marny said, "What is it, Owen?"

"They've fired the ranch," he said. He pointed to the smoke. "It's burning . . . or has been."

"What about the Kernohans?" she asked, suddenly frightened for them.

"I don't know," he said. "I just don't know."

TWELVE

Pa was just a-gettin' hitched up when I seen 'em comin'. He had the harness on when I glimpsed the dust on the trail, an' I yelled at him.

"Pa! The Mowatt gang!"

Well, I never seen him act so fast or so sure. I didn't know he had it in him. Pa seemed to me a ord'nary sort of man, and when I picked out heroes he wasn't among 'em. But he wasted no time.

The saddle was already on my horse for I'd been fixin' to take off yonder to the hills. Pa had bound me up tight round the chest and waist, like I was in a cast, and although he didn't know what I aimed to do, he wanted my ribs to knit nice and clean so he done what seemed best to him.

So my horse was ready, an' my rifle was there with extra bullets. An' a bait of grub. An' when Pa seen that dust cloud he run for the house.

I started after him and he yelled back to turn the stock loose. That meant the cows he had up, the one we were milkin', and the heavy stock, so I threw down the corral bars and shied 'em out and into a run down the meadow.

Pa come out with clothes and a few extries. He'd been thinkin' on this. That I figgered out after, 'cause he knew just what to take. He run for the horses.

"Pa!" I yelled. "What about the house?"

"We didn't have a house when we come here, boy, but we did have ourselves and our stock. Let's go!"

We taken out.

The way Pa led off I knowed he wasn't just runnin' wild. He had a bee in his bonnet and soon I seen what it was.

He was ridin' right into Lost Canyon.

Sometime or other he'd found him a trail, and we went for it. Afore we got there, we rode through several big clump of trees, and he done what he could to cover our trail. Then he headed for that place he'd found.

Right where we hit the canyon she probably wasn't much more'n fifteen hundred feet rim to rim, but she was at least five hundred feet deep. And both walls was covered with trees 'cept right at the rim. It was thick cover.

We didn't waste no time. Pa went over that rim and dropped plumb out of sight. When I got that close I seen his horse slidin' on his haunches down a trail that made you catch your breath to look at.

I taken out after him. I wasn't goin' to have Pa sayin' I showed the white feather 'cause of no cliff. But I was sweatin' blue water by the time I'd gone down a hundred feet.

We bottomed out in that there canyon close by a stream, that went rushin' by—a fine trout stream if ever I seen one, and me with no pole nor no time to fish.

Sometime or other, Pa had done some scoutin' without sayin' a word to me about it. He'd been here afore and he led off almighty fast to a place where, some time or other, the stream cut back into the cliff to make of a holler faced off with trees. Some fallen logs had made a natural corral, and here we bunched our stock and Pa got down off his horse.

"You stay here, Doby. I've got somethin' to do up yonder."

"You goin' back, Pa?"

"They ain't gonna burn that house 'thout me showin' 'em I disapprove," he said. "I'll just fire a few rounds and then come on back."

"I'll go along."

"Now, son, you stay here with the stock. I ain't put in my years raisin' you from a penny-grabbin', candy-suckin' kid to a growed up man just to see you killed by no outlaws. You set tight and I'll be back, and then we'll plan what to do."

"Pa, if'n you raised me to set still and watch my Pa go into a fight by hisself, you surely wasted your time. I'm a-goin' with you."

We went up together, me an' Pa, and I never felt closer to him than right at that time. We went up together and we run back through the trees. The Mowatt gang was circlin' round the house, yellin' and shootin'.

There was smoke from the chimney, and I guess they didn't know we was gone. It was too far away for good shootin', but we had to git back to that canyon if they took out after us, so Pa hunkered down among some rocks and he taken a long sight and squeezed her off. I seen that ol' rifle jump in his hands and one of them horses r'ared up like it was burned and its rider went tumblin'. Then you never seen folks scatter like they done.

But not before I put in some lead. I'd had my eye on one big gent with white suspenders, and I held my sight a mite below where those suspenders crossed on his back, and though it was a good long shot I tightened up the finger until that rifle went off.

I didn't kill him, but I burned him. I made him know he'd been shot at. I sent him a yippin' out of there. But they kept ridin' around. One of 'em throwed a torch at the house that fell on the roof an' rolled off.

Both Pa an' me we opened up an' dusted 'em around with lead. It taken 'em a few shots to realize we weren't inside but outside, and then they turned around and charged at us.

Well, you never seen such a fine sight.

There must've been fourteen or fifteen of 'em an' they was all mounted up on fine horses and they come at us like cavalry chargin'. It was a real sight. A better sight I never saw nor had, lookin' right down the rifle barrel at 'em, and that time when I fired there wasn't no mistake. A man just throwed up his hands and fell off his horse. He hit dust and rolled over and he lay all sprawled out. And Pa took a shot and then he said, "Son, let's get out'n here."

So we taken off.

We taken off a-runnin'. Pa was a better runner than I thought. He was really a-leggin' it when we heard a yell behind.

They'd seen us.

"Here, boy," Pa said. He dropped behind a log and he hadn't hit dirt 'fore he fired. And me, I was just a hair behind him, firing standin' up behind a good thick tree.

They'd set the house afire. We could see the smoke goin' up.

Them riders split around us and we hightailed it. We was close to the rim then and bullets was kickin' the dust all around us when we went over the rim and flopped down. We was shootin' fast.

They turned right and left into the trees and I started reloadin' and looked over at Pa. And there was blood all over his shirt, and his face had gone white and me, I was scared.

I crawled over to him and slung him over my back, and carryin' both rifles I slid and fell and crawled to the bottom of the canyon. It was no way to handle a hurt man, but I didn't have no choice. I got him to our corral and bathed off his face a little, then tried to peel off his shirt.

I got it off and his undershirt down to his waist. I seen the bullet had hit his shoulder bone and tore through the meat on his shoulder, and down his back a mite. It was pressin' against the skin of his back, a bluelike lump, and I figgered the thing to do was get shut of it. So I slid out my bowie and cut a slit in the skin and the bullet, it just popped out in my hand.

He'd lost some blood. He'd lost a-plenty of blood, but it didn't look to me like no death wound. Still, a body couldn't be sure. So I plugged up the wound with pieces of his undershirt, bathed him off some, and stretched him out.

The bullet hittin' that shoulder bone must have been a shock 'cause he'd passed out, somewheres.

I taken his rifle and reloaded it and set a-watchin' for the Mowatt gang. But didn't none of 'em come. I was all set for 'em, and I was aimin' to kill me some men. But they never come.

I guess they thought they'd killed us. Or scared us off, or somethin'. Or maybe they didn't relish comin' into that canyon against two rifles that had the drop on them from the trees.

So there I was in the bottom of Lost Canyon, with Pa bad off from lost blood and me not knowin' a thing 'bout what to do.

Time to time, I'd figgered Pa didn't know much. But he was always able to patch up folks or doctor 'em somehow. And me, for all my windy talk, I didn't know what to do.

Right then I surely wasn't thinkin' of no blonde and blue-eyed girls. I was just wishin' I known what to do 'cause there wasn't nobody else around to help.

I kindled us a small fire and started heatin' water in one of the kettles Pa had slung on the horse. I swear, he must have thought it all out ahead of time 'cause he'd took along everything a body might need.

Unpackin' the horses I started rummaging around to see what I could find. I come on a can of white powder Pa had been give by an old man once that was supposed to be good for bob-wire cuts. Now I'd never seen no bob-wire, but I'd heard of it, and a bob-wire cut was a scratch. And this here wound wasn't too different, so when I'd bathed it again, I scattered some of that white powder around it.

Them days, when folks was far from doctors, they just concocted their own medicine, and some of it worked almighty good. I put on the coffeepot and scouted for firewood. And I built our cover a little higher.

For all I knew they might just be a-settin' up there atop the rim waitin' 'til it was sure-enough dark to come at me.

Leavin' Pa for a moment I slipped down and got some water to heat up for broth after I'd made the coffee.

When I got back Pa was stirrin' a mite. How long he'd been bleedin' before I seen he was wounded I don't know. It might have been after the first burst of gunfire, but the way his clothes was soaked up with blood had scared me somethin' awful.

Nobody showed. I guess they never come down off the rim but I wasn't taken no chances going up there. If they nailed me, Pa would be left to die down here. Or tough it out alone.

So I set and waited and listened, longing for *somebody* to come. Only there wasn't nobody goin' to, 'less Owen Chantry come back, and he'd not find us easy, way down in this hole.

I was real scared for Pa and never felt so helpless in all my days.

It was long after midday 'fore Pa opened up his eyes. I was right there with some coffee, and I held the cup for him and let him have a sip or two.

"What happened?" he asked.

"You caught one, Pa. Ain't too bad, but you surely lost blood. You got to sit quiet an' rest. Ain't nobody come. I got the stock took care of and some deefenses built up an' the guns loaded an' I been settin' by just a-waitin' for 'em to come. . . ."

He closed his eyes, then taken a mite more of coffee. It seemed to do him some good, and so I shaved off some jerky into a kettle and stirred it up real good with a fire under it. Soon I'd have us some broth.

"Chantry'll come," he said. "We'll be all right then."

Well, that sort of ired me. "He won't find us, if'n he does. An' even if'n he does come, he'll likely run afoul of them Mowatts. We got to set here 'til you feel better, then climb up yonder and get out of here."

"This here's our home, boy. We're not goin' to leave. We're goin' back an' build up that house again. I've done wandered all I'm a-goin' to, son. I've been a mover all my born days, but this here's where I intend to stay. Maybe it ain't the finest land, maybe it's far from city places, but it's land I can say is mine. We'll stay."

By the time I'd fed him all he would take of that broth, the sun was out of sight and shadows were climbin' the walls of the canyon. I drank what was left.

Then I taken the stock to water and found a patch of open grass along the stream. I dragged some poles into place and made a corral, using rocks, trees, and the side of the canyon. That would keep my stock a-feedin'.

Then I taken up my rifle. "Pa?" I said.

He answered somethin'. Only what he said weren't right. He had him a fever and was wandering in his head. I'd figgered on going up to the rim for a look around.

I was turning back when I noticed the ears on Mary. Mary was a plow horse, and she was a big, powerful brute, but gentle as could be. And she could sense whatever was goin' on around. Mary had her head and ears up. . . . Something was a-comin'.

There wasn't no sound. Not a smidgin. And I listened hard.

Mary's ears were still up, though she seemed less concerned. Maybe it was a varmint of some kind, a catamount, or the like. I started to set down my rifle when somebody spoke.

"Doby? Is it all right to come in?"

It was that Chantry. It was him, sure 'nough.

"Come on in," I said. I was never so relieved in all my born days. I wasn't alone no longer with nobody to help with Pa but me.

Chantry come out of the trees afoot and stopped there 'til I had a good look at him. Then he come on up to the fire. He looked at Pa. "How bad is he?"

So I told him. Pa was sleeping, so Chantry said to let him sleep, which was the best doctor of all. But when Pa was awake he'd have a look at the wound. And then he said, "Marny is with me, and an old man."

"An old man?"

"He's been here in these mountains for years. . . . Or so he says."

"I never seen no old man round here. You sure he ain't one of them?"

"He's not. We've been doing some shooting of our own." Chantry went to the edge of the woods and called softly.

They come in. There was that girl, lookin' tired-like but

still almighty pretty, and an old, old man who looked like somebody had woke him up from his grave, he was that gray an' old. But he moved about spry enough, an' the way he taken for that coffeepot, you'd a thought he owned it.

"Get some sleep, Doby," Chantry said to me. "I'll look after your pa."

Well . . . I was tired.

They built up the fire some and when I'd stretched out to sleep they set around drinkin' coffee.

Our house had been burned, our stock scattered, an' Pa was wounded. I had me a couple of busted ribs, and there was folks up on the canyon rim that wanted to kill us, but I slept. I just taken off to sleep, and it was full day 'fore my eyes opened up. And there was no more sound than nothin'.

I sat up and looked around. There was Marny Fox, a-settin' by the fire. Pa was a-layin' on the ground not far off, his head on a folded coat.

Chantry was nowhere about.

"Where's Chantry?" I asked.

"He went up to the house."

"Ain't no house. He's wastin' his time. It's done burned down."

"No, it isn't, Doby. The old man looked at it through his telescope and the house is standing. It's been partly burned, all right, but it's still standing."

Course, I should have maybe figgered on that. Heavy timbers like them would take time to burn. A sudden flash fire might not hold long enough to get them tight-fitted, squared-off logs to burnin'.

I went to the creek and splashed water on my face and washed my hands. I taken a mouthful of water and kind of sloshed it around inside, then spit it out. Then I combed my hair with my fingers the best I could.

When I come back to the fire, Marny poured coffee for me. And about that time Owen Chantry come in with that old man who looked like the walkin' dead.

Chantry had an armful of books, some of 'em charred a mite, but that was all. "The house didn't burn, Doby. Only part of the roof and part of the porch."

"You saved you some books," I said. "Is that all you looked for?"

"It's Tennyson I wanted," he said, "I. . . ." A kind of funny look come over his face, and he stared hard at Marny. "Tennyson. . . . Now that *is* a thought."

THIRTEEN

They were huddled together in a bunch.

"I used to read," Marny said, "but we've few books here. If it wasn't for Mac—"

"Mowatt reads?"

"As a matter of fact, he does. My feeling is, considering where he's lived, he's had a better than average education."

"My brother liked Tennyson," Chantry said, "and we had a mutual favorite, a poem called 'Ulysses.' "

It wasn't the right time to be talking of books and poetry. It was time to figure a way to get out of the fix.

The Mowatts had bled and they'd not take it lightly. They'd come back.

"I think we should pay us a visit to Mowatt," said Doby.

"Clive would have his own way of doing things," Chantry mused, "and if he wanted to tell me something he'd have his own way of doing it."

"Them Mowatts got a way of tellin' things, too," Kernohan said, cross-like. "They'll be comin' back and here we set, like an ol' ladies' tea party!"

"You're right, of course," Chantry said. "But I don't think they'll come now. Sooner or later, we must leave this canyon, and when we do it will be easier for them to attack."

Marny brought Chantry a cup of coffee. He took it gratefully and glanced over at Doby.

Chantry knew the younger Kernohan had a chip on his shoulder, and it was probably over Marny. Well . . . that was to be expected. The important thing was not to let it get out of hand. Chantry was, he knew himself, inclined to be impatient, but he must not be impatient with Doby, who was a good lad and had the makings of a man.

Despite his assurances to the others, Chantry also knew the situation was uncertain. How much control could or would be exerted by Mac Mowatt remained to be seen.

He was tired and he needed a shave. Suddenly, he was irritated. Doby was right. It was time to wind this thing up.

"I'm going to see him," he said suddenly.

They looked at him, uncomprehendingly.

"I'm going to see Mac Mowatt and have him call off his dogs."

"You're plumb crazy!" The old man spoke before any of the others could. "They'd kill you afore you got to 'im. An' he ain't callin' nobody off, even if he could."

"We'll see."

Marny was on her feet again. She was wide-eyed and still, staring at him. "They won't listen," she protested. "They'll kill you."

They were right, of course, but he was right, too. Mowatt might see reason. If he did, that would take most of the load off their backs, anyway. Getting to him would be a problem but, despite his normal caution, there was in Owen Chantry a streak of wild Irish rebellion—foolhardiness some would call it. Others would call it plain damn foolishness. . . . But it was his way to bow his neck and plunge in. And better him than the others.

"They won't expect it," he said, more quietly. "I could walk in on them."

"You can walk in," Doby said grimly, "but you'll never walk out again."

In a flash of anger, Chantry spoke and was instantly sorry. "You'd like that, wouldn't you, Doby?"

All their heads came up. Doby flushed. "Nossir, I wouldn't," he said. "You an' me may not see eye to eye, but I'd surely not like to see you get killed. I surely wouldn't."

Doby swallowed.

"Fact is, you go in there an' I'm a-goin' with you," Doby said. "I can shoot, an' I can stand steady. You go in there with me an' you'll see you ain't the on'y one's got hair on his chest."

"I never doubted it, Doby," Chantry said, sincerely. "But I'll have to go by myself. After all," he added, "it was my brother they killed. Whatever it is they're looking for belongs to me."

"Maybe it does," Doby said stubbornly, "an' maybe it don't. It's buried in the ground, or hid. So maybe it's just treasure-trove belongin' to the finder."

Chantry shrugged. "Wherever and whatever it is," he said calmly, "my brother intended me to find it, and so he will have left it."

He wanted it over, done with. He was getting the old urge to get out, to leave. Yet how many times had he done just that? Was that not, in itself, a form of cowardice?

Chantry brushed the wood ashes from his sleeve. He would need a new coat. This one was getting threadbare. He straightened it and walked over to his horse. This was no place to leave his friends, yet. . . . He glanced up the canyon.

He hated to leave. Kernohan was hard hit. Reluctantly, Chantry gave up the idea of moving their camp. They would have to chance it here.

"Sit tight," he said, "I'll go out and take a look."

"If you're goin' after 'em, I'm comin' along," Doby insisted.

"You stay. What about your pa?"

Doby looked trapped, but he argued no longer. "You're takin' a long chance," he said.

Chantry glanced over at Marny. "I'll be back," he said and, touching a spur to his horse, he started for the trail.

He had no certain plan, nor could a plan be devised until he saw the situation at close hand.

It was a good scramble for his horse to get up the trail to the top of the mesa, and Chantry dismounted and led his horse when they reached the crest.

Birds were everywhere about. A squirrel sat on the ground near some rocks.

Every move must be made with caution now, for the renegades who rode with Mowatt were frontiersmen, all of them. His only advantage lay in the fact that they might also be careless.

He walked his horse in the deepest shadows, pausing from time to time to listen. He was disturbed by a vagrant but unfocused notion that kept slipping around at the edge of his mind. Every time he tried to pin the thought into position, to guide it into focus, it slipped away, eluding him.

. . . Something about Tennyson and his brother and himself. They used to write each other letters.

His horse walked softly through the grass and wild flowers that edged the woods. It was the long way around, but he had no desire to trust himself to the open out there, where the distance was shorter.

When he was well away from Lost Canyon, he moved more swiftly.

The air was cool, there was a dampness of dew on the underbrush now. Something stirred and he drew up suddenly. Several shadows moved out into sight. He waited, holding his breath. Then he slowly relaxed. . . . Elk. They liked to feed in high meadows at night.

He caught a faint smell of smoke. He waited, trying to locate the source. The smell faded. He walked his horse on, keeping his eyes on its ears.

The ears were up, and Chantry could sense the interest of his horse. It smelled something too. The smoke, other horses, or men. . . .

A faint breeze stirred the leaves, they rustled, and the

breeze passed. He walked on, a few steps further. Chantry had a feeling he was near their camp, but so far he had no definite indication of it.

He caught a gleam through the trees . . . water. He rode closer. It was a small lake, yet he still saw no fire, nor smelled any more smoke. He rode around the lake, taking his time. He glanced at the stars. He still had plenty of darkness before daybreak. Suddenly he caught a whiff of smoke again . . . very faint, but definite.

It seemed to be coming from straight ahead. He kept in the darkest shadows and rode on.

He saw the horses first, felt his own horse swell his sides with a deep breath. "Easy, boy," Chantry whispered. "Take it easy now!" He wanted no whinny that would arouse the camp.

Chantry stepped down from the saddle and with a slipknot tied his horse in the deepest shadows. They were downwind of the Mowatt horses, yet it could be only a few minutes, perhaps a few seconds, until they scented his horse.

He glanced around at the sleeping camp. There was no guard, for obviously they doubted that anyone would have the courage to attack them. Chantry's sense of the fitness of things rebelled at the careless, dirty, ill-kept camp. One by one, he let his eyes slide over the sleeping men until he picked out Mowatt—a bit to one side, an enormous figure of a man covered with a buffalo robe.

Stepping lightly, Chantry walked right through the middle of the camp and squatted on his heels beside Mowatt. It was only then that he realized the old man's eyes were open and on him, and that Mac Mowatt held a pistol in his right hand.

"Mr. Mowatt," he spoke softly.

"Been watchin' you," Mowatt whispered and heaved himself up. "Been watchin' you ever since you showed up . . . listenin' to you come afore that. Got ears like a cat," he said proudly. "Always could hear more'n anybody else."

He rubbed his face, then squinted at Chantry. "You got you a nerve . . . ridin' in here like this. When the boys wake up they'll carve their names in your hide."

"In your own camp?" Chantry acted surprised. "I understood *you* were the man in your outfit. Even an Apache respects an enemy in an Apache's camp. . . ."

"Some Indians do. All right. What d'ya want?"

"Marny tells me that you read."

"*Read?* What in the hell's that got to do with anything? 'Course I read! I had schoolin'. Most of it's been forgot, but I had it. My pa was a reader. Had him a house full. Must have been eight or ten books."

"That's why I came here. I want to talk to you before anybody else gets killed. There is no gold, Mowatt. There never was."

Mowatt snorted. "You 'spect me to believe that? We done heard about this treasure already. How all that gold was brought up from Mexico—"

" '*All that gold?*' Think, man. When my brother came into this country he came out of Mexico with one, maybe two pack mules. He had a small outfit, some grub maybe, and he rode through Apache country. There was no way he could have carried enough gold to matter, even if he had it. And I know enough about him to know that he never cared much for money.

"If he'd had any gold, why would he stop *here?* Where he couldn't use it? Why stop here after riding all that distance out of Mexico?"

"You got you a point there. Always did wonder 'bout that. Figgered he was crazy or a miser or something."

"I believe he brought something with him," Chantry continued, "but I do not think it was treasure. I want to talk to you because you might understand, you might grasp the idea . . . which I am sure they," Chantry gestured at the camp, "would not.

"Although," he added, "Frank Mowatt might." Chantry looked straight at Mac Mowatt. "You know, Mr. Mowatt, Frank is the best of the lot. He'll stay by you because he's loyal and a good son. But he's the only one of you who's worth a tinker's dam, and that includes you."

Mowatt stared at him. "You got you a nerve. Talkin' that way to Mac Mowatt."

Even Chantry was amazed at what he'd said.

"I had nerve when I rode in here, and whether you believe it or not, I'll ride out, too. But I thought maybe I could talk some sense into you. You've got a tough bunch of boys here, but you'll waste them trying for something that would keep the least of you in whiskey for less than an hour. Believe me."

"You know what it is?"

"No . . . but I've a hunch. My brother was interested in the old civilization of Mexico. He was a thoughtful, intelligent man. Most of us Chantrys have gone off wandering for no special reason, but when he went to Mexico and Central America, I think it was for a special purpose. And I think he found something down there that has some bearing on history."

Chantry paused. "He never cared much for money, and he passed up a dozen chances to have an easy life. All he ever wanted was to see what lay over the horizon, to study the ways of man."

"Maybe." Mowatt hitched himself around and reached for a boot. "Did you ride in here just to tell me that?"

"No." The two were moving quietly away from the camp. "I wanted to talk some sense into you. I have nothing against you. So why should I kill you? Or any of your outfit? I came into this country to stay. I'm going to hang up my guns and do some ranching."

"You?" Mowatt was skeptical. "I'd have to see that to b'lieve it."

"You should do the same thing, Mowatt. Get yourself some land while you can, settle down and raise cattle." Chantry paused. He had to say it. "The real reason I came into camp tonight was because of Marny."

"Marny?" The old man's face turned toward him. "She's got nothing to do with you. Don't bring Marny into this."

"She has everything to do with it. I had to shoot a couple of your boys yesterday. They'd chased her over a dozen miles of country. I killed one of them and put lead into three others."

"Marny? My boys? You lie, Chantry!"

His voice was choked up.

Finally, he said, "What do you know about Marny?"

"That's she's a fine, beautiful young woman who respects and loves you, despises your outfit, and deserves a better chance. In fact, that's the real reason I rode in here tonight. You're her stepfather. I want to ask Marny to marry me. And I want your permission."

FOURTEEN

"**Y**ou *what?*"

"You're her oldest living relative. I suppose that legally you're her guardian. So I came to you."

"Well, of all the damn gall! You—!" Mowatt stared at Chantry, then began to chuckle. "I'll be a yeller-livered coyote if that don't take first prize! You ridin' in here with my boys huntin' your hide, just to tell me that!"

"She's a lady," Chantry continued quietly, "and somewhere under that tough old hide of yours there used to be a gentleman. A man who knows how things should be done."

"You said anything to her 'bout this?"

"No. . . . She'd be surprised. She might even laugh at me. But I had to do it."

"Well, I'll be damned," Mac Mowatt threw his cigar butt into the ground and rubbed it out with his toe. "You'd think we was back in Richmond or Charleston or somewheres like that." He shook his head. "No . . . you're a gunfighting drifter, Chantry."

"It would take a gunfighter to get her out of this. You've lost your control. I—"

"Lost my control? Like hell, I have! I can—"

"I told you I was settling down. I'm going to ranch, if you'll put your outfit off my back."

"What do you mean, I've lost control?"

"Well, they went out after her, didn't they? Said she was uppity, that they'd just show her."

"I hope you killed that man."

"He took one in the leg that didn't do him any good, and so far as I know he's still out there."

Then Owen Chantry got to his feet. "Now you know, Mac Mowatt. I want to court Marny, and I've come to you as a gentleman should. You call off your boys, or there's going to be war."

"How long do you think you'd last?" Mac Mowatt had risen too.

"Jake Strawn is trouble."

"And Tom Freka?"

"I thought he was leading the chase after Marny. I'm pretty sure he's killed at least one woman. Get him out of the country or I'll kill him."

Mac Mowatt rubbed his hand over his face. "Damnit, Chantry, I like you! Damned if I don't. You shape up like a man. But I've got these boys. And when you lead an outfit like this you got to *lead*. You got to stay ahead of them. I dunno . . . I really dunno. Why don't you and Marny light out? There's a preacher in the San Luis valley, and there's always Santa Fe."

"This is my country, Mowatt. I've come home. If your boys want war, they'll get it. My advice to you is to latch onto Strawn. He and your son Frank are *men*."

Mowatt shrugged. His mind was made up. "You an' them farmers don't count for much, Chantry. Those boys will cut you down."

"Then it's war?"

"It is," Mowatt said. "But I'll say this Chantry, if you pull through somehow, and Marny wants you for her man, you've got my permission. If it plays that way, Chantry, give her a good life. She's a mighty fine young woman."

Chantry turned and walked into the trees. He had gained nothing.

He worked his way back toward his horse, moving slowly, taking every precaution. Twice he paused to listen . . . ready for an instant shot.

He caught the vague glisten of moonlight on the polished leather of his saddle and heard the black shift its hoofs. Something moved in the shade and a low voice said, "I always wanted to kill me a big man, one o' them special fightin' men. I always figgered they was just so much talk. You know who this is, Chantry? This here is Thrasher Baynes, an' I got you dead t' rights!"

Chantry felt suddenly very tired. Almost bored. Would they never learn? He wanted to kill no one. He had never wanted to kill. He had fought in wars, he had fought in the service of the law, but he had never, even as a boy, wanted to be known as a killer of men.

Thrasher Baynes stood in the darkness. Thrasher Baynes had spotted him. He was expecting Chantry to reply, and he needed that reply to know exactly where he was.

Owen Chantry waited, alert to the slightest sound. If Thrasher moved. . . . On his own right Chantry had a tree, on his left an open space some six feet across. And beyond that, his horse.

Thrasher spoke again. This time his voice was a tone higher. "What's the matter, Chantry? You scared? You too scared to talk? I'm a-gonna kill you, Chantry."

Chantry didn't move. His rifle was on that voice, his finger on the trigger, the slack taken up. . . . He was only a hair from firing a shot, and he knew when he fired he would fire three times—one right down the middle, one somewhat lower right, and a third to the left.

If his first shot scored and Thrasher started to fall, Chantry'd have a good chance of nailing him a second time.

"Yaller, ain't you?"

They would all be coming now. It was only a matter of time.

Chantry fired into the sound. Fired once, then as fast as

he could work the lever, twice more. Then he walked to his horse, pulled the slipknot, and climbed into the saddle.

Behind him something groaned and thrashed about on the ground. Then all was silent.

Owen Chantry knew where the trail was and how it lay. He went down it at a dead run. He had done what had to be done. What happened now would be on their own heads. He had had no hope of talking them out of their battle. That would have been asking too much of human nature. Yet now Mac Mowatt had been told of the growing lack of discipline in his own gang.

He slowed his pace among the trees, but rode steadily onward. The air was cool, the light wind from off the mountains chilly. Bright moonlight bathed the trail.

He had asked for a girl's hand in marriage before he had even asked the girl, or even talked to her of love. Was he a fool? Could she, or any woman, love him?

Was he the kind of man who would make a fit husband for Marny Fox . . . if he lived?

He had declared war. And although he might have help, it was a one-man war. They had killed his brother. It was his own land over which they were fighting. What his brother had left was his legacy, whether it was wealth or knowledge or a dream.

The ranch house had not burned down. Its timbers were solid, allowing no air holes. Some had just charred. A part of the roof had burned, but a late afternoon shower—usual in these mountains—had put out the fire. Nothing a good man with tools couldn't repair in a few days, and clean up in a week.

However, the place was exposed. They could not return there yet.

They'd come after him, the Mowatt gang. He dismounted and led his horse to water. Some distance away, he stretched out on the grass with his saddle for a pillow and watched the declining moon.

He dozed, awakened to listen, and dozed again. He knew all the sounds of the night and what they meant, and his horse was alert as only a former wild horse is, having lived too long with danger.

The nights when he slept through without awakening were few. He had taught himself to awaken at the slightest change in sound or air.

When the sky was gray and the landscape still black, he got up, sat on a log, and tugged on his boots, stamping his feet to settle them well. He led his horse to water again, saddled up, and considered what lay before him.

To kill every one of the gang might be necessary, but he had no wish for such an end. Yet he was one man alone, and the enemy was many. And victory would mean life for others than himself.

He thought about these things ruefully. The only gallant and dashing thing about him at the moment was the fine black horse he rode.

When he reached the house, he gathered a few half-burned rags and wrapped them up with string, the coarse twine Kernohan used to tie up bundles of corn.

Then Owen Chantry mounted the black horse and rode into battle. There were no banners flying, but the Irish were accustomed to fighting gallantly for causes already lost.

He was riding forth to battle. And his only weapons were wit and the bitter wine of his experience.

FIFTEEN

On his long night ride back from the ranch house, Owen Chantry had crossed Turkey Creek Canyon and turned west along the south rim, scouting it all the way to Lost Canyon.

If they followed his trail, they would ride where he had ridden. . . . And they *would* ride his trail, because otherwise they might lose him.

In a patch of woods overlooking his trail, but several hundred yards off, he dismounted. He caressed the black and talked to it. The horse turned its head and pushed at Chantry with its nose.

The grass along these trails and back in the cul-de-sac was tall and dryer than elsewhere. There was sparse timber. He glanced at the sky. It was scattered with the usual white puffballs of cloud. By midafternoon they would bunch up and there would probably be rain.

He knew a way to box them in.

He saw their dust before he saw them. Just a thin trail rising up from the dry grass. He walked back to his horse, took up the reins, and mounted. They were following his trail, just as he intended.

Putting a finger in his mouth he wetted it well and held it up. The wind was from the east, toward Lost Canyon. They'd have a little trouble at the canyon's rim because there was a shelf of rock there, bare rock, and the trail would be lost for a little way.

When they had gone on by he rode down toward them. He would have to be quick, for the ride into and out of the cul-de-sac would be no more than a mile.

He drew up when he'd cut their trail and glanced along a line toward a smaller canyon. Then he struck a light and lighted a bundle he'd made of dry cloth and grass. The bundle was big, and took longer than he liked to flame up. Then he got into the saddle and took a turn around the pommel with the other end of the twine. He walked his horse west, dragging the burning bundle. Behind him the grass caught fire and began to burn toward the rim. The wind was not strong enough, but it was there, and the fire would generate wind of its own.

He walked the black along, and first the grass began to burn, then the brush. He started to trot his horse and rode up to the other canyon rim. Then he loosed the twine and turned away, riding swiftly. A half mile off, he glanced back. Smoke was billowing up, and he saw a sudden arrow of fire as a tree loaded with sap exploded into flame.

He knew he wasn't going to burn them. They were too smart for that. They would find a gap in the line where the fire had not taken hold, or they would ride into the small lake near the rim. What he wanted to do was worry them, make them wonder what was coming next. He wanted them to know it wasn't going to be easy for them. He wanted them to think about losing, about coming up with nothing for all their trouble, about dying. He wanted them to sweat. He wanted them to get so disgusted they'd quit.

He trotted the black, watching for the home trail. He had no fear of the fire burning over into Lost Canyon because of that strip of bare rock.

*   *   *

I was puttin' sticks on the fire when I seen him coming down from the rim. Seems like no matter how long he'd been ridin' or where, he always sat his saddle like he was on parade. It bothered me some, but at the same time I envied him. He surely was a fine-looking man, even if he was wore out a little around the edges.

"You smell that smoke?" I asked him.

"Nothing to worry about, Doby. It'll burn out in a few more minutes."

Marny came up from the stream, brushing her hair as she walked. The gladness in her eyes worried me more than Chantry. What did she see in him, old as he was?

"How's Kernohan?" Chantry asked.

"He's better. He's had some soup and he drank some more coffee. I think he's gaining a little." She looked at him, his face haggard in the morning light. "Have you slept at all, Owen?"

Calling him by his first name like that!

"Enough. But if there's anything to eat. . . ."

"It's ready."

"Where's the old man?"

"He's disappeared into the timber."

Trees shaded the ground, but there were spots of sunlight. Chantry ate a bit, then sat down under a tree, his rifle across his lap. He weren't never far from that rifle. And sleepy he might be, but when he woke up he was ready.

Marny came up with a refill for his coffee, but he had his head back, plumb asleep. "He looks beat," I commented. "Ridin' all night, likely. I'd give a coon to know what he's been up to."

"I am glad he's back with us," Marny said. "Between the two of you and the old man—"

"I don't cotton to that old man. Says he's been around since Noah's ark, but I never seen him before. I don't know what he's up to, but I don't like it no how . . . or him either."

"Has he told you his name?"

"He's mentioned a couple, but I don't believe either one of 'em is right. He sorta smiled when he told me. Likely he don't even remember. I don't believe he's been here long. We woulda seen him."

"Doby? How many bears have you seen in these mountains?"

"Ain't seen any. Nor cougars, neither, but they're around here."

"That's right."

Well, I taken another look at her. "I see what you mean," I admitted, "you figger he's like them. If I ain't seen a bear or a cougar, that don't mean they ain't here."

She went over to where Pa lay. His eyes opened and he looked up at her. His mind wasn't wanderin' this morning and he seemed better, like she'd said. I was never no hand with sick folks and was uncomfortable bein' around 'em, because I never known what to do. Ever' once in a while I figgered to ask Pa what a body did at them times, and I kept telling myself to listen and watch other folks. Womenfolks, they just seemed to know. But how, I never could figger out. Just come natural to 'em, I reckon.

I taken my rifle and edged out toward the creek to where I could listen, but the creek was so noisy itself I couldn't hear much. Yet I worked upstream about half a mile, but I couldn't see nothin' except plenty of trout in the stream. And when I got back to camp, Chantry was awake and cleaning his guns. I never did see a man fuss so much over guns. Them guns and his horse. I said somethin' about it, and he looked up at me.

"We live by them, Doby. A man without a gun and a horse in this country is downright helpless. You take care of them, and they'll take care of you."

'Course made sense, but it was a mighty lot of fussing to do, seemed to me. Pa was always after me, too. Couldn't bear to see a used gun set down without cleaning.

The old man come back then, and he was chucklin'. He filled his cup with coffee and kept looking at Chantry, chuckling some more. "You sure played hob," he said. "You surely did. That outfit is fit to be tied. Run 'em all into the lake, you did, an' some of 'em got in up to their ears. You fairly trapped 'em."

Well, when we asked him he told us about Chantry catchin' them with a grass fire.

"Taken a shot at 'em m'self," the old man said, "just to bugger 'em a mite. I was a mite far off for good shootin', but I burned one of 'em. Burned him good . . . dropped his rifle an' he taken off. He come back for his rifle after a while, but somebody's snuck down there an' packed it, packed it right off."

"Good!" Chantry smiled. "A man doesn't find a rifle every day."

He surely didn't, and I felt sorry for the man who lost it, at the same time thinkin' it was one more we wouldn't have to worry about aimin' at us.

Chantry kept sizing up the old man and finally he asked him when he come into the country. That old man, he canted his head and his old eyes twinkled. He gulped down some more hot coffee an' he says, "I don't pay no mind to years. Ain't seen a clock or a calendar since I was a boy. But this here much I'll say. When I first come over on the dry side I already had hair on m' chest. I was fit to handle m'self or anybody that come to catch me. Only nobody come."

"But you knew Clive?"

"I knowed him. Had his head in a book most o' the time. But he was a good man for all of that . . . a good man. Kept the coffee on . . . never had to wait in his house. Rode with Clive once. Down in Mexico with another feller named Mowatt. But we got chased out. They ran us awhile, but one of Clive's friends was an Otomi Indian. He knowed the country, an' he taken us out.

"We had us a fight an' the Indian was killed, but 'fore he died he tol' Clive 'bout some papers. He'd seen him readin', so he told him his people had papers, too. Told him where they was hidden. . . . Old papers, and carvin's and such.

"Clive, he'd have it no way but to go lookin', an' sure enough, he found 'em. Wasn't all he found, neither. He found a heap of grief and trouble.

"Clive Chantry was the one built the cabin on the rampart. And buried or hid whatever it was."

"How much gold did he have?" I put in.

The old man chuckled. "Gold? Laddie, you'd of had a hard time fillin' a thimble! I know! I was there! We three had us some gold until the big fight in Mexico, an' then we was lucky to get out with our skins! We had us some horses and two mules, an' we had some grub. We had powder an' lead, an' mighty little else. Gold? I should smile!"

Well, there it was! Unless this old man was a-lyin', or had found where the gold was hid and had it hid someplace hisself. I taken another look at him. Old he might be, but he was no damn fool. He was smart as a hill-country fox.

"I never heard of no Otomi Indians," I muttered.

"There are many tribes in Mexico," Chantry said, "with many languages. I know nothing of the Otomis either, except that I've heard their language is very different, with no kinship to the other Indian tongues. Of course, that may be just hearsay."

"That Otomi was a good man," the old man said, "but he was a drifter and a wanderer, never stayed put nowheres."

"I still believe there was gold," I declared. "Or gems and such. I don't see why a man would waste his time totin' old papers or whatever all the way from Mexico. What I want to know is where it was hid?"

The old man shrugged. "Who knows? Clive was mysterious. Wherever he hid the stuff, nobody ever knowed. You'll play hob findin' it."

Chantry went off under a tree and rolled up in his blankets, and the old man, he just set awhile staring into the coals of the fire an' talkin' to hisself. I taken my rifle an' started scoutin' out again up toward the rim. When I finally got there I set down amongst the rocks and brush where I could see, and I started watchin' the trails.

That was a mean outfit and I didn't trust them no way at all. Chantry said he'd talked to Mac Mowatt, but I didn't know whether to believe him or not. I didn't figger anybody could walk right into an outlaw camp and talk to the leader without getting killed. But maybe he done it.

I couldn't figure that old man out either. It was hard to believe he'd lived in that country so long and we never even seen him. Yet it could be so. It was right what Marny said about bears and lions, and if they could do it maybe a man could too. It made a body downright uneasy to think there's folks around, peerin' at him without him knowin'. Made me look around.

Settin' there like that, nothin' on my mind, thoughts kept edging their way up front, thoughts I'd put out no welcome for. It kept nagging at me there might be men who set such store by papers they'd risk their lives to save 'em. That was a new thing to me.

Shifting my rifle, I squinted down the trail. No dust. No smoke. Yet somethin' about that trail worried me.

I oughta be thinking of meat, too. We didn't have much left. Maybe some fish. I could rig myself up a pole and catch a bait of mountain river trout, be mighty tasty.

I taken another sight down trail and still seen nothin'. I studied the country round, then backed out the brush and went down the trail to the Lost Canyon camp.

Owen Chantry was polishin' his boots when I got there. "See anything, Doby?" he asked.

"All quiet," I told him. "What you reckon they're figurin' on?"

"If they're smart, they're pulling out about now. But I don't think they're that smart, or that willing to believe they've wasted their time. What they should do, not being smart enough to quit, is to hole up and hide out until I've found whatever it is they think is so valuable."

"Might be a long time," I said, thinking about that. For how could any man alive read the thoughts of a man long dead? There were miles of country in which to hide something, clefts in the rock, hollow trees, boulders, places where holes could be dug. An' I said so.

Chantry agreed. "Clive knew me, and I knew him. He would think of something, some clue we would both understand. But whatever it is, I can't figure it out from here. I've got to go back to the cabin. I have to be where he was and try to think his thoughts."

"However could you do that?" Marny asked.

Chantry put down the cloth he'd been using to polish his boots. "Put myself in his place. He may have known they would try to kill him."

Marny flushed. "I had no idea they'd kill him. You see, they thought whatever it was was in the house . . . the ranch house. I thought so, too."

"So?" Owen Chantry was lookin' right at her, kinda cold and steady.

"They told me they were going to kill him if he didn't tell them where it was, and I begged them not to. I'd met him, you see, while riding. We'd talked. . . . He was much older. . . . He seemed much older than you, Owen. I liked him. He was a gentleman. And after being with them. . . . Oh, I liked it! I liked being treated like a lady, I liked listening to him. I was anxious to learn things. How to be a lady, how to act, what women wore. Clive seemed to know something about everything. Then they told me they were going to kill him, so I begged them to let me try to find it. They agreed.

"So I went down. I told Clive I'd run away, that I was afraid of them, and that much was almost true. I *wanted* to run away, but I was always afraid . . . always.

"He let me stay there. He told me he'd protect me until he could figure out how to get me away safely. And when he was out of the house, I looked for treasure. The only thing I ever discovered was that it could not possibly be hidden in the ranch house.

"We used to talk a lot. Suddenly he'd seem very lonely. And most of all, Owen, he talked of you. He'd read poetry to me, and to himself, and he read other things. And when I realized he had nothing of value hidden in the house, I went to them and tried to tell them. I begged them, pleaded with them but they wouldn't listen. They thought he'd made a fool of me.

"Finally, Mac promised they'd do nothing. Or I thought he'd promised, at least. And then they killed him. And ransacked the house, and found nothing . . . nothing.

"And he was dead. Clive Chantry was dead."

SIXTEEN

Mac Mowatt sat hunched on the butt end of a log in Hell's Hole, a small hollow on the course of the middle fork of the range. Above him, the great bulk of the hogback loomed, rising over a thousand feet to its crest.

It was not a good campsite and Mowatt was not in a good mood. He stared gloomily into the flames, Owen Chantry's words of the night before sticking like spurs into his brain.

Suppose Chantry was telling the truth. Suppose all this searching was for nothing at all. Suppose all this waiting, all this grief, plus the loss of several good men, and the trouble they were in now was in vain.

All of them had reached the lake before the flames burned anyone bad, but several had been singed and were suffering. A burning leaf had set Ollie Fenelon's hair afire before he could slap it out, and he had a raw scalp. And Tom Freka's big horse had a burn across his hip from a bullet that had come out of nowhere.

His own clothes were still damp from the soaking, for most of them had gone in up to their necks. Their blanket-rolls were wet, and a lot of their grub had been soaked. Pierce Mowatt, his half-brother and the best cook among them, was contriving something at the fire. Several coffee-pots were on the coals, and things might soon be looking better.

"I'll kill him!" Freka yelled suddenly. "I'll break both his legs and show him what the feel of fire is!"

Jake Strawn rolled the tobacco in his jaws and spat. "You get a chance to kill him, you better not try no fancy touches."

"You think he's really somethin', don't you?" Freka sneered.

"Uh-huh. He's the best I ever seen . . . unless it's me." Strawn was complacent. "He's right handy, an' you choose your weapon. Knife, pistol, or club, he's rough an' randy."

"I'll kill him!" Freka repeated.

"Pa?" It was Frank, and Mac Mowatt looked up. "I'm takin' a ride to Santa Fe. Maybe El Paso. I'd be pleased not to ride alone."

There was a momentary silence, then Mac shifted his boots. "Don't talk that way, Frank. We need you here."

"I got no liking for this dodging about in the brush, all on somebody's say-so that there's gold." So much was what Frank thought and felt. When he continued, he was speaking partly to affect the others. "I want to see a woman. I want some lights and some fancy grub. Or at least some grub we don't have to fix for ourselves. There's stages down near the border. And there's cattle can be stole across the border an' sold this side. An' vice versa. We're a-wastin' time here, Pa."

"There's got to be a mint o' gold," Mac said. "Why, they was comin' out of Mexico with an army after 'em! What was they after 'em for? Just those fool papers Clive was supposed to have?"

"Who told you about that army, Pa?" Frank inquired mildly. "That's just border talk, you know that. An' if they had any gold, why didn't they spend it? Why would a man bury gold in the ground? Did we ever bury any of ours?"

"Why should we bury it?" Pierce asked.

"That's what I'm saying," Frank said quietly. "Why should anybody bury gold? If there's a posse after 'em and they need to lighten their load, maybe. If they got so much they can't carry it, maybe. But if there was an army after Ben Mowatt and Clive Chantry, what happened to the army?"

Fenelon looked up. "Whad'ya mean?"

"They were after them, weren't they? This was Spanish territory them days, wasn't it? So if they was after them, why did they stop short? Mowatt got killed, and Clive settled down right here an' stayed, so they wouldn't have had no trouble findin' him."

"Aw, hell!" Fenelon said. "We know an army chased 'em! Why, Charlie Abrams down to Socorro, he knowed all about it. He said they was Mex soldiers, and he was on the border when they was chasing Mowatt an' Chantry."

"Wasn't any border," Frank said quietly. "Not them days. I heard tell Charlie never even come into this country 'til just before the war."

He got out his pipe and loaded it. He didn't want to talk anymore. They were out-of-sorts and sore at the world. Let them stew about it.

Treasure! Lost mines! How many stories had he heard? Some of them made sense. Some of them had some basic logic behind them, but most of them wouldn't hold water.

He got up and started for the river bank. He'd taken no more than a step when he heard the rumble. He started to turn, saw what was happening and yelled, "Run! Rockslide! *Run!*"

They ran. They scattered. Somebody charged into Frank full-tilt and they both fell, sprawling on the ground just in time to be missed by a boulder the size of a mule. It hit a rock above them and bounded over their heads. Men were falling, cursing. Somebody screamed. There was a roaring behind them, then a few scattered rocks falling down, a trickle of pebbles, and silence.

And then the swearing began.

"Help!" a voice called. "I got a busted leg!"

Men came out of the creek, stamping the water from their legs, pausing to empty their boots.

"Where's the horses?" Mac Mowatt yelled. There was more cursing.

"Gone, god damnit!" Pierce said.

Their fire was out, buried under a deluge of rocks and gravel. Their coffeepots were spilled, smashed, or buried. Their food was under a heap of rocky debris from off the cliff.

It hadn't been a big slide, but big enough to frighten the horses, wipe out their camp, and ruin their supper.

"Now why in hell," Pierce muttered, "did that have to happen?"

"Happen, hell!" Ollie Fenelon shouted. "That didn't *happen*! It was done! Somebody had to start that rockslide!"

Mowatt swore, and Freka said again, "I'll kill him, damnit. I'll kill him!"

Jake Strawn gathered up what he could find of the camp gear. When Frank came over to help, Strawn said, "El Paso sounds better'n better."

Strawn found one dented but intact pot, and they found most of their gear and bedding, after some digging. One rifle had a broken stock, and the wooden stirrup on a saddle was broken. But that could be repaired, and the gun stock also, with time.

When the coffee was ready they took turns, for they needed more than one pot. It was a slow, tiring supper they ate and finally, on ground a hundred yards from their original campsite, they bedded down.

It was after midnight before the camp was quiet. Within the hour that followed, all were asleep. Even Mac, who'd been doing some serious thinking.

The moon rose later and finally shone into the canyon. Suddenly the perfect stillness of the mountain night was split wide open by the heavy explosion of a rifle shot, unnaturally loud in the quiet.

Tom Freka came to his feet with a scream of pure fury, and as he lunged erect a bullet hit the ground within inches of his toes. He sprang back, tripping over Frank Mowatt to fall in a heap. Another shot followed, and then stillness.

Bleary-eyed from weariness, only half-awake, the men stared around, and then from the cliff above them came a mocking voice, singing, "We're tenting tonight on the old campgrounds, give us a song to cheer—"

Tom Freka emptied his rifle toward the sound high above.

"Goodnight, boys!" It was Owen Chantry's voice. "Sleep late in the morning."

Wiley swore bitterly, and after a minute or two they rolled in their blankets. But it was a long time before they could sleep. Pierce Mowatt came out of the darkness and walked down by the stream, lighting his pipe, half-expecting a shot. But no more shots were heard.

The trouble was, Mac Mowatt reflected, now they would never know. Nobody would strike a match, try to make coffee, or settle down for a meal without wondering when the shots were going to come.

There were two possible solutions: leave the country or track down Owen Chantry and kill him. He said as much to Freka.

"There's another," Freka said. "I think he's got a case on Marny. If'n we could get Marny back, he'd come for her."

"No!" Mowatt's voice was flat and harsh. "Marny's kin. Keep her out of this."

"It's your funeral," Freka said, but he was doing his own thinking. If he could get Marny, then he'd have Marny and he could get Chantry at the same time. Bait him right into a trap . . . a juicy trap.

Jake Strawn—big, tough, and raw-boned, a gunhand in many a cattle war, a man who'd done time in two prisons—looked across at Freka. Tom Freka might be a mystery to some, but he was an open book to Strawn. Jake turned on his side with disgust and closed his eyes. The trouble with being on the wrong side of the law was the kind of company you had to keep.

Daylight came to the camp on Lost Canyon with a red glow on the rimrock. Owen Chantry, who had slept two hours, went down to the river and bathed his face in the cold water, cupping it in his hands to dash into his eyes. He stood up, shaking water from his fingers. The trouble with doing what he had done was that the other side could do it too.

It was time to move. Kernohan was better and might be strong enough to sit a horse, if they didn't have to go too far. Chantry watched a squirrel run out on the rocks near the water, then turned back to the camp.

He was tired, dog tired, and it was catching up with him. Yet he knew he could go for days . . . might have to go for days.

"Ten," he said aloud. "Ten, eleven, twelve—" What had Clive been trying to say? The other day he'd again had a fleeting idea that had disappeared as quickly as it came . . . some haunting thought that had come to him.

He walked back to the camp and sat down. Marny was up and combing her hair. The filtered sunlight caught the light in it, and Chantry watched. She was uncommonly graceful, her every move.

"Nice morning," he said quietly

"Where were you last night? I was worried."

He chuckled softly, amused. "I went serenading. I wanted to sing those boys to sleep."

She stared at him, not knowing what he meant. He picked up the book of poetry and turned the pages under his thumb. Clive had read it a lot. "Locksley Hall" had been a favorite of his and Clive's too. There was a copy of "Marmion" by Sir Walter Scott, tucked in the pages, written in Clive's own hand. It gave him a sudden pang of loneliness. He would never see Clive again.

Suddenly, he knew. Suddenly Owen believed he knew where Clive Chantry's treasure was hidden.

SEVENTEEN

At least he had a clue. Even with the clue, it would take some searching to find. But at least he now knew how Clive was thinking.

Clive Chantry had been a considerable scholar, yet he had taken his linguistic skills casually, learning several languages before he was fifteen, and acquiring others as the need developed or as his interests demanded. In several years of wandering, much of it in South and Central America as well as Mexico, he had mastered several Indian tongues.

Although not pretending to be a scholar, he was keenly aware of the demands of scholarship, and his wanderings had taken him into places, and brought him into contact with people, who were relatively unknown.

There might actually be a treasure.

Owen Chantry watched Marny brush her hair but, attractive as she was, his thoughts were far away.

Mac Mowatt would not take the midnight attack on his camp lying down. He dare not, if he expected to lead his outfit. They would be angry, eager to retaliate. And this time they would come in for the kill with no nonsense about it.

"We've got to move," Chantry said, suddenly.

"Move to where?" Doby said. He was sitting quiet with his thoughts. "All we're gonna do is get out in the open where they can wipe us out."

Chantry glanced at the old man, who was leaning on his rifle, watching them with his bright-gray eyes. "You know this country best. Is there a good hideout nearby?"

"A couple. Figgered you'd be wantin' to go back to the cabin on the rampart. There's places up there—"

"How about water?" Doby protested. "I seen no water." At least if he had, he didn't remember it.

The old man chuckled. "You youngsters, you never look. Got no *eyes*! Why, there's a passel o' water right near to the door! Off there to the right, hid behind the brush. Ol' Clive, he was no fool! A man needs water, an' he built hisself a dam. Across the gully to catch the runoff. Got a drain for her, too, an' a rock to stop off the drain when need be, so's the water keeps fresh.

"Rained there t'other night, so there'll be water . . . maybe five hundred gallons . . . maybe twice that much."

"I don't want to get Pa stuck in no cabin. You can't get out up there, an' you're caught in a trap."

"No need, son. Chantry, you're an army man. Move out from the cabin, set up a perimeter defense. Give y'rself room to move in. Why, there's a-places up there a good man with a rifle could stand off an army! I can show y' where. Now, if y' really—"

"I do," Chantry said bluntly. "Let's go!"

Within a matter of minutes they were moving, with the old man to ride point, followed by Marny and Kernohan, then Doby, with Owen Chantry riding well back to cover their flight, if need should be.

"Wrong time o' day," the old man grumbled. "Of a night-time I could take y' there easy as pie. This here way we got t' keep under cover, got t' ride careful, like."

"We can hole up somewhere on the way," Chantry said. "Just get us away from here!"

The old man spat, shifted his rifle in his hands, and then said. "Got just the place! Take 'em a while t' find us there!"

"How far?"

"Four, five mile. 'Bout that." He pointed with a long bony finger. "South."

He led off down canyon. Curiously, the canyon's walls grew less steep, and the canyon itself flattened out into a series of meadows. The old man skirted a low hill, then led them up the slight bank and into the trees.

Chantry rode behind, rifle in hand. He was worried. They had left the canyon almost too easily, and his every sense told him trouble was near, though the old man was wily. The way he had taken them was hidden from view, and there was a chance they'd escaped observation.

The day was hot and still. And it was quiet, altogether too quiet. He trotted his horse to catch up. Doby was leading the packhorses, including his own buckskin.

How many were left in Mowatt's crowd? Several had been killed, although he could be certain of only a few . . . three, perhaps. And several injured.

Chantry ducked his head under a low branch, glimpsed Doby ahead with the packhorses and at a bend in the trail, he watched Marny's red hair catch the sun. Not really red, but when the sun caught it—

He heard the faintest of sounds and turned sharply in the saddle.

Nothing. . . .

Had it been some animal or bird? Or a branch stirred by the wind? Entering a thick grove, he drew up to look back again. . . . There was nothing.

He cantered his black across a small meadow and glanced around again.

Where was the old man taking them? They had been traveling slowly to take advantage of every bit of cover, and they must have covered three or four miles. Now they were leaving the cover behind, the best of it, at least. The trees were mostly cedars now, some piñon pines. This country was broken and rocky. It was very dry. Chantry saw no tracks but their own.

He looked around again. . . . Still nothing.

Owen Chantry mopped the sweat from his face. He wished again that he owned a hat. He had borrowed an old one from Kernohan for a few days, but it had been left in the house. His own hat had been lost when he was riding north.

It was growing hotter. A grasshopper flew up and winged away in the distance. Overhead, a vulture circled. Chantry took off his coat and put it over the saddle before him.

Finally they reached a cave, which was perfectly screened by trees. The old man chuckled, pleased with himself. "Cain't see this here place from hardly nowheres. You got to know it's here, or come right down the canyon to it. Indians used to stop here. We'll just set tight an' leave 'em hunt for us, an' come tomorry we'll get goin' afore light comes."

There was no talking. They ate, slept, rested, waited. From time to time Chantry or the old man slipped out from behind the screen of trees and went up the canyon or down, scouting, listening.

Late in the day, they were all lying quiet when they heard the drum of hoofs on the rocks above, then silence.

"Hell," they heard somebody say. "They'd never go down there! It's a trap!"

"Damnit," said somebody else, "they can't just disappear! They got to be around here somewhere."

"Did you see any tracks? I found some back yonder in the dust but they faded out. Anyway, they wouldn't come this way! Why, this here heads right out into open country, an' there'd be no place to hide! I figure they went to the high country up yonder, where they can see round the country."

Then the riders went away, and Chantry grounded his rifle. The sun slowly sank, tinting the peaks of the mountains with gold and crimson.

The old man went up the rocks. When he returned he shook his head. "No sign of 'em. Might's well have some coffee. Eat up, 'cause we got a round-about ride to the rampart."

The stars came out. The tiny glow of the fire was lost in the vast darkness. The air around the cave was damp from the waters of a spring and the grass around it. The horses were picketed near the spring where they could browse or drink as they chose.

Chantry went to where Kernohan lay. The flickering firelight shone on his gaunt cheeks and sunken eyes. "How are you?" he asked.

"All right. Feel mighty tired, but I don't hurt much."

"We've a long ride ahead."

"So I heard. Let's go on an' ride, Mr. Chantry. I'll not hold you back." He was silent for a few minutes, and Chantry sat on a slab fallen from the overhang and sipped his coffee. "That boy's doin' all right, ain't he?" asked Kernohan.

"He sure is. He's carrying his weight and more. You've no need to worry about him."

"I reckon. 'Though a body does worry. Times are hard for a boy his age. No young folks, no dances, socials or such. Why, he ain't seen a box supper since he was eight!"

"This is a beautiful country," said Chantry. "There will be people along soon, lots of them. There're a good many in the San Luis valley already, and just a few years ago a man named Baker led a party into the San Juans. We're just the first. Doby will have plenty of company soon."

At moonrise, they moved off with Chantry leading. He started at a rapid trot and held it. The trails were narrow, but they were plain to see in the moonlight.

The old man moved up beside Chantry. "You ride keerful, young feller. Them boys might be most anywheres about."

From time to time Chantry drew up, listening, trying the air for smoke. He doubted if the renegades were so far east, but they could be.

The night was cool and still, almost cold. The peaks were harsh against the blue black sky and bright stars. There was no sound but the creak of saddles and the fall of hoofs. Once Kernohan coughed. Owen Chantry looked ahead. The rifle felt good in his hands.

The old man dropped back to spell Doby at leading the packhorses, and the boy rode forward to join Chantry.

"Where you think they are?" Doby asked, low-voiced.

Chantry shrugged. "No telling, Doby."

*   *   *

The fire had gone out.

Mac Mowatt was hunched against a tree, chewing on a chunk of elk meat. He felt sour and old, and there was no pleasure in him.

Frank was gone. Pulled out. He'd never believed that Frank would leave him—although it was obvious he was discontented. Mac Mowatt was sore as an old grizzly with a bad tooth. He stared at Ollie Fenelon, who was rubbing his burned scalp, which was now beginning to peel. Then his eyes went to Pierce, at the fire.

Jake Strawn had drawn away from the others and was sitting by himself. Strawn was something of a loner, anyway. And tonight Mowatt was especially remembering what Chantry had advised. To get close to Strawn and keep him close.

How many of them could he trust? Mowatt knew the answer . . . probably not one of them, unless it was his own kinfolk, and he was none too sure about them. The losses they had taken, the wounded men, the man with the broken leg. They'd been outmaneuvered by Chantry every time. It rankled. They'd spent too much time in these hills with nothing to show for it. And despite all his arguments, he knew some of the men were beginning to doubt there was anything here.

Frank was gone. Mac knew that some of them had set great store by Frank. He was solid. He was *there*, and you knew he was there. Strawn was just lingering on, and Tom Freka paid almost no attention to Mowatt's orders anymore.

They were a sorry bunch . . . a sorry bunch.

He lifted the coffee cup to his lips, and at that very moment he heard the horse. He saw Tom Freka come to his feet like a cat. Mowatt dropped his cup and got up fast.

Chantry had slowed his horse to let the old man come abreast. Doby had turned in his saddle to look for his father. And the next thing they knew they were right in the middle of the Mowatt camp.

The shock was complete on both sides. It was Freka who came to life first, leaping to his feet and grabbing for his gun.

But Owen Chantry had quickly lunged his horse forward. The horse's shoulder hit Freka as his gun came up, and he was knocked sprawling into Strawn, who was just rising off the ground.

Wiley raised up, grabbing a rifle. Using his rifle in one hand like a pistol, Chantry thrust it at him and fired. Wiley gave a choking cry and fell backward, his arms and legs all spread out, his chest bloody. And then there was only a roar of sound, of guns and screams and yells, leaping men and charging horses. Mac Mowatt got off a shot, charged forward and then fell back just in time to escape being run over by the packhorses.

Then it was over.

It had been a wild, crazy two minutes of gunfire and screams. Then the gunfire was scattered, and clothes were burning, the coffee was spilled, and Mowatt's men were scrambling back around the burned out coals of their campfire.

The riders were gone. Freka, on his feet, was still grabbing about for his gun, dropped from his hand. When he found it, he turned and ran for his horse.

Mowatt swore and shouted orders. "Get your hosses an' git!" he yelled. "Get 'em, damn it! *Get 'em!*" . . .

They followed his orders.

Strawn got up and brushed off his clothes. The others, save Mac Mowatt and Pierce, who was looking at their last shattered coffeepot, were already gone. Mac Mowatt had started for his own horse, then hesitated. After a moment he walked over and picked up his fallen cup. It was empty, and he swore.

"Let 'em go, Mac," Strawn suggested. "They won't find anything. And if they do, they'll wish they hadn't."

"You think they did it a-purpose?" Pierce asked.

"Uh-uh," Strawn said. "They come up on us by accident. Surprised them as much as us." He nodded to indicate Wiley's body. "You better have you a look. I figure he's dead. Owen Chantry don't miss very often."

Pierce crossed to the fallen man. "Dead, all right. Through the heart, looks like." He turned to Mac. "Let's get out of here. Next thing we know it'll be one of us."

"Get out?" Mowatt rumbled. "I'll be damned if I will! There's gold up there, I tell you! Gold!"

Jake Strawn glanced around. "And what if there is? How far do you think it would take you with this outfit? They'd murder you for what's in your pocket, most of 'em. I say we get out and stay out. And then, after a while, we come back nice and quiet like, with only a few of us . . . the ones who can be trusted."

Pierce nodded. "I like that. I really do. Catch 'em off guard, an' by that time Chantry'll have the gold."

"Will they leave for good?" Mac Mowatt asked.

"They will . . . chances are, except for Freka. He wants Marny."

"*What?*" Mowatt's head came up. "Tom Freka? I'd kill him first!"

"You ain't noticed?" Strawn asked. "Well, I have. And the man's not normal. Not human. There's something wrong with him."

"I'll kill him," Mac Mowatt muttered.

"You may have to," Strawn said quietly. "You may just have to."

EIGHTEEN

The cabin on the rampart lay still and cool under the dawn light. The sentinel pines stood straight and dark, austere as nuns at prayer. The leaves of the aspens trembled, and the high peaks of distant mountains were crowned with the gold of sunrise.

Their horses walked into the stillness, tired from the miles behind them, grateful for the scent of water and the end of their journey.

Owen Chantry dismounted and reached up to help Marny down, just a second before Doby reached her. Doby scowled and dropped his hands as if to imply that he had not even intended to help. Then he walked to his father, helped him from the saddle, and half-carried him into the house.

"Old man," Chantry said, "do you want to explore out there? Have a look around? You're probably the best scout among us."

"Maybe. Y'do pretty well your own self. Ain't nothin' to fear from this place right here. A man could come up, but he'd make a powerful lot of noise gettin' through all that brush."

When the gear was stripped from the horses, the packs carried inside, and a bed made for Kernohan, Owen Chantry took his rifle and went out along the rim. The shadows were pulling back from the vast expanse to the west, where hundreds of miles of land lay open to the eye.

The land at the rim sloped off, then ended abruptly in a tremendous escarpment, a sheer wall of two hundred feet dropping away to talus slopes below.

Yet the cliffs were not smooth, but were fluted and broken. Suddenly, near the place where the walls of two escarpments met, he saw a narrow gap between a boulder and a raised portion of the wall. He peered through.

Here, hidden at the edge of the escarpment, was a secret place—a descent to the ground below, but an excellent firing position also. Several possible trails were in full view from here, and a man with a rifle—

"It shall be me," he said aloud. "Or the old man. Somebody who's good with a rifle."

Marny came up to meet him. "Can you see them?"

"They haven't found us yet."

"Have you found out where it is? I mean, whatever it is that's hidden?"

"I think I know how to find it now."

She looked out over the forest and meadows below. "It is beautiful. With all God's bounty, why must there be so much trouble?"

"That is the hardest question of history, Marny, the question people have asked in every age, in every time. Many men want what other men have. Men are often greedy, jealous, and vindictive. Or they look across the fence at what they think is greener grass. They pursue will-o'-the-wisp dreams, such as this 'treasure.' "

Chantry scanned the horizon. "Men have died, months of time have been wasted, and all to get something for nothing, to profit from someone else's spoils. And the end is not yet in sight."

"What will happen?" Marny looked up at him.

"They will come after us. They have committed themselves to a course of action. If they gave up now, all their efforts would go for nothing. So they will not give up."

"When will they come?"

"I don't know. But we must stop them . . . if we can."

"I hope that Mac Mowatt does not come with them. I wouldn't want to see him shot."

"Nor I."

Bright now was the land below, bright with the early sun, with the clearness of the sky.

It was a good land. Grazing land for the most part, but here and there a plain where something could grow well. A man could make a living here. And as mining increased—as it was bound to—he could sell beef cattle to the miners. And vegetables and grain also.

Chantry stooped and picked up a handful of the soil. Good . . . very good. . . . Many trees and plants grew here, and others could also grow. Down there on the flat, still others could grow. There was more water there. A man might choose crops by studying what already grew in the soil, and choosing those crops which needed the same soil, water, and climate.

He leaned on the rock and put his rifle beside him. His eyes again swept the vast green land that lay below. What a place Clive Chantry had chosen for his cabin! The rampart! There could not be a more beautiful view anywhere, nor one encompassing a wider lookout.

He was tired. The warm sun baked his muscles and he slowly relaxed.

"When this is over, Owen, where will you live?"

"Here. . . . If I'm alive. Or down there," he gestured below.

Then he saw them. Four riders in a small, neat group, coming out of a narrow draw near a canyon. They rode up out of the draw and came at a canter across a meadow, rode into the trees, then emerged again.

He pointed. "Marny? Look!"

She looked. They rode in a tight group, occasionally stringing out, then coming together again like figures in a square dance. "From here," she said quietly, "they look beautiful!"

"Yes," he agreed, watching them appear and disappear along the trail they followed.

"How far away are they?"

He shrugged. "A mile and a half. Two miles. They're slowing down now, and I think they're looking at us."

"You mean they see us?"

"No. They couldn't pick us out from here . . . I think they're scanning the wall for a way up."

"We'd better tell the others," Marny said.

"All right." But he hesitated, his eyes reaching out to the horizon. "There will be others, you know, coming by some other route."

"Do you want Doby?"

"No, tell him to check on his father, then locate the old man and work with him. They will have to cover the trail from the spring side. This may be a long fight, and it may be over quickly."

The riders below were closer now. Chantry caught the gleam of light from a rifle barrel. He watched them, and there were few places their trail led that could not be seen from his vantage point.

He tucked the rifle butt against his shoulder and lowered his cheek to the stock, sighting along the barrel, tracking them. They were too far away for a shot, but he was in no hurry. Nor had he any wish to waste his ammunition.

Suddenly, he was anxious. The riders must know they were up here. The riders must surely know that they could be seen. Then why . . . ?

He turned sharply and ran to the cabin.

He got to the door and saw Kernohan inside. He was sitting up in bed. "What's happened? What's wrong?" Kernohan asked him.

Kernohan's rifle was in a corner near the door, and Chantry caught it up with his left hand and threw it to the sick man. "We've got trouble," Chantry said.

He ducked away from the door and started for the trees. Suddenly a shadow loomed in the trees. He saw a rifle come up and then he shot from the hip. The bullet hit a tree near the man's face, scattering splinters and bark. Chantry worked the lever and fired again. The man's gun banged but no bullet sound followed. Chantry saw the man clinging to a tree, one arm around it. The man was staring at him with wide, empty eyes, his lips working with words that would not come out, that would never come out.

Owen Chantry ran past the dying man, catching up his rifle as he went. It was a Henry, and a good rifle. Suddenly he halted and went back to the man, now down on the ground, his shoulder and chest against the tree, his head hanging forward.

Without ceremony or hesitation, Chantry unbuckled his gun belt and jerked it free. There were twenty loops in the man's belt, all filled with .44s.

They had timed it nicely. The four horsemen below must have waited under cover until the others had circled around to come up to the house. While Chantry was watching the riders below, the men near the house had simply closed in. Luckily, he had guessed their strategy in time. Or had he?

There must be others. Where were they? Where was Marny? Where were the old man and Doby?

No sounds, no shots.

Was the man he had wounded or killed the only one near the house? He didn't think so. Where were the others?

He crouched behind a thick ponderosa at a point where another had fallen against it, offering a kind of cover.

A voice called out from somewhere in front of him. "Come on out, Chantry! Give yourself up! We've got the kid and we've got Marny Fox!"

"Is Mac Mowatt with you?" Chantry called back.

A momentary silence. Then: "No, he ain't. That ain't got nothing to do with it. You come out or we'll kill 'em both."

"I'd like to hear you say that to Mac Mowatt," he called back.

"You come on out. Throw down your guns and come on out."

Chantry eased his position, seeking a place to move, giving a glance to the ground cover to see how much noise he would make in moving. He thought he had the threatening voice located.

Where was the old man? Did Mowatt's gang even know about him?

"Come out, damn you, or we'll start busting the kid's fingers!"

"Who killed Clive?" Chantry asked, just loud enough to be heard. "I told you I wanted him . . . or them . . . hung. Have you done what I want?"

"Are you crazy? We're in command here!"

"Are you now?"

How many were there? Chantry was suddenly quite certain that there were no more than three, possibly two, and that if they *had* captured Doby and Marny, the boy and girl were not with these men.

He moved swiftly, silently, twenty yards in the trees and knelt down.

Where were Mowatt, Freka, and Strawn?

Chantry was poised for a move when he heard the sudden boom from a heavy rifle. There was a yell, then a volley of shots, then after a slight interval, the heavy boom again. Then swearing.

He crept toward the noise, carrying both rifles. Suddenly, he dropped his own rifle and threw the other to his shoulder. Several men had broken out of the brush and were running diagonally across from him. He opened fire. One man stumbled and fell, and another turned swiftly and levered three quick shots at Chantry. Something struck him a wicked blow and he fell. A second shot spat bark from the tree where his head had been just a moment ago. Chantry fired again but the men were gone.

He was on his knees, rising, when a man broke through the brush coming right straight at him. Chantry swung his rifle and caught him across the shins. The man's mouth opened in a scream, and Chantry left the ground in a lunging dive that knocked the man to the ground. The man tried to get up, swinging his gun to bring it to bear, and Chantry, lacking purchase or room for a proper swing, thudded the butt of his rifle against the man's chin.

Chantry himself staggered and fell against a tree.

The man, whoever he was, was out cold. Chantry threw

the man's rifle into the trees and jerked off his gun belt. His left leg hurt bad, but he could see no blood.

Chantry decided to give up his spare rifle. It was too awkward to carry. He leaned it against a tree, half-hidden by low-growing branches.

Then he moved to another tree and limped into a thicker stand. Now he could see the corner of the cabin, some distance off through the forest. He had started toward it when his move was cut short.

"All right, Chantry! This is Strawn! Don't move!"

There was nothing else to do. Chantry stood perfectly still and they came up to him and took his gun.

NINETEEN

Awrong move—a move of any kind, and he was dead.
There was no nonsense about Strawn. He was not a
vicious man, but he had killed and would kill again, and his
shots were true.

To move was to die, and Owen Chantry was not ready to
die.

"Looks like you win the hand, Jake," he said mildly. "I
was hoping you weren't around."

"He's around, all right, and I am, too!" That would be
Ollie Fenelon. Two more of the Mowatt men were coming
up through the trees.

"Hell!" one of them exclaimed. "This ain't no buffalo gun!
This here's a Henry!"

"Well? You heard it, didn't you? Sure sounded like a
buffalo gun! Sounded like a big Sharps fifty! I'd a swore—"

"Mac wants to see you, Owen," Strawn said. "You just
walk easy now and don't make me kill you."

Chantry had no choice but to follow.

When they came to Mowatt's camp, a fire was going, and
Mac Mowatt was waiting for them.

"Well, Chantry," Mowatt was sitting, his heavy forearms locked about his knees. "You've given us some trouble. But now you're goin' to make it all worthwhile."

"Always glad to oblige," Chantry said, seating himself on a rock, "what can I do for you? Now, if you want to leave the country, you just take this trail along here—"

"Leave? Who said anythin' about leavin'?" Mowatt asked him.

"Well," Chantry said seriously, "it seems to me that if you want any of your men left, that's what you should do. I figured Strawn here took me because you needed a guide through the mountains, and there's nothing I'd rather do."

"Damn you, Chantry," Mowatt said. "Go to hell. All we want from you is treasure. Show us where it is and we'll let you go free."

Chantry smiled. "Now, Mac. Let's be honest. You'd never turn me loose. You know I'd only get another gun—"

Tom Freka had joined them. "Not without hands, you wouldn't. What if we took off your hands, Chantry? You got two hands now, but I got a bowie, an' Pierce has an ax to cut firewood."

"That sounds just like you, Freka," Chantry replied quietly. "You'd cut off my hands because you know I can draw faster and shoot straighter than you. You're scared, Freka. You're just plain scared."

"Am I?" Freka took a big burning stick from the fire. "You also got two eyes. How would you like to try for one?"

"Put it down, Freka," Mowatt said. "I'll kill a man, but I'll be damned if I'll torture one."

"Then how do you expect us to find that treasure?" Freka asked. "You think he'll just up an' tell us?"

"Why not, Freka?" Chantry said. "Mowatt's a gentleman. And Strawn here's a man of his word. I'd trust either one of them." He stretched his stiff leg out before him. "Mowatt, do you have Marny and the boy . . . Doby?"

"I do. Catched 'em unexpected like. Yeah, I got 'em all. Back yonder."

Mowatt pointed back over his shoulder.

"Turn them loose. Let them get out of here with their

horses and Doby's father, and I'll take you to whatever it is, if I can."

"You think we gonna believe *that*?" Freka demanded.

"I believe him, Freka," Strawn said.

Mowatt shifted his position and took out his pipe. "Figure it this way, Chantry. We got you. We got them. The boy's old man is mighty sick hurt. We ain't got to argue with nobody, an' we ain't got to deal with nobody. Either you tell us what we want, or we let that man die. We might even shoot Doby."

Mowatt drew on his pipe to test the stem, then began to tamp tobacco. "We might even kill you."

"You might. But I don't think you will," said Chantry. "Not if you know what's good for Marny."

"You don't seem to get the idea," Mowatt said. "You ain't in no position to bargain, Chantry. You got no place to stand. Just get us that treasure an' you'll have no more trouble."

"Release my friends," Chantry said quietly, "then hang the man who killed Clive, and I'll show you the treasure."

"You goin' to listen to that talk?" Freka snorted.

"Well, I don't know about that," Pierce Mowatt said. "It might be a right good deal."

"Might be at that," Jake Strawn said. "We got nothing against the boy, or his pa either."

"Chantry's a troublemaker," Freka said angrily. "Can't you see? He's tryin' to get us fightin' amongst ourselves."

"Seems to me," Chantry said, "that the killer should volunteer to be hung, just for the good of his friends."

He was smiling easily, but his mind was working swiftly.

"Where's the treasure, Chantry?" Mowatt asked bluntly.

"You boys have kept me so busy I haven't had time to look." Chantry shrugged.

They had his gun, and they had his rifle, but somewhere not half a mile away the captured rifle still leaned against a tree.

"Chantry," Mowatt spoke slowly and carefully, "I want you to get this straight. You've given us a sight of trouble, an' we ain't goin' to put up with it. You got you one more chance. Find whatever it was Clive Chantry brought out of Mexico. If you don't, I'll not leave you to the boys. I'll shoot you myself."

"Looks like I don't have much choice," Chantry said. "But all I've got is a clue."

"What's the clue?" Pierce demanded.

"I know what the clue is," Chantry admitted, "but I don't know how to read it. Like it or not, I'm going to need time.

"When Clive was murdered, he wasn't quite dead when he was left behind. So he left me something to work on."

"What could he leave if he was dyin'?" It was Freka again.

"He wrote something on the door step. He wrote the word ten."

They stared at him.

"Ten? What's that mean?" Freka demanded. "Ten what?"

"My thought exactly, gentlemen," Chantry said. "Ten what? Then I wondered, if it was ten feet, ten miles, ten inches, then why didn't he write the numeral? Why the word *ten*?"

"Don't make no sense," Ollie Fenelon muttered. "It surely don't."

"You figgered it out yet?" Mowatt asked.

"Maybe. I think he was trying to write *Tennyson*," Chantry said.

"Tennyson? What's that?" Pierce demanded.

"It ain't what," Mowatt said. "It's *who*. It's a man's name."

"Name of who?" Ollie asked. "I never heard such a name."

"It's a writer," Mowatt said. He glared around at the others. "If you would *read* once in awhile you'd know somethin'. Tennyson is a writer." He glanced at Chantry. "English ain't he?"

"English . . . and a poet. A very good poet."

"Poet?" Ollie was shocked. "What would a man write a poet's name for when he was dyin'?"

"I like his poetry," Chantry said quietly. "And so did Clive. Whatever he'd hidden he didn't wish anyone to find it but me. So he was trying to conceal it in such a way that only I *could* find it."

"Hell!" Freka spat. "If one man can find it, another man can too."

"You've tried, I think," Chantry said. "But what have you found? You're welcome to go on trying. There's room enough for every one to look. Be my guest."

"If you know something sure, stop talkin' so much an' tell us," Mowatt said. "Was it somethin' in one o' them books he left?"

"Of course." Chantry got to his feet and stretched. Three guns were on him, and the men who held those guns were ready to kill him. But not quite yet. They wanted to know what he knew.

"We both liked Tennyson," Chantry said. "Certain of Tennyson's poems we both liked very much, so Clive naturally thought of something he knew I would think of also. The secret to the hiding place is hidden in one of Tennyson's poems."

"In a poem! Who'd a thought of that?" Fenelon was disgusted. But suddenly his mood changed. "I don't believe it! I don't believe one cottonpickin' word. You made the whole thing up!"

"Maybe some of it," Strawn said, "but I seen that ten. Never paid it no mind."

Mac Mowatt was watching Chantry with careful eyes. "All right, what next?" he asked finally.

"I'll need a copy of Tennyson," Chantry said.

"You sure?" Mowatt stared at him, eyes hard. "Don't you remember? Didn't you learn it by heart?"

"No," said Chantry, "I didn't. I don't even know which poem it's in. I'll need the book, and I'll need some time to study it at the cabin."

"We ain't got no time to waste," said Freka.

"We'll all go along," Mowatt said. "All but Whitey and Slim. Just so's the rest of us stay together. Wouldn't want nothin' to go wrong now."

Under his breath, Chantry swore. His mouth was dry, the taste bitter. This was his last chance.

TWENTY

"You're not gonna need us all," Freka said, "I'll just stay here with Whitey and Slim and the prisoners."

"You'll come with us," Mowatt said sternly.

Tom Freka got to his feet slowly and he spat into the fire. "Whitey can stay," he said, "but I'll stay, too."

Owen Chantry felt his muscles slowly relax, yet all his senses were alert. This might be a showdown, and if—

"All right, Tom," Mowatt was suddenly easy. "Maybe you're just wore out. You set by while the rest of us pick up that gold. You just set by." He let his eyes shift to Whitey, a hard-faced man. "Whitey, I'm holdin' you responsible for the people I'm leavin'. That goes for all of 'em. They're not to be hurt, y'understand?"

Whitey nodded. "I hear you, Mowatt. They won't be."

Mowatt led the men off. When they were out of earshot of the camp, Pierce suggested, "Maybe I should go back?"

"They'll be all right," Mowatt said.

"I wouldn't leave any woman where Freka is," Chantry said.

154

"Ain't none of your damn business, Chantry," Mowatt told him roughly. "Just lead us to that treasure now."

They walked the distance to the cabin.

Chantry stopped in the clearing just shy of the cabin. A gun prodded his back.

"What y' stoppin' for?" Pierce demanded.

Chantry didn't answer.

"All right, get goin'," Mowatt said.

Chantry walked forward, and seeing the door partially open, he pushed it gently with his hand. The door swung inward.

The room was empty, the bed was made. A few coals were gleaming in the fireplace. A blackened pot on the hearth steamed slowly. Chantry glanced quickly around. He saw no gun, nothing he could use for a weapon. He felt like he'd been struck in the belly. He had hoped . . . he scarcely knew any longer what he had hoped.

Mowatt pushed him hard from behind, and he staggered. "Damnit, get in there!" Mowatt shoved in after him, glaring around.

The books were on the table where he'd put them. Chantry glanced out of the north window. Like the south window, it was small, almost like a porthole, though somewhat larger. It was rounded at the top.

"Now look at them books!" Mowatt said. "And you better find somethin' quick!"

Mowatt took up the books one by one and riffled their pages.

At one point a torn scrap of paper had been used for a bookmark. It was at the poem, "Ulysses." Mowatt read the poem slowly, his lips moving, occasionally scowling over some word or meaning. "Hell," he said, at last, "there ain't nothing there!"

Only there was.

He offered Chantry the book. Chantry made a show of turning the pages as if searching for a clue. Ollie Fenelon and Pierce Mowatt went outside, and he could hear them muttering over "Stuff an' nonsense."

Chantry knew that "Ulysses" had been a special favorite of

Clive's. They had quoted it to each other in letters and written of certain passages in it.

One passage that Chantry especially remembered began: "Yet all experience is an arch wherethrou'/Gleams that untravell'd world whose margin fades/For ever and for ever when I move."

Reading quickly from first one poem and then another Chantry paced the floor.

Pausing in his pacing, he looked out of the north window. Only trees in a dense stand beyond an area of rock, scattered shrubs and young aspens.

Yet the top of the window could be called an arch. He went back to turning the pages.

Chantry sat down on the edge of the bed. "Damn it," he muttered, with a great show of irritation, "it's got to be here."

"It better be," Mowatt said.

Again Chantry paced the floor. This time he stopped in the middle of the room, reading a couple of lines from "Locksley Hall" aloud as though searching for something in them. Then he looked out through the south window.

The sky was a brilliant blue. The sun shone brightly.

A big granite rock was visible above the green of the grass.

Chantry had started to turn away when something flashed across his vision . . . a faint gleam. He took his eyes from the window and slowly turned a page.

"What was you lookin' at then?" Mowatt demanded.

"I was just thinking," Chantry replied. "Clive was never a simple man. I've got to put myself in his shoes and try to think like him. I may seem to be daydreaming, but I'm not."

Mac Mowatt hitched around in his chair. "Your funeral," he said shortly. "But I'm gettin' mighty impatient. And so are the boys."

"You haven't yet hung the killer of my brother," Chantry said. "And I gave your men two weeks."

Mowatt came off his chair with a lunge and backhanded Chantry across the mouth. He staggered, falling against the wall. Instantly, the men outside were in the doorway.

Mowatt waved a hand. "It's all right. He just gave me some lip. You boys relax. I can handle this."

Mowatt sat down again and Chantry picked up the fallen book. He tasted blood, and his lip was swelling where it had smashed against his teeth.

"You keep a still tongue now," said Mowatt. "I got no time to waste."

Chantry lifted his eyes to the window. There, by the big granite rock where the secret way went down the mountain, there was a gleam . . . a bit of mica in the rock reflecting light. Chantry turned his eyes away and knew what he intended to do. It was a long, long chance to take, and it meant some close-up shooting, and a chance that he'd be killed.

He smiled.

"What you smilin' at?" Mowatt demanded.

Chantry continued to smile. "I was just thinking of your faces when I find it," he said, "because I know it isn't what you think. You've been a fool, Mowatt, leading your men on a wild-goose chase, getting several of them killed, and several hurt. And all for nothing."

Chantry wanted him close. He wanted him to hit again. He had to get him close.

"I was smiling, too," he added, "to think how foolish we all are. Everybody dies sometime. The one thing we know about life is that we never get out alive, so why not live like a proud man? Mowatt, you're a yellow-bellied coward to hit an unarmed man. You are no gentleman, not even a shadow of one. You're leading a murdering, cowardly band of renegades, and not one of them would stand up to a man in a fair fight.

"And you, Mac Mowatt, supposed to be a fearless leader. I heard you back up for Freka . . . afraid to face him down. You're nothing, Mowatt, nothing at all. You haven't the guts of a mouse."

Chantry was ready, poised for attack, but it didn't come. Mac Mowatt leaned back in his chair and grinned at him, his eyes cold and crafty.

"You talk a lot, Chantry," he said, "but you ain't got what

it takes. I know just what you're thinkin'. Like I'll get mad, jump you, you'll try for my gun, an' then you'll shoot it out. Well, it ain't a-gonna work.

"Oh, I'm mad, all right! As for Freka, I'll handle him my own way, and I need no help from you. Meanwhile, you got you one minute. You tell me where that gold is." Mowatt drew his gun and balanced it in his palm, muzzle upward.

"Read it," growled Mowatt.

" 'Yet all experience is an arch wherethrou'/Gleams that untravell'd world whose margin fades/ For ever and for ever when I move.' "

"Don't mean nothin' to me," Mowatt said. The gun was steady in his hand, its muzzle lined on Chantry's chest.

"Look, Mowatt. The window is the arch. And looking out the window, you can see the sun reflecting off the mica. That's the gleam. If you shift your head a mite, the gleam fades and you lose it. That's 'whose margin fades/ For ever and for ever when I move.' "

"Thanks, Chantry." Mac Mowatt was smiling. "Now you've given me all I need."

He eared back the hammer on his gun.

What was happenin' to 'em I couldn't find out. All I knew was that if me an' Marny was to get out of this alive I surely had to do somethin', an' fast.

Whitey was a tough, mean man, an' nobody to tangle with if it could be avoided, and there he set behind a slab of pine he'd picked up from a lightnin'-blasted tree, a-playin' solitaire with a greasy deck of cards. He sat there facin' us where we could never move without his seein', his cards in his hands, his six-shooter lyin' on the slab right there beside him.

Slim had come back and was watching Whitey's game an' I happened to glance up an' seen something wavin' at me. It was a hand, and it was that old man. He was in the edge of the woods and he had that ol' buffalo gun and he was kind of gesturin', seemed to me, toward Slim and then himself.

It taken me no time to see what he meant. He was going

to take Slim and that left Whitey for me. Well, he sure
picked the easy one. Tacklin' that Whitey was like jumping
right down a grizzly's throat, but I aimed to do it.

I reached over an' taken Marny's wrist and kinda squeezed,
puttin' my feet back for a quick getup as I done it, so she'd
know somethin' was up. First time I ever touched her.

That old coon hunter out there, he taken aim with that ol'
buffalo gun and I looked up at Slim just a minute, an' I
couldn't help but say it. I said, "Good-bye, Slim," and his
eyes come to mine, and then that gun boomed.

What the buffalo gun done to him, I never seen, 'cause
when it boomed I left the ground in a lunge, and I swung
one from the hip that clobbered Whitey right in the face. He
went over backward, grabbin' for his gun that was falling off
the slab, and Slim, he was on the ground near me, kickin' an'
squawlin'.

Whitey come off the ground but I swung another fist into
him and the gun somehow landed near my feet. I ducked an'
grabbed for it, but Whitey kicked me in the head, knockin'
me back to the ground. And then I heard a gun go off close
up, and I was certain I was shot.

When I opened my eyes and started to get up, Marny was
standin' there with a gun in her hand an' Whitey was dead.

Then something slammed into my skull, I heard a scream
an' another gunshot, and then I was rolling in the dust and
branches from a fallen tree an' my head was roaring with
sound an' a stabbing pain. I fought to get up. Got up,
staggered, and scraped my palms on tree bark when I tried
to hold myself from fallin' again.

Blood was streamin' into my eyes and all I could see was
Tom Freka up on a horse. He had Marny and she was unconscious, seemed like, and they were ridin' away through the
trees.

Whitey was on the ground where Marny had shot him to save
me, and I jumped for him, trying to find the gun Marny must
have dropped near him. I found it and came up holding it.

Then a man I never seen before come running at me. He
skidded to a halt when he seen me and he says, "Drop it,
kid, or I'll kill you!" and I shot him right through the brisket.

TWENTY-ONE

Chantry had no faith in the breaks, but he knew one when he saw it.

The hammer on Mac Mowatt's gun eared back and from somewhere outside a buffalo gun boomed. The boom of that big gun, unexpected as it was, froze Mac Mowatt for one instant. Chantry needed no more.

He swung a long-stretched kick at the tilted-up leg of Mowatt's chair and hooked it. The chair went over and Mowatt with it. And the gun went off into the ceiling.

Chantry threw the Tennyson at him and followed it in, and as Mowatt floundered in the tangle of book and chair, he kicked him in the belly and wrenched the gun from his hand. He heard the snap of a bullet past his ear and the thud of it into the wall, and then he fired. Mowatt lay still.

His next bullet caught Ollie Fenelon filling the doorway and a second one hit Ollie as he fell into the room, Ollie's gun falling from his hand. Snatching Ollie's gun, Chantry jumped for the door: Pierce Mowatt had a rifle and it was lifting as Chantry stepped into the door and chopped down on him with both guns. Pierce took a step back and fell, tried to get up and then lay still.

And there, across a small clearing, his six-shooter in its holster, stood Jake Strawn.

"Chantry, take my horse," he said, "Tom Freka's prob'ly got your girl."

That big blood bay was standing there, saddled for traveling, and Chantry swung into the saddle. "Thanks!" he yelled, and then the bay was running.

Jake Strawn had need of a fast horse from time to time, and this was the horse that could outrun anything in the country.

Chantry had heard some gunshots from far away and feared the worst.

Doby was at the Mowatt camp, standing all spraddle-legged, only half aware of what was happening. There was blood all over his head and two men down. Doby yelled and pointed out the direction, and the bay began to run again.

Freka's tracks were fresh, and the bay seemed to know that was where they were going.

The trail was narrow, and the slender stems of aspens bent over the trail in arches, like the crossed swords at a military wedding. It was like riding down a tunnel, only there was dust in Chantry's nostrils until they broke into open meadow.

Not knowing the country, Freka had been riding blind and, in his haste, had reached a dead end.

He was seeking a trail out when he saw the big bay, believing its rider to be Strawn. "Lay off, Jake!" Freka shouted. "This gal is mine!"

Then he saw it was Chantry, and his face went white. He let go of Marny, who slid from the saddle to the ground. Freka's horse stepped away from the fallen girl, and Freka snarled, "How'd you get that horse, Chantry?"

"Jake let me have him, Freka. He said you had my girl."

"Never knowed she was yours," Tom said, "or I'd a taken her sooner. I see you got a drawn gun. That gives you a edge."

"You never had an edge, Freka?" Chantry was relentless.

Marny was stirring. She was going to get up, and he wished she would stay where she was.

"I didn't think the almighty Owen Chantry needed an edge. You holster your gun an' I'll beat you."

"You might . . . and you might not. But I'm not aiming to give you a break. You're a woman-killing snake."

Chantry dropped his gun into its holster. He saw Freka's hand move to cover him. His hand already just above his own gun, Chantry simply brought it out again and fired.

Freka had white pearl buttons on his dark blue shirt. The button on his left pocket flap vanished and was replaced by crimson.

Chantry walked the big bay closer as Freka tried to bring his suddenly too heavy gun to bear. "I'm not a woman, Freka," he said. "You should have stuck to killing women."

There was no need to waste another bullet. The gun slid from Freka's fingers and he slumped in the saddle, still holding the reins and looking at Owen Chantry with staring eyes.

"He let you have that horse. I never knowed him to—"

"Jake Strawn is a man, Freka. A bad man, but a man."

Freka fell from his horse, his boot hanging in the stirrup. The horse walked off a few steps, dragging Freka face down in the dirt.

Owen Chantry rode the bay over, disengaged Freka's boot, and let his leg fall. Then he rode back to Marny Fox, leading Freka's horse behind him.

"We'd better go back," he said gently. "They'll be worried."

When Marny rode in with Chantry beside her, Strawn was waiting near the cabin. Chantry swung down. "Thanks, Jake. Lucky you had him saddled."

"Glad to oblige, Chantry," Strawn said, "I've had enough of Mowatt's crew. Them that's still alive has scattered. I figgered I'd ride down El Paso way and see Frank."

"Frank's a good man, Jake. One of the best."

Jake Strawn mounted his bay, then turned in the saddle. "How'd it go, Owen? With Freka, I mean?"

"He won't kill anymore," said Chantry.

"He was the one killed Clive," said Strawn.

"That's what I guessed," said Chantry. "But much obliged. I'm happy to know for sure."

Strawn started to ride away.

"Jake?"

He pulled up. "If you ever want to sell that horse—?"

"Not a chance!" Jake replied, and rode away.

Chantry looked slowly around. Kernohan, looking pale and weak but on his own feet, came in from the aspens. Doby was with him, and the old man—looking even grayer now and leaning on his buffalo gun as he walked.

"Is it over, Owen?"

"I think so, Doby." Chantry smiled. It felt like his first smile in months. "Except for burying the dead and finding the treasure. How'd you like to find the treasure?"

"Now?" Doby asked.

"Now," said Chantry. And slowly he led the way to the boulder, followed by Marny, Kernohan, and Doby.

The foot of the boulder where the hidden trail went steeply down offered a splendid view. Chantry paused there for a moment, drinking in the magnificence of it.

Clive had sighted well. Close up, the bit of mica was hard to find. Chantry stepped back and looked thoughtfully at the rock, then studied to the right and left of it. Finally, he stepped into the cleft and began a close examination of the rock.

Once he found it, the hiding place seemed obvious and scarcely could be termed anything of the kind. More than likely, Clive's only thought had been to put it away from the danger of fire, always something to be reckoned with in cabins with open hearths.

It was just a little hole in the bolder, the opening blocked off by a rock. After displacing the rock, Chantry removed a rusted metal box. He broke it open. Inside was a roll of parchment covering a sheaf of papers. The parchment was wrapped in oilskin.

Doby leaned over and peered into the hole, then at the now empty box. "Is that treasure?" he asked.

Carefully, without answering, Owen Chantry removed the oilskin cover and gently unrolled the parchment. It was a deep tan in color and written upon with firm and elegant handwriting: *"This manuscript to be delivered to my friend Jean Jacques Tremoulin, Paris, France. The Legends of the Otomi as Collected by Clive Chantry."*

Chantry read the words aloud. They stared at the manuscript in wonder, as Chantry turned the oilskin inside out. When he did so, a tiny gold nugget slipped free and fell to the ground.

Doby was struck with awe. He'd never seen real gold before, but he knew what it was.

Treasure . . . gold . . . and value. . . .

It was a whole lot to understand at once, Chantry knew, especially for a poor country boy.

"Anyway," said Chantry, "we're going to be neighbors now. The war is over." He reached for Marny's hand.

For war it had been.

"I'm mighty glad," said Kernohan. "Us down there and you up here. You're a mighty generous man, Chantry." He was weak on his feet, but he could walk.

"And you must visit us often, Doby," said Marny, "being as close by as you are."

Doby grinned. She was a little too old for him anyway. One of these days, he'd just take him a trip to El Paso.

In the stillness of a mountain grove high above, the old man looked down at the people, dead and alive.

He'd helped. He'd taken his shots, and made them when they counted, *where* they counted.

Enclosed by the silence around him, broken only by a bird call, the old man bent down, drank from a small stream, and wiped his mouth.

"The trouble with people is," he said, aloud to himself, "they make too damn much noise!"

Son of a Wanted Man

TO BADIE-GUY
  My Ponca Friend . . .

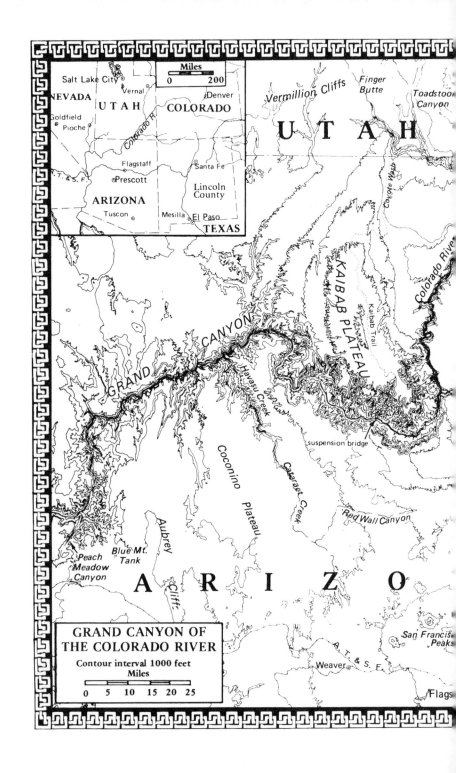

GRAND CANYON OF
THE COLORADO RIVER

Contour interval 1000 feet
Miles

0   5   10   15 20 25

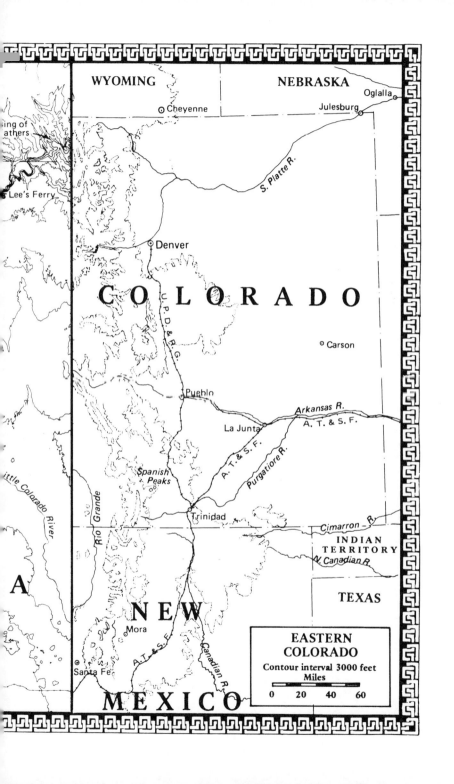

WYOMING

NEBRASKA

Cheyenne

Oglalla

Julesburg

S. Platte R.

ing of
athers

Lee's Ferry

Denver

C O L O R A D O

U. P. D. & R. G.

Carson

ttle Colorado River

Pueblo

Arkansas R.

A. T. & S. F.

La Junta

A. T. & S. F.

Purgatiore R.

Spanish
Peaks

Rio Grande

Trinidad

Cimarron R.

INDIAN
TERRITORY

N. Canadian R.

A

TEXAS

N E W

Mora

A. T. & S. F.

Canadian R.

Santa Fe

M E X I C O

EASTERN
COLORADO
Contour interval 3000 feet
Miles

0   20   40   60

Author's Note

To defend against the kind of outlaws I write about in *Son of a Wanted Man*, and as the towns of the western frontier began to develop and become more populated, there was a great need for law enforcement officials to become more professional in their approach to dealing with lawbreakers. Dave Cook, whom I mention in this novel, was a real marshal who began to organize the individual marshals of towns in the West in an effort to get them to cooperate in tracking down criminals and bringing them to justice.

There are two town marshals who play important roles in this story and who support the ideas of Dave Cook, and they will both be old friends to my readers: Bordon Chantry and Tyrel Sackett. Tyrel Sackett, of course, appears in a number of the novels I have written over the years about the Sackett family. I know from the mail I get that the "Mora gunfighter" is a particular favorite of many readers so I am glad to have been able to work him into this book. Tyrel has met up once before with Chantry in the novel *Borden Chantry*, where Chantry solved the murder of Joe Sackett, Tyrel's brother.

One

The winter snows were melting in the forests of the Kaibab, and the red orange Vermilion Cliffs were streaked with melting frost. Deer were feeding in the forest glades among the stands of ponderosa and fir, and trout were leaping in the sun-sparkled streams. A shadow moved under the ponderosa, then was gone.

Five deer fed on the grass along the bank of a mountain stream back of Finger Butte, their coats mottled with the light and shadow of sunlight through the leaves.

It was very still. Water rippled around the roots of a tree where the soil had washed away, and gurgled cheerfully among the rocks. A buck's tail twitched, twitched again, and the regal head lifted, turning its nostrils to the wind, reading it cautiously, but the reading was betrayal, for the shadow under the pines was downwind of him.

A faint breeze sifted through the grass and stirred the leaves, and with the breeze the shadow moved into the sunlight and became a man, standing motionless not twenty feet from the nearest deer.

Straight and tall he stood in gray buckskins. He wore no hat, and his hair long. Lean and brown, his black hair loose, he waited until the buck's head lifted again, looking right at him.

A startled snort and the buck sprang away. The others followed. Mike Bastian stood with his hands on his hips, watching them go.

Another man came through the trees behind him, a lean, wiry old man with a gray mustache and blue eyes alive with humor.

"What do you think of that, Roundy?" Bastian asked. "Could your Apache beat that? Another step and I could have touched him."

Roundy spat into the grass. "No Apache I ever knowed could do better, son. An' I never seen the day I could do as well. You're good, Mike, really good. I am surely glad you're not huntin' my hair!" He drew his pipe from his pocket and began stoking it. "We're headin' back for Toadstool Canyon, Mike. Your pa sent for us."

"No trouble, is there?"

"None I know of, although things don't look good. They don't look good at all. No, I think your pa figures it's time you rode out with the bunch."

Mike Bastian squatted on his heels, glancing around the glade. This was what he liked, and he did not want to leave. Nor did he like what he was going back to face. "I believe you're right, Roundy. Pa said I was to ride out in the spring when the boys went, and it is about time."

He tugged a blade of grass and chewed on it. "I wonder where they will go this time?"

"Whatever it is, and wherever it is, it will be well planned. Your pa would have made a fine general, boy. He's got the head for it. He never forgets a thing."

"You've been with him a long time, haven't you?"

"Mighty long. I was with him before he found you. I met him in Mexico during the War, longer ago than I care to remember. I was just a youngster then, myself."

From the grass he took up a fallen pine cone. "Son! *Look!*" He tossed the pine cone into the air.

Mike Bastian palmed his gun and it belched flame, then again. The second shot spattered the pine cone into flying brown chips.

"Not bad," Roundy said, "but you shot too quick. You've got to get over that, Mike. Most times one shot is all you'll get."

Side by side they started back through the woods. The earth was spongy with a thick bed of pine needles. An occasional break in the trees offered a glimpse of the far-off San Francisco peaks, with clouds shrouding their summits. Roundy was not as tall as the younger man, but he walked with the long, easy stride of the woodsman. Coming to a break in the forest that permitted them a long view of the wild, broken canyon country to the east, Roundy spoke. "Your pa picked mighty well. Nobody in God's world could find him in all that."

"There's Indians," Bastian reminded, "and some of the Mormons know that country."

"He doesn't bother them and they don't bother him," Roundy said. "That's why his outfit needs a tight rein."

They walked on, in silence. Several times Bastian paused to study the ground, reading the tracks to see who or what had passed since they had passed. "This here is somethin' you better not do again," Roundy suggested, "comin' back the way we went out. Somebody could be layin' for us."

"Who?"

"Ah, now. That's the question. Nobody is supposed to know your pa's plans for you, but there's always the chance somebody might. Believe me, son, nothin' is a secret for long, an' you can just bet some of the boys have been doin' some thinkin' about you."

They paused again, studying the country around, and Roundy put the question that had been bothering him for months. "Mike? If Ben's ready for you to go out, what will you do?"

"Go, I guess. What choice do I have?"

"You're sure? You're sure you want to be an outlaw?"

"Wasn't that why he raised me? To take over from him?" There was an edge of bitterness in Mike's tone. "Wasn't I to take over when Ben Curry stepped aside?"

"That's what you were raised for, all right." Roundy poked at the pine needles with his toe. "But it's your life you have to live. Ben Curry can't live it for you, and you can't live his life for him, no matter how much he wants it.

"The thing to remember, Mike, is that things have changed since Ben an' me rode into this country together. It's no longer wild and free like it was. Folks are movin' in, settlin' the country, buildin' homes.

"Getaways won't be so easy no more, and the kind of men you ride with will change. Fact is, they have already changed.

"When Ben an' me rode into this country it was wide open. Most banks had been mighty hard on a poor man, ready to foreclose at the slightest chance, and the railroads gave all the breaks to the big cattle shippers, so nobody cared too much if a train was robbed or a bank. If you killed somebody, especially a man with a wife and kids—well, that was something else. If you just robbed a bank or train the posses would chase you more for fun than actually to catch you. It was a break in the work they were doin'. They'd get out, run an outlaw for a while but not too serious about it.

"Kill a man? That was different. They'd chase you for keeps then, and they'd catch you. That's why Ben Curry wouldn't stand for killin', an' he's been known to personally kill a man who disobeyed that order."

"He actually did?"

"Seen it myself. It was Dan Peeples, and Dan was a high hand with a gun. They'd robbed a bank in Wyoming an' as they were ridin' out of town this young feller came out of an alley, blundered right in the way, and Dan Peeples shot him.

"Folks seen it. Folks knew it was deliberate. Well, we rode on three, four miles an' Ben pulled up. He turned to Dan Peeples an' he said, 'I said no killin', Dan.'

"Dan, he just grinned an' said, 'Well, he got in the way. Anyway, what's one farm kid, more or less?'

"Ben Curry said, 'When I say no killin', I mean it.'

"Dan, he says, 'So?' And Ben shot him. Dan saw it comin' and reached but he was too slow, so Ben left him layin' there for the posse to find."

"What if they got cornered?"

"That was different. If they had to fight their way out, well an' good, an' a time or two that happened. Your pa was against needless killin', an' the word got around. The outlaws knew it, but the townsfolk, ranchers, an' lawmen knew it, too."

"I've heard some of the stories."

"No way you could miss. Ben Curry's kind breed stories. In them old days many a man rustled a few head to get started, and sometimes a broke cowhand would stand up a stage and nobody took it too serious, but it isn't like that anymore. The country is growin' up and changing viewpoints. More than that, it is Ben himself."

"You think he's too big?"

"What else? Your pa controls more country than there is in New York State! Right under his thumb! And he's feared over much of the west by those who really know about him, but not many do.

"Outside of his own crowd nobody has seen Ben Curry in years, at least, not to know who he was. Mighty few know his power, although there's a rumor around that somewhere there lives a man who rides herd on more than a hundred outlaws. Much of his success lies in the fact that nobody believes it.

"His men ride out and meet at a given point. They ride alone or in pairs, never more than three together at a time until the job is pulled, then they break up an' scatter.

"He plans ever' job himself, with maybe one or two settin' in. He's scouted or had the job scouted by somebody he can trust. It is planned, rehearsed, then done.

"Mostly folks lay the robberies to driftin' cowhands, to Jesse

James or somebody else. He pulls jobs anywhere from Canada to Mexico, and from San Antone to Los Angeles."

Roundy started off along the trail. "He's been the brains, all right, but don't ever forget it was those guns of his kept things in line. Lately, he hasn't had to use his guns. Kerb Perrin, Rigger Molina, or somebody else will handle discipline. He's become too big, Ben Curry has. He's like a king, and the king isn't gettin' any younger."

He stopped in the trail and turned around. "How d'you suppose Perrin will take it when he hears about you takin' over? You think he'll stand still for that?"

"I doubt if he will," Mike said thoughtfully. "I imagine he's done some planning on his own."

"You can bet he has! So has Molina, and neither one of them will stop at murder to get what they want. Your pa still has them buffaloed, I think, but that won't matter when the showdown comes. And I figure the time has come."

"Now?" Mike was incredulous.

"Mike, I never told you, and I know Ben hasn't, but Ben has a family."

"A *family*?" Mike Bastian was shocked. "But I—!"

"He has a wife and two daughters, and they have no idea he's an outlaw. Wouldn't believe it if you told 'em. Their home is down near Tucson someplace, but occasionally they come to a ranch he owns in Red Wall Canyon, a ranch supposedly owned by Voyle Ragan. Ben visits them there."

"Who else knows this?"

"Nary a soul, and don't you be tellin' anyone. Ben, he always wanted a son, and never had one, so when your real pa was killed down at Mesilla, Ben took you to raise. That was nigh onto eighteen years ago, and since then he's spent a lot of time an' thought on you. A long time later he told me he was going to raise you to take over whatever he left."

"What about my real father? My family?"

Roundy shrugged. "I never did get the straight of that, and there may be other stories. The way I heard, it was your real pa was killed by 'Paches whilst you was off in the brush somewhere. They come down, killed your pa, stole your horses, and looted the wagon. They were bein' chased by soldiers out of El Paso or somewhere an' it was a sort of hit-an'-run thing. The soldiers brought you back to town an' Ben took you to raise."

"Kind of him."

"Yes, it was. Not many men would do such a thing, them days. Most of them just didn't want the responsibility or wouldn't take the time. For several years it was just you an' him, an' he tried to teach you everything he knew.

"Look at it. You can track like an Apache. In the woods you're a ghost, and I doubt if old Ben Curry himself can throw a gun as fast and accurate as you. You can ride anything that wears hair, an' what you don't know about cards, dice, roulette, and all the rest of it, nobody knows. You can handle a knife, fight with your fists, and open anything made in the way of safes and locks.

"Along with that he's seen you got a good education, so's you can handle yourself in any kind of company. I doubt if any boy ever got the education and training you've had, and now Ben is ready to step back an' let you take over."

"So he can join his wife and daughters?"

"Uh-huh. He just wants to step out of the picture, go somewhere far off, and live a quiet life. He's gettin' no younger and he wants to take it easy in his last years. You see, Mike, Ben's been afraid of only one thing. That's poverty. He had a lot of it as a youngster. I reckon that was one reason he taken you to raise, he knowed what you were up against, if you lived at all.

"Now he's made his pile, but he knows he can't get out alive unless he has somebody younger, stronger, and smarter to take control of what he's built. That's where you come in."

"Why not let Perrin have it?"

"You know the answer to that. Perrin is mean and he's dangerous. He'd have gone off the deep end long ago if it hadn't been for Ben Curry. He's a good second man but a damn poor leader. That goes for Molina, too. He'd have killed fifty times if he hadn't known that Ben would kill him when he got back.

"No, neither could handle it, and the whole shootin' match would go to pieces in sixty days left to either of them. More than that, a lot of people would get killed, inside an' outside the gang."

Little of what Roundy was saying was new to Bastian, yet he was curious as to why the old man was saying it. The two had been together a lot and knew each other as few men ever did. They had gone through storm, hunger, and thirst together, living in the desert and mountains, returning only occasionally to the rendezvous in Toadstool Canyon.

Obviously there was purpose in Roundy's bringing up the subject, and Bastian waited, listening. Over the years he had learned that Roundy rarely talked at random. He spoke when he had something to say, something important. Yet even as they talked he was aware of all that was about him. A quail had moved into the tall grass near the stream, and ahead of them a squirrel moved in the crotch of a tree, and only minutes ago a gray wolf had crossed the path where they walked.

Roundy had said he was a woodsman, and it was true that he felt more at home in the woods and wild country than anywhere else. The idea of taking over the leadership of the outlaws filled him with unease. Always he had been aware that this time would come, and he had been schooled for it, but until now it had always been pleasantly remote. Now, suddenly, it was at hand.

Was he afraid of responsibility? Or was he simply afraid? Searching his thoughts he could find no fear. As for responsibility, he had been so prepared and conditioned for his role that it was a natural step.

He thought of Kerb Perrin and Rigger Molina. Was he afraid? No, he was not. Both men had been tolerant and even friendly when he was a boy, Molina especially. Yet as he grew older and became a man they had withdrawn. Did they realize the role that he was being prepared for?

They knew him, but how much did they know? None of them had seen him shoot, for example. At least, none that he knew.

Roundy interrupted his thoughts by stopping to study the country ahead. "Mike," Roundy said, "the country is growing up. Last year some of our raids raised merry hell, and the boys had a hard time getting away. Folks don't like having their lives disrupted, and when the boys ride out this year they will be riding into trouble.

"Folks don't look at an outlaw as they used to. He isn't regarded as some wild youngster full of liquor and excess energy. He's a bad man, dangerous to the community, and he's stealing money folks have saved.

"Now they see an outlaw like a wolf, and every man will be hunting him. Before you go into this you'd better think it over, and think seriously.

"You know Ben Curry, and I know you like him, as well you should. He did a lot for you. At the same time, Ben had no right to raise you to be an outlaw. He chose his own way, of his own free will, but you should be free to do the same.

"No man has a right to say to another, 'This you must be.' Nobody ever asked you did you want to be an outlaw, although as a youngster you might have said yes. Looked at from afar it seems romantic an' excitin'. Well, take it from me, it ain't. It's hard, dirty, and rough. It's hangin' out with mean, bitter people; it's knowin' cheap, tricky women who are just like the outlaws, out to make a fast buck the easiest way they can."

The old man stopped to relight his pipe, and Mike kept silent, waiting for Roundy to continue. "I figure ever' man has a right to choose his own way, and no matter what Ben's done for you, you got that right.

"I don't know what you'll do, but if you decide to step out of the gang I don't want to be around when it happens. Old Ben will be fit to be tied. I don't figure he's ever really thought about how you feel. He's only figuring on gettin' out and havin' somebody to take over.

"He's built somethin' here, and in his way he's proud of it. Ben would have been a builder and an organizer in whatever direction he chose, but he's not thinkin' straight. Moreover, Ben hasn't been on a raid for years. He doesn't know how it is anymore.

"Oh, he plans! He studies the layout of the towns, the banks, and the railroads, but he doesn't see how folks are changin'. He doesn't listen to them talk. It isn't just saloons, corrals, honky-tonks, and gamblin' anymore. Folks have churches an' schools. They don't want lead flyin' whilst their kids are walkin' to school.

"Right now you're an honest man. You're clean as a whistle. Once you become an outlaw a lot will change. You will have to kill, don't forget that. It is one thing to kill in defense of your home, your family, or your country. It is quite another thing when you kill for money or for power."

"Do you think I'll have to kill Perrin an' Molina?"

"Unless they kill you first. You're good with a gun, Mike. Aside from Ben Curry you're the best I ever saw, but shootin' at a target isn't like shootin' at a man who's shootin' back at you.

"Take Billy the Kid, this Lincoln County gunman we've been hearin' about. Frank an' George Coe, Dick Brewer, Jesse Evans, any one of them can probably shoot as good as Ben. The difference is that part down inside where the nerves should be. Well, that was left out. When he starts shootin' or they shoot at him, he's like ice.

"Kerb Perrin is that way, too. He's cold, and steady as a rock. Rigger Molina's another kind of cat. He explodes all over the place. He's white-hot but deadly as a rattler.

"Five men cornered Molina one time out of Julesburg. When the shootin' was over four of them were down and the fifth was holdin' a gunshot arm. Molina, he rode out under his own power. He's a shaggy wolf, that one! Wild, uncurried, an' big as a bear!"

Roundy paused, puffing on his pipe. "Sooner or later, Mike, there'll be a showdown. It will be one or the other, maybe both of them, and God help you!"

Two

Listening to Roundy, Mike remembered that time and time again Ben Curry had warned him to confide in no one. Betrayal could come from anyone, at any time, for even the best of people liked to talk and to repeat what they knew. And there were always those who might take a drink too many or who might talk to get themselves off a hook. What nobody knew, nobody could tell.

Obviously, Ben practiced what he preached, for until now Mike had not even guessed Ben might have a life other than the one he lived in and about Toadstool Canyon. Of course, he did ride off alone from time to time, but he was understood to be scouting jobs or tapping his own sources of information.

Nobody knew what the next job was to be, or where, until Ben Curry called a conference around the big table in his stone house. At such times the table would be covered with maps and diagrams. The location of the town in relation to the country around, the possible approaches to and routes away from town, the layout of the bank itself or whatever was to be

12

robbed, and information on the people employed there and their probable reaction to a robbery.

The name of the town was never on the map. If it was recognized by anyone present he was advised to keep his mouth shut until told.

Distances had been measured and escape routes chosen, with possible alternatives in the event of trouble. Fresh horses awaited them and first-aid treatment if required. Each job was planned months in advance and a final check made to see that nothing unexpected had come up just before the job was pulled.

There were ranches and hideouts located at various places to be used only in case of need, and none were known criminal resorts. Each location was given only at the time of the holdup, and rarely would a location be used again.

Far more than Roundy imagined had Mike Bastian been involved in the planning of past ventures. For several years he had been permitted to take part in the original planning to become acquainted with Ben Curry's methods of operation.

"Some day," Ben Curry warned, "you will ride out with the boys, and you must be ready. I do not plan for you to ride out often. Just a time or two to get the feel of it and to prove yourself to the others. When you do go you will have charge of the job, and when you return you will make the split."

"Will they stand for that?"

"They'd damn' well better! I'll tell 'em, but you'll be your own enforcer—and no shootin'. You run this outfit without that, or you ain't the man I think you are."

Looking back, he could see how carefully Ben Curry had trained him, teaching him little by little and watching how he received it. Deliberately, Ben had kept him from any familiarity with the outlaws he would lead. Only Roundy, who was no outlaw at all, knew him well. Roundy, an old mountain man, had taught him Indian lore and the ways of the mountains. Both of them had showed him trails known to no others. Several times outlaws had tried to pump him for information, but he had professed to know nothing.

The point Roundy now raised worried him. The Ben Curry he knew was a big, gruff, kindly man, even if grim and forbidding at times. He had taken in the homeless boy, giving him kindness and care, raising him as a son. For all of that Mike Bastian had no idea that Ben had a wife and family, or any other life than this. Ben had planned and acted with care and shrewdness.

"You ain't done nothin' wrong," Roundy suggested. "The law doesn't know you or want you. You're clean. Whatever you knew about those maps an' such, that was just a game your pa played with you."

And that was how it had been for the first few years. It was not until recently that he had begun to realize those maps and diagrams were deadly serious, and it was then he had begun to worry.

"Nobody knows Ben Curry," Roundy said. "Any warrants there may have been have been forgotten. He ain't ridden out on a job in fifteen year. When he decides to quit he'll simply disappear and appear somewheres else under another name and with his family. He'll be a retired gentleman who made his pile out west."

Roundy paused. "He'll be wanted nowhere, he'll be free to live out his years, and he'll have you trained to continue what he started."

"Suppose I don't want to?"

Roundy looked up at him, his wise old eyes measuring and shrewd. "Then you'll have to tell him," he said. "You will have to face him with it."

Mike Bastian felt a chill. Face that old man? He shook his head. "I don't know," he said, "if I could."

"Is it you don't want to hurt him? Or are you simply scared?"

Mike shrugged. "A little of both, I guess. But then, why shouldn't I take over? It's an exciting life."

"It is that," Roundy commented dryly. "You got no idea how excitin' until you tell Kerb Perrin and Rig Molina who's boss."

Mike laughed. "I can see them," he said. The smile faded. "Has Ben Curry thought of that?"

"You bet he has! Why's he had you workin' with a six-gun all these years?"

Here, around the Vermilion Cliffs was the only world he knew. This was his country, but what lay outside? He could only guess.

Could he make it out there? He could become a gambler. He knew cards, dice, faro, roulette, all of it. Or he could punch cows, he supposed. Somewhere out beyond this wilderness of rust-red cliffs there was another world where men lived honest, hardworking lives, where they worked all day and went home at night to a wife, children, and a fireside. It was a world from which he had been taken, a world in which his father had lived, and his mother, he supposed, although he knew nothing of her.

"Roundy? What do you know about who my parents were?"

The old man stared at the ground. He had known the question would be asked someday. He had wondered how he would answer it. Now, faced with it at last, he hedged.

"You were in Mesilla when he found you. The way I heard it, your pa was killed by 'Paches. I reckon your ma was dead before that, or why else wouldn't she be with you, young as you were?"

"I've wondered about that," Mike said quietly. "I suppose she had died before." He paused. "I guess a man is always curious. Pa, I mean Ben, he never speaks of it."

They had reached their horses, grazing on a meadow among the aspen. Roundy spoke. "You'd better be thinkin' of the future, not the past. You'd best be thinkin' of what you're goin' to tell Ben when he tells you you're ridin' out with the boys."

Roundy stared after Mike as he walked toward the horses. He had never had a son, none that he knew of, anyway. Yet for years he had worked with Mike Bastian, leading him, training him, talking to him. He had spent more time with him than most fathers did with their sons, and not only because it was his job.

Now he was scared. He admitted it, he was scared. He was

scared for more reasons than one, because Ben Curry had made a mistake.

Roundy only heard of it after the fact. Usually he sat in on the planning, keeping well back in a corner and rarely putting in a comment, but in this case he had been out in the hills with Mike and had not heard until later.

When they were alone, he faced Ben with it. "Mora? You've got to be crazy!"

Ben Curry pulled up in his walking across the room. "What's that? Why?"

Roundy had never spoken to him like that, and Ben was startled. He stared at the old man. "What's wrong?" he asked.

"You said Mora. You sent the boys into Mora. That's Tyrel Sackett's town."

"Who?"

"Ben, you've been back in the hills too long. You don't listen anymore. Tyrel Sackett is that gunfighter who was in the land-grant fight. He's hell on wheels."

"I never heard of him. Anyway," he added, "he was in Santa Fe. I made sure of that."

"And when he comes home?"

"The boys will be long gone and far away."

"Ben, you don't know him. He won't stand for it, Ben. He'll never quit until he knows who, how, and why. I know him."

Ben shrugged. "Too late now. Anyway, there's no tracks. Rain washed everything out, and the boys never even raised a whisper. Sixty thousand on that one. Most of the town's savings in one swoop."

Roundy said no more, but in the weeks that followed he grew increasingly worried. Mike would be going out soon, and the country was tightening up. That was bad enough without incurring the anger of a man like Tyrel Sackett, a man who was a master at tracking and trailing.

A few months later, Ben had commented on it. "What did I tell you? Nothing came of that Mora business."

Roundy, squatted on his heels at the fireplace, nursing a cup of coffee, had glanced up. "It hasn't been a year yet. You can bet Sackett hasn't forgotten."

Approximately four hundred miles to the east a train was stopping even as he spoke, stopping at a small, sandblasted town in eastern Colorado, a town with only a freight car for a depot.

One man stepped down from the train, a tall young man in a black suit. He stood there, watching the train pull away.

Glancing out the window, Borden Chantry had seen the train slow, then come to a stop, and as it rarely stopped, he waited, watching.

He had been doing his accounts, never a job he liked, but the taxpayers demanded to know where every dollar went, and as town marshal he had to account for every fine, every cent spent feeding those in jail.

He saw the lone man swing down, and he got up. "Ma?" He spoke to his wife, Bess. "Set another place. We're goin' to have comp'ny. Tyrel Sackett just got off the train."

Three

When the dishes were put away and the table wiped clean, Borden Chantry refilled their coffee cups. He swung a chair around with its back to the table and straddled it, leaning his thick forearms on the back.

"This is a long way from Mora," he suggested.

"Things are quiet over there, and I've got a good deputy. Thought I'd ride the cars over and have a little talk."

Borden sipped his coffee, and waited.

"Ever hear of Dave Cook?"

"Officer up Denver way, ain't he?" Borden paused. "My wife says I shouldn't say 'ain't' but I keep forgettin'."

"That's right. Denver. He's got an idea of organizing all the officers so we all work together. You know how it's been—you keep the peace in your town and I in mine. If somebody kills a man here, why should I care if he keeps out of trouble in Mora? Well, Dave thinks we should all work together."

"I'm for it."

"About a year ago we had a holdup in Mora. Store holdup,

18

but a store that banked money for folks. Had quite a lot of money, sixty thousand dollars, in the store safe. I was out of town," he added.

"Handy," Chantry commented.

"I thought so. Just too handy. Sixty thousand in the safe and the sheriff out of town. Makes for easy pickin's, 'specially when the note that got me down to Santa Fe was a fake."

"Forged?"

"No, and that's another interesting part. It was a note from my brother Orrin and it simply said, *Need you*. When a Sackett gets that kind of word he just naturally comes a-running. The trouble was that note was one Orrin wrote to his former wife a couple of years ago.

"Now the question is, how did somebody get hold of that note and where's it been all that time?

"Orrin wrote that note. He remembered it well because it was a troublesome time, but he never saw it again." Tyrel paused. "Seems to me somebody was mighty farsighted. They come on that note somehow, some way, and they just kept it against a needful time."

"It doesn't seem reasonable. How would anybody know they might need such a note years in advance?"

"Think of it, Bord. That note doesn't explain anything and there's no date, so somebody saw it might be useful and filed it away, and that somebody had to be a crook."

"They robbed your bank."

"Exactly. That says that somebody two years ago thought that note might be useful, somebody who was probably a thief at the time."

Sackett put down his cup. "Let me lay it out for you. At noontime folks are home eating. The streets are empty, only one man in the store, and then of a sudden there are three other men. The storekeeper was bound and gagged, money taken from the safe, as it was rarely locked in the daytime, and the shade drawn on the front door window. The three men leave by the back door.

"Nigh onto two hours later a fellow comes to the store, finds it locked, and goes away. Sometime later another comes, only he don't go away but walks around to the back door. He's out of tobacco and he'll be damned if he's goin' to go without.

"The back door is closed. He knocks and it opens under his fist and he hears thumpin' inside. He goes in and finds the teller all tied up an' the money gone."

"Any descriptions?"

"Three youngish, middle-sized men, one of them wearin' a polka-dot shirt. The teller says they moved fast, knew right where the money was, and weren't in the store more than five minutes, probably not more than three. Nobody said a word amongst them, just to the teller to keep his mouth shut if he wanted to live."

"Nobody saw them comin' or goin'?"

"Yes, a youngster playing in his yard. He saw a man settin' a horse an' holding the reins on three others. He saw three men come out of an alley and mount up and then another man rode in from the street and they all trotted off down the lane.

"That youngster was nine years old, but canny. He noticed one of the horses. It was a black with three white feet and a white splash on the rump."

Borden Chantry put his cup down carefully. Then he looked across the table at Tyrel Sackett. "What are you sayin'?"

"I described a horse."

"I know you did, and I have a horse like that."

Sackett nodded. "I know you have. I saw him when I was down here right after Joe was killed. A mighty fine horse, too."

Borden Chantry took up his cup. His coffee was lukewarm, so he went to the stove for the coffeepot. He filled Sackett's cup, then his own. Returning the pot to the stovetop, he sat down, straddling his chair. "Sackett," he said slowly, "maybe we've got something. Let's run it into the corral and read the brands."

Chantry paused. "This here job was wished on me, but when it was offered I sure needed it. I'm no detective or even a marshal excep' by the wish of these folks in town. I went broke ranchin', Sackett. Drouth, rustlers, an' a bad market did me in, and when I was mighty hard up these folks asked me to be marshal. I've done my best."

"You solved the murder of my brother, Joe."

"Well, sort of. It was kind of like tracking strays. You know where the feed's best, where there might be water, an' where you'd want to go to hide from some dumb cowhand. It was just a matter of puttin' two an' two together."

"Like this."

"Sort of. You done any work on this?"

"A lot of riding an' thinking. Sort of like picking up the cards and shuffling them all together again, then dealing yourself a few hands faceup to see what the cards look like.

"Only in this case it wasn't cards, but news items." Tyrel Sackett reached in his breast pocket and brought out three clippings and spread them on the table facing Chantry.

All three were of holdups, and the dates were scattered over the last two years. Robberies, no shooting, no noise, no clues. The robbers appeared, then disappeared. One robbery was in Montana, one in Washington, one in Texas.

"Mighty spread out," Chantry commented. Only in Montana had there been an organized pursuit, and the bandits had switched to fresh horses and disappeared. "Had the horses waitin'," he commented.

"The rancher says no. They were horses he kept in his corral for emergencies, like going for a doctor or something like that."

"And somebody knew it."

Chantry looked over the descriptions. They were vague except for a tall, slim man wearing a narrow-brimmed hat.

"Funny-lookin' galoot" was the description of the man in the bank.

"I think he was meant to be," Sackett suggested. "I think he was meant to be noticed, like that man wearing the polka-dot shirt in Mora."

"You mean they *wanted* somebody to be able to describe him?" Chantry asked.

"Look at it. What happens is over in minutes, and your attention focuses on the obvious. You're asked to describe the outlaws, and that polka-dot shirt stands out, or your tall man in the narrow-brimmed hat. You see the obvious and ignore the rest. You don't have a description, just a polka-dot shirt or a tall man in a narrow-brimmed hat. What were the others like? You don't recall. You've only a minute or two to look, so you see what's staring at you."

Chantry ran his fingers through his hair. "Sackett, until now I've been wonderin' if I'm foolish or not." He got up and walked to the sideboard and opened a drawer, taking out a sheaf of papers. "Looks like you an' me been tryin' to put a rope on the same calf."

He sat down and spread out the papers. They were wanted posters, letters, news clippings.

"Nine of them," he said, "Kansas, Arkansas, Wyoming, California, Texas, and Idaho. Two in California, three in Texas. Seven of them in the last four years, the others earlier. Nobody caught, no good descriptions, no clues.

"Nor were any strangers noticed hanging around town before the holdups. In four cases they got away without being seen so as to be recognized."

Chantry picked a wanted poster from the stack. "But look at this: *Four bandits, one described as a tall man wearing a Mexican sombrero.*"

"The same man, with a different hat?"

"Why not?"

Sackett finished his coffee. "All over the west, the same pattern, clean getaways, and nobody saw anything."

Borden Chantry nodded toward the stack of papers. "Got two of those in the mail on the same day, and there seemed to be a similarity. I was comparing them when I remembered the wanted poster. Since then I been collecting these, and then I went over to the newspaper and went back through their files.

They keep a stack of Denver and Cheyenne papers, too, so I ran a fairly good check."

Chantry got up and went over to the stove and, lifting the lid, glanced at the fire, then poked in a few small sticks, enough to keep the coffee hot.

"I'm glad you came over, Sackett. Now we've got to do some figuring."

"Let's start with your horse."

"You don't suspect me?"

Sackett smiled. "I suspect everybody, but I've got a theory. Suppose you tell me how you got him."

"It was roundup time, and it was late. Work had been held up and we got off to a bad start, so we were working our tails off when this gent came riding up to the chuck wagon leading five horses.

"He asked the cook if he could eat, and of course we fed him. I came in for coffee about that time, and he commented that we were shorthanded. I agreed, but added that what we were really short of was horses.

"He set there chewin' for a minute like he was thinkin' it over, and then he waved a hand at his stock. 'I've five head there you're welcome to use,' he said, 'all good stock horses. All I ask is that when you've finished the roundup you keep them up close to your house, in the corral or a small pasture where I can pick 'em up when I come back through. An' keep 'em together.'

"That gent got up, threw his coffee grounds on the grass, and started for his horse. 'When will you be back?' I ask him, an' he says he's ridin' on to the coast and it may be six months or even a year, but don't worry. He'll be back. Maybe if we're drivin' stock we may just leave the horses we're ridin' an' pick up these. He turned his horse around and said, 'Treat 'em gentle. They're good stock.' An' he rode away.

"Those horses made all the difference, and so when we finished the roundup I did like he said, only once in a while I'd catch one of them up and ride him to town, like that black.

"That sort of thing isn't that unusual, and I gave it no thought until after they appointed me town marshal. When I was cleanin' out my desk over in the office I come on this reward poster. Seems like there'd been a holdup over east of here, just a few days before.

"Our newspaper wasn't operatin' then, and I'd been too busy tryin' to make ends meet, and nobody had mentioned any holdup to me.

"Four or five men, they said. Nobody seemed right sure. Well, I filed it with the others and gave it no thought, but I was roundin' up and sellin' off some of my own cows, tryin' to pay bills, and ridin' past my horse pasture I saw those five horses were gone but there were five others in their place.

"Five horses, all good stock, but they looked like they'd been used mighty hard, an' just lately. That's when I started puttin' it all together."

The fire crackled in the stove, and the clock ticked in the silent room. Neither man spoke for some time. "Smart," Sackett said, at last. "Somebody is all-fired smart."

"How could they guess that a two-bit, rawhide rancher like me would someday be marshal?" Chantry said.

Sackett answered, "And they plan, they plan way ahead, like with your horses and that note of Orrin's." He gestured toward the papers. "There's twelve holdups or more, an' who knows anything?"

"I wonder how long it's been goin' on?"

Sackett shrugged. "Who knows? Or how many other robberies there have been of which we have no record? It would be my guess this is only the fringe. We're only two men in two mighty small towns." He tapped the stack of papers with his finger. "This makes the James boys look like pikers."

"They were pikers," Chantry said. "They advertised themselves too much. Everybody knew who they were, and they were two bloody, too many people killed for no reason, like that schoolboy who ran across the street in front of them."

"They've been getting away with this for years," Sackett

commented, "but when they picked you to keep some horses for them they made their mistake. It only takes one."

"So what do we do now?"

Sackett indicated the stack of papers. "We go through that and look for something common to all of them. That tall man, for instance, who wears funny hats. And we write to places where there have been holdups. We look for some item common to them all, and there will be something."

"We've already got something," Chantry said. "We've got one thing, anyway."

"What's that?"

"Utah. There have been no robberies in Utah."

Four

Borden Chantry got to his feet, stood there for a moment thinking, then went over to a big, hide-covered chair and dropped into it.

"You think they're Mormons?"

"No," Sackett replied, "I don't. Most Mormons I've known were law-abiding folks, although there's a bad apple in every basket.

"But look at it like this: there's thousands of square miles of rough, wild country in southeastern Utah and neighboring parts of Colorado, Arizona, and New Mexico.

"This outfit seems to be operating all over the west, so why not Utah? My guess is he doesn't want trouble on his own doorstep."

He tapped the clippings. "Look here, a robbery in Montana and a day later, in Texas. That means, if we're figuring this right, that he has more than one bunch of men. My guess would be five or six, and to control that number of men and keep them disciplined their boss man has got to be both tough and smart. So far we haven't tied this outfit to a single killing, nor has anybody caught one of them."

Chantry studied the man at the table. He had heard all the stories, as had everyone. Tyrel Sackett was known to be one of the most dangerous gunfighters in the west, a quiet young man who had come out from Tennessee, never hunting trouble, yet never backing away from it, either. Chantry had met Tyrel before when investigating the murder of his brother, Joe, but Sackett made him uncomfortable. He did not want such men, no matter how law-abiding, in his town. They had a way of attracting trouble.

He himself had never had the reputation of being a good man with a gun, yet deep inside him he was confident he could handle the best of them. He had not wanted to be a peace officer, yet when he needed money the job had been there, and he had accepted it.

Keeping the peace in a small western town was not that hard. Most of the cowboys who came into town and went on a drunk were men he had worked with. Some had worked for him, and some had worked trail drives and roundups beside him, so they were prepared to listen to him when he suggested they sleep it off.

He had been successful so far, but he made no claims to being a good officer. He was, well . . . he was competent. Up to a point, anyway. This job Sackett was talking about was out of his depth. He said as much.

Sackett gave him one of his rare smiles. "You're better than you think." He tapped the papers on the table. "You saw these and smelled something wrong. You've got an instinct for the job, Bord, whether you think so or not."

He tapped the papers again. "You know what we've got here? Something nobody would or will believe. Holdups are by local gangs, cowboys who need drinking money, something like that. By the very nature of them folks are going to say such men can't be organized. My guess is that in the last four years this outfit has pulled over a hundred holdups and robberies, gettin' away with every one.

"Somebody has to come in and scout the layout, somebody has to plan the getaway, somebody has to be sure there are fresh horses where they'll be needed."

"I don't know." Chantry shook his head. "Somewhere, somehow, something's got to give."

Sackett took out a billfold and extracted a news clipping. "They've had their troubles. Look at this."

SUSPECT ARRESTED AT CARSON

A man who gave his name as Dan Cable was arrested last night at Jennings' Livery. He had in his possession sacks containing $12,500 in freshly minted gold coin. He stated that he was en route to buy cattle.

Three days ago the bank at Rapid City was robbed of $35,000 in freshly minted gold coins. Cable is being held for investigation.

"So?"

"The next morning his cell was empty. He was gone, the gold was gone, his horse was gone. Nobody knows how it was managed."

"They moved fast," Chantry said thoughtfully. "They must have had somebody close by."

"There was no jailer at Carson. Small jail. The same key opens both the cell door and the outer door. Left alone like that he might have managed it himself."

"The gold?"

"Left in the desk drawer at the jail. The door was locked and it seemed safe. They'd had no trouble at Carson and the bank was closed, so the marshal just locked it up and left it.

"Carson's quiet now, so the two saloons close at midnight. After that the streets are empty. Cable just unlocked his door somehow, broke into the desk, then unlocked the outer door and went around to the livery stable, saddled his horse, and rode out."

"I'll be damned."

They talked until after midnight, carefully sifting the little they knew and going over the wanted posters, the news clippings, and a few letters from other peace officers and bankers.

"Maybe," Chantry said at last, "we'd better try to think ahead. If we could pick out several likely places we might beat them to it and be waiting."

"I thought of that. The trouble is there's so many possibilities. Of course, they'll be wanting a big strike."

"No stage holdups," Cantry suggested, "because when they carry big shipments they have a shotgun guard. Most of them will fight, so somebody is going to be killed."

Tyrel reached for the coffeepot and filled his cup. "I've been thinkin' about what you said about tryin' to beat them to it." He paused. "How about right here? How about your town?"

Chantry shook his head. "The trouble with that is nobody here has any big money. Nobody—" He stopped, then sat up slowly. "Yeah," he muttered, "maybe. Just maybe."

Chantry looked up at Sackett, at the table. "You heard about that deal?"

"Heard about it? Everybody has been talking about it. Old man Merlin bought cows from ever'body around and paid them in scrip. Merlin had several gunmen riding with him, and nobody dared argue the point, so he drove off half the cattle in the county.

"About a year ago, I think it was, young Johnny Merlin told everybody he was coming back to redeem that scrip, a hundred thousand dollars worth, and he'd pay off in gold. His old man may have been a highbinder, but young Johnny was going to do the right thing.

"Next month Johnny will be in town, and he'll have a hundred thousand in gold here to pay off."

"Bait for a trap," Chantry said. He glanced up. "Seven

thousand dollars of that is coming to me," he said. "I wouldn't want anything to happen to it."

"All right," Tyrel said quietly, "it's you and me, then. That outfit seems to have good information, so don't tell anybody who might repeat it. Just you and me. You've a good deputy, but don't tell him until the day. I'll bring a man along, too, and we'll be waiting."

"I hope they try it," Chantry said grimly.

"They will, Bord. I'm bettin' on it. You still got some o' their horses in that pasture?"

"I have."

"They'll come, Bord. This time they will get a surprise."

In the massive stone house at the head of Toadstool Canyon, Ben Curry leaned his great weight back in his chair and stared broodingly at the valley below. The door stood open, and the day was a pleasant one, yet Ben Curry was not feeling pleasant.

His big face was as blunt and unlined as the rock from which the house was built, but the shock of hair above that leonine face had turned gray. No nonsense about it, he was growing old. Even such a spring as this did not bring the old fire to his veins again, and it had been long since he had himself ridden on one of the jobs he planned so shrewdly. It was time to quit.

Yet, for a man who all his life had made quick and correct decisions, he was uncertain now. For six years he had ruled supreme in this corner of the mountains and desert. For twenty years he had been an outlaw, and for fifteen of those twenty years he had commanded a bunch of outlaws that had grown until it was almost an empire in itself.

Six years ago he had moved to this remote country and created the stronghold from which he operated. Across the southern limit was the Grand Canyon of the Colorado, barring all approach from that direction. To the east, north, and west was wilderness, much of it virtually impassable unless one knew the trails.

Only at Lee's Ferry was there a known crossing, but further along was the little-known Crossing of the Fathers. Both places were watched, day and night.

There was one other crossing, of an entirely different sort, that one known only to Ben himself. It was his ace in the hole.

One law of the gang was never transgressed. There was to be no lawless activity in the Mormon country to the north. Mormons and Indians were left strictly alone and were, if not friends, at least not enemies. Both groups kept what they knew to themselves, as well as what they suspected. A few ranchers lived on the fringes, and they traded at stores run by the outlaws. They could buy supplies there closer to home and at cheaper prices than elsewhere. The trading posts were listening posts as well. Strangers in the area were immediately noticed— usually they stopped by the stores, and their presence was reported to Ben Curry.

Ben Curry had not made up his mind about Kerb Perrin. He knew the outlaw was growing restive, aware that Curry was aging and eager for the power that went with leadership. What would he do, and how would he react when Mike Bastian took over?

Well, Curry reflected grimly, that would be Mike's problem. He had been trained for it.

Old Ben himself was the bull of the herd, and Perrin was pawing dust, but what would he do when a strange young bull came in to take over? One who had not won his spurs on the outlaw trail?

That was why Ben had sent for Mike. It was time for Mike to go out on his first job. It would be big, sudden, and dramatic. It was also relatively foolproof. If brought off smoothly it would have an excellent effect on the gang.

There was a sharp knock on the door, and Ben Curry sat back in his chair, recognizing it. "Come in!" he bellowed.

He watched Perrin enter and close the door behind him, then cross the room to him with his quick, nervous steps, his eyes scanning the room to see if they were alone.

"Chief, the boys are restless. It's spring, and most of them are broke. Have you got something in mind?"

"A couple of things. Yes, it's about time for them to move out." He paused. "Are they all back?"

"Most of them. Of course, as you know some of them never left."

"I've got one or two that look to be really tough. Seems it might be good for the kid to try one."

"Oh?" Perrin's irritation was obvious. "You mean he'll go along?"

"I'm going to let him run it. The whole show. It will be good for him."

Kerb Perrin absorbed that. For the first time he began to seriously consider Mike Bastian. Until now the only rival for leadership if Curry stepped down was Molina. He knew little about Bastian except to see him ride in and out of camp. He hunted a lot, was often with Roundy, and he knew Bastian had sat in on some of the planning at times. Yet for some reason he had never considered him as vying for leadership.

Perrin had accepted the fact that there would be trouble with Rig Molina, but Bastian? He was the old man's adopted son, but—

A quick, hot anger surged through him. It was all he could do to keep his voice calm. "Do you think that's wise? How will the boys feel about a green kid leading them?"

"He knows what to do, and they'll find he's as trailwise and smart as any of them. This is a big job and a tough one."

"Who goes along?" Kerb paused. "And what job?"

"Maybe I'll let him pick 'em. Good practice for him. What job? I haven't decided. Maybe the gold train, or maybe a job over in eastern Colorado. It's one I've been thinking about for some time."

The gold train? To Kerb's way of thinking that should be his job. He had discovered it, reported it, dug out most of the background detail. It was the job *he* wanted. It was a shipment from gold mines high in the mountains, gold brought down by muleback to the railroad, rich beyond dream.

Months before, in laying out the plan for Curry, he had it vetoed. He had recommended killing every man jack of them. Burial nearby, no witnesses, nothing. The gold train would simply have vanished into thin air. And he could do it. He knew he could.

"Too bloody," Curry objected. "You're beginning to sound like Molina."

"Dead men can't talk," Perrin insisted.

Ben Curry nodded agreement. "Maybe not, but their families can. A thing like that wakes people up, stirs their curiosity. Whenever people are killed some others want revenge or justice or whatever they call it. Whenever gold disappears it starts everybody in the country to looking."

Curry drummed his fingers on the table, thinking. "No," he said finally, "we won't do it. Not that way."

Even then as he spoke Curry was thinking of the effect upon the men if he let Bastian pull it off. Perrin was too bloody. Bastian would not be. Moreover, he could probably come up with a plan.

Many of the men knew Bastian slightly. Some of them had helped to train him in various skills. Some of the older men were as proud of Mike as if he had been their own son. If he brought off this job his position in the gang would be established. Yet what of Perrin?

Now, much later, he thought again of giving the job to Bastian. It was big, the biggest in years.

Fury surged up within Perrin. Curry had no right to do this! The gold train was his job! He found it, he scouted it, and as for killing them, if Curry was squeamish he was not. A total washout, that was the way to go. And now he was being sidetracked for a kid! Curry was shoving Bastian down their throats!

His rage died, but in its place there was resolution. It was time he acted on his own. For too long he had done what the old man directed. If Curry wanted the kid to handle the gold train, he would pull the other one whether Curry liked it or not. Moreover, he would be throwing a challenge into Curry's teeth because he would plan this job without him. If there was to be a struggle for leadership let it begin here.

"He'll handle the job," Curry said. "He has been trained and he has the mind for it. You boys couldn't be in better hands."

Kerb Perrin left the stone house filled with a burning resentment, but also with a feeling of grim triumph. After years of taking orders he was going on his own. To hell with Ben Curry! He'd show him! He would show them all!

Yet a still small voice of fear was in him, too. What would Ben Curry do?

The thought made him shrink inside. He had seen the cold fury of Curry when aroused, and he had seen him use a gun.

He was fast, but was he as fast and accurate as Ben Curry?

In his innermost being Perrin doubted it. He shook off the doubt. He could beat him. He knew he could. Yet maybe it would not be necessary. There were other ways.

One thing he knew. He would have to do something about Ben Curry, and he would have to do it soon.

Five

Mike Bastian stood before Ben Curry's table and the two men stared at each other.

Ben Curry was huge, bearlike, and mighty. His eyes were cool and appraising, yet there was kindliness in them, too. This was the son he had always wanted, tall, lithe, powerful in the shoulders, a child of the frontier grown to manhood, skilled in all the arts of the wilds, trained in every dishonest practice, every skill with weapons, but educated enough to conduct himself well in any company.

"Take four men and look over the ground yourself, Mike," Ben Curry was saying. "I want you to plan this one. The gold train leaves the mines on the twentieth. There will be five wagons, the gold distributed among them, roughly five hundred thousand dollars of it.

"We've scouted the trail three times over the past couple of years, so all you'll have to do is ride over it to be sure nothing has changed.

"Don't be seen if you can help it. Don't ask questions or

loiter around anyplace where people are. If you speak to any-body ask how far it is to Prescott. Let 'em think you're just passin' through.

"When you've pulled off this job I'm goin' to step down and pass the reins to you. You'll be in command. You've known I intended to do this for some years now.

"I'm gettin' up there in years, and I want a few years of quiet life. This outfit takes a strong hand to run it. Think you can handle it?"

"I think so."

"I think so, too. Watch Perrin. He's got a streak of snake in him. Rigger is dangerous, but whatever he does will be out in the open. It's not that way with Perrin. He's a conniver. He never got far with me because I was always a jump ahead of him, and I still am!"

Curry fell silent, staring out the window at the distant peaks of the San Francisco mountains.

"Mike," he said, more quietly, "sit down. It's time you an' me had a talk. Maybe I've taken the wrong trail with you, raisin' you the way I have, to be an outlaw an' all.

"I'm not sure what's right an' what's wrong, an' to tell the truth, I never gave much thought to it. When I came west it was dog eat dog and if you lived you had to have big teeth. I got knocked down and kicked around some. Cattlemen pushed me off the first homestead I staked, and killed my sister.

"When I struck it rich in the mines some men moved in and took it away from me. They done it legal, but it wasn't right or just, so I decided it was time to bite back.

"I got some boys together, and when those fellers shipped gold from my claim we stole it back. Then I rode east and with a big outfit I moved in and ran off five hundred head of stock from that outfit that pushed me off my homestead.

"They took in after me and I let the boys take the cattle over into Mexico and I went back and ran off another five hundred head whilst they were chasing the first batch. When I had those cattle started south with some of the boys I went back and pulled down his corrals, and stamped my brand on the door of his house. I mean, I burned it deep. I wanted him to know who hit him.

"They taken in after me, the law did. They wanted me in prison, but I stayed clear of them. Now I was an outlaw, whether I liked it or not, and stamping that brand on his door had been a fool thing to do.

"That's the trouble with outlaws, they want to brag about what they've done. Well, I'd made my mistake but decided I would never do that again.

"So all these years we've kept quiet about what we were doin'. My boys move in, get what they came after, and drop from sight. Those James boys now, ever'body knows who they are, so they have to stay hid out most of the time."

He paused. "Who you want to take with you? I mean to do your scouting?"

"Roundy, Doc Sawyer, Colley, and Garlin."

Curry nodded slowly, then looked over at him. "Why?"

"Roundy has an eye for terrain like nobody in this country. He says mine's as good, but I'd like him along. Doc Sawyer is completely honest, and if he thinks I'm wrong he'll say so. As for Colley and Garlin, they are two of the best men in the outfit. They will be pleased if I ask their help, which may put them on my side when I need them."

Curry nodded. "That's good thinking. Yes, Colley and Garlin are two of our best men, and if there's trouble later with Molina an' Perrin, it will be good to have them on your side."

Later, when Bastian had gone, Ben Curry got up and walked to the window. He was feeling restless and irritable and he did not know why, unless—

For the first time he was having doubts as to his course of action. What right did he have to start Mike down the outlaw trail? Maybe Roundy was right, and the time for all that was over and past. The country was filling up and the old days were fading. Even the Indians were settling down, unwillingly perhaps, but settling nonetheless. For several years past he had been careful in picking the spots for his boys to operate. Some of the small-town marshals were very tough men, and the townspeople were changing, too. Just look what happened to the James boys up there in Minnesota, shot to pieces by a bunch of farmers and businessmen.

Bill Chadwell, Clell Miller, and Charlie Pitts had been killed, all three of the Youngers wounded and one of them so bad he could travel no further. Jesse had wanted to shoot him and leave him behind but the Youngers stood by their brother, so Jesse and Frank had gone off by themselves. And one of them wounded.

The James boys had gotten a lot of sympathy because they were supposed to be still fighting for the Lost Cause. That just wouldn't wash because most of the banks they robbed were southern banks operated by former Confederates or other southerners.

Ben Curry turned away from the window and walked to the fireplace. Picking up his pipe from the mantel, he knocked out the ashes and refilled the pipe.

Hell, he had trained the boy for what he was to do, and he would be handling a couple of hundred of the toughest men around. Although, come to think of it, the time was coming when the outfit should be cut down in size. Some of the boys didn't take to this life. They liked to drink and carouse more, and they wanted to spend their money as fast as they made it.

He thought back to Mora. Despite his scoffing at Roundy's worries, he was having doubts himself.

Tyrel Sackett? He had heard the boys talking about him but had paid little attention. After all, they were always talking about some gunfighter, some bucking horse, or something of the kind. Yet Roundy was right, he had been back in the hills too much. He was losing touch.

That little town in Colorado, now? That should be an easy touch. Maybe he should start the kid on that one? And he had left some horses there with a rancher. Big, strong-looking man, ranching a rawhide outfit.

He relit his pipe. He would have to watch Kerb Perrin. Perrin had not liked it a bit when he had suggested Mike to handle the treasure train. Perrin had not said much, but he knew him all too well.

Kerb Perrin was dangerous. Perrin was shrewd, a conniver and a plotter, good at planning but apt to fly off the handle. He was given to impatience and sudden rages. Frustration infuriated him.

Mike Bastian was excited. At twenty-two he had been considered a man for several years, but in all that time except for a few trips to Salt Lake City he had rarely left the mountain and canyon country where he had grown up.

Roundy led the way, for the trail was a familiar one to him, an old Indian trail the outlaws used when they rode out of the country to the south.

Snow still lay in some of the shadowed places, but as they neared the canyon the cliffs towered even higher and the trail dipped into a narrow gorge with sheer rock walls that gave way to rolling red waves of solid rock enlivened by the green of scattered cedar that seemed to grow right from the rock itself.

In this wild country, seeing another human, even an Indian, was a rare thing. The Navajo country lay south of them, and there were still a few scattered Paiutes, who probably knew this country better than anyone. Ben Curry had established a friendship with them right from the start, traded horses with them, left them occasional presents, and kept his men away from their camps.

Mike followed Roundy, riding hump-shouldered on his ragged gray horse that seemed as old as himself but was mountain-wise and reliable in any kind of a pinch.

Behind them rode Doc Sawyer, his lean, saturnine features showing little of what he thought, his eyes always alert and faintly amused. Tubby Colley was short, thick-chested, and confident, a hard-jawed man who had been a first-rate ranch foreman before he killed two men and had to hit the outlaw trail.

Tex Garlin was tall, rangy, and quiet. Little was known of his background aside from the fact that he came from Texas, although it was said that if he had been that kind he might have carved a dozen notches on his gun.

Roundy turned his horse around a gray boulder and struck a dim trail along the face of the cliff, following a route that led them right down to the river.

There was a small cabin and a square plot of garden. The door opened and a man awaited them with a rifle. His cold old eyes went from one to the other. "Howdy! I been expectin' comp'ny." His eyes went to Mike Bastian. "Ain't seen him before."

"It's all right," said Roundy. "This is Ben Curry's boy."

"Heard of you. Can you shoot like they say?"

Mike flushed. "I don't know what they say, but I'll bet a lot of money I can hit the side of that mountain if it will hold still."

"Don't take no funnin' from him," Roundy said. "If he has to, he can shoot."

"Let's see some shootin', son," the old man said. "I always did like to see a man who can shoot."

Bastian shook his head. "A man's a fool to shoot unless there's reason. Ben Curry taught me never to draw a gun unless I meant to use it."

"Go ahead," Colley urged. "Show us."

The old man pointed. "See that black stick over there? That's about fifty, maybe sixty paces. Could you hit that?"

The stick was no wider than a piece of lath, barely discernible against the backdrop of rock. "You mean that one?" Mike Bastian palmed his gun and fired and the end of the black stick pulverized.

The move was so smooth and practiced that no one of the men even guessed he intended to shoot. Garlin's jaws ceased their methodical chewing and he stared as long as it would take to draw a breath. He glanced at Colley, spat, and said, "I wonder what Kerb Perrin would say to that?"

Colley nodded. "Yeah," he said softly, "but the stick wasn't shootin' back at him."

Old Bill took them over the swollen river in one hair-raising trip, and with the river behind them they started south. Several days later, after exchanging horses at several points along the way and checking the stock available at each stop, they rode into the little mining town of Weaver.

Colley and Garlin rode in about sundown, followed an hour or so later by Roundy and Doc Sawyer. They kept apart, and when Mike Bastian rode in alone he did not join the others.

Most of those gathered in the saloon were Mexicans who kept to themselves, but there were three tough-looking white men at the bar whom Mike eyed warily.

One of them glanced at Mike in his beaded buckskins and whispered something to the others, at which they all laughed.

Mike leaned nonchalantly at the bar, avoiding the stares of the three men. One of them moved closer to him.

"Hi, stranger! That's a right purty suit you got there. Where can I get one like it?"

Garlin heard and glanced over at Colley. "Corbus an' Fletcher! And trouble hunting! Maybe we should get into this."

"Wait, let's see how the kid handles it."

Mike's expression was mild. "You want an outfit like this? Almost any Indian can make one for you." He had taken their measure at once and knew the kind of men he had to deal with. There is at least one such in every bar. Given a few drinks they hunt trouble.

"Just that easy?" Corbus asked.

He was in a quarrelsome mood, and Mike looked too neat for his taste.

Trouble was coming and there was no way to avoid it. If he walked out they would follow him. It was better to meet it head-on. "Just like that," Mike said, "but I don't know what you'd want with it. A suit like this would be too big for you."

"Huh?" Corbus was startled by the brusque tone. "You gettin' smart with me, kid?"

"No," Mike replied coolly, "nor am I about to be hurrahed by any lamebrain, whiskey-guzzling saddle tramp.

"You commented on my suit and I told you where you could get one. Now you can have a drink on me, all three of you, and I'm suggesting we drink up." His voice became softer. "I want you to have a drink because I want to be very, very sure we're friends, see?"

Corbus stared at Bastian, a cold hint of danger filtering through. This might be dangerous going, but he was stubborn, too stubborn to laugh it off and accept the drink and end the trouble. "Suppose I don't want to drink with no tenderfoot brat?"

Corbus never saw what happened. His brain warned him as Bastian's left hand moved, but he never saw the right. The left smashed his lips, and the right cracked on the angle of his jaw. He hit the floor on his shoulder blades, out cold.

Fletcher and the third tough hesitated. Corbus was on the floor and Bastian was not smiling. "You boys want a drink or do we go on from here?"

"What if a man drawed a gun instead of usin' his fists?" Fletcher asked.

"I'd kill him," Mike replied.

Fletcher blinked. He had been shocked sober by what happened to Corbus. "I reckon you would. All right, let's have that drink. The boot hill out there already has twenty graves in it."

Relieved, the bartender poured. Nobody looked at Corbus, who was still out.

"What will Corbus do when he gets up?" Colley wondered.

Garlin chuckled. "Nothing today. He won't feel like it."

There was silence and then Garlin said, "I can't wait to see Kerb Perrin's face when he hears of it." He glanced over at Colley. "There's a whisper goin' around that the old man intends the kid to take over."

"That is the rumor."

"Well, he can shoot and he doesn't waste around. Maybe he can cut the mustard."

Mike Bastian finished his beer as he heard a stage roll into the street. It offered an easy way out and he took it, following several men who started for the door.

The passengers were getting down to stretch their legs and eat. There was a boardinghouse alongside the saloon. Three of the passengers were women, all were well dressed, with an eastern look to them.

Seeing him, one of the younger women walked up to him. She was a pale, pretty girl with large gray eyes. "What is the fastest route to Red Wall Canyon?" she asked.

Mike Bastian was suddenly alert. "You will make it by morning if you ride the stage. There is a cross-country route if you have a buckboard."

"Could you show us where to hire one? My mother is not feeling well."

Doc Sawyer was on the steps behind him. "Be careful, Mike," he spoke softly. "This could be trouble."

Six

Mike stepped down into the street and walked back to the stage with her. The older woman and the other girl were standing near the stage, but he had eyes only for the girl.

Her hair seemed to have a touch of gold but was a shade or two darker than the hair of the girl who had spoken to him. She who had approached him was quiet and sweet. This other girl was vivid.

Their eyes met and he swept off his hat. The girl beside him spoke. "This is my mother, Mrs. Ragan, and my sister, Drusilla." She looked up at him. "I am Juliana."

Mike bowed. He had eyes only for Drusilla. "I am Mike Bastian," he replied.

"He said we could hire a rig to take us by a shorter route to Red Wall Canyon."

"Just where in the canyon did you wish to go?" he asked.

"To the V-Bar, Voyle Ragan's place."

He had started to turn away, but stopped in midstride. "Did you say—Voyle Ragan's?"

"Yes. Is there anything wrong?"

"No, no. Of course not. I just wanted to be sure." He smiled. "I wanted to be sure. I might want to come calling."

Juliana laughed. "Of course! We would be glad to see you. It gets rather lonely at the ranch sometimes, although we love it. Sometimes I think I could spend the rest of my life there."

Mike walked swiftly away, heading for the livery sign he had seen along the street. These then were Ben Curry's wife and daughters, and somehow Doc Sawyer knew it. How many others knew?

He was their foster brother, but obviously his name was unknown to them. Nor would he have guessed who they were but for what Roundy had told him. Yet he was, as Sawyer had warned, treading on dangerous ground. He must reveal nothing of what he knew, either to them or anyone else. This was Ben Curry's secret and he was entitled to it.

Hiring the rig was a matter of minutes, and he liked the looks of the driver, an older man with a lean, weathered face and an air of competence about him.

"No danger on that road this time of year," the driver said. "I can have them there before the stage is more than halfway. I don't have to take that roundabout route to pick up passengers."

"Take good care of them," Bastian said.

He left while the man was harnessing his team and walked back to the boardinghouse.

Drusilla looked up as he came in. "Did you find a rig?"

"He'll be around in a matter of minutes. It will be a long drive but you could lie down in the back if you like. He was putting in some buffalo robes when I left."

"You're very kind."

"I hope I am," he said, "but all I could think of was that you were beautiful."

She blushed, or seemed to. The light wasn't very good.

"And I can come to visit?"

"My sister invited you, didn't she?"

"Yes, but I'd like the invitation from you, too."

"All right. Now why don't you ask my mother, too? She likes visitors as much as Julie and I do."

"I'll have to take the invitation from you and your sister as being enough. If I ask your mother I might have to ask your father, too."

"He isn't with us. His name is Ben Ragan and he is probably off buying cattle or looking at mining property. He travels a great deal. Do you know him?"

"I've heard the name," he said.

He sat with them, eating a little, drinking coffee, and listening to them talking of the trip. Drusilla was very cool, saying little. Twice he caught her eyes upon him but each time she looked away, though without embarrassment.

"You won't be able to see much but stars," he said. "My advice is to lie down in the back and get what rest you can."

"Do you live over that way?" Juliana asked.

"Sort of," he said, "when I'm home." He hesitated, not wanting to lie. "I've always been a kind of hunter, so I keep to the wild country." He paused, thinking that being a hunter did not seem like much of a life to such girls as these. "I'm thinking of going into ranching."

Drusilla glanced at him coolly, curiously. She was disturbing, in more ways than one. Did she believe him? Why did she look at him like that?

When they had gone he walked back to the saloon, dissatisfied more than ever. At the bar he listened to the talk and had another beer. All such places were clearinghouses for information. Men did business there, found jobs, sought entertainment, often even attended church services in saloons. Certainly, if one wanted to know what was happening in the country, that was the place to go.

There was talk of the gold shipment as men were being hired to make the trip. The guards, he heard, had been chosen. Now, more than ever, it seemed fantastic that he could actually be planning to steal all that gold, with the possibility of resistance, of even killing men.

He considered that. Killing a man in a fair fight was something that could happen to anyone, but killing men who were defending property was something else. He stared gloomily into his beer. What would Drusilla think of that? And what would Ben Curry think of an outlaw visiting his daughters?

The idea that he might someday lead the gang had been with him for years. He knew he had been trained for it, conditioned for it. He knew Curry had based all his plans on him, Mike Bastian. So now what?

Often he had thought of what he would do and how he would do it. He supposed many a man had considered a holdup and how it should be done but with no idea of ever doing it. It was a form of daydreaming, but with no connection to reality. The trouble was this was no longer a daydream, this *was* reality. Now, suddenly, he was uneasy.

Yet he was thinking not only of himself but of Drusilla.

What a girl she was! And her father was an outlaw. Was she aware of it? He doubted that. Roundy said Ben Curry had kept his family life completely away from his other side. Ben Curry himself was a strange man, one who, had he gone straight, might have directed his energies into cattle, mining, or some other business, even into politics. He knew men and had a genius for organization and control. A strange life, turned off suddenly down the wrong roads. But that was Ben Curry. What of him? What of Mike Bastian?

Doc Sawyer cashed in his chips and strolled to the bar, offering to buy him a drink. It was a casual meeting, like many that occur in saloons.

"The twentieth," he said, "and there will be five shotgun guards, but twelves guards in all. The big fellow at the poker table is one of them." He paused. "It looks bad, Mike. It looks very bad, indeed."

What Roundy said was true, of course. He was still an honest man. This was the turning point. Once he stepped over that boundary that separated the thieves from honest men it would not be the same. Of course, later he might be able to step out of it as Ben Curry would do. If he was able to do it.

Listening to Sawyer made him wonder. Why had such a man, brilliant, intelligent, and a skilled surgeon, why had he taken to the outlaw trail?

"Doc"—he spoke softly—"whatever made you take this route?"

Sawyer glanced at him. "Having doubts, Mike?"

"Doubts? It seems all I have these days are doubts."

"I've wondered about that. You've said nothing, so I assumed you were perfectly willing to go along with Ben's plans for you.

"It means power and money, Mike. If it is the future for outlaws that disturbs you, don't let it. From now on it will be different than in Ben Curry's day. You will have to have the best lawyers, the right connections, and spend some money for bribes, but with the money you will have that should be easy.

"Roundy told me he had spoken to you about it. He can see it more clearly than Ben. The old days are over. Up to now all those robberies were considered to have been pulled off by free-wheeling outfits like the James boys and the Renos. Nobody has thought there might be an organization behind it. That will change. There are some pretty shrewd officers out there and when they begin getting organized themselves outlaws will have no chance. Still, with the connections, the lawyers, and the money you should manage."

"Yes, it could be," Mike agreed. "Only maybe I don't want it that way."

Sawyer smiled wryly. "Does conscience rear its ugly head? Can it be that Ben Curry's conditioning has fallen on fallow ground? What started this sudden feeling? Is it fear? Or a woman?"

"Would that be so strange?"

"That it was a woman? I've wondered it hasn't happened before, except that you've been such a recluse. If it is a woman, take a second look and time to think about it."

"It wasn't her. I've been thinking about it for the past two years. I've been wondering what I should do. I hate to disappoint Ben Curry, and actually, I've no other place to go. What can I do? Hunt? Punch cows?"

Doc Sawyer put his glass down hard. "Either is better, Mike. Anything is better. And it's easier to get in than get out. Once you have the name, it follows you.

"But don't ask me. I made a mess of my own life. Partly a woman and partly for what I thought would be easy money. Well, let me tell you, there's no such thing as easy money. You make your own decision. What was it Matthew Arnold said, I think you learned the quotation."

" 'No man can save his brother's soul, or pay his brother's debt.' "

"That's it! You save your own and you pay your own. But remember this, Mike. No matter which way you go, there will be killing. If you take over from Ben you'll have to kill either Kerb Perrin or Rig Molina, maybe both of them. And if you decide to step out you may have to kill them and even Ben Curry."

"Oh, no! Not pa!"

"Mike, get this through your head. There is no easy way out. Do you suppose you're alone in this? Roundy an' me have talked this up one side and down the other. After all," he added, "neither of us ever had a son. We've helped to train you and teach you, and it has meant a lot to us.

"But remember this. No man is a complete ruler or dictator. He is only the mouthpiece for the wishes of his followers. As long as he expresses those wishes, he leads them.

"Ben is the boss because he is strong, because he has organization, because he is good with those guns. Also he is boss because he has made them money, kept them out of trouble, sometimes even against their own wishes. He has offered them security. If you walked out there would be a chink in the armor. No outlaw ever trusts another who turns honest. He always fears betrayal."

"Let's check with Roundy."

He was coming across the room to them. "Get the horses. We've got to blow town. Ducrow and Fernandez just rode in, and they are drunk and they are talking. If they see us they are apt to spill everything."

Garlin was there. "Ducrow's a pal of Perrin's. He thinks he can get away with anything."

"Here they come now!"

"All right! Drift!" Bastian ordered. "Be quick with the horses!"

Seven

The world of most criminals is incredibly small, consisting largely of others like himself. He wants to be considered a big man, a tough man, a smart man among his own kind. If not that, he wants to be associated with somebody who is big, tough, and smart, even if only to run errands for him.

Few can stand alone, most are afraid to try. The gang is their protection and their strength. It is also their refuge.

Their world is a few hangouts, a few saloons, a few places where the lawbreakers meet. If in the city it comprises a few city blocks, in the western lands a few towns, a few hundred square miles of territory. When escaping they will almost invariably return to old associations, to areas they know, people with whom they are familiar.

Ben Curry had provided the refuge, the planning, access to money, but most of his men did not like it. They were restless for freedom, to go as they pleased, act as they wished. Most of them wanted the reputation of being bad men, they wished to swagger and strut. Over the years Ben had tried to weed them

out, to keep the cool and careful men, to eliminate the brag-
garts and the show-offs. He had only been partially successful.

Usually he managed to weed out the undesirables before
they knew anything about the ramifications of his operations.
Ducrow had been a tough man, a quiet man, but lately he had
become a close ally of Perrin. Also, he had begun drinking too
much.

Saloon doors slammed open and the two men came in. One
glance and Mike knew there was trouble, not only for him but
for Ben Curry, all of them. Tom Ducrow was drunk and ugly.
Behind him was Snake Fernandez. An unpleasant pair, they
had made trouble before this, always protected by Perrin.

Bastian started toward them but had taken scarcely a step
when Ducrow saw him. "There he is! The pet! The boss's pet!"

"Tom," Bastian said mildly, "I'd suggest you go sleep it off.
This isn't the place."

"Look who's givin' orders! Gettin' big for your britches, ain't
you?"

"Your horses will be outside the door," Bastian suggested.
"Get on them and start for home."

Ducrow planted his feet. "Suppose you make me!"

"Tom," Mike protested, "this isn't the place!" He stepped
closer and lowered his voice. "Ben wants no trouble, you know
that."

"Ben? Who the hell is Ben? Kerb Perrin's the man, an' don't
you forget it!"

It was a challenge, and more words might reveal too much.
Mike Bastian struck swiftly. A left to the body, a right to the
chin. Ducrow was not a fistfighter and the blows were totally
unexpected. He went to his knees, then slumped facedown to
the floor.

With an oath, Fernandez went for his gun and Mike had no
choice. He shot him through the shoulder. The gun dropped
from Snake's fingers. Mouthing curses, he reached for his
left-hand gun. Garlin, who had stayed behind when the others

went for their horses, grabbed him from behind and disarmed him.

Mike pulled the groggy Ducrow to his feet and started for the door.

He found himself facing a big man with a stern look and a star on his chest. "What's going on here?" he demanded.

Mike smiled pleasantly. "Nothing at all, Officer. A couple of boys from our outfit with too much red-eye. We'll take them back to camp and we're moving out in the morning."

The sheriff looked from Mike to Doc Sawyer. The apparent respectability of the two calmed him somewhat. "Who are you? I don't know you."

"No, sir. We've come up from the Mogollons, driving a few head of cattle to a ranch in California. It has been a rough trip and the boys got a little too much to drink."

The sheriff was suspicious. There was something here he did not understand. "You may be a cowhand," he said, "but that gent with you looks like a gambler!"

Mike chuckled. "Officer, I've played with him, and if he had to make his living with cards he'd starve. As a matter of fact, he's a doctor, a surgeon, and a mighty good one. He's a friend of the boss."

A tall, gray-haired man had strolled over beside the sheriff. "What outfit did you say you rode for? I'm from the Mogollons, myself."

Garlin had hustled Fernandez and Ducrow outside as they talked. Doc Sawyer was wishing he had gone with them.

"I don't ride for a Mogollon outfit," Mike said, smiling, "but Jack McCardle can vouch for me. Doc Sawyer is a friend of his and has handled the sale of some of his beef."

The sheriff glanced at the gray-haired man. "Do you know this McCardle, Joe?"

"I do, and he's a good man. He has the Flying M, but I didn't know he was selling cattle."

"Guess you're all right." The sheriff was reluctant to let go. He studied Mike. "You sure don't talk like no cowhand."

"Officer, cowhands come from everywhere and anywhere. We had a puncher working with us last year from Norfolk, England. However," he said gravely, "I was studying for the ministry but my interests led me in more profane directions. I am afraid I'm a backslider. An interest in draw poker isn't conducive to a place in the pulpit."

"I guess not." The sheriff chuckled. "All right, you ride out of here, but no more trouble, do you hear? And Doc, you better look at that man's shoulder."

Mike turned away and Doc followed. Outside, the men had disappeared. They rode out of town, heading north. It was not until they were several miles on the road that Doc rode up beside Bastian.

"You'll do!" he said. "You handled that better than anybody I know."

"Hell!" Garlin said. "I was gettin' ready to shoot our way out of town. You sure smooth-talked 'em!"

"That sheriff," Mike said thoughtfully, "wasn't satisfied. He'll ride out come daybreak and check for tracks."

Garlin chuckled. "I figured on it. We're ridin' somebody's cow trail right now. I seen 'em passin' when we rode into town. I figure they were headed for a grassy patch with a spring about four mile west, and they'll be gone by daybreak. I doubt if that sheriff is ready to ride that far just to check up on us."

Kerb Perrin and Rig Molina were sitting around the table in the stone house when Mike and Doc returned to the canyon. Both men looked up sharply, and Ben Curry was suddenly watchful.

Bastian wasted no time. "Kerb, what were Ducrow and Fernandez doing in Weaver?"

Perrin looked around, irritated by Mike's tone but puzzled, too.

"In Weaver! And drunk! We nearly had to shoot our way out of town because of them. They were drunk and talking too much. When I told them to get on their horses and head for home, they made trouble."

"How?"

"Ducrow was attracting too much attention. If I hadn't stopped him there's no telling what he'd have said."

"*You* stopped him?"

Ben Curry had leaned back in his chair and was watching with attention.

"I knocked him out," Mike said coolly, "and when Fernandez went for his gun I put a bullet into his shoulder."

"You should've killed him," Molina said. "You'll have it to do sooner or later."

Kerb Perrin was stumped. This was something he had not wanted to happen, nor would he have believed Mike Bastian could handle Ducrow, let alone Fernandez as well.

"We got what we went after," Bastian told Curry, "but another break like we had and we'll walk into a trap. As for that, I think we should drop it for now."

"Are you crazy?" Perrin said. "That's the big one. That's the one we've been waiting for!"

"The sheriff in Weaver," Mike said, "is a good man, a tough man, and a smart one. I talked our way out of it, but he may do some checking. He struck me as a careful man."

"To hell with him!" Perrin said.

When Perrin and Molina had gone, Mike left for his own room and Doc Sawyer turned to Ben. "It would have done your heart good! He had a run-in with Corbus and Fletcher, too! He flattened Corbus with a punch and backed Fletcher down. He'll do, that boy of yours!"

"I knew he had it," Ben said, with satisfaction.

"He met a girl, too," Doc added.

"Good for him! It's about time."

"This was a very particular girl, Chief. If I am any judge of such things he fell and fell hard, and I'm not sure it didn't happen both ways."

Something in his tone caught Curry's attention. "Who was she?"

"A girl who came in on the stage. Mike got her and her family a rig and a driver to take them to their ranch. Out to the V-Bar."

Ben Curry turned on him. For a moment their eyes held. So Doc Sawyer knew! The one secret he had been determined to keep, the one he wanted none of them to know! How many others knew? How many had guessed? Or discovered some clue? And he had believed his tracks had been covered. For the first time Ben Curry knew fear, real fear.

"The girl's name is Drusilla Ragan. She's a beautiful girl, Ben."

"I won't have it!" Ben slammed his glass down. "I'll be damned if—!"

Doc Sawyer's tone was ironic. "You mean the foster son you raised isn't good enough for your daughter?"

"Don't use that word here! Who knows besides you?"

"Nobody of whom I know. It is only accident that I know. Remember the time you were laid up with that bullet wound, and I took care of you myself? You were delirious, and you talked too much." Doc lighted his pipe. "They made a nice-looking couple," he added, "and I believe she invited him to Red Wall Canyon."

"He won't go! I'll not have any of this crowd there! If you think I want my daughter associating with outlaws—!"

"He isn't—yet." Doc puffed on his pipe. "He could be, and he might be, but if he does, the crime will be on your shoulders because I don't think he wants to be."

Curry went to the window and looked down the canyon.

"Chief, the boy has it in him. He could be all of it, believe me! He's quick! You should have seen him throw that gun on Fernandez! And when that sheriff walked up to him he handled it like a veteran!"

Ben Curry was silent. Doc glanced at the broad back and

went over to the sideboard and took up a cup and filled it with coffee.

"He may be deciding he doesn't want to take over. That boy's smart, Ben, *smart!*"

"He'll do what I tell him."

"Maybe. He's got a mind of his own, Ben."

Ben swore under his breath. All his plans, all of it falling apart after all the thinking, all the years!

A small voice of doubt was whispering within him, a voice that made him remember that quiet, determined little boy whom he brought home with him, that boy who would not cry, a boy who listened and obeyed and who tried very hard to do what was expected of him. Yet despite that Ben had always been aware the boy had a mind of his own, that he listened and weighed everything in some balance of his own.

Long after Doc Sawyer was gone, Ben Curry sat alone, thinking. If Doc knew, somebody else might know, yet he thought not. Doc was canny, and Doc always had his ear to the ground. Doc would know if anybody else knew.

His thoughts reverted to the discussion over what had taken place in Weaver. What were Ducrow and Fernandez doing there, anyway? It had always been the policy for none of the gang to show up in the town where a job was to be pulled off except the scouts who went in, got the lay of the land, then rode out as unobtrusively as possible.

Now there had been trouble, attention had been drawn to them, and Ducrow had been drunk and shooting off his mouth. Mike warned that the sheriff was a canny man, and he would remember their faces. So none of them could be used. The boy was out of it.

Despite himself, Ben felt relief. The risk had worried him. Twelve guards, several with shotguns. How were they to handle *them*?

Kerb Perrin wanted the job, so let Kerb have it. For the first time the thought of betrayal entered his mind. He shook his head.

No. Perrin was his problem. He would cope with it himself, as he always had. But what were Ducrow and Fernandez doing in Weaver? And Doc had reported the words Ducrow had spoken in anger, that it was no longer Ben Curry who mattered, but Kerb Perrin.

Something brewing there.

He was getting old. For the first time he began to doubt his rightness. What about the boy? He had wanted a man he could trust to take over, but had he any right to raise the boy to be an outlaw?

He walked to the window again. He had a reason, or thought he did, but Mike had none beyond his father's wish. Suddenly, Ben stopped, staring at the partial reflection of himself in the glass. Mike was the son he had never had, why not Mike and Drusilla?

He shook his head. No, no. Never. Yet—how many fathers could raise their own son-in-law? He smiled at the thought, but put it aside. There was too much else to think about now.

Kerb Perrin was planning rebellion. Planning to go his own way.

His thoughts reverted to Dru. Suppose she wanted Mike Bastian, outlaw or not? Had it been Juliana now, he could have bluntly told her no and she would have, might have, listened. But Dru? He chuckled. She would laugh at him. She was too much like him.

What to do? Ben Curry moved away from the window. He must remember not to stand there again. Once, he need not have worried but now there were enemies among his own men, something he dared not tolerate.

What had Ducrow and Fernandez been doing in Weaver? Scouting the job for Perrin? For themselves?

He walked back to the fireplace and stared at the sullen coals. He was growing old, and it was time to quit. He wanted the last years with his wife and the girls. He wanted to get out, to get away. He was a man born out of his time, and in the past he might have been a Viking, a robber baron, a freebooter. Now he was an outlaw.

He had liked planning their forays. He had liked playing his chess game with the law, but lately—

Was he changing? Or was it the times? Was it like Roundy kept telling him, that the old days were gone? An outlaw was an enemy of society, a different society from that rough, casually tolerant west in which he had spent his early years.

He walked over to the clothes tree and took down his gunbelt. He checked each pistol, then slung the belt about his hips.

From now on he had better wear them, all the time.

Eight

M ike Bastian rolled out of bed and sat up. Rarely did he sleep during the day, but on his return he had been tired. Now he felt better.

Darkness had come while he rested, and the sky was spangled with stars. From his window he could see a few lights glowing from the settlement below, a settlement of outlaws.

Only Doc Sawyer and himself shared the stone house with Ben Curry, and on the occasional visits when others discussed future jobs with Ben, they never left the spacious living room with its big table where the planning was done.

The doors leading to other rooms were closed and conferences were kept to the big table. Ben Curry had always been a private person and nobody had ever ventured to intrude on that privacy, not even Mike himself.

He was restless and uneasy. There had been a sampling of what he could expect in the facing of Corbus and later with Ducrow and Fernandez. Was that what he wanted? Or did he want a more respectable life? Such a life as Drusilla Ragan might wish to share?

Hey! He flushed. What was he thinking of? She had scarcely noticed him, and who was he, after all? He was nothing, he had nothing. He did not have a home, other than this provided by Ben Curry, he had no job, he had nothing to offer. Although he knew there were some people who admired outlaws, largely because they had never known any, he did not think Drusilla would be of that sort.

He had not needed Roundy's questions, nor Doc's, to start thinking. Whenever he went into a town he wondered about the people there. They did not have to worry about being recognized by some lawman or some former victim. They did not have to be hiding out in the hills, seeking shelter from cold and rain or suffering from a gunshot wound they dared not have treated.

Ben's operation was the most successful, but he had his failures, too. Only a few weeks before four of the boys had arrived on hard-ridden horses, one man wounded, with only fourteen dollars to show for their trouble. At the last minute, plans had been altered and the shipment of gold had gone out early, going through the day before they arrived.

Down there in town they had probably told the story of his meeting with the sheriff, of his coping with Ducrow and the others. The majority liked him, and this would tell them he could handle himself. Molina and Perrin stood between him and leadership of the gang.

Molina, Perrin, and himself. He shook his head, trying to clear it. Did he want to be an outlaw?

Blowing out the light, he opened the door and stepped out into the night. For a moment he stood listening. It was very quiet. Distant music came from the saloon. He walked down the path toward the town, hoping to see no one, simply to walk and to think. There was no more time. He must decide. Yet how could he leave Ben?

Avoiding the main street of the little settlement, which was composed of a saloon, a store, and a livery stable, as well as a boardinghouse and what was called a hotel but was actually just a big cabin with bunks, he walked down one of the lanes toward the creek.

Several cabins were scattered along the lane, with corrals, stables, and a well or two. He was passing the last cabin before reaching the trees along the small creek when he overheard ". . . at Red Wall."

Abruptly, he stopped. The cabin door was open and light streamed out, but he was in the darkness out of sight.

Kerb Perrin was speaking. "It's a cinch! We'll do it on our own without anybody's say-so. There's about two thousand head of cattle on their range, but there must be at least five hundred head gathered for a drive, and I've got a buyer for them. We'll hit the place about sunup."

"Who's on the place?"

"Only four hands now. If we wait a few days there will be a dozen. They'll be expectin' nothing."

"How many men will we have?"

"A dozen, maybe less. Keep the divvy small. Hell, that Ragan ranch is easy! The boss won't even hear about it until it's too late to stop us. Anyway, he'll never know it was us."

"I wouldn't want him to," Fernandez said.

"To hell with him!" Ducrow said. "All I want is a crack at that Bastian kid!"

"Stick with me," Perrin said, "and I'll set him up for you."

"You said there were some women?" Ducrow suggested.

"Two white girls are visiting there, and there's two Mexican maids and the mother of the girls. I want the younger girl. What happens to the others is none of my business."

Fernandez looked uneasy. "It is not good," he said. "The women, I mean. Steal cattle, yes. But women? They will hunt you forever."

Perrin shrugged. "Who will be left to talk?"

Ducrow glanced at him, wetting his lips. Fernandez said nothing. After a bit he muttered, "Killing a man is one thing."

"You want to be left out?" Perrin demanded. "You don't have to go."

"I'll go."

"What happens if Ben Curry finds out? He doesn't miss much, you know."

"What happens? If he opens his mouth I'll kill him." There was a pause, then he added, "I never wanted to kill anybody the way I've wanted to kill him. He thinks he's the big man! I'll show him who's top dog!"

"What about Bastian?"

Perrin waved a dismissing hand. "He's your problem! If you an' Fernandez can't figure a way to handle him, then you aren't the men I think you are."

"He's quick," Ducrow remarked. "It won't do to think he's easy."

"You handle him."

"And you handle Ben Curry?" The voice was that of the man named Bayless. "He may not be young anymore, but he's hell on wheels with a gun."

"Forget him! You three, along with Clatt, Panell, Monson, and Kiefer, will go with us. Nine out of ten will be with us in makin' the break. There's been a lot of dissatisfaction lately. The boys don't like bein' tied down so much. Sure, they've got money, but what good does it do them?"

"Molina wants to raid the Mormons," Bayless commented. "They've a lot of fat stock and some damn good horses."

Mike Bastian waited no longer. The chance of discovery was too great. His first thought was to go at once to Ben Curry, but he might betray his interest in Drusilla and the time was not ripe for that.

What would Ben Curry say if he learned the foster son he had raised to be an outlaw was in love with his daughter? A foster son who had nothing, and no prospects?

Yet what could he do?

Ben Curry would know the girls and their mother were at Red Wall, and he would be going to see them. If he kept an eye on Ben he might find Ben's shortcut to the V-Bar.

Recalling other times when Ben had left, Mike knew the

route had to be much quicker than any he could guess at. It was probably further west and south, possibly some way across the Grand Canyon, although knowing the enormous depth of the canyon he could not picture a possible route.

He would have to wait. He wanted to see Drusilla again but now he must wait here, watch Perrin, and do what he could to protect Ben.

How fast was Ben now? And how tough? Speed of draw was the least consideration. Nerve and a steady hand were infinitely more important.

If there was as much unrest in the gang as Perrin implied, something might break loose at any moment. He had known the outlaws were restless. Most of them had become outlaws to avoid discipline. Ben had commanded them longer than anyone would have believed, their loyalty due in part to the returns, in part to the carefully prepared escapes, as well as fear of his far-reaching power. Now there was fear that he was losing his grip.

Mike felt a sudden urge to saddle his horse and ride away forever, to escape all the cruelty, conniving, and hatred that lay dormant here. He could ride now by way of the Kaibab Trail through the forest. Living as he did, it might be a week before they even knew he was gone.

Yet to run now, no matter how much he wished to be away, would be to give up all hope of seeing Dru again. Moreover, whatever future he chose he could not abandon Ben in his hour of need.

Returning to his room he sat down on his bed to think. Roundy first and then Doc Sawyer, each seemed to be hoping he would give it up and get out before it was too late. Doc said it was his life, but was it?

There was a light tap at the door. Gun in hand, he reached for the latch. Roundy stepped in, glancing at the gun.

"Gettin' jumpy, Mike? I don't blame you."

Mike explained what he had heard. Roundy heard him out and then asked, "Mike? Have you heard of Dave Lenaker?"

"You mean that Colorado gunman?"

"He's headed this way. Ben Curry just got word that he's coming out to take over the gang."

"I thought he was one of Ben's best men?"

"So did we all, and so he has been, but more than likely he's afraid Perrin will climb into the saddle, and they have never liked each other."

"Does Ben know?"

"You bet he does! He's mighty wrought up, too. He'd planned on bein' away a few days on one of those trips to Red Wall. Now he can't go."

Doc came in and the three talked, trying to foresee what might happen and what the best strategy would be. Perrin was hot for a break.

"Roundy," Mike suggested, "either me, you, or Doc had better be here at all times, but you two had best sift around and get some of the men on whom we can depend, like Garlin and Colley. Don't get any you have doubts about. Have them drift up this way and be ready for trouble."

"Garlin's with the horse herd," Roundy said, "no way to reach him today without riding down there."

"All right, get him when you can."

When Roundy had gone, Mike went out to the porch overlooking the canyon. The night was dark, although the stars were bright and there were no clouds.

Somehow he must warn them at the V-Bar, but whom could he trust? The secret of the ranch and its people was not his, but Ben's. Nobody in the canyon would carry any message in any way harmful to another member of the gang. He could get a dozen men by using Ben's name, but that was just what he dared not do.

Ben knew how to get over there in a hurry, but how? And how could he find out in time?

The date for the raid on the treasure train was the twentieth, and there had been talk of a raid into eastern Colorado. Was that to be the twentieth also?

Dave Lenaker was on his way here. If Ben knew that, Perrin might know also. Such things were hard to keep secret, especially when there seemed no reason for keeping them secret.

For a long time he lay awake, trying to think his way to a solution. He must talk to Ben Curry. He must warn him and tell him what he knew.

His window was open and he could hear the far-off howling of coyotes. He found himself wishing he was out there in his wilderness, away from all this, walking down one of those long, long valleys or climbing among the aspen, up to timberline, where the spruce ended and the tundra began. Up to the sliderock slopes where the springs were born.

There was freedom there, and peace, and there was no worry about such men as Kerb Perrin.

He sat up suddenly. He was not cut out for an outlaw, and he had known it all the time. He had played with the idea because it was what was expected of him, but now he knew it was not for him. Yet much as he wished to just ride away from it all, there was no way it could be done. No matter what he was to other men, Ben Curry had been a father to him, gruff but kindly, his affection only shown through a friendly squeeze on the shoulder or, when he was younger, a casual cuff and a ruffling of his hair.

Now Ben's back was to the wall, his lovely daughters and wife in danger and nobody to help but him.

Of course there was Roundy and there was Doc and a few loyal men, but nobody who could stand up to Molina or Perrin or Lenaker, if it came to that. There was only him, and this was what he had been raised for.

He lay down again, staring wide-eyed into the darkness. He would need all his training, all his skill. Perrin was a wily, dangerous man, good with a gun, but cunning as well. And he would know Ben Curry because he would have studied him all those years.

Tomorrow, he told himself. I've got to move tomorrow, and

I must talk to Ben. I must make him see what is happening and how he must tell me how to reach his family in a hurry.

His eyes opened again. This was the end. He could see it clearly now. Ben Curry had held them together but he could do so no longer, nor could anybody else, no matter how well trained.

Many of them were good men who just got started off down the wrong track, but others were murderers and thieves, and the wild animals were about to turn on their keeper.

Tomorrow . . . tomorrow he would see what could be done. Tomorrow. . . .

Nine

The Red Wall Ranch, also called the V-Bar, lay at the head of a small canyon, an isolated oasis at the upper end of a network of small canyons watered by scattered springs and runoff from the cliffs.

It was such a place as only an Indian, an outlaw on the run, or a wandering prospector might find. During a wet year the range would support cattle, but in a dry year much of it was semidesert, offering little.

Ben Curry had found the place a dozen years before and had with the help of some Indian friends put up a stone house, stable, and corrals. He had piped water into the house from a spring, had kept some cedars growing close by, and had planted a few other trees, carefully watered until their roots were down.

By handling cattle judiciously, taking advantage of the wet years and cutting the numbers during dry periods, a man might do well with a small ranching operation. Ben Curry did not intend to live out his life there, simply to maintain it as a secret base of operations. Doc Sawyer knew of the place, but only Roundy had actually been there.

The ranch house was a low building almost lost to view against the cliffs some distance behind, and partly screened by trees. A man might easily ride by the lower end of the canyon without even seeing the house, which was on a low knoll. Behind it and between the house and the canyon wall were the corrals, a stable, a storage shed, and a smokehouse.

"It's so alone!" Juliana said, looking down the long narrow valley. "I love it here, but it scares me, too!"

Drusilla said nothing, but she, too, was looking down the long valley. It was beautiful, it was remote, it was wild and strange. Maybe that was why she loved it so much, and maybe that was why she so looked forward to coming back, even though the visit would be a short one.

"I often wonder why papa chose such an out-of-the-way place," Juliana went on. "He could have a ranch anywhere. I don't believe anyone lives within a hundred miles of us."

"We aren't that far from Flagstaff. It just seems far."

"But what if something went wrong?"

"We'd have to fend for ourselves," Dru said. "That's why you should learn to shoot. Someday you may have to."

"There was trouble in town after we left," Juliana said. "I heard the men talking about it. Some sort of a fight."

"I wish papa would come."

It was very quiet. From the steps before the bunkhouse where the men slept they heard the low murmur of voices. It was a comfortable sound. Night was falling and already they had a light on out there.

"It gives me the shivers."

"There's nothing to be afraid of. There are four men out there."

They were silent, and Juliana drew the shades. Walking back to the table Dru took the chimney from the lamp, struck a match, and touched it to the wick. Replacing the lamp globe she drew back a chair. "It's almost time for supper."

"I don't like it, Dru. I don't feel right. Something's going to happen."

Dru looked at her sister, a cool, appraising glance. Juliana had these feelings once in a while, and they were often right. It was foolish to be afraid. Still—

By day anyone approaching could be seen for some distance, but at night?

"I'll speak to the men," she said, "after supper."

Juliana left the room and Dru walked slowly back to the window. Standing at one side she could still see far down the valley, but in a few minutes it would be too dark.

Now she was feeling it, too. Suddenly she turned and went to her room. From her duffel she took a derringer her father had given her, and checked it.

Loaded, and both barrels. She slipped it into her skirt pocket.

It *was* lonely! Where was pa? He had warned them not to expect him at any particular time but that he would come. They could depend on that.

Of late Drusilla had been doing some wondering of her own. Several times her father had met them at the ranch, but it was not until the last time that she had noticed anything strange. The first thing was his horse. Pa said he had come far, but his horse did not look it or act it. Thinking back she remembered that his horses had never seemed hard ridden, yet if pa came from somewhere near, where could it be?

There was nothing near. There was only wilderness.

She looked down the valley again. Now all was darkness, with only a few stars hanging in the sky.

Supper was a quiet meal. None of them felt like talking very much, but then her mother had never been much of a talker.

"How did you meet Papa?" Dru asked suddenly.

"Papa? Oh—?" Her mother hesitated, then laughed. "It was at a party, back in Texas. Some riders stopped by, and of course, everybody was welcome in those days, so we invited them to join us.

"We danced, talked a little, and finally ate supper together.

Two of the men who came with him stayed with their horses, although once in a while one of the others would change places so they could come in and enjoy the party, too.

"He was so *big*! And so very good looking! He wasn't from anywhere around there, and when I asked him he said he was from Colorado but he had been back farther east to buy cattle.

"They left before daylight but he was back a week later, but that time he was alone. He stayed several days and we went driving and riding, and something about him kind of scared the others away. There were several young men who—"

"Courted you?"

"You could call it that. But after he came they were all frightened away."

"He frightened them? What did he do?"

"Oh, nothing, really. There was just something about him. He was very romantic, you know. So mysterious! He would come, stay around a while, then be gone."

"He is still mysterious," Dru said quietly.

Her mother glanced up quickly, defensively. "Not really. His work just keeps him away. I have always understood that."

When supper was over, Dru went out back. The door of the bunkhouse was open, and Voyle Ragan was coming toward her.

"Uncle Voyle? When will papa be here?"

"I don't know, honey. He can't always get here when he wants. What's the trouble?"

"Juliana is scared. I don't know why, but she is. She says something's wrong, and when she feels that way she is usually right."

He was a tall, lean man. He managed the ranch, talked little, but was a kindly, thoughtful man.

"Nothing to worry about," he said. "Not many folks even know about this place. We don't see many strangers."

She was silent. If she were to ask, would he tell her? "Uncle Voyle—?" She hesitated. "What does Papa *really* do?"

She watched him turn his head and glance down the canyon, then he said quietly, "Why, you know as well as I do. He buys cattle, drives 'em sometimes, sells 'em to the best buyer. He does right well, but it keeps him on the road."

He spoke hastily, before she could interrupt. "He never talks business at home. It just ain't his way. Buyin' like he does he goes out to ranches, deals with some pretty rough men, time to time. Sometimes he buys an' sells cows without ever movin' 'em. Knows the buyer before he buys. He's a shrewd man."

"I believe he is. I believe you are, too, Uncle Voyle, and that story will satisfy mama and Juliana but not me. I want to know where papa is, and I want to know why he always comes from over toward the canyon."

"Where'd you get that idea?"

"I've seen him. Once when I was riding I saw him coming up through the draw. And when he gets here after those long rides his horses are always so fresh."

Voyle Ragan was disturbed. For years he had been afraid of this. Juliana would accept things as they seemed to be, but not Drusilla. She was like her father, and missed nothing.

"Have you talked to anybody else about this?"

"Who would I talk to? I've seen no one."

"Well, don't. Not even the men here. Your papa knows what he's about, but you leave it lay. The less you know the better, and the fewer questions you ask the fewer other folks are apt to ask."

"So that's it." Her voice fell. "He's an outlaw, isn't he?"

"Well—"

"I've suspected it for a long time, but somehow he never seemed the type."

"No, Dru, he surely doesn't. That's just it, he never did. Your ma, well, I think she *knows* but she'd not mention it, and she'd not admit it, even to herself.

"He'll be along soon, and when he does you get him alone if you're of a mind to, and ask him, hisself. But not where anybody can hear you."

"Uncle Voyle? I don't believe he'll come tonight. I think

there has been trouble. Call it intuition, whatever you wish. I have a feeling."

Her uncle shifted his feet. "Now, don't you be gettin' scared," he said. "There's nothing—"

"Yes, there is." She paused. "Uncle Voyle, when we were coming up from Flagstaff, we were followed."

"Followed?" He was startled.

"By a man who came out of a draw from the east. He kept back out of sight most of the time, like he did not wish to be seen, but he was following us. Just before we came into Red Wall he disappeared."

Voyle Ragan was worried. The fact that Ben Curry owned the V-Bar was a well-kept secret, and Voyle knew Ben had prevented any raiding of ranches close to the hideout in Toadstool Canyon. His argument had been simple. Leave the nearby ranches alone and they would be friendly in time of need. Yet Voyle had never trusted Curry's leadership. Sooner or later some of the outlaws would break loose and go to raiding on their own.

Who would be scouting the place? The law? There was none within miles, and no breath of suspicion invited their interest.

Outlaws? What would be more likely, with cattle already gathered and ready for moving?

"Don't scare your sister or your mother with this, Dru. You can use your rifle, so keep it handy. I'll have a talk with the boys." He paused. "Just where did you see that rider?"

He listened to her description, recognizing the area at once. "Tomorrow I'll have a look," he told her.

"You be careful," she said. Then she changed the subject. "Uncle Voyle? Did you ever hear of a cowboy named Mike Bastian?"

Voyle Ragan was glad of the darkness. "Can't say I have," he said cautiously. "What about him?"

"We met him on the way up here. In fact, it was he who helped us get a rig to bring us in after we left the stage."

"Most any western man would have helped you."

"I know, but it was he who helped, and—there was something about him—"

"I'll bet I know," Voyle said, amused. "He was probably young and good looking."

She laughed. "He was that, too, but it was the way he moved. Like a big cat. But like somebody else, too. I can't think who he reminded me of, but somebody I know very well."

"Mike Bastian? I'll remember the name. He tell you what he did?"

"No. No, I don't believe he did. I thought he might be a cowboy, or even a hunter. He was wearing buckskins. You know, like the Indians do." She paused again, then trying to keep her tone casual she said, "He asked if he could come calling."

Voyle Ragan chuckled. "And I'll bet you said yes."

It was her turn to laugh. "Of course. Could I be less than hospitable? After all, this is the west!"

After she had gone inside Voyle Ragan walked to the bunkhouse. Two of the hands were already asleep or pretending to be. The other had one boot off and one on. "You," Voyle said to him, "put that other boot back on. You're taking the first watch."

"Watch? For what?"

"Somebody followed that buckboard when it brought the womenfolks. I don't like it."

One of the other men, Garfield, sat up. "Been meanin' to tell you, Voyle. I come on some hoss tracks up on the rim a few days back. Looked like somebody had been scoutin' us."

"All right, you boys all know your business. Make like it's Injun times again, only these Injuns will be white men and outlaws, more than likely.

"We're bunchin' cows for a drive. In a few days we'll have a dozen more hands on the place. I'd guess they know that, so if anything happens it will be before the other hands get here.

"Don't any of you get more than two, three miles from the

place. Watch your back trails, and if anything happens you hightail it back here to stand by the womenfolks."

"Hell, I never knowed any outlaw to bother women!" Garfield protested.

"I know, but we're away out in the hills. Mighty few folks even know we're here, an' there's outlaws an' outlaws."

Garfield pulled on his other boot and straightened up, hitching his suspenders over his shoulders. Then he slung on his gunbelt.

"Take your Winchester, too, you may need it."

Garfield gave him a bleak look. One of the hands started to snore, and Voyle indicated him. "Wake him up at midnight. He can stay on watch until three, and then Pete can take over until daybreak."

Voyle Ragan went outside and stopped, listening. It was quiet, very quiet. He walked up to the house and to his room. After he had hung his gunbelt to the headboard of his bed, he placed his Winchester across the washstand, close by.

It had been a long time since he had been in a shooting fight and he wasn't sure he was up to it.

Ten

Morning was cool and clear, yet Mike Bastian could feel disaster in the air. Dressing hurriedly, he headed for the boardinghouse. Only a few men were eating, and there was no talk among them. They glanced up when he entered, but only one nodded briefly. Mike was finishing his coffee when Kerb Perrin entered.

Instantly, Mike was on guard. Perrin walked with an arrogance that was unusual with him. He glanced at Mike Bastian, then seated himself and began to eat.

Roundy came in, then Doc Sawyer. That meant that Ben Curry was alone in the stone house. A moment later Ducrow entered, followed by Kiefer, then by Rocky Clatt, Monson, and Panell.

His cup halfway to his mouth Mike remembered suddenly that these were the men Perrin planned to use in the raid on the Ragan ranch. That could mean the raid was to happen today!

He looked up to see Roundy push back from the table, his

coffee unfinished. The old woodsman hurried outside and disappeared.

Mike put down his own cup and stood up. Instantly, he was motionless. The hard prod of a gun was in his back and a voice was saying, "Don't move!"

The voice was that of Fernandez. Perrin was leaning back in his chair, smiling.

"Sorry to surprise you, Bastian," Perrin said, "but with Lenaker on the way here we had to move fast. By the time he arrives I'll be in the saddle. Some of the boys wanted to kill you but I figure you'd be a bargaining point with the old man.

"He might be a hard kernel to dig out of that stone shell of his, but with you for an argument I think we can make him listen."

"You're mistaken," Mike said quietly. "He doesn't care what happens to me. He can afford to be rid of me and recruit somebody else. He won't let you get away with it."

"I shall, though. You see, Rigger Molina left this morning with ten of his boys to knock over the gold train."

"That was to be my job," Mike said.

"I swapped with him. He could have the gold train if he left me the bank job. I must admit"—Perrin smiled—"that I neglected to tell him about the twelve armed guards, and the number who had shotguns. In fact, I told him only three guards would be along. I believe that will take care of him for me."

Perrin turned abruptly. "Take his gun and tie his hands behind his back, then shove him into the street. I want the old man to see him."

"What about him?" Kiefer pointed a gun at Doc.

"Leave him alone. We may need a doctor, and he knows where his bread is buttered."

Mike Bastian was coldly, bitterly angry with himself. He should have been more careful! His attention had been on Perrin, and Fernandez had slipped up behind him. He was shoved into the street. The morning sun was warming things up and he was pushed out in its full glare, facing up the street toward the stone house.

He felt a fierce triumph. No matter what happened to him the old man would be tough to move out of that house. The sun was full in his face as it would be in the faces of any attackers, and the old man would be up there, ready, with a high-powered rifle. From the doors and windows he could command the whole settlement.

Perrin had moved out behind a wall of logs and sandbags hastily thrown up in the street. "Come on down, Curry!" he shouted. "Come down with your hands up or we'll kill your son!"

There was no reply, no evidence they had been heard.

"I'm not his son," Bastian said. "We're not even kin. He raised me to do a job, and he can get along without me. He doesn't give a tinker's damn about me."

"He hasn't heard you," Clatt said. "Let's just rush the place."

"You rush it," Kiefer said. "I'll just set back an' watch!"

Despite his helplessness, Mike felt a glow of satisfaction. Ben Curry was a wily fighter. He knew that once he responded, their threat would have force. It was useless to kill Bastian unless Curry could see it, useless to waste him when they did not know Ben was even listening.

Perrin had been positive Curry would come out rather than sacrifice Mike, and now they were not even sure their message was reaching him. Nor, Mike knew, were they sure Curry would give himself up to save him. At first, it had seemed logical. Now he knew Perrin was no longer sure. Nor were those who followed him.

"Come on out!" Perrin shouted. "We'll give you an' Bastian each a horse and a mile's start. Otherwise you both die! We've got dynamite!"

"Perrin," Mike said, "you've played the fool. Curry doesn't care whether I live or die. He won't come out, and there's no way to get him out. Don't you think the old man has planned for this? When did you ever know him not to plan for everything?"

Mike was talking as much for the effect on Perrin's men as for Perrin himself. If he could make them doubt his leadership, they might, out of fear of Ben Curry, turn on Perrin.

Perrin ignored him. Some of the men stirred restlessly, and one or two looked around as if wondering if someone was creeping up on them. Ben Curry was a shrewd fighter. Suppose he had planned for this? What would he have done?

"All he has to do, Kerb," Mike said, "is wait for Dave Lenaker to show. Then he can make a deal with Dave, and where will you be? Out in the cold with these men who were crazy enough to listen to you!"

"Shut up!" Perrin's tone was angry. "He'll come out, all right. He's just stallin'!"

"Let's open fire on the place!" Ducrow was impatient. "Or rush it, like Clatt suggested!"

"Hell!" Kiefer was disgusted. "Why bother? Let's take all we can get away with an' leave! There's the cattle, at least two hundred head of the best ridin' stock in the country, and what all. Rigger's gone. Lenaker ain't here yet. We've got a clear field."

"Take pennies when there's millions up in that stone house?" Kerb's veins swelled with anger. "There's the loot of years up in that house! A strong room with gold in it, stacks of money! With all that to be had you'd run off with a few head of cows?"

Kiefer was silent but unconvinced.

"There is no strong room," Mike told them. "I sleep in one room, Doc Sawyer in another, and there's one for the old man. The only thing he's got stored up there is ammunition. He's got enough ammunition to fight a war, and he's got the range of every place in town. Any time he's good an' ready he can start takin' you out, one at a time."

Standing in the bright sunlight of the dusty street, Mike looked toward the stone house. All the love and loyalty he felt for the old man up there came back with a rush. Whatever he was, good or bad, he owed Ben Curry. Perhaps Curry had reared him for a life of crime, but to Ben Curry it had not been a bad life. He lived like a feudal lord and had no respect for any law he did not make himself.

Wrong though he might be he had taken the orphan boy Mike Bastian and given him a start. He could never, Mike now realized, have become an outlaw. It was not in him to steal, rob, and kill. That did not mean he could not be loyal now to the man who had reared him and given him a home when he had none.

He was fiercely proud of that old man up there alone. Like a cornered grizzly, he would fight to the death. He, Mike Bastian, might die here in the street, but he hoped only that Ben Curry would stay in his stone shell and defeat them all.

Kerb Perrin was stumped. He had planned quickly when he heard Lenaker was on his way to Toadstool Canyon. When Lenaker arrived he would have men with him, and the fight for control could turn into an ugly three- or four-way battle.

With Molina out of the way he had been sure he would take over from Curry and be ready for Dave Lenaker when he arrived. He would be waiting in ambush for Lenaker and his men. They would never live to enter the canyon. Now, suddenly, both his planning and his timing had gone awry.

The idea that Ben Curry would not even reply had not occurred to him. That he might not surrender, Perrin had foreseen, and he had a sniper posted to pick him off if he so much as showed himself.

"If you boys want to make a strike"—Mike spoke casually—"there's that bank in eastern Colorado. According to all we hear it is ripe and waiting to be taken."

Nobody said anything but he knew they would be thinking. He doubted if any of them really wanted to face Ben Curry. He might be old, but how old was he? And how tough?

There was simply nothing he could do. At any moment Perrin might decide to kill him where he stood. Out in the open as he was, hands tied behind him, there was nothing he could do but think.

What had become of Roundy? The old trapper had risen suddenly and left the table, and Roundy had left his coffee unfinished, an almost unheard-of move for Roundy. Could he be in league with Perrin? No, that was impossible. Roundy had always been Ben Curry's friend and had never liked Kerb Perrin.

Yet where was he? Up there with Ben? That was likely, yet Roundy had a dislike of being cooped up. He liked to range free. He was a moving fighter, not given to defense unless forced to it. Wherever he was he would be doing what was necessary, of that Mike was sure.

"All right," Perrin said suddenly, "there's no use all of us watchin' one old man." He glanced at Bastian. "That was a good idea of yours, about that bank. We'll just hold you, knock off that Ragan place, and then the old man will be ready to quit. We'll take care of him an' ride east an' pick off the bank."

Bastian was led back from the street. His ankles were tied and he was thrown into a dark room in the rear of the store.

His thoughts were in a turmoil, and he fought to bring them to order. If he was to get out of this alive he must *think*. There was always a way if one but tried.

If Perrin's men rode to the Red Wall they would find only four hands on the V-Bar. They would strike suddenly, and they knew how to do what must be done. Juliana, Dru, and their mother would be helpless. Four men, five counting Voyle Ragan, could not stand against a surprise attack.

And here he was bound hand and foot.

Desperately, he fought the ropes that bound him, but those who did the tying were skilled with ropes and had tied many a head of cattle and horses.

As his eyes became accustomed to the darkness he looked for something he could use to free himself, but there was nothing. No projecting corner, no nail, nothing.

Outside all was still. Had they gone? He had no way of

knowing, but if Perrin was not gone he soon would be, leaving enough men to watch Ben Curry. Mike ceased struggling and tried to think. If he could get free and discover Ben's secret route across the river he might beat Perrin to it and be waiting when the outlaws arrived.

Where was Roundy? And Doc Sawyer?

Just when he had all but given up a solution came to him so simple that he cursed himself for a fool. Mike rolled over to his knees. Fortunately he was wearing boots instead of the moccasins he often wore in the woods. Bracing one spur against another to keep them from turning, he began to chafe the rawhide against the rowel of the spur. He wore big-roweled Mexican spurs, given him by Sawyer, spurs with many sawlike teeth instead of long spikes.

Desperately, he sawed until his muscles ached and he was streaming with perspiration. Once, pausing to rest, he heard a rattle of hoofs from outside. Several horses being ridden away.

Were they just going? He might have a chance, if only—

Boots sounded on the floor. Someone was coming! And just when he was cutting through the rawhide! Fearful they would guess what he was doing, he rolled to his side.

The door opened. It was Snake Fernandez. In one hand he held a knife. The other shoulder was still bandaged from Bastian's bullet.

"You shoot Fernandez, eh? Now we see! I am Yaqui! I know many ways to make a man bleed! I shall cut you into pieces. I shall cut slowly, very slowly. You will see!"

Bastian lay on his shoulder, staring at the half-breed. Stooping over him, the Yaqui pricked him with the knife point, but Bastian did not move.

Enraged, Fernandez tossed up the knife and caught it in his fist. "You do not jump, eh? I make you jump!"

Viciously, he stabbed down, and Mike, braced for the stab, turned to his back and kicked out with both feet. The heels of his boots caught Fernandez on the knees and knocked him over backwards. As he fell, Mike rolled to his knees and jerked hard at the rawhide binding his wrists.

Something snapped, and Mike pulled and strained.

Fernandez was on his feet, recovering his fallen knife.

Fighting the ropes that tied him, Bastian threw himself at Fernandez's legs, but the Yaqui leaped back, turning to face him with knife in hand. Bastian turned himself, keeping his feet toward the other man, then as the outlaw moved in, Mike lifted his bound feet and slashed downward.

His spurs caught the outlaw on the inside of the thigh, slashing down, ripping his striped pant leg and cutting a deep gash in his leg.

Fernandez staggered, cursing, and Bastian jerked hard on his bound wrists and felt something give. The rawhide ropes started to fall away, and shaking them loose he whirled himself around and grabbed at the outlaw's ankle, jerking it toward him.

Fernandez came down with a crash, but fighting like an injured wildcat, he attempted to break free. Mike, grasping Fernandez's wrist with one hand, took his throat with the other, shutting down with all the strength developed from years of training for just such trouble.

Struggling, the man tried to break free, but Mike's grip was too strong. Fernandez's face went dark with blood. He struggled, thrashed, and his struggles grew weaker. Releasing his grip on the man's throat, Bastian slugged him viciously on the chin, then hit him again.

Taking the knife from the unconscious man's hand, Mike cut his ankles free and stood up, chafing his wrists to get the circulation back.

Now—!

Eleven

A moment, he hesitated. Looking down at the unconscious man. Fernandez was wearing no gun but usually had one. It could have been left outside the door. Careful to make no sound, as he had no idea what awaited, he moved to the door and opened it cautiously.

The street before him was deserted. His hands felt awkward from their long constraint and he worked his fingers continually. He pushed the door wider and stepped into it. The first thing he saw was Fernandez's gunbelt hanging over the back of a chair.

He had taken two steps toward it when a man stepped out of the bunkhouse. The fellow had a toothpick in his hand and was just putting it to his mouth when he saw Mike Bastian. Letting out a yelp of surprise he dropped the toothpick and went for his gun.

It was scarcely fifteen feet and Mike threw the knife underhanded, pitching it point first off the palm of his hand. It flashed in the sun as the gun lifted. The man grunted and dropped his gun, reaching for the hilt of the knife buried in his stomach, his features twisted with shock.

Mike grabbed Fernandez's gunbelt and slung it on, one gunbutt forward, the other back. Then he ran for the boardinghouse where his own guns had been taken from him. He sprang through the door, then froze.

Doc Sawyer was there with a shotgun in his hands. Four of Perrin's men were backed against the wall. "I've been waiting for you," Doc said. "I didn't want to kill these men but wasn't about to try tying them up."

Mike's gunbelt was on the table. He stripped off Fernandez's guns and belted on his own, then thrust both of Fernandez's guns into his waistband.

"Down on the floor!" he ordered them. "On your faces!"

It was the work of minutes to hogtie all four. He gathered their weapons.

"Where's Roundy?"

"I haven't seen him since he walked out of the boardinghouse. He just stepped out and disappeared. I've been wondering."

"Forget him. Let's go up to the house and get Ben Curry, then we can figure this out. We don't have much time. They're headed for the V-Bar."

Doc looked sick. "I didn't know. My lord! And those womenfolks—!"

Together they went out the back door and walked along the line of buildings. Mike carried his hat in his hand, the easier to be recognized. He knew that Ben could see them, and he wanted to be recognized.

Sawyer was excited but trying to be calm. He had seen many gun battles but had never been directly involved in one.

Side by side, gambling against a shot from the stone house or someone of the Perrin outfit they had not rounded up, they mounted the stone stairs to the house.

There was no sound from within. Opening the door they

stepped into the living room and looked around. There was no sign of life. On the floor was a box of rifle cartridges scattered over the carpet.

A muffled cry reached them, and Mike paused, listening. Then he ran out of the room and up the staircase to the fortress room. He stopped abruptly. Sawyer was only a step behind him.

This was the room no outsider had seen, not even Doc. A thick-walled stone room with water trickling into it from a stone pipe, falling into a trough and then out through a hole in the bottom of a large stone basin. The supply of water could not be cut off, and there was a supply of food stored in the room.

The door was heavy and could be locked from within. Nothing short of dynamite could blast a way into this room.

This was Ben Curry's last resort, but he lay on the floor now, his face twisted with pain. "Broke m' leg! Tried to move too fast an' I'm too heavy!

"Slipped on the steps, dragged m'self up here." He looked up at Mike. "Good for you, son! I was afraid they'd killed you. Got away by yourself, did you?"

"Yes, Pa."

Ben looked at him, then away.

Sawyer had dropped to his knees, examining the older man's leg. "This is a bad break, Ben. We won't be able to move you very far."

"Get me a mattress to lay on where I can see out of the window. You an' me, Mike. We'll handle 'em!"

"I can't stay, pa. I've got to go."

Ben Curry's face turned gray with shock. He stared, unbelieving. "Boy, I never thought—"

"You don't understand, pa. I know where Perrin's gone. He's off to raid the V-Bar. He wants the cattle and the women. He figured he could get you any time."

The old man lunged with a wild effort to get up, but Doc

pushed him back. Before he could speak, Mike explained what had happened, then added, "You've got to tell me how you cross the Colorado. With luck I can beat them to the ranch."

Ben Curry relaxed slowly. He was himself again, and despite the pain Mike knew he was feeling, Curry's brain was working. "You could do it, but it will take some riding. They're well on their way by now, and Kerb will know where to get fresh horses. He won't waste time."

He leaned back, accepting the bottle Sawyer brought to him. "I never was much on this stuff, but right now—" He took a long drink, then eased his position a little. Quickly but coolly, he outlined the trip that lay ahead. "You can do it," he added, "but that's a narrow, dangerous trail. The first time we went over it we lost a man and two horses.

"Once you get to the river you'll find an old Navajo. Been a friend of mine for years. He keeps some horses for me and watches the trail. Once across the river you get a horse from him. He knows about you."

Mike got to his feet and picked up some added ammunition. "Make him comfortable, Doc. Do all you can."

"What about Dave Lenaker?" Doc protested.

"I'll handle Lenaker!" Curry flared. "I may have a busted leg but I can still handle a gun. You get a splint on the leg and rig me some kind of a crutch. I'll take it from there!"

He paused. "I'm going to kill him when he shows in that street, but if something happens and you have to do it, Mike, don't hesitate. If you kill either Perrin or Ducrow you'd be doing the west a favor. I've been thinkin' of it for years.

"But remember this about Lenaker. If I miss out somehow or you see him first, *watch his left hand!*"

Mike went down the steps to his own room and picked up his .44 Winchester rifle. It was the work of a minute to throw a saddle on a horse. Ben Curry and Doc could hold out for weeks in that room if need be, but the risk was dynamite thrown through or against the window. He would have to ride to the Red Wall and get back as quickly as possible.

Mike Bastian rode from the stable on the dappled gray and turned into a winding trail that led down through the ponderosa and the aspen to the hidden trail leading to the canyon. He had never ridden this trail, although he had discovered it once by accident. The gray was in fine fettle, and he let it have its head. They moved swiftly, weaving through the woods, crossing a meadow or two, and twice fording the same stream.

As he rode he tried to picture where Perrin would be at this time. He knew nothing of the secret crossing, of course, and must ride the long way around. Even with fresh horses and getting little sleep it would take time. His own ride would cover less than a quarter of the distance but was steeper and rougher. Nor could Mike even imagine how he would cross the river. All Ben had told him was there was a crossing and he would see when he got there.

"It'll take nerve, boy! *Nerve!* But remember, I've done it a dozen times, and I'm a bigger man than you!"

This was all new country to him, for he was heading south-west into the wild, unknown region toward the canyon of the Colorado, a region he had never traversed. It was unknown country to everyone but Ben Curry, the Indians, and perhaps some itinerant trapper.

Occasionally the trail broke out of the trees and let him have a tremendous view of broken canyons and soaring towers of rock.

He must ride fast and keep going. He was sorry now that he had not picked up some jerky before leaving Ben, for there would be nothing to eat until he reached the ranch, and then there might not be time.

Once, atop a long rise, he drew up to let the gray catch its wind and sat the saddle, looking out across the country. In the purple distance he could see the gaping maw of the great canyon. He spat into the dust, feeling a chill. How could any lone man hope to cross *that*?

And at the end of the ride, if he made it, there would be Kerb Perrin.

He had seen Perrin shoot. The man was fast with a gun and deadly. He was almost too fast.

Patches of snow still showed themselves around the roots of trees or on the shaded slopes. He dismounted, letting the gray drink from a clear, cold mountain stream that cascaded down a steep slope, disappearing into the brush, then appearing once more. Beaver had built a dam, formed a wide pool, and built a house at the pond's edge. He drank well above the pond and let the gray rest for a few minutes while he stood, listening to the silence and watching a beaver push through the water with a green branch which it would bury in the bottom of the pond against the days when snow fell and the pond was covered with ice.

He walked back to the gray and, putting a toe in the stirrup, swung to the saddle. "All right, boy, we've got a way to go."

The gray trotted down a narrow path covered with pine needles, then suddenly out of the ponderosa and into an eyebrow of trail that clung hopefully to a cliff's sheer face. One stirrup scraped the wall, the other hung in space. The drop was a thousand feet or more to the first steep slope, and if one slid off that it was another thousand to the bottom. The gray was a good mountain horse who went where only the imagination should go, and picked its way with care until the trail dipped into the forest again.

Shadows fell across the trail, and he glimpsed a white rock he had been told to watch for. He turned sharply left and went down through a steep cleft of sliderock where his horse simply braced its legs and slid to emerge at the foot of the mesa with a long, rolling plain before him.

A whiskey-jack flew up, flying ahead to light in a tree he must pass. It knew where men were there was often food, and it followed along, perhaps as much for the companionship as for whatever he might leave. "No time, old boy," he said. "I've a long way to go while the sun's still up."

He was tired, and he knew the gray was slowing down, but that meant nothing now.

Would he arrive in time? What was it like there? If he did not arrive in time, what then? There was a coldness in him at the thought, something he had never known before, but he knew what he would have to do. He would hunt them down, every man of them, no matter how long it took or how far the trail led. He would find them.

Mike rode down through heaped-up rocks, which had been falling for ages down upon this slope, rolling into position and lying there. Here the trail dipped and wound, and he thought of what lay ahead.

He had never been in a gunfight. He had drawn and fired at Fernandez without thinking, but he knew he had been lucky. In a gun battle you were shooting at living men who could fire back, and would. How would he react when hit by flying lead? He must face that, make up his mind, once and for all. If he got hit he must take it and fire back.

He had known men who had done it. He had known men hit several times who kept on shooting. Cole Younger at Northfield had been hit eleven times and escaped to finally survive and go to prison. His brothers had each been hit several times yet had survived, at least for the time. If they had done it, he could do it.

Perrin and Ducrow, those two he must kill, for they were the worst. If they fell the others might pull out. No matter what, he must kill them. He could not die trying. He had it to do.

Suddenly the forest seemed to split open and he was on the edge of that vast blue immensity that was the canyon. He drew the gray to a stand, gasping in wonder. Even the weary horse pricked its ears. Here and there through the misty blue and purple of distance red islands of stone loomed up, their tops crested with the gold of the last light.

The gray horse was beaten and weary now and Mike turned the horse down another of those cliff-hanging trails that hung above a vast gorge, and the gray stumbled on, seeming to know its day was almost done.

Dozing in the saddle, Mike Bastian felt the horse come to a halt. He could feel dampness rising from the canyon and heard the subdued roar of rapids as the river plunged through the narrow walls. In front of him was a square of light.

"Hello, the house!" he called out. He stepped down from the saddle as the door opened.

"Who's there?"

"Mike Bastian!" He walked toward the house, rifle in hand. "Riding for Ben Curry!"

The man backed into the house. He was an old Navajo but his eyes were bright and sharp. He took in Mike at a glance.

"I'll need a horse. I'm crossing the river tonight."

The old Indian chuckled. "It cannot be done. You cannot cross the river tonight."

"There'll be a moon. When it rises, I'll go across."

The Navajo shrugged. "You eat. You need eat first."

"There are horses?"

The chuckle again. "If you wish a horse you find him on other side. My brother is there. He has horses, the very best horses.

"Eat," he said, "then rest. When the moon rises, I will speak." He paused. "Nobody ever try to cross at night. It is impossible, I think."

Mike Bastian listened to the water. No man could swim that, nor any horse, nor could a boat cross it. He said as much, and the old Indian chuckled again. "If you cross," he said, "you cross on a wire."

"A *wire*?"

"Sleep now. You need sleep. You will see."

A wire? Mike shook his head. That was impossible. It was ridiculous. The old man was joking.

He crossed to the bunk and lay down, staring up into firelit darkness, and the sound of the rushing waters filled the night, and then he slept.

And in his dreams a red-eyed man came at him, guns blazing. . . .

Twelve

Borden Chantry glanced out the kitchen window toward the train station. When the tracks were built through town they fortunately passed within fifty yards of his home, so he could drink coffee, eat his breakfast or supper, and watch people get on and off the trains. Not that very many ever did. Four days out of five the train just whistled and went on through.

He liked seeing the trains come in, and so did Bess. She brought coffee to the table now, and with it the old subject. "I wish you would give it serious thought, Borden. This is no place to raise a boy."

"I grew up in the west," he replied mildly.

"That's different. You enjoy this life, but I want something different for Tom. I want him to go to school back east. I want him to have a fine education. I don't want him to grow up riding after cows or wearing a gun."

He glanced toward the station again. He knew how she felt, but what could he do back east? She just didn't understand. He had always been somebody wherever he was, but that was because all he knew was the west. Back east the best he could do would be to manage a livery stable or do common labor. He was a fair hand at blacksmithing but not at the kind of work he would have to do back east.

Right now he was holding down two jobs and getting paid for them both. He was sheriff of the county and marshal of the town, and for the first time in years he was saving money. If he could work a couple of years more he could buy cows and go back to ranching. All he had now was about sixty head running on open range and about thirty head of horses, five of which did not belong to him, but ran with his stock.

"I have thought about it, Bess. How would I make a living back there? All I know is cattle and range country. I got my start hunting buffalo and went to cow punching and then ranching. Drouth and a tough banker broke me, and these folks were kind enough to give me a job as town marshal."

"You'd find something, Borden. I know you would. I just don't want Tom growing up out here. All he does is run with that orphan McCoy boy, and he thinks about nothing but guns and horses."

"Billy's a good boy," Borden said. "Ever since he lost his pa a few years ago he's been batching. You should see that cabin. Keeps it spotless. That's a good lad, and he will do well."

"At what?"

He shifted uncomfortably. This discussion occurred at least once a week, and Bess was living a dream. She wanted to go back where she'd come from, wanted Tom to grow up as her brothers had, as her father had. What she wasn't realizing was that they would be poor. You could be poor in the west and if you worked nobody paid much attention, but back east you fell into a different class. There were things you were left out of, places you weren't invited. At least, that was the way he heard it. He had only been east twice, for a few days each time.

The first was when he took Bess east after they were married. He saw at a glance the money he was earning out west wouldn't take them far in the east. If he could just get started ranching again . . . well, he knew he could make it. Right now, for example, the range was good. What he needed was three to five hundred head. With that kind of a start and a break on the weather he could soon build himself a herd.

Back east? He would be a poor relation, and that was all.

"You just wait, Bess. I'll get back to ranching again. I've been thinking about those cows of Hyatt Johnson's. He's going to sell out, and I could pick them up if I had a little cash. Maybe—"

"Borden? Why did Mr. Sackett come over here to see you? Is there trouble?"

He sipped his coffee. "No, not really. Just something we're interested in. Maybe it's a fool idea, Bess, but you recall those letters I had? The one I wrote to Fort Worth? And El Paso?"

"Well, Sackett thinks the same as I do. He believes most of those robberies were pulled off by one big outfit, with one man in charge."

"What kind of a man would it take to keep that many outlaws in line?"

Of course, that was it. Bess, as usual, had put her finger on it. The kind of man needed to ramrod that sort of operation wouldn't be any average sort of man, he would be something special, and he would have been noticed, and if noticed, remembered.

Between them Sackett and he had now come up with eighteen jobs in which the robberies were pulled off with quick, neat work—nobody shot, nobody caught, no trail left. Men appeared, pulled off the robbery, and disappeared.

Usually one or more of the men loafed around town beforehand, studying the bank, getting the layout. No strangers had been spotted that could not be accounted for.

Yet a few days ago he'd had an idea and had written to Sackett. Whoever was ramroding that gang had been keeping his men under cover, so how about checking up on known outlaws who hadn't been showing themselves and were not in prison?

It had been his experience that they couldn't stay under cover for long. They showed up in another robbery, got into a saloon brawl, something of the kind. Most of them were the sort who craved attention, and it was unlike them to stay out of sight for long.

His thoughts returned to the kind of man to control such an operation, and suddenly, he had a hunch.

Bess, who had come up with the key question in the Joe Sackett murder when she asked how he got to town, had done it again. *What kind of a man would it take to keep such men in line?* Or words to that effect.

And he knew. At least, he had a hunch. That big man who had left the horses with him, the big man who might have been a big cattleman or something. He might not be the man but he was the kind of man who could do it. If anybody could.

Borden Chantry pulled out his watch, glancing at it. Barely nine o'clock. Mary Ann would be up even if the rest of her girls were sleeping. Bess wouldn't like it but he would have to see Mary Ann, and it was best to tell her first. Somebody else certainly would mention it if he was seen going to her house. Police business occasionally called him there, and she had been a help in that murder case. Moreover, Mary Ann had been around. There was little she did not know about outlaws.

He emptied his cup and got to his feet, reaching for his hat. "Bess, I've got to see Mary Ann."

Her face stiffened. "Is that necessary?"

"Bess, you just gave me a lead when you spoke about the kind of man it would take. You're right, as always. Remember how your question opened up that murder case? I think you've done it again."

"Then why see Mary Ann?"

"That woman knows more outlaws than anybody in the country, and she's on the grapevine. Whatever is going on, she knows."

"But will she tell you?"

"Bess, this is her town, too. She has money in that bank."

Mary Ann was in the kitchen drinking coffee when he rapped on the door. "Come in," she said, "but keep your voice down. The girls worked late last night."

He accepted the coffee she offered. Mary Ann was no longer young but she was still a beautiful woman, and during her rare appearances on the street she dressed sedately and conducted herself modestly. She was a shrewd, intelligent woman who listened as he laid it out for her.

"What I want to know," he said, "is who the boss man is, or the name of any other outlaw who has dropped from sight."

He paused. "And it is just possible that boss man stopped overnight here in town five or six years back. Maybe less."

She gathered her kimono a little tighter. "What's happening?"

"I think, among other things, the local bank. It's just a hunch, but Tyrel Sackett thinks so, too."

"I've money in that bank. Most of my savings."

Chantry waited, letting her think. Most of the outlaws were known to girls such as these, and the girls moved around a good bit and talked among themselves. There was not much they did not know.

"Rigger Molina," she said.

"I don't know him."

"Not the boss. He hasn't brains enough, but he's big, tough, and very, very good with a gun."

"And . . . ?"

"Nobody has seen anything of him for two or three years. That's unlike him. The girls were talking of it the other day with some fellow who was in here. Molina isn't the sort of man you can miss.

"He's big, powerful, thick arms and legs, shock of hair, broad jaw, small eyes, moves like a cat, and he swaggers. He doesn't brag, doesn't have to, you can look at him and you know he's got it. The point is that he is not a man to remain unnoticed. If he had been around he would have been seen, talked about."

"Odd that I don't know him."

"No, it isn't. Not really. He's out of Vernal, up in Utah. He worked in Montana, the Dakotas, and Idaho. He killed a man in Catlow Valley, up in Oregon. Some dispute over a steer. When they came after him he killed two more and wounded the sheriff. He loaded the sheriff on his horse and took him to a doctor, banged on the door, and left him.

"The thing was, Molina rode ten miles out of his way to get help for that sheriff. He could have let him die."

She got up. "Wait . . . I'll get Daphne. She's the new girl."

Daphne was a tall, slinky blonde who looked from the badge on Chantry's vest to his face. "How'd a good-lookin' man like you start to wearin' that thing?"

"Lay off, Daph. He's married, and happily."

"All the good ones are." She sat down and lit a cigarette. "You want to know about the Rigger? He's a good badman, sheriff."

"Where is he?"

She drew on her cigarette. "This guy really a friend of yours, Mary Ann?"

"Yes, he is. He will be a friend of yours, too, if you level with him."

She waited, dusted ash from her cigarette, and said, "The Rigger was nothing to me but he was to a girlfriend of mine. They saw each other reg'lar. Then one day he told her to take care of herself, he'd be out of circulation for a while, but when he came back he'd be loaded.

"We hear that sort of talk all the time, but not from Molina. He never had to brag.

"He said he was tying up with an outfit that would make it big, and then he went away. One of the girls I ran into said she saw him eating in a restaurant in Pioche with some tall, thin galoot."

She paused. "I hope this isn't trouble for him. He was an all right guy. Didn't have an enemy in the world unless it was Kerb Perrin."

"I hope he kills him," Mary Ann said. "Perrin beat up one of my girls once, when I was working in Goldfield. He beat her up and he liked doing it."

She paused. "Come to think of it, I haven't heard anything of him for a long time, either."

Borden Chantry walked back to the office, mulling it over in his mind. He might have something.

Kim Baca, his own deputy, had been a skilled horse thief at one time, and he knew everybody on what some called the owl-hoot trail. He had never heard it called that himself.

An hour later he knew much more. Kim Baca knew both Molina and Perrin, liked Molina, didn't like Perrin. Both had dropped from sight. So had Colley, the Deadwood outlaw. When Baca thought about it, there were a dozen or more he could name who simply hadn't been around.

Chantry was having his supper and watching the train when he remembered the big man who had left the horses with him. He should have asked Mary Ann about him. Thinking about it, he remembered detecting a change in her face when he spoke of the man stopping over in town a few years back. She had sort of tightened her kimono, and he knew Mary Ann, somewhat. It was a gesture she made when she had an idea or made a decision.

What did she know?

He wished Sackett was here. And it took too long for a letter—

What was he thinking of? The telegraph! Why couldn't he get used to the idea of the telegraph? Ever since they put the railroad in it had been here, available.

He walked through the twilight to the station and wrote out his message.

Rigger Molina—Kerb Perrin—Colley. Big man, middleaged or older. Six three, two forty. Strong face, big hands. Deep scar below right earlobe.

*   *   *

Sitting beside the fire that night Borden Chantry drew a long breath and waited, and then he spoke quietly. "Bess? If you're set on it, I mean if you want it that much, we could try it back east."

She stopped sewing and lowered her hands to her lap. "I haven't wanted it because this is my world, but for you—for you I'd do it." He hesitated again. "One reason I haven't wanted to go is that I don't want you to see me a failure.

"I've been enough of one so far." He waved a hand around. "They like me here. I was a good marshal, I guess, so they elected me sheriff. I didn't make it ranching because of the weather. Maybe I wouldn't have made it, anyway. I don't know what I'd do back east where nobody knows me and where I've no skills they can use.

"The thing is, I want you to be happy, and you've thought about little else these past few years. When my term's up, we'll go."

"Borden, I—I don't know what to say. I do want to go back. You can't realize how much I've hated all this. The shooting, the killing—"

"That could happen anywhere." He brought his knee up and pulled off a boot. "This thing I'm into, the thing I'm helping Sackett with. We've got to finish that first."

He pulled off the other boot and got up. "I'm going to bed, Bess. I'm a little tired. You an' Tom make your plans. I'll go with you."

He carried his boots into the bedroom and put them down. Then he took off his gunbelt and hung it on the back of the chair that stood beside his sleeping place. Taking off his vest he sat down.

He was being a damned fool. What *could* he do back east?

Bess wanted to live in town. She was remembering how it had been for her father, who had kept a store or something. He couldn't keep a store, and he had too little education to compete. He would be—

There was a rap at the door. He stood up, reaching for his

gunbelt. He listened, heard Bess replying to something, then the door closed.

She came into the room with a sheet of paper in her hand. "It was the telegrapher. He was going home but he brought this over, thinking it might be important."

It was from Tyrel Sackett, and it was just two words: *Ben Curry*.

Thirteen

He knew the name.

Borden Chantry was at his battered office desk when Kim Baca came in. Chantry glanced up at his young deputy. Baca had been one of the most skillful horse thieves in the country before he became Chantry's deputy, and he knew the men who rode the outlaw trail and their ways.

"Kim? What do you know about Ben Curry?"

"Leave him alone."

Chantry shuffled some papers on his desk. "I may have some horses of his. If I am not mistaken he left some at the ranch a while back."

"If he did he will pick them up in his own good time. Leave him alone, Chief. He's trouble, big trouble."

"When he picks those horses up he will be on the run. We want him, Baca."

Kim ran his fingers through his dark hair. "If the horses are here they are here for a purpose. Ben Curry doesn't make many mistakes, and he doesn't make any false moves."

"I think he wants our bank," Chantry commented mildly.

"He won't do it himself, and my suggestion is stay out of the way and let him have it. You aren't gettin' paid to get killed."

"I'm paid to do a job, Kim. So are you."

"Yeah, I know." Baca paused. "I'm told you could pick up an easy thousand dollars by bein' out of town for a few days. You're sheriff, too. You could be investigatin' that counterfeit money that's been showin' up."

"Kim, you can tell whoever passed that word along that I'm not for sale. An officer who turns crooked is worse than any thief. A thief is out to steal and is at least honest in his intentions. A police officer takes an oath to support the law." Chantry pushed back from his desk. "If I was a judge and a crooked officer came up before me, I'd give him the stiffest sentence the law permitted."

Kim shrugged. "I figured you'd think thataway but I was told to pass the word along."

"Let them know that I'll be here," Chantry said, "and I'll be ready."

"It won't be Ben Curry," Kim said. "More than likely it will be Molina or Perrin or somebody new. There's a word out that Ben's got a new man, specially trained for the work."

"Do you have friends in that outfit?"

Baca hesitated, then shrugged. "No, I can't say I do. I never ran with a gang, you know. Worked alone. I know some of those boys, and there's good men among 'em or they wouldn't have stayed together so long. The word is that the old man is lettin' go, and the boys are restless."

"Thanks, and if you hear anything, let me know."

Baca shook his head. "Since I pinned on this badge I don't hear as much. However," he added, "I could put it in my pocket and ride over to Denver. Down along Larimer Street I might hear something."

"Do that. Here." Chantry held out a couple of gold coins. "I'm not carrying very much but use that. Let me know what you hear."

He paused. "Kim, Tyrel Sackett is workin' with me on this. I think there's going to be a lot goin' on this spring. Something can happen wherever there's a gold shipment, a payroll, or a bank that looks easy.

"They've been quiet all winter, so I think they'll be lookin' for a big one."

Kim Baca walked outside. Well, now! A ride to Denver, all expenses paid and some money to spend!

There were few secrets. Somebody always talked, and somebody always listened. Most of the western outlaws were known, and when they traveled they were noticed. No matter what their orders were there was always one who wanted to see an old girlfriend or stop off for a drink with old acquaintances.

For not the first time he was glad he was no longer a wanted man. He could see what was happening. Chantry and Sackett were comparing notes, and if they were, others would be, and then the law would start to close in.

He would have to be very, very careful. Ben Curry, or so the word was, wanted no killings during the commission of a holdup, but that was a matter of policy, and he would and had killed when pursued.

His own knowledge of Ben Curry's operation was limited to a comment here and there or a rumor. He had not thought about a pattern to the crimes until Chantry pointed it out, showing his series of clippings, reward posters, and notifications from other peace officers. There *was* a pattern, and a pattern meant a trail one could follow, and not all trails were tracks on the ground. Behavior patterns were difficult to eliminate, and in moments of stress one reverted to them.

The outlaw might believe he was winning for a time, but someone—like Chantry or Sackett—somebody was carefully working out the trail.

His weakness had always been horses, better horses than he could afford to buy. He loved them for their speed, their beauty, and just for themselves. He had stolen some of the finest horses in the west, but the trouble was such horses were usually known. Just a few weeks ago Chantry had taken him out to Chantry's old ranch and pointed out a handsome bay gelding.

Kim caught his breath when he saw the horse. It was a beauty.

"The man who owned that horse," Chantry said, "I sent to prison. He'll do twenty years if he lasts that long, and as he's a sick man now neither of us believes he will. I asked him what to do with his gear.

" 'Keep my guns, rope, and saddle,' he told me. 'I never sold my saddle and never will.'

" 'What about the gelding?' I asked.

" 'That's the finest horse I ever rode, and I wouldn't want him in the wrong hands,' he told me."

Chantry said, "I knew how he felt, and I told him I had a man who loved horses and would care for him as long as he lived. He asked me who, and I told him 'Kim Baca.'

"He laughed, Kim, laughed real hard. 'Kim!' Well, I'll be damned! Sure, I'll write a bill of sale for him. I'll bet that's the first bill of sale Kim ever had, and I'll bet it was the first horse he was ever given!' "

"You mean he gave that horse to me?"

"He surely did. Here's the bill of sale. And Kim?"

"Yes, sir?"

"When you ride that horse, carry the bill of sale with you. Anytime the law sees you on a fine horse they are apt to ask questions."

Kim had caught up the gelding and saddled it. Across the pasture, bunched together like they were old friends, were five other horses, all of them fine stock.

"That them?" he asked, knowing the answer.

"That's them, just waiting to be picked up when somebody is traveling fast and needs fresh horses to outdistance a posse."

He turned as Chantry followed him outside. They rode out of town together.

"Take me a few days to get to Denver," Kim suggested.

"Take the steam cars. They'll put your horse in a stock car, or if there isn't one, I'll get him in the baggage car."

"Why didn't I think of that? I can't get used to thinking of trains and railroads and such." He turned his horse away. "See you in about a week."

Borden Chantry sat his horse, watching Kim ride away. The sky was clear and blue, the air fresh and cool with morning. From the low hill on which he sat his horse he could see the distant Spanish Peaks far off to the westward. Some day he'd ride over that way again, a beautiful country. Closer, he saw a coyote trotting across the distance, stalking some antelope.

The coyote was wasting his time unless there was an old one or a cripple amongst them. No fawns yet that he had seen, but several of the antelope looked about ready, which was probably why the coyotes were closing in, waiting until the does were down and helpless.

No wolf or coyote could catch an antelope running, and several times he had seen antelope run right away from the fastest greyhounds and stag hounds.

He looked around slowly, drinking in the vast distances. Bess wanted him to leave this. He loved her, but could he do it? And she did not realize what a position she was putting before him. She had always seen him in a position of strength, as a rancher and then as a town marshal and sheriff. Back east he would have none of the needed skills, nor had he the education required there.

He started his horse and walked it slowly down the slope. Kim Baca was, of course, right. He should be paying more attention to counterfeiting. For years now it had been one of the major crimes in the west, and a comparatively safe one. A bogus bill might be months or even years in reaching a bank where it could be identified, and a lot of queer money had been showing up. Both he and Baca believed the source was close by.

First, he must prepare for an attempted robbery. The Ben Curry boys had refrained from killing, but he knew that if capture appeared to be a possibility, they would fight. He was going to alert the town and select a couple of deputies for the emergency. If Ben Curry wanted his bank he would have to get it the hard way.

This new man Baca mentioned? What about him? Who would he be?

Whoever it was, they could expect a shooting fight, and with the kind of men Ben Curry recruited that meant somebody would get killed.

Unless he could figure out a way, a plan.

He didn't want to kill anyone or see anyone be killed, but the choice might not be his.

At the Red Wall it was quiet. A few cows grazed on the meadows below the house. Dru Ragan stood on the wide porch and looked broodingly down the canyon. There had been nothing friendly about that rider she had seen. Nor was he an Indian. An Indian might not have approached the house and out of curiosity might just have looked it over, but it had been a white man and had he been friendly he would have come on up to the ranch for a meal or at least for coffee.

Most of her life had been spent in the east, but she was instinctively western in her thinking. From first sight she had loved all this wild, lonely, wonderful country with its marvelous red canyons, its blue distance, its green forests, and the golden leaves of the aspen when autumn came to the hills. She loved seeing the cattle out there, and riding through the sage on horseback, topping out on a high ridge with magnificent views in every direction.

This had long been sacred land to the Indians, and the great peaks they revered had become important to her, also.

Now there was this other thing, this lurking danger. Or was it danger?

Riding around she scouted the country, knowing little about tracking but looking for the obvious. She came upon the tracks of the rider she had seen, and followed them. Several times, from several positions, he had looked at the ranch. That was obvious enough, for she could see where he had stopped and his horse had moved restlessly, leaving many tracks in the one position.

She wanted to follow the tracks, as they seemed plain enough, but the hour was late. She glanced off to the north where the great canyon lay. Someday she wanted to see it. Someday she would stand on its rim.

Voyle Ragan was waiting when she rode up. He was standing on the porch where she had looked over the country before beginning her ride.

He was worried, she could see that. "See anything?"

"Tracks," she said. "Somebody has definitely been looking us over."

With its shielding canyon walls darkness came early to the V-Bar. The Red Walls lost their color to shadows, and the night lay like velvet upon the meadows and the range. Only the stars were bright, and the windows of the house and the bunkhouse.

They would need to keep watch again. Voyle walked back into the house and took his rifle from the rack. He would keep it at hand. He should put on a belt gun but hesitated because of the women and as he rarely wore one around the house.

He had never thought of the night as an enemy. Now he was no longer sure.

Ben had a means of crossing the canyon. How, he could not imagine, but it worried him that others might discover that route. Ben's success had been due to keeping it a secret and to the fact that no one suspected he had a reason for crossing.

He blew out the lamp in the living room, returning to the kitchen where the girls and their mother were already seated for supper.

The night was very still. He sat down, and there was little talk where usually there was much, only a pleasant rattle of dishes and an occasional low-voiced request for something. Voyle kept his ears sharp for the slightest sound from outside.

Why couldn't all this have waited until the roundup and trail-drive hands were here?

That was why it was happening now. Or was he just worrying too much? Maybe that cowhand who was looking them over was just shy. He had known them to be. Maybe there was nothing to worry about at all.

A soft wind blew down the ranges, whispering in the pines, stirring the leaves of the aspen. Out on the open country beyond the canyon an antelope twitched its ears, listening.

A sound whispered across the stillness, a far-off sound as of something moving. The antelope listened as the sound faded, and then it rested again.

A cloud blotted out the moon, the wind stirred again, and a tumbleweed rolled a short distance and stopped as the wind eased. Overhead a bat swooped and dived and searched for insects in the night.

At the V-Bar the women had gone to bed. Voyle Ragan blew out the last lamp and walked to the porch to listen. The night was still.

Walking back through the house he went down the back steps and crossed to the bunkhouse. Garfield was sitting outside.

"Better get out in front of the house or on the porch," he suggested. "You can hear better."

Garfield got up. Taking his rifle he walked around to the front steps. This was kind of silly. What was Voyle afraid of, anyway? He put the rifle down and lit his pipe.

He looked at the stars. Mighty pretty. A man out in this

country looked at the stars a lot. The trouble was a man was so busy he forgot to take time to enjoy.

Garfield did not know he was looking at the stars for the last time. He did not know that within a matter of hours he would be dead, sprawled on the ground, cold and dead.

Fourteen

Mike Bastian awakened with a start. For a few minutes he lay still, trying to remember where he was and why he was there.

He sat up. His guns were there, and his rifle. He was in a small stone house and he could hear the river. He was supposed to cross that river, although from the sound he could not imagine anyone crossing it. The old Indian was seated by the fireplace, smoking. He glanced over at Mike.

"You had better eat something. The moon is rising." He paused. "Not even he ever tried to cross at night."

"You speak very good English," Mike commented, thinking his own was none too good.

The Indian gestured with his pipe. "I was guide for a missionary when small. He was a kind, sincere man, trying to teach Indians something they already knew better than he, although the words were different."

"He taught you to speak well, anyway."

"He did. I spoke English with him every day for six years.

111

He taught me something about healing, and I think my mother taught him something about it. She was very wise about herbs.

"He asked me one time why I never went to church, and I told him that I went to the mountains. I told him my church was a mountainside somewhere to watch the day pass and the clouds. I told him, 'I will go to your church if you will come to mine.' I think by the time he left us he liked mine better."

The old Indian turned to Mike. "When you are tired and the world is too much with you, go to the mountains and sit, or to some place alone. Even a church is better when it is empty. So it is that I think, but who am I? I am an old Navajo who talks too much because he wishes to speak his English."

When Mike had eaten they walked together to a trail that led them up even higher and then to a place where there was a ledge. "Ben Curry needed two years to build this bridge," the Indian said, "and nobody has crossed it but him, and only a few times."

Mike stared into the roaring darkness with consternation. Cross there? Nothing could. No man could even stay afloat in such water, nor could any boat live except, with luck, riding the current downstream. The river was narrow here. At least, it was narrower than elsewhere. The water piled up at the entrance to the chasm and came roaring through with power. Of course, this was spring and snow in the mountains was melting.

"There! You see? There is the bridge. It is a bridge of wire cable made fast to rings in the rock."

He stared across the black canyon where two thin threads were scarcely visible, two threads of steel that lost themselves in the blackness across the canyon, one thread some five feet above the other. On the bare cold rock he stood and stared and felt fear, real fear for the first time.

"You mean . . . Ben Curry crossed *that*?"

"Several times."

"Have you crossed it?"

The old Navajo shrugged. "The other side is no different

than here. If there is anything over there I want I shall ride around by Lee's Ferry or the Crossing of the Fathers. I have too little time to hurry."

A faint mist arose from the tumbling waters below. Mike Bastian looked at the two wires and his mind said *No!* He wet his lips with his tongue, lips gone suddenly dry. Yet, Ben Curry had done it.

How far was it across there? How long would it take?

He was deep in the canyon, deep in this vast cleft cutting to the red heart of the earth. Around him were rocks once bare to the world's winds, rocks that had been earth, pounded by rain, swept by hail, crushed down by eons of time's changing. Looking up he could glimpse a few stars, looking out across the deep he could see nothing but looming blackness. Somewhere, somehow, the cables were made fast, and if they were strong enough to hold Ben Curry, who was forty pounds heavier, they would be strong enough for him.

He put his rifle over his head and across one shoulder. Again he hesitated, but there was no other way. Kerb Perrin was riding to the V-Bar. He must be there before Perrin arrived. Taking hold of the upper cable he put a tentative foot on the lower and eased himself out. A moment passed, then he glanced back. The old Navajo was gone.

A slow wind whispered along the canyon walls, stirring the night with ghostly murmurings, then was lost down the blackness of the canyon. Mike Bastian took a deep breath. He had never liked heights and was glad the depths below were lost in darkness except where white water showed around the rocks, catching the few last rays of light.

He edged out. It was not too late. He could go back. He could return for his horse and ride back to Toadstool Canyon, but what of Drusilla and Juliana? What of their mother? And the cowboys . . . would they be warned? Would they have any idea until death swept down upon them?

He edged out further, clinging to the upper strand, not

lifting his feet above the cable but sliding them. One slip and he would be gone.

How far to the water? Two hundred feet? More like five hundred, although he was already deep in the canyon. He remembered now, hearing some talk of this when he was a small boy and it was being done. Roundy it had been, he told Ben of finding an iron ring in the wall, wondering why it was there. No doubt the idea had come from that.

He tried to keep his mind away from the awful depth below, and the roaring waters of the spring floods. Many times he had seen the river when it was like this, although never from this point. He moved on. At places the wire was damp from mist thrown up from the raging waters. Once he slipped, his foot touching some mud left from the boot of a previous traveler. His foot shot from under him and he was saved only by his tight grip on the wire. Slowly, carefully, he pulled himself erect once more, feeling for the cable with his foot.

Now he was at the lowest point above the river, and from now on he would be climbing a little, pushing his foot along the slanting cable. Carefully, he worked himself along. He could see the loom of the cliff on the opposite side.

Was there a good place to get off? Would the rock be wet and slippery? He remembered climbing out of a cliff dwelling once when the ladder stopped below the top of the boulder against which it rested, a smooth, polished boulder, and he had to work himself to the edge, turn himself around, and clinging to that polished surface, feel for the steps of the ladder with a five-hundred-foot drop behind him. He had not liked it then, and would not now.

Little by little he edged along until he was under the loom of the cliff, and he was trembling when he stepped off the cable into the safety of a rocky cavern at the cable's end. He was so relieved to be safely across that he did not immediately notice the Indian who sat awaiting him.

The Navajo got up and without a word led him along a trail to a cabin built in a branch canyon. Tethered at the door of the cabin was a huge bay stallion. With a wave for the Indian, Mike stepped into the saddle and was off, the stallion taking the trail it obviously knew.

Would Perrin travel by night? Bastian doubted it. After all, what was the reason for hurry? His victims awaited him, practically helpless, and with no warning of what impended. The trail led steadily upward. No doubt Curry himself had ridden this horse. It obviously knew where it was going, and he was eager to be there.

As the trail widened the horse broke into a swinging lope that ate up the ground.

The country was rugged, red rock, cedar, and occasional flats where the purple sage grew, only not purple tonight, merely dark patches here and there. As for the cedar, he could smell it, and the pinyons, too.

Dawn came slowly, breaking through long streaks of gray cloud. He drew up at a pool of snow water and drank, then let the stallion drink. He took a strip of jerky from his small pack and chewed on it while he unslung his rifle and edged it into the boot.

His approach must be with great care. He was not sure as to the exact position of the ranch, and Perrin might already be there. As he drew nearer he must ride slower to make the beat of his horse's hoofs less loud.

He knew the men he was facing, and they were skilled and dangerous fighting men.

The shadows were almost gone, but the sun was not yet up. Mike slowed the stallion to a walk although the animal tugged at the bit, eager to go.

Now he must listen, listen for any sound, a movement, a distant shot—

Drusilla Ragan brushed her hair thoughtfully, then pinned it up. She could hear her mother moving in the next room, and the Mexican girls who cared for the house were tidying up.

Juliana was outside talking to the young blond cowboy who had been hired to gentle some horses.

Suddenly Drusilla heard Juliana's footsteps. She came into the door, cheeks glowing. "Aren't you ready? I'm famished!"

"I'll be along." Then as Juliana turned away, she asked, "What did you think of him, Julie? That cowboy or whatever he was who got the buckboard for us? Wasn't he the best-looking thing you ever saw?"

"Oh? You mean Mike Bastian? I was wondering why you were mooning around in here. Usually you're the first one up. Yes, I expect he is good looking. And you know something? He reminded me of pa. Oh, not in looks, but some of his mannerisms."

Drusilla was no sooner seated at breakfast than she decided to ask Uncle Voyle about Mike Bastian again.

Ragan knew the girls had met Mike Bastian in Weaver, and he knew about the gold train, so he tried to keep his expression bland. "Did you say his name was Bastian? I don't place it. You said he was wearing buckskin? Sounds more like a hunter than a cowboy, but you can never tell."

"He's probably a hunter from up in the Kaibab. It's unlikely you will see him again. It's pretty wild up there on the other side of the canyon."

"The driver of the buckboard said there were outlaws up there," Juliana said.

"It could be. It is very wild up there," and he added truthfully, "I've never been up there."

He lifted his head, listening for a moment. He thought he had heard horses coming, but it was too soon for Ben to arrive. If anyone else stopped by he would have to get rid of them, and promptly. Visitors, however, were extremely rare.

Then he heard the sound again, closer. He got up quickly. "Stay here!" He spoke more sharply than intended.

His immediate fear was a posse, and then he recognized Kerb Perrin. He had seen Perrin many times, but doubted if Perrin had ever seen him or had any idea who he was. There were several riders, and they were Ben's men, but Ben had always assured him the outlaws knew nothing of the V-Bar or his connection to it.

He walked out on the porch. "How are you?" He spoke mildly, suddenly aware that he was not even wearing a gun. "Anything I can do for you?"

Where were his hands? Why had the sentry not warned him?

"You can make as little trouble as possible," Kerb Perrin said harshly. "You can stay out of the way and maybe you won't get hurt. We heard there were women here. We want them and we want your cattle."

Voyle Ragan stood tall and alone. "My advice is for you to ride out of here, and ride fast. You aren't welcome."

He paused, stalling for time. "The only women here are decent women, who are visitors."

Ducrow slid from his horse and shucked his Winchester. At that moment Garfield appeared at the corner of the corral. "All right!" he shouted. "Back off there!"

The others were on the ground, spreading out. Garfield was cool. He stepped out, his rifle up. "Back off, I said!"

He saw a movement and his eyes flickered and Ducrow shot across the saddle. Garfield took the bullet and fired back. A man beyond Ducrow spun and fell, Garfield worked the lever on his rifle and Ducrow shot into him. The cowhand backed up, going to his knees, fighting to get his rifle up. Another shot knocked him over, yet he still struggled.

Ignoring the shooting, Kerb Perrin started up the steps and Voyle Ragan hit him in the mouth. The blow was sudden, unexpected, and it landed flush. Perrin put his hand to his mouth and brought it away, bloody.

"For that, I shall kill you!"

"Not yet, Perrin!"

The voice had the ring of challenge, and Kerb knew it at once. He was shocked. Bastian *here*?

He had left Bastian a prisoner at Toadstool Canyon, so how

could he be here, of all places? And if he was free that meant Ben Curry was back in the saddle.

He must kill Mike Bastian and kill him now!

"You're making fools of yourselves! Ben Curry is not through and this place is under his protection! He sent me to stop you. All those who get in the saddle and ride out of here now will be in the clear. If you don't want to fight Ben Curry get going, and get going *now*!"

Kerb Perrin went for his gun.

Fifteen

Kerb Perrin knew he was going to kill Mike Bastian.

There had never been a time when he was not sure of his skill with a gun, and now even more so. Who did this kid think he was, anyway?

Kerb Perrin was smiling as his hand dropped to his gun, yet even as his gun cleared its holster he saw a stab of flame from the muzzle of Bastian's gun and something slugged him hard in the midsection.

Staggered and perplexed, he took a step backward. Whatever hit him had knocked his gun out of line, and the shot he fired went into the dirt out in front of him. He lifted his gun to swing it into line when something hit him again, half turning him.

What was wrong? He struggled with his gun, which was suddenly very heavy. There was a strange feeling in his stomach, something never experienced before. Suddenly he was on his knees and could not remember how he got there. A dark pool was forming near his knees, and he must have slipped.

He started to rise. He was to kill Mike Bastian, he had to kill him. He peered across the space between them. Bastian was standing with a gun in his hand, holding his fire. What was the matter with Bastian? Did he think he, Kerb Perrin, needed time? He lunged to his feet and stood swaying. His legs felt numb and he was having a hard time getting his breath.

That blood . . . it was *his* blood! He had been shot. Mike Bastian had beaten him. Beaten *him*? Like hell! His gun muzzle started to lift, then fell from his fingers. He had another gun. He would—

He reached for it and fell into the dust. His eyes opened wide, he tried to scream a protest but no sound came. Kerb Perrin was dead.

In the instant that Kerb Perrin's gun came up too late, Ducrow wheeled and ran into the house. Kiefer, seeing his leader fall, grabbed for his own gun and was killed by a shot from Voyle Ragan's rifle, hurriedly grabbed from its place beside the door.

The others broke and ran for their horses, and Mike got off one quick shot as they fled. He had lifted his gun for a final shot when he heard the scream.

Ducrow had come to the ranch for women, and it was a woman he intended to have. Dashing through the house while all eyes were on the shooting, he was just in time to see Juliana, horrified at the killing, run for her bedroom. The bedroom window was open and Ducrow grabbed her and threw her bodily from the window. Before she could rise he was through the window and had caught her up from the ground. Swiftly, he threw her across the saddle of a horse and with the few swift turns of the experienced hand she was bound hand and foot. Her scream was partly stifled by a backhanded blow across the mouth, then Ducrow leaped to the saddle of Perrin's mount, which was better than his own. Catching up the bridle of her horse he went out of the yard at a dead run.

Mike had wheeled, running for the house, believing the scream had come from inside. By the time he glimpsed them they were disappearing into the pines. He saw two horses, one rider and—

"Where's Juliana?" he shouted.

He had already glimpsed Drusilla standing on the porch. Voyle Ragan ran around the house. "He's got Julie!" he yelled. "I'll get a horse!"

"You stay here! Take care of the women and the ranch! I'll go after Juliana!"

He walked to his horse, thumbing shells into his gun. Dru Ragan started toward another horse.

"You go back to the house!" he ordered.

"She's my sister!" Dru flared. "When we do find her she may need a woman's care!"

"Come on then, but you'll have to do some riding!"

He wheeled the big bay and was off in a jump. The horse Dru mounted was one of Ben Curry's big horses, bred not only for speed but for staying power.

Mike's mind leaped ahead. Would Ducrow try to return to Toadstool? Or would he join Monson and Clatt? If he did, then Mike was in trouble. He worried about no one of them—but all three?

He held down the bay's pace. He had taken a swift glance at the hoof tracks of the two horses he was trailing.

Mike Bastian went over the situation, trying to view it from Ducrow's standpoint. Ducrow could not know that Juliana was Ben Curry's daughter, but at this stage he probably would not care. Yet he would realize Ben was back in the saddle again, so a return to Toadstool was out of the question. Also, Ducrow would want to keep the girl for himself. That he would kill her had to be understood, for any attack upon a decent woman was sure to end in hanging if he was caught.

Long ago Roundy had taught him that there were more ways to trailing a man than merely following tracks. One must follow the devious trails in a man's mind as well. He tried to think as Ducrow would be thinking.

The fleeing outlaw could not have much, if any, food. On

previous forays, however, he must have learned where there was water. Also there were ranch hangouts that he would know. Some of these would be inhabited, others would not. Owing to the maps Ben Curry had him study, Mike knew the locations of all such places.

The trail veered suddenly, turning into the deeper stands of brush, and Mike followed. Drusilla had not spoken since they started, but glancing back he saw her face was dusty and tear streaked, yet he noted with a thrill of satisfaction she had brought her rifle. She *was* Ben Curry's daughter, after all, a fit companion for any man.

He turned his attention to the trail. Ducrow must know he was followed or would be followed, and he would want to leave no trail. Nor was he inexperienced. In his many outlaw raids as one of Ben Curry's men and before he would have had much experience with such things.

And now it had happened. Despite the small lead he had, Ducrow had vanished!

Turning into the thicker desert growth he had dipped down into a sandy wash. There, because of the deep sand and the tracks of cattle and other horses it needed several precious minutes to decide whether he had gone up or down the wash. He searched, trying not to disturb the sand until he had worked it out. Then he saw a recognizable hoofprint following the winding of the wash as it led up-country. Ducrow would not stay in the wash long, as it was tiring for the horses to walk in the deep sand, and he would wish to save his horses' strength.

From there on it was a nightmare. Ducrow rode straight away, then turned at right angles, using every bit of cover he could find and mingling his tracks with others wherever found. At places he had even stopped to brush out tracks, but Roundy's years of training had not been wasted, and Mike clung to the trail like a bloodhound.

Following him, Dru saw him pick up sign where she could

see nothing. Once a barely visible track left by the edge of a horseshoe, again a broken twig on a bush they had passed.

Hours passed and the sun began to slide down the western sky. Dru, realizing night would come before they found her sister, was cold with fear for her.

Mike glanced back at her. "You wanted to come," he said, "and I am not stopping because of darkness."

"How can you trail them in the dark?"

"I can't, but I believe I know where they are going and we will have to take a chance."

Darkness closed down upon them. Mike's shirt had stuck to his body with sweat, and now he felt the chill of the night wind, but grimly he rode on. One advantage he had. He had never ridden with the gang, so Ducrow might not suspect he knew of all the hideouts. Ducrow could not know of the hours he had spent with Ben Curry and Roundy going over the trails and checking the hideouts and what he could expect at each one.

The big bay horse seemed unwearied by the miles of travel, yet at times Dru heard Mike speak encouragingly to the big horse. At the edge of a clearing he suddenly drew up, so suddenly she almost rode into him.

"Dru," he whispered, "there's a small ranch ahead. There might be one or more men there, and Ducrow is almost surely there with your sister. I am going to find out."

"I'll come, too."

"Stay here! When I whistle, come and bring the horses. I have skill at this sort of thing, and I have to get close without making a sound."

Removing his boots he slipped on the moccasins he always carried in his saddlebags. He was there a moment, and then he vanished into the darkness, and she heard no sound, nothing. Suddenly a light appeared in a window . . . too soon for him to have reached the cabin.

Moving like a ghost, Mike reached the corral. There were horses there, but it was too dark to make them out. One stood near the bars, and putting a hand out he touched the horse's flank. It was damp with sweat.

Without so much as a whisper of sound, Mike was at the window, his head carefully to one side but peering in.

He saw a square-faced man with a pistol in his hand, and as Mike watched, the man placed the pistol on the table with a towel over it.

Soundless in his moccasins, Mike walked around the house and stepped into the room.

Obviously the man within had been expecting the sound of horse's hoofs or even a jingle of spurs and a sound of boots. Mike's sudden appearance startled him, and he made an almost inadvertent move toward the pistol under the towel.

Bastian closed the door behind him, and the man stared at him. This black-haired young man in buckskins did not look like the law, and he was puzzled but wary.

"You're Walt Sutton. Get your hands away from that table before you get blown wide open! *Move!*"

Sutton backed off hurriedly, and Mike swept the towel off the gun. "If you had tried that I'd have killed you."

"Who are you? What d'you want here?"

"You know damn' well what I want! I am Mike Bastian, Ben Curry's foster son. He owns this ranch. He set you up here, gave you stock to start with! Now you double-cross him. Where's Ducrow?"

Sutton shook his head. "I ain't seen him," he protested.

"You're a liar, Sutton! His horses are in the corral. You're going to tell me where he is or I'll start shooting."

Walt Sutton was unhappy. He knew Ducrow as one of Ben Curry's men who had come for fresh horses. He had never seen this young man before, yet so far as Sutton was aware nobody but Ben Curry and himself knew the facts about the ranch. If this man was lying, how could he know?

"Listen, mister, I don't want no trouble. Least of all with old Ben. He did set me up here, and I been doin' well. Yes, I seen Ducrow, but he told me the law was after him."

"Do I look like the law? Ducrow's kidnapped Voyle Ragan's niece, and they are friends of Ben's. I've got to find him."

"Kidnapped Voyle Ragan's niece? Gosh, mister, I wondered why he wanted two saddle horses."

Mike backed to the door and whistled sharply. "Where did he go?"

"Damned if I know. He rode in here about an hour ago wanting two packhorses with grub and blankets. He took two canteens and then lit out."

Drusilla appeared in the doorway and Sutton's eyes went to her. "I know you," he said. "Evenin', ma'am."

"Get us some grub, and make it quick. Then I want the two best horses Ben left here, and I want them fast!"

Sutton put bread and meat on the table and ducked out of the door. Mike watched him hurry to the corral and saw him bring two horses from the stable. They were typical Curry horses, big, handsome animals.

Sutton led them to the door and then sacked up some supplies and tied them behind the saddles.

"You've been a help," Mike said, "and I'll tell Ben about it. Now—have you any idea where Ducrow might be going?"

"Well—" Sutton hesitated, obviously frightened. "He'll kill me if he learns I told, but he did say something about Peach Meadow Canyon."

"Peach Meadow?" Bastian frowned. The canyon was a legend in the red rock country, and Roundy had talked of it. "What did he ask you?"

"If I knew the trail there and if it was passable."

"What did you tell him?"

Sutton threw up his hands. "What could I tell him? I've heard of that canyon ever since I came into this country, and I've looked for it. Who wouldn't, if all they say is true?"

As they moved out Mike put his hand on Dru's arm. "Dru? This is going to be rough, so if you want to go back—?"

"I wouldn't think of it."

"Well, I won't say I'm sorry. I like having you with me. In fact—" His voice trailed off.

There was more he meant to say, and Drusilla realized it. She also knew he was very tired. She had no idea of the brutally hard ride before he arrived at the Ragan ranch or the crossing of the canyon, but she could see the weariness in his face.

They rode side by side when the trail permitted, and Mike explained. "I doubt if Ducrow will stop for anything now. There isn't another good hideout within miles, and he will know he's pursued, although not by whom or how many. I almost wish he knew it was me."

"Why?"

"Because he wants to kill me," he said simply, "and he might stop long enough to try."

Sixteen

Then they were alone in the night, with only the horses under them, only the stars to watch. "Is it far?"

"I do not know," he said. "If Ducrow knows where it is he has found the perfect hideaway. Outlaws often stumble across such places in making getaways from the law, or they hear of them from some Indian, some trapper or prospector, and file the knowledge away against future need."

"What is Peach Meadow Canyon?"

"It is said to be near the river, one of those deep canyons that branch off from the Colorado or one of its tributaries. According to the stories somebody discovered it years ago, but the Spanish had been before him, and Indians before them. There are cliff-dweller ruins in the place, but no way to get into it from the plateau. The Indians had a way, and the Spanish are supposed to have reached it by boat.

"The prospector who found it told folks there was fresh water and a small meadow. Somebody had planted some peach trees, probably from pits he carried in his pack. Nobody ever saw

him or it again, so the place exists only on his say-so. The
Indians now say there's no such place, but they may just not
want anybody nosing around. Ducrow might be trying to throw
us off, but he might actually know something."

"You'll try to follow him in the dark?"

"No, not actually. It is night and he will be taking it easy as
this is rough country. He can't get out of this area where we're
traveling, so we'll stay behind him until he leaves the canyon.
By that time it will be daylight and we can pick up his trail."

"I am worried for Juliana."

"Of course, but I think he knows somebody is following, so I
don't think he will stop until he reaches the canyon or turns
into rough country."

For several miles they rode down a high-walled canyon from
which there was no escape. Ben Curry and Roundy had both
told him of it, as one of the approaches to Walt Sutton's place.
Once they emerged from the canyon, however, he must be
extremely careful.

At the canyon's end, where it opened upon a wide stretch of
semidesert, he pulled up and swung down. "We can't have a
fire," he said, "because in this country a man can see for miles,
and we want him to think we're pushing hard on his trail."

He put his folded poncho on the ground near a flat-faced
boulder and handed Dru a blanket. "Rest," he said. "You'll
need it."

She was feeling the chill and gathered it close about her.
"Aren't you cold? If we sat close together it would be warmer,
and we could share the blanket."

He hesitated, then sat down beside her and pulled the
blanket across his shoulders. He was desperately tired but
feared to fall asleep. Ducrow might leave Juliana and double
back to kill him. He had unsaddled and ground-hitched the
horses but had no worry about them drifting off. This was one
of the few patches of grass anywhere around.

Yet he did sleep. When the sky was faintly gray he awakened

suddenly, listened, looked at the horses who were cropping grass contentedly, and then eased from under the blanket.

He caught the horses, smoothed the hair on their backs with his hand, and saddled up. From time to time he glanced at Dru, who was sleeping peacefully. He was amazed that he should be here, in this lonely place, with this beautiful girl. He, an orphan and foster son of an outlaw.

Some movement of his must have awakened her, for her breath caught and then her eyes opened. She looked up at him with a sleepy smile. "I was tired!" She sat up and watched as he kindled a small fire in the shadow of a boulder. Using very dry wood that would offer almost no smoke, he got his small coffeepot from the pack and started coffee.

Digging into his pack he found some hard biscuits and beef jerky. "Better eat what you can," he said. "We won't be stopping again."

She drew on her boots and stood up, shaking out her hair.

Squatting by the fire he studied the terrain that lay before them, trying to recover from his memory all he had been told about it.

Ducrow would have no trail to find and would have moved swiftly. By now he would probably have reached his goal or was nearing it. When they were in the saddle again they picked up the tracks of the three horses they were following. It was easier because the packhorse Ducrow was leading was a horse Mike remembered, and the tracks were familiar.

What sign there was he could follow from the saddle, and they gained distance, moving swiftly. Dawn broke and the sky was streaked with rose and gold. The warming sun began to ease some of the stiffness from their muscles.

The trail crossed a small valley, skirted an alkali lake and dipped into a maze of boulders and rocky outcroppings before entering a pine forest. Nowhere did he see any signs of a camp. Juliana, who lacked the strength and fire of Drusilla, must be almost dead from fatigue. Obviously, the outlaw knew exactly where he was going and that his destination was not far off. He was making no effort to save his horses.

The trail became more difficult to follow. Mike slowed his pace, then suddenly stopped.

The tracks had vanished as if the three horses had stepped off a cliff!

"Stay in the saddle. I've got to look around a bit."

Mike studied the ground, then walked back to the last tracks he had seen, which he had taken care not to cross in the event he needed to examine them again.

He knew the stride of each horse now, and he measured the distance with his eye, knowing where each hoof must fall.

Nothing . . .

He paused, studying the ground, then the pine timber that surrounded the spot. It seemed absolutely uniform and as he would expect it to be. Avoiding the trail ahead he went into the woods and walked a slow circle around his own horses, studying the ground, the trunks of the trees, everything. He found no tracks.

He stopped, hands on his hips, scowling in concentration. They were gone, and seemed to have left no trail.

Dru was watching him, worried now. She started to speak but he lifted a hand. "Wait! I want to think."

He studied, inch by inch, the trail ahead and the trail on his right. Nothing offered a clue. The three horses and the two riders had vanished as if they had ridden off into space.

On the left the pine woods were thick, so dense as to offer no means of passing through. He had studied the trees and brush, and even if a horseman turned that way there was no place to go.

As the trail ahead was trackless it had to be on the right. Again he walked into the woods, and found no tracks. It was impossible, yet it had happened.

"Could they have backtracked?" Dru asked.

"There were no tracks except those going ahead. I believe—" He stopped, swore softly. "I'm a fool! Lend me your hat."

Puzzled, she removed her hat and handed it to him. Using the hat as a fan he began to wave it over the pine needles, letting the wind he created move the needles. He worked for several minutes, then suddenly stopped.

"Got it!" He pointed. "There they are!"

Dru stepped her horse closer. With the pine needles wafted away, the tracks were plain.

"Ducrow is smart. He rode across the open space, then turned back the way he had come, riding over on the far side close to that wall of pines. Then he dismounted, and probably in his sock feet came back and scattered pine needles over the tracks, letting the wind sift them down naturally."

Mounting again, they started back, but from time to time he dismounted to check for tracks. Suddenly the trail turned into a narrow gap in the pine forest, and they followed, winding their way through thick woods. Once Mike indicated a scar on a tree where a stirrup had brushed.

"Move as quietly as you can," he whispered, "and don't speak aloud. Voices carry. He may try to ambush us."

"Do you think he knows we're following?"

"I'm sure of it, and he knows I'm a tracker but not whether I am any good or not."

The trail was now no longer hard to follow and they made better time. Mike Bastian had a hard time keeping his thoughts from the girl with whom he rode. What would she think when she discovered her father was an outlaw? And that he himself had been raised to be an outlaw?

Pine trees thinned, and before them was a vast misty blue distance. Mike stepped down from the saddle and walked forward on moccasined feet. On the rim of the canyon were a few cedars and a pinyon pine or two. Scouting the rim he stopped suddenly, feeling the hair prickle on the back of his neck.

Had they gone down *that*? He knelt on the rock. Yes, it was the scar of a horse's shoe on the rock. He moved a little further, looking down. The cliff fell away for hundreds of feet, but the trail was there, a rock ledge scarcely three feet wide.

He walked back and explained. Dru nodded. "If you are ready, I am." She paused. "Mike, he may be waiting for us. We may get shot."

He shrugged. "I knew that when I started, Dru. These are rough men, and Ducrow has reason to hate me. Of course, he will try to kill me."

"But you needn't have come, Mike."

He shrugged again. "I didn't think much about it. Your sister was kidnapped. I was there and knew what to do. It is as simple as that."

"Who are you, Mike? Uncle Voyle seemed to know about you, and that man, the one who tried to kill you, he knew you. And I heard you say Ben Curry sent you to stop them from raiding the ranch. Who is Ben Curry? And are you an outlaw?"

For as long as a man might have counted to a slow ten Mike looked out over the canyon. "No," he said at last, "I am not an outlaw, although I was raised to be one. Ben Curry raised me like his own son, planning that I should inherit the leadership."

"You lived with them?"

"When I wasn't out in the woods. Ben Curry taught me and had me taught. How to shoot, track, ride, even to open locks and safes."

"What is he like, this Ben Curry?" Dru asked.

Mike hesitated, and then said, "In any other time he might have been considered a great man. In his own way, he is. Back in the days of robber barons he would have wound up with a title, I expect.

"When he came west it was wild, there was little law and much of that was enforced by men big enough to get away with it. If they rustled cattle they were building their herds. If a cowboy did it he was rustling. He had a small outfit and he branded loose cattle like they all did, but the trouble was he wasn't big enough. They came after him and he fought. He fought altogether too well, but that made him an outlaw.

"He accepted the role, but he's one of these men who can do nothing small. Soon he was organizing a bigger outfit, planning the jobs like a general plans a campaign, arranging getaways.

"He no longer went out himself, he was behind the scenes, planning it all. I doubt if any other man could have done it, for outlaws do not take to organization, and when they have money they want to spend it where there are bright lights."

"He has killed men?"

"Two, that I know of. One was a justified killing. The second one? Well, he was in a hurry."

"Are you apologizing for him? After all, he was an outlaw and a killer of men."

"He was all of that, but I am not apologizing for him. He's a man who always stood on his own two feet.

"He may have been wrong but he was always good to me. He took me in when I had no place to go, and he cared for me."

"Was he a big man, Mike? A big old man?"

His eyes avoided hers. So she knew, then?

"In many ways he was one of the biggest men I ever knew. . . . We'd better get started."

It was like stepping off into space, but the horses accepted it calmly enough. After all, they were mountain-bred and would go anywhere as long as there was a foothold.

The canyon gaped to receive them, and they went down the narrow, switchback trail. Here and there Mike could see that work had been done. Somebody with a pick and perhaps high explosives of some kind had made a trail where none had been before.

It was late afternoon when they started down, and soon shadows began to creep up the canyon walls, reaching with hungry fingers for the vanishing sunlight. At a wider spot Mike dismounted and Dru did also. Mike carried his rifle in his right hand, ready for instant use. What was to happen could begin at any moment and he had not wanted to be caught in the saddle on a narrow trail where a wounded horse might rear and fall.

His eyes sought the shadows, searching the canyon below for some sign of a house, for a fire, for movement. He saw nothing.

Supposing they were not here at all? That Ducrow had tricked him somehow?

He shook his head. He could not accept that. He had to be right. He thought of Juliana and Ducrow. She could never cope with such a man. Dru, now—

He grinned despite himself. He had an idea Dru would have made Ducrow wish he'd never been born. She was lovely, but there was steel in her, too.

They could hear the river now, not the roaring that he heard when crossing on the cable, but swift, silent, rushing water. Silent, at least, by comparison.

The tracks led back from the river and into a high-walled, almost hidden canyon. It seemed only a gap in the canyon walls, but it angled off to the east. He followed the tracks. It would soon be dark.

The canyon turned a little and he glimpsed a fire reflecting from canyon walls. He paused and passed the reins to Dru. "You will have to stay with the horses."

"Is—is it them?"

"It couldn't be anyone else." He paused. "I'll have to kill him, you know."

"Don't you be killed."

He started forward and she caught his arm. "Mike, let me go. Maybe he would listen."

"He won't. You know that. I've got it to do."

"Why are you doing this? She isn't your sister."

"No . . . but she's yours."

His moccasins made no sound in the sand or on the rocks. He could see a figure moving about the fire. Then he saw Juliana, her head on her arms, sitting near the fire. Ducrow glanced over at her, then said impatiently, "Get some of this coffee into you! This is where you stay, here in Peach Meadow Canyon. You're my woman now!"

He straightened up from the fire. "Monson an' Clatt! They ran like scared foxes! No bottom to them! I come for a woman an' I got one!"

"Why don't you let me go?" Juliana lifted a tear-streaked face. "My father is a wealthy man. He will pay you well."

"Your pa? I thought Voyle Ragan was your uncle?"

"He is. My father is Ben Ragan. He ranches north of the canyon."

"North of the canyon? Not unless he's a Mormon, he don't." Suddenly he straightened from the fire again. "What's he look like, this pa of yours?"

"He's a great big man with gray hair, a heavy jaw—" She stopped talking, staring at Ducrow. "What's the matter with you?"

"Your pa, this Ben Ragan—a big man with a scar on his jaw. That him?"

"Oh, yes! Take me to him. He will pay you well!"

Ducrow was laughing. "Well, I'll be damned! So I latched onto the old rooster's chick, did I?" He chuckled sourly. "Now I'm really goin' to enjoy this here. So the old devil had hisself a family, did he? I thought all he had was that damned brat, that Mike Bastian!"

Seventeen

Kim Baca was on the town. It had been three years since he leaned on a bar in Denver, and he had headed for Gahan's opposite the courthouse. He was known there, and friends often dropped in. Moreover, it was a place to pick up news and information, and that was what he wanted.

With money in his pocket and time on his hands, Kim was content. He played a couple of games of pool, bowled a little, had a few drinks here and there, and ate in some of the best restaurants. He spoke to old acquaintances, talked with some of the girls along the street. But it was not until he reached the bar at Gahan's that he actually heard anything.

Kim was young, he was attractive, and he was friendly. He had removed the badge from his vest and carried it in his pocket, as he did not want to inhibit any old friends or arouse suspicion in others.

At Gahan's he ordered a beer and looked around. George Devol was having a drink with two shady-looking characters at a nearby table, and at the other end of the bar Bill Cody was surrounded by a group of friends. It was as Kim had remembered it. He was thinking of another beer when a man stopped beside him and a low voice said, "Rounded up any good stock lately?"

Kim glanced around and found himself looking into Doc Middleton's smiling face. Doc was said to be the most successful horse thief in the west, but they both knew Kim had been every bit as good and perhaps better.

"Not so's you could notice," Kim said. "I resigned in your favor. You were makin' the competition too tough."

Doc chuckled. "Your only trouble was you *loved* fine horses," he said. "I took 'em an' sold 'em and went back for more. You just had to have the best horses in the country, and such horses are remembered. No way you could get away with it."

Doc turned his back to the bar and leaned his elbows on it, watching the crowd. "I see you ain't wearin' your badge. You quit?"

"No," Kim replied. "I think I'm locked in for good, Doc, so do me a favor and stay away from my town, will you? I'd hate to jail an old friend."

"If you could catch me." Doc's expression changed and he turned around, facing the mirror. "You workin' with Bord Chantry?"

"I am."

"I like him. When he was ranchin' down there he always set a good table. I put my feet under it time to time when ridin' the country." Doc turned and looked into his eyes. "This is no time for you to be away from home, Baca. Bord's goin' to need all the help he can get."

"What is it, Doc?"

"You know about Ben Curry's outfit?"

"Just talk around. Not much."

"It's been big, the biggest, but the whisper is that it's breakin' up. The whisper is that the bank in your town is the next one up, and the outfit ridin' that way are sayin' Ben's lost his grip an' that he was a fool, anyway, him wantin' no shootin'."

"When?"

"Next couple of days. Maybe tomorrow. Remember Clatt? Yeah, he's one of them. He's talkin' it around that he's going to kill Bord if Chantry so much as shows on the street."

Doc Middleton touched the spot on Kim's vest where the badge had been pinned. "I never wore one of those, but some of the men who do are mighty square. I've been treated right here an' there.

"Far as that goes"—he spoke more softly—"as I come up the street I ran into Bat Masterson. We shook hands, talked over old buffalo huntin' days, and then he suggested I not stay around Denver too long. Too many people know me.

"He knows I'm wanted, but we also fit a couple of Injun fights together. He's square."

Kim Baca nodded. "Know him myself. He's a good man." His thoughts were racing ahead. He was miles from home and Bord would need him, need him desperately. There was no way—

He swore. Why couldn't he remember the *train*? Just hadn't got used to the idea, and the telegraph, too. He thought the thing through quickly, running over in his mind his every move. First, the telegraph station, then a ticket on the train. "Damn it!" he said bitterly. "I had me a bed in a fine hotel and was fixin' for a late breakfast of whatever was available. Now I got to light out."

"Was I you, with Borden Chantry for a friend, I wouldn't waste around."

Kim finished his beer and left a coin on the bar. "Thanks, Doc. I'll not forget this."

"You just tell Bord that I didn't forget. Monson an' Clatt have never been anything but trouble. Bord Chantry's a good man."

Kim Baca went outside, heading for the railroad. At the despatcher's office he sent his telegram.

Not five. Seven or eight. Monson and Clatt, today or tomorrow. Coming a-running.

KB

"When's the next train goin' east?"

The despatcher looked up from under his green eyeshade. "Tomorrow mornin', eight o'clock."

"I need one tonight." Baca flashed his badge. "I need anything that will roll, a place for myself and a horse. Will it help if I call Dave Cook?"

"What's goin' on?"

Briefly, Baca explained. The despatcher replied, "Monson an' Clatt, is it? I'll get the trainmaster. We'll see." He started for the door and over his shoulder he said, "They've robbed trains. Four, maybe five years back Clatt killed one of our boys."

An hour later, with his horse in a stockcar and himself in a caboose, Kim Baca was racing east. With luck he would make it.

There was only the locomotive, the stockcar, and the caboose, but they had a clear track.

There was coffee on the stove. Baca found a cup and helped himself. Somewhere out there Monson and Clatt with several friends were riding for Chantry's town.

He had warned Bord there would be seven or eight but that was guessing. With Ben Curry it was nearly always five men to a job, but Ben was no longer the big man, and Clatt had always run with a gang. He would take all he could get together and they would plan to hit fast and hard.

Monson and Clatt would be shooting to kill.

If Bord got his telegram he would do some planning and round up a couple of good men. The bank was opposite the store, and the building next to the store was the express office. A man placed there could cover the door of the bank and the side door as well. If Bord was at the jail, where his office was, he could cover the bank door as well as the other side of the bank. With a man at the big barn, which was behind the bank and a little further along, they could cover the front, both sides, and the rear.

He finished his coffee and stretched out on a bunk. He was

thinking of how the men should be placed and the probable action when he fell asleep.

He was awakened by a slowing of the train. He sat up abruptly. Taking out his watch, he glanced at it. They were scarcely an hour out of Denver.

The brakeman, watching the track, spoke to him. "Baca? Fire up ahead, right alongside the track, one man and a horse. He's tryin' to flag us down."

Baca slung on his gunbelt and picked up his rifle. "One man? Are you sure?"

"Mister, you couldn't hide a sick goat out yonder. It's all wide-open country. This gent looks like he wants a train. There's a dirt ramp there, for loadin' stock, an' he's atop it."

"All right, slow down."

At the brakeman's signal the locomotive slowed down still more. Baca rested his Winchester on the windowsill and waited. He could see the man plainly now, but not his face. But that horse—!

Slowly the train braked to a stop.

"All right, out there! You're covered by a .44 Winchester. So speak your piece!"

"I need a ride for my horse and myself, I am—" The voice broke off. "Baca? Is that you? Sackett, here. There's going to be a holdup."

"That's why I'm headed home. Load up and let's get on with it."

"I was headed your way when I stopped off at the Wiggins place for supper. They've got a telegraph operator at the station there where they load stock. I didn't know of any train, so when the message came through I headed off to join Chantry."

He went to the stove for coffee, hotter and blacker now. Baca filled a cup also and laid out his plan. "I think Bord will have it set up just that way."

"Monson an' Clatt? Tough boys," Sackett said.

Baca sipped his coffee. "With this here telegraph an' the trains it's gettin' so a poor robber doesn't have much chance."

"It's changing things," Sackett agreed. "Look at us. A couple of years back we wouldn't have a chance of gettin' there in time."

"And we may not now."

The train rumbled along, and the two men alternately slept, drank coffee, and talked, watched the wild countryside slip past them.

Wagon trains had crossed this country, and cattle drives. Before that there were Indians, various branches of the Plains Apache, most of them wiped out by the Comanches.

Baca spoke of it, and Sackett nodded. "More Indians were killed by other Indians than by white men," he said. "I've talked to a few who were the last of their kind."

He peered from the window of the caboose. Antelope went skipping away over the plain, then paused to look back and ran on again. A half dozen buffalo lay on a low hill, watching the train.

"We've got to hope he got that telegram you sent," Tyrel said. "But even so he's a careful man. Nobody's goin' to catch him off guard."

"He knows they've set this place up," Baca agreed.

The brakeman came back over the cars and dropped into the caboose. "Goin' to have to stop for water," he said. "You boys better stand by. Somebody might be wishful of takin' a ride."

The long plains twilight faded as they waited alongside the water tank. The plains stretched out for miles with here and there a gully, and far off a light from a distant window. Somebody else was in the world, anyway.

The brakeman released the water pipe and swung it back into place, tying the rope. Baca and Sackett swung aboard.

"When I first came west," Tyrel Sackett said, "I tied up with a cattle drive, Orrin an' me. Went through to Abilene with it. Then we came on into this country right south of here, rounded up wild cattle, and sold 'em."

"You were in that land-grant fight, weren't you?"*

---

*As described in *The Daybreakers* by Louis L'Amour.

"Uh-huh. Orrin an' me were. Orrin was sheriff there for a while, too. Then he studied more law and went into politics."

"Best get some sleep. Be daylight before we know it."

"The shack said, I mean the brakeman, that we'd get to town just after daylight."

"Ben Curry always timed his robberies about openin' time at the bank," Baca said. "Fewer folks on the street, and in the bank they're gettin' money out for the day's business."

They dozed, slept, and awakened with gray light in the distance. Tyrel Sackett checked his guns.

Baca walked to the window of the caboose and peered out. For a moment he just looked, and then he said, "Sackett?"

Tyrel turned, struck by an odd sound in his voice. "What is it?"

"Look!"

Tyrel bent to look out.

They were there, three abreast, the others strung out behind. Baca counted aloud. " . . . seven, eight . . . nine. Nine of them. I hope Chantry has some help."

Nine men riding to a town where Borden Chantry waited. "Well," Sackett said quietly, "one thing we know."

"What's that?"

"We're gettin' there on time."

Eighteen

Borden Chantry finished his coffee and stood up, reaching for his hat. "I'd best get over to the office."

He turned and looked at his wife. "You goin' to be around, Bess?" His eyes met hers. She was as lovely as ever, and never a day passed that he did not thank the good Lord for letting him find her before he made a fool of himself with somebody else.

"Where would I go?"

"Oh, I thought maybe over to Mary's or something."

"I'll be here." She adjusted his coat collar. "Be careful, Borden. You never walk out of that door but that I worry."

"I'll be all right."

A train whistled, and he turned sharply. "That's funny! We don't have any train comin' in this morning."

He glanced out, and he could see it coming, just a locomotive, a stockcar, and a caboose. *Now what the hell?*

He stepped outside and looked toward the station. The station agent had stepped out on the platform and was shading his eyes along the track. Borden Chantry slipped the thong from the hammer of his gun. He glanced toward the street, but the cafe cut off his view of most of it.

Two men were standing in front of the other cafe, which was across the street, facing toward his house and the railroad. Mary Ann's house was behind it, some distance back, but nobody was stirring there, although a thin trail of smoke rose from the chimney.

The small train was pulling in alongside the unloading ramp, and two men swung down from the caboose before the train was fully stopped.

They ran up the ramp and began opening the stock-car door. One of them was Kim Baca, and the other?

Tyrel Sackett!

Chantry stepped back into the house and took his Winchester from the rack. Bess stared at him, her face gone white.

"Borden? What is it?"

"Trouble," he said, "Kim's back and Sackett with him. They're in a hurry." He checked the rifle, jacked a cartridge into the chamber, and said, "If they stop here, I'm at the office."

"Shouldn't you wait for them?"

"If there's trouble I'd better alert the town. I think it is coming, and fast, or they wouldn't be in such a hurry."

He stepped down off the porch and strode quickly toward the opening between the cafe building and the post office. As he stepped up on the boardwalk he saw Prissy sweeping the walk in front of the post office.

"Priss," he said quickly, "get off the street. I think we have trouble coming."

"Borden Chantry, if you think I am afraid—!"

"Priss, there's goin' to be some shootin'. I think we've got a robbery coming. You get off the street, or if you want to help, run up the street and tell George an' Hyatt."

"Not me, marshal! I've my own rifle to get. You tell them!"

Somebody tugged at his sleeve and Chantry turned. It was Billy McCoy, a friend of Tom's. "Can I? Let me!"

"All right. Run up the street and tell them all to stand by. I think there's going to be an attempted holdup." He turned and spoke loudly. "Everybody! Off the street!"

Big Injun, his jailer and occasional deputy, had come to the jail door, a shotgun in his hands. "Stand by," Borden said.

He was going to look the fool if nothing happened. After all, Sackett and Baca might be just hurrying for breakfast. But why the special train?

He glanced along the street. Three saddle horses standing in front of the cafe, one down the street in front of the Mexican cafe. A buckboard at the grocery store. No time to move it now, so the horses would just have to take their chances.

Kim Baca walked out on the street, hesitated, and then came over. "They're comin', Bord. We passed 'em just outside of town. There's nine of them, led by Monson an' Clatt."

"How far?"

"How far away? They should be ridin' into town any minute unless our train scared 'em, but I doubt it."

Two miles out of town Monson drew up to let the others gather around him. "You boys know the drill. Clatt, me, an' Porky will ride up the street to the bank. Klondike, you come in from behind the Corral Saloon and hold our horses. The rest of you boys cover the street."

"What if there's trouble?"

"You got a gun. The old man ain't in charge now," Monson said. "Me an' Clatt are. We'll show this bunch what we're made of."

"All right," Clatt said impatiently. "Let's go!"

Klondike hesitated. "Monny, what about that train? I didn't like the looks of it."

"Forget it! Just shiftin' a stockcar in to pick up some cattle. Let's go!"

Borden Chantry was in his office door with the jail behind him. Big Injun was at the window. Hyatt Johnson, up at the bank, had been a major in the Confederate cavalry, and George

Blazer at the express office had been a sharpshooter with Sherman and was a veteran of a number of Indian battles.

He glanced down the street. Here they were, three men riding abreast, coming right up the street. A trail of dust where one man had cut over behind the saloon.

"Big Injun?" He spoke over his shoulder. "There's one comin' up behind the Corral. You take him."

Borden Chantry stepped out of the door and went to the edge of the boardwalk.

Down the street Tyrel Sackett, his badge in plain sight, stepped out from the shadow of the McCoy house as the last two riders rode into town. The others were a good fifty yards ahead of them and intent on the street and the town.

"Boys? I'm Tyrel Sackett, and I'd like to talk to you. Get down off those horses and come over here. And boys? Keep your hands in sight."

Tyrel Sackett? *The Mora gunfighter?*

Denny Dinsmore felt himself go a little sick in the stomach. What the hell was this? Sackett here?

He hesitated. Sweat broke out on his brow. Clyde Bussy was beside him, and Clyde was a good, tough boy, but—

"What is this?" he protested.

Sackett's tone was sharp. "Get off those horses and get over here. *Now!*"

"You want us to drop our gunbelts?" Denny asked.

Sackett seemed to smile, but it was not a smile Denny liked. Why did he ever want to be an outlaw, anyway?

"Oh, no! Keep your guns on! I'd never like it said that I shot an unarmed man!"

Clyde wasn't offering any argument. Slowly and carefully, the two men dismounted.

When the three advance riders drew almost abreast of Chantry, he lifted his left hand. "Just a minute, boys! I'm Borden Chantry, the sheriff. I'd like a word with you."

Something clicked in Monson's brain. *Chantry?* It was his

place where the horses were. What had happened? An old man named Riggin was supposed to be marshal here.

Monson laughed. "Sorry, mister sheriff, we ain't got time to talk. Supposin' you just shuck them guns an' walk ahead of us. Walk slow, up to the bank. That all right with you?"

Monson turned in his saddle. "Anybody shows along the street, shoot 'em!"

Monson was cocky, and he was sure of himself. No hick town sheriff—

He never saw the draw. Borden Chantry had stood there, big, formidable, his gun in his holster. Monson went for his gun but as Chantry drew he stepped to the left, and Monson shifted his gun to cover him, firing as he did so, and he shot his horse, the bullet grazing the black's neck. The horse plunged and Monson was already falling.

There was a burst of gunfire all along the street, the stab of flame from pistols, plunging, rearing horses, the smell of gunsmoke.

Riding from behind the Corral Saloon to become the horse holder while the robbery took place, Klondike heard the shots, saw Monson down, his horse racing away up the street. Somebody was shooting from the bank, and he saw a man kneeling in front of the express office with a Big Fifty Sharps. This was no place for a man who wanted to spend his old age sitting in the sun. Klondike wheeled his horse and headed for the shelter of a barn, from which point he hoped to make the wide-open country beyond.

Klondike had never heard of Big Injun, a big, slow-moving, quiet man who rarely smiled. He did not know that the year Klondike was born Big Injun had taken his ninth scalp. All Klondike knew was that things had exploded all around him and he wanted to get away from there, and fast. He turned his horse to go and the horse made at least two jumps in the right direction. Big Injun, kneeling in the doorway, fired his Sharps, and the bullet, because of the movements of the horse, was a little low. It grazed the cantle of Klondike's saddle and, badly deformed, careened upward. The jagged metal took off the back of Klondike's skull.

What remained of Klondike stayed in the saddle for a quarter of a mile before it fell, toppling into the dust. The horse ran off a little way and, missing its rider, stopped, trotted off a few steps, and waited.

Klondike lay where he had fallen. Klondike, a tough man, was tough no longer. He stared up at the sky. "I wish . . . I just wish . . ."

The sun faded and a grasshopper leaped to his shirtfront, then hopped again. A few yards off his horse started to graze.

Back in the street Clatt, who had always been proud of his silver belt buckle, had no chance to regret it. Up the street George Blazer was kneeling beside a post on the boardwalk in front of the express office. His days with Sherman were long since gone, but his skill with a rifle was not.

The belt buckle flashed an invitation and George accepted it. He was a quiet man who liked to read his newspaper over coffee in the evening, but he did not like a bunch of would-be tough men shooting up his hometown. You could have laid a silver dollar over the spot where the two rifle bullets went in, but you couldn't have covered with a bandana the place where they emerged.

Clatt was down, and nobody knew who accounted for the other two, as several men were shooting and all showed evidence of skilled marksmanship.

Suddenly the thunder of guns, suddenly the flashes of gunfire, the plunging horses, the shouts, cries, dust, and then silence with the smell of dust and gunsmoke.

A horse walked away up the street. Another ran away between the buildings. Others, faithful to their training, stood where their reins had fallen.

Borden Chantry thumbed cartridges into his almost empty gun. People emerged on the street. Prissy came from the post office. "Sheriff Chantry! You should be ashamed of yourself!

What did we elect you for! So this sort of thing wouldn't happen! What will people say?"

"I'm sorry, ma'am," Borden said. "We tried to spread the word that this was a quiet town. I'm afraid somebody didn't get the message."

Big Injun, his rifle across the desk, came outside. "I'll get the buckboard an' pick 'em up."

Tyrel Sackett came up the street with two frightened outlaws. They stared at the fallen bodies, faces gray. Denny Dinsmore felt like throwing up. He didn't want to, not in front of all these people.

Clatt and Monson, dead.

Kim Baca was looking at his gun. He had fired two shots and could not remember when or how. He had no idea whether he had even hit anything.

Denny licked his dry lips. "What's for us?" he asked, glancing at Chantry.

Men who tried to steal the money others worked hard to earn got no sympathy from him. "For you? If you're lucky you may get no more than twenty years."

Denny stared at him. Denny was twenty-two. He had thought an outlaw's career would be wild and exciting. He turned and stared at the bodies in the street. He had never really liked any of those men, especially Monson. He had always been a little afraid of Monson, but he had eaten with them, told stories and talked, he had slept in bunkhouses with them and in camps.

Now they were dead.

Twenty *years*? Why, he would be over forty when he got out! His youth gone. He'd be an old man, he'd—

What about Mag? Why, she would never even know what happened to him! And after a little while she wouldn't care.

"Mister," he pleaded. "I—"

"You put your money on the wrong card," Chantry said. "You dealt your own hand, and in this life a man pays to learn. You just didn't learn fast enough."

He walked away and held out his hand to Sackett. "Thanks," he said. "Thanks very much."

"I'll buy you a drink," Tyrel said, "or coffee."

"Later," Borden said. "I'd better go speak to the wife first. She'll have heard all that shootin'."

She was standing waiting, her face white and still. "Borden? Bord? Are you all right?"

"All right, Bess. They were going to rob the bank. We had to stop them before somebody got hurt. We stopped them."

"You're all right? You're sure?"

"I'm all right, Bess. I will have to go back and see everything straightened up, though. There was some shooting."

"I heard. Was anybody—? I mean, was—?"

"Some outlaws. Tyrel Sackett arrested two of them. There were some pretty bad men among them. Some men just can't understand there isn't any free ride. Everything has its price."

"I can't stand it, Borden. I just can't! I'm not cut out for this. Borden, I want to go home. I want to go back east! I want to get away from all this!"

"I know, Bess, but what would I do back there?"

"I don't care. Anything is better than this!"

"Well"—he turned away—"I'll give it some thought, honey. Now I've got to go finish my job."

He walked to the cafe and stopped outside. Already the bodies were gone, dust thrown over the blood, the loose horses tied up.

What could he do back east? What would he do?

Sackett stood in the door of the Bon-Ton. "Come on in, Bord. Hyatt Johnson's here, and George. We'll have some coffee."

He turned toward the door, looking back once more. This was his town, and it was safe once more.

Nineteen

Firelight flickered on the canyon walls, somewhere in the distance a coyote howled. Wind stirred through the pines and fluttered the flame of the fire.

"You set up an' eat. You an' me, we're goin' to have a long time together. How long you live depends on how I get treated, understand? You give me any back talk or any trouble an' I'll kill you.

"Wouldn't be the first woman I killed, although the others were squaws. I never had nothin' like you."

"You will hang for this."

He chuckled harshly. "Yeah? Who is goin' to know it ever happened? You sure ain't goin' to be in no shape to tell anybody, an' who could find this place? Nobody's been in here for fifty year! Maybe more'n that."

Out in the darkness a horse stamped and blew. Ducrow straightened up from the fire, listening.

"Monson an' them," he said, thinking aloud, "I'll bet they

went to do that bank job! Well, that will be an easy one! Then if they are smart they'll head for Mexico."

He glanced around at Juliana. "Your pa thought he was king bee!" He paused, then shook his head. "And for a while there, he was. He could plan 'em, I'll give him that." He glanced at Juliana. "Your pa's dead, you know. Perrin an' them, they'll have killed him by now. I mean whoever Perrin left to do it. There was nobody but him, all alone in that stone house of his."

Juliana sat up straighter. "Don't be too sure," she said, "and when he has time he'll hunt you down. Don't you suppose he knows this place? Who knows this country better than he does?"

Ducrow stared at her. "What makes you think he knows this place?"

"Peach Meadow Canyon?" Juliana was frightened, but desperation was making her think. "I've heard him speak of it," she lied.

Ducrow was uneasy now, and she sensed the doubt. He had believed himself secure, but her comment had injected an element of uncertainty. If she had a chance it lay in that doubt. He had believed himself secure, but if she could make him wary, make him hesitate—

"Aw, he don't know nothin' about this place! Nobody does! Anyway, those boys back at Toadstool have taken care of him. All that damn' discipline! Do this, don't do that! Makes a man sick! This here's been comin' for months!"

"The man you call Perrin," Juliana said, "was killed! I looked back. He was down, and Mike Bastian was standing over him."

Ducrow squatted by the fire. Rig Molina would be killed attempting to rob the treasure train, Monson and Clatt were gone, and if Perrin was dead, then what would stop him from moving in and taking over?

Juliana had been afraid but was so no longer. She was like a trapped animal fighting for its life. Dru would have known what to do . . . but what *would* she do? There had to be something, some way to outwit him, some way to trick him. . . . How?

The fire—if she could only get him into the fire! If she could trip him, push him! If she could get hold of a gun! She could shoot, even if not so well as Dru.

Or a knife, something she could hide until the proper moment. Even a sharp blade of stone. Indians used them, and some of the scrapers she had seen seemed hardly to have been shaped at all. Her eyes searched the ground for a sharp-edged stone.

She would slash him across the face . . . no, not the face. It must be the throat. She must try to kill him or hurt him badly, she must—

"Here! Eat up, damn you! I haven't time to be stallin' around! Eat!

"Come daylight we're movin' further up the canyon! There's a place—"

"This is the place, Ducrow. Right here!"

He couldn't believe it. Ducrow put the frying pan down and slowly he straightened. Was the thong off his gun or not?

"Ol' Roundy was right." Ducrow was stalling for the moment he wanted. "He said you could track a snake across a flat rock.

"Well, now that you're here, what are you goin' to do about it?"

"Whatever you like, Ducrow, but I'd suggest you just carefully unfasten your belt and let your guns drop. If you don't want to do that you can always shoot it out."

"You're too soft, Bastian! You'll never make a gang leader like ol' Ben was! Ben would never have said aye, yes, or no, he'd just have come in blasting! You got a sight to learn, youngster. You're too soft! Too bad you ain't goin' to live long enough to learn it.

"Perrin always thought he was good with a gun. Never a day in his life I couldn't have beat him!" He lifted his right hand and wiped it across his tobacco-stained beard. The right made a careless gesture but at the same time his left hand dropped to his gun. It came up, spouting flame!

Mike Bastian simply palmed his gun and fired. It was smooth, it was fast, but most important it was accurate. He fired and then stepped to Ducrow's left and fired again.

Ducrow stood staring at him and then his gun dropped from loose fingers. His knees sagged and he fell forward, facedown in the sand. One hand fell into the fire and his sleeve began to smolder. Bastian stepped forward and pushed the hand away from the fire with his toe.

Then he loaded his gun and holstered it.

Dru came running, rifle in hand. "Oh, Mike! I thought you'd been killed! I thought—!

"Juliana!" She dropped on her knees beside her sister, and Mike walked back to the horses. For a long moment he stood leaning on the saddle.

After a while he heard the girls coming and he said, "There's the ruins of a stone house over yonder. Go there. I'll come along in a minute and build a fire. We'll go home in the morning."

He went to where Ducrow lay, and dragged him over against a low ridge of sand and gravel. Then he caved sand over him. "That's good enough for now, Ducrow. When we come back, I'll bury you right and proper."

The coffee was already made, so he brought it to the new fire he built.

Later, as the coals burned down, Dru asked, "Mike? What will you do now?"

"Go back to Toadstool," he said. He sipped his coffee and stared into the cup, then at her. "I've got to go back to Ben. I've got to make sure he's all right."

"And then?"

"Go someplace and start over."

"Not as an outlaw?"

"I never was one, never really wanted to be one." He looked up at her. "Dru, folks have to live together, and it can only be done if they work together to keep things right. There's no room for outlaws in a decent world, not even the kind of world they would try to create.

"Ben was wrong. Wrong from the start, and even as a small boy, I knew it."

"So?"

"He was all I had. I'd no place else to go, and he was kind. I'll say that for him. He was always kind."

Sunlight lay white upon the empty street at Toadstool Canyon when Mike Bastian rode into the lower end of town, his rifle across his saddle. Beside him was Dru Ragan.

Juliana had stayed behind at the Ragan ranch, but Dru refused. Ben Curry was her father and she was going to him, regardless, outlaw camp or not. Besides, she would be returning with Mike beside her.

If Dave Lenaker had arrived, Mike thought, the town was quiet enough for it. No horses stood at the hitching rails, and the door of the saloon gaped wide.

Something fluttered in the light wind, and Mike's eyes flickered. Torn cloth on a dead man's shirt, a man he did not know.

He walked his horse up the silent street, and the hoof falls were loud in the stillness. A man's hand and wrist lay across a windowsill. A pistol lay on the ground beneath it. There was blood on the stoop of another house.

"There's been a fight," Mike said softly, "and a bad one. Better get yourself set for the worst."

At the mess hall a man lay sprawled in the doorway.

They drew up at the foot of the stone steps and Mike helped her down. "Stay a little behind me, if you must come."

Up the steps, across the wide veranda, and into the huge living room. Shocked, they stopped in their tracks.

Five men sat about a table, playing cards. A coffeepot bubbled on the stove.

Doc Sawyer, Roundy, Garlin, and Colley were there, Garlin's head was bandaged, and Colley had one leg stretched out stiff and straight, as did Ben Curry, who was on the sofa. All were smiling.

Dru ran to her father and dropped on her knees beside him. "Oh, Dad! We were so scared!"

"What happened?" Mike demanded. "Did Dave Lenaker get here?"

"He surely did, but what do you think? It was Rigger Molina who got him! The Rigger got to Weaver and discovered Perrin had double-crossed him before he ever made an attempt on the train. When he found out that Perrin had lied about the number of guards on the treasure train he simply rode back.

"When he found that Ben was crippled and Perrin had run out, with Lenaker coming, he waited for Lenaker himself!

"He was wonderful, Mike! I never saw anything like it! He paced the veranda like a bear in a cage, muttering and waiting for Lenaker. 'Leave you in the lurch, will they? I'll show 'em! Lenaker thinks you're gettin' old, does he?'

"They shot it out in the street down there, and Lenaker beat him to the draw. He put two bullets into Rigger, but he wouldn't go down. He just stood there spraddle-legged in the street and shot until both guns were empty.

"Lenaker must have hit him at least five times but when Lenaker himself went down Molina went over and spat in his face. 'That's for a double-crosser!' he said. Mike, he was magnificent!"

"They fooled me, Mike," Roundy said. "I saw trouble comin' and figured I'd better get to old Ben. I never figured on them slippin' in behind and grabbin' you.

"Then I heard Lenaker was comin'. I knew him and I was afraid of what he would do, so I headed down the trail to meet him. Mike, I never killed a man in my life except some

Blackfeet that attacked us when I was livin' with the Crows, but I was sure aimin' to kill Lenaker.

"Then Lenaker come in by the old creek trail, and him and his boys went after Ben and the gold he was supposed to have."

"Doc was here," Garlin said, "an' Colley. Roundy slipped through and joined us. Oh, it was some fight while it lasted. We got scratched up some, but nothin' to what they got."

Briefly, Mike Bastian described his fight with Kerb Perrin and the pursuit of Ducrow.

"They've pulled out," Roundy said, "all that's alive."

"The only man who ever fooled me was Rigger Molina," Ben Curry said. "I never guessed he was that loyal, but he took that fight when I was in no shape to, and soaked up lead like a sponge soaks water."

Doc Sawyer idly shuffled the cards. "Ben," he said, "I think we should move out, as soon as you're able to ride. I think we should all move out."

Ben Curry looked up at Dru. "Now you know. Your old man's an outlaw. I never wanted you to know, and I planned to get shut of this whole outfit and live out my days with your ma, over there on the V-Bar."

"Why don't you?" Dru asked.

"Funny," Ben said, "I never figured it would get this big, never at all. One thing just follered another until it got too big to let go of."

"It was over, Ben. You held men together who did not like being held. You made things work. Now some of them will slip away and probably disappear just like you can."

"You shuffle them cards any more, Doc," Garlin said, "and I'll get worried what you're doin' to that deck. Set up an' deal."

Mike and Dru walked outside and looked down over Toad-stool Canyon. There were no lights in the town where dead men lay, sprawled in their last moments.

Inside they heard argument. "He's a fine lad, Ben, and well educated, if I do say so who taught him all he knows."

"All he knows!" Roundy exploded. "Book larnin' is all well an' good but where would that gal be tonight if'n I hadn't taught him to read sign an' foller a trail? I ask you, where would she be?"

On the wide veranda, with the stars brushed by the dark fingertips of the pines, Mike said to Dru, "I can read sign, all right, but I'm no hand at reading the trail to a woman's heart. You will have to help me, Dru."

She laughed, resting a hand on his arm. "Mike, you've been blazing that trail ever since we met in Weaver! You need no help at all!"

She turned him to face her. "Mike, I love this country! Every bit of its red rock canyons, its green cedars, the pines, the distance . . . all of it! Why don't we get some cattle and go back to Peach Meadow Canyon?

"Why don't we build a cabin, plant some more peaches, and start a place of our own? You said you could make a better trail better than the one we used."

From inside Garlin was saying, "Monson an' Clatt? Wherever they went, we'll hear of them soon enough!"

"That Clatt," Ben commented, "he was one I was going to drop. Liked to brag too much! He wanted to tell around the saloons what a tough man he was. He wasn't content with my kind of operation, wanted to be pointed out as a bad man and an outlaw."

"The trouble with that," Garlin remarked, "is that the law listens, too." He glanced at Ben Curry. "He favored that bank back over the mountains. He always did think well of that job."

Curry glanced at his cards. He would keep what he had. He looked over them at Garlin. "I was calling it off. The old marshal, Riggin was his name, he got himself killed, and that rancher where we left the horses, Borden Chantry was his name, he took over as marshal."

He watched Doc draw two cards. Three of a kind, maybe?

"There at their wagon I drank coffee with Chantry. I looked across my cup at him and I knew then he was one man I wanted no part of. When he became marshal I decided I'd just forget that job. Not that I didn't think back to it every now and again, but it always came up as a bad bet."

"Come daylight," Doc said casually as he laid down three nines and took the pot, "we should ride out of here. If somebody happened by there'd be explanations." He stacked his winnings in neat piles. "I'm glad it's over, Ben. You an' me, we're the past. Those youngsters outside there, they are tomorrow."

Ben hitched himself into a more comfortable position. "You're right, of course. All of us, you, me, Wyatt Earp, Billy the Kid, Bill Hickok, we've lived out our time in a world we never made.

"Take Billy now, I knew him as a youngster. Not a bad kid, but in Lincoln County them days you took sides. You had to. Billy took the right side, too. Tunstall and Maqueen were good men, and then of the whole two hundred or so involved in that fight Billy was the only one ever brought to trial."

Garlin, gathering the cards, suddenly stopped. On the back of a nine of spades there was a small fingernail scratch. Quickly he ran through the deck. There was another on the nine of diamonds, a third on the nine of hearts.

"Doc!" he yelled. "Damn you for a four-eyed pirate! You—!"

Ben chuckled and hitched himself around to get his foot on the floor. "Gar, you ought to know Doc by now. With him it ain't the money, it's the winning. How many times has he staked you?"

Garlin shrugged, smiling. "Nevertheless—"

Out in the dark a coyote pleaded plaintively to the silent stars, and Ben heaved himself to his feet, leaning on the heavy cane.

On the porch, nearing the low stone wall, Mike Bastian

stood with Dru. He stood staring for a minute, then muttered, "Well, why not?"

He looked down the dark and empty street. Tomorrow it would be alone with its ghosts.

"Garlin?" Mike called out. "See that Rig Molina gets a proper marker, will you? Say *He was a good man*. And carve it in stone."

About Louis L'Amour

"I think of myself in the oral tradition—
as a troubadour, a village tale-teller, the man
in the shadows of the campfire.
That's the way I'd like to be remembered—as a storyteller.
A good storyteller."

It is doubtful that any author could be as at home in the world re-created in his novels as Louis Dearborn L'Amour. Not only could he physically fill the boots of the rugged characters he wrote about, but he literally "walked the land my characters walk." His personal experiences as well as his lifelong devotion to historical research combined to give Mr. L'Amour the unique knowledge and understanding of people, events, and the challenge of the American frontier that became the hallmarks of his popularity.

Of French-Irish descent, Mr. L'Amour could trace his own family in North America back to the early 1600s and follow their steady progression westward, "always on the frontier." As a boy growing up in Jamestown, North Dakota, he absorbed all he could about his family's frontier heritage, including the story of his great-grandfather who was scalped by Sioux warriors.

Spurred by an eager curiosity and a desire to broaden his horizons, Mr. L'Amour left home at the age of fifteen and enjoyed a wide variety of jobs, including seaman, lumberjack, elephant handler, skinner of dead cattle, miner, and officer in the transportation corps during World War II. During his "yondering" days he also circled the world on a freighter, sailed a dhow on the Red Sea, was shipwrecked in the West Indies and stranded in the Mojave Desert. He won fifty-one of fifty-nine fights as a professional boxer and worked as a journalist and lecturer. He was a voracious reader and collector of rare books. His personal library contained 17,000 volumes.

Mr. L'Amour "wanted to write almost from the time I could talk." After developing a widespread following for his many frontier and adventure stories written for fiction magazines, Mr. L'Amour published his first full-length novel, *Hondo*, in the United States in 1953. Every one of his more than 120 books is in print; there are more than 300 million copies of his books in print worldwide, making him one of the bestselling authors in modern literary history. His books have been translated into twenty languages, and more than forty-five of his novels and stories have been made into feature films and television movies.

His hardcover bestsellers include *The Lonesome Gods, The Walking Drum* (his twelfth-century historical novel), *Jubal Sackett, Last of the Breed,* and *The Haunted Mesa.* His memoir, *Education of a Wandering Man,* was a leading bestseller in 1989. Audio dramatizations and adaptations of many L'Amour stories are available as audio downloads and on CDs from Random House Audio publishing.

The recipient of many great honors and awards, in 1983 Mr. L'Amour became the first novelist ever to be awarded the Congressional Gold Medal by the United States Congress in honor of his life's work. In 1984 he was also awarded the Medal of Freedom by President Reagan.

Louis L'Amour died on June 10, 1988. His wife, Kathy, and their two children, Beau and Angelique, carry the L'Amour publishing tradition forward with new books written by the author during his lifetime to be published by Bantam.

FIC
LAM

3-13

DISCARDED

Newfoundland Area Public Library

Newfoundland, PA 18445 (570) 676-4518